PAVING THE NEW ROAD
The Fourth Rowland Sinclair Mystery

"The combination of famous historical figures, detailed descriptions of a troubling time, and plenty of action makes for a tale as rousing as it is relevant."

—*Kirkus Reviews*

"This installment takes the aristocratic Sinclair into a much darker place than did the previous three entries in the series but does so without losing the stylish prose and the easy way with character that have given the novels their appeal."

—*Booklist*

MILES OFF COURSE
The Third Rowland Sinclair Mystery

"Gentill's third reads like a superior Western, alternating high adventure with social and political observations about prewar Australia."

—*Kirkus Reviews*

"Set in Australia in 1933, Gentill's entertaining third mystery featuring portrait artist Rowland Sinclair will appeal to fans of Greenwood's Phryne Fisher ... Gentill matches Greenwood's skill at blending suspense with a light touch."

—*Publishers Weekly*

"Rowland is an especially interesting character: at first he comes off as a bit of a layabout, a guy who feels he's entitled to a cushy life by virtue of his aristocratic roots, but, as the story moves along, we realize he has a strong moral center and a compulsion to finish a job once he's started it. A great addition to a strong series and a fine read-alike for fans of Kerry Greenwood's Phryne Fisher novels."

—*Booklist*

A DECLINE IN PROPHETS
The Second Rowland Sinclair Mystery

"I thoroughly enjoyed the glamour of the ocean voyage, the warmth and wit among the friends, and yet all the time, simmering beneath the surface, was the real and savage violence, waiting to erupt. The 1930s are a marvelous period. We know what lies ahead! This is beautifully drawn, with all its fragile hope and looming tragedy. I am delighted this is a series. I want them all."

—Anne Perry, *New York Times* bestselling author

"Set in late 1932, Gentill's lively second mystery featuring dashing Australian millionaire Rowland "Rowly" Sinclair takes place initially aboard the luxury cruise ship Aquitania, as it steams along toward Sydney … The witty and insightful glimpses of the Australian bourgeoisie of this period keep this mystery afloat."

—*Publishers Weekly*

"A delightful period piece."

—*Kirkus Reviews*

A FEW RIGHT THINKING MEN
The First Rowland Sinclair Mystery

"Fans of Kerry Greenwood's Phryne Fisher series, rejoice: here comes another Depression-era Australian sleuth! Along the way there is plenty of solid discussion of politics and social status, with enough context to both draw in those new to the era and keep those more well-versed in their history interested."

—*Historical Novel Society*

"As series-launching novels go, this one is especially successful: the plot effectively plays Sinclair's aristocratic bearing and involvement in the arts against the Depression setting, fraught with radical politics, both of which he becomes involves in as he turns sleuth. And Sinclair himself is a delight: wining us over completely and making us feel as though he's an old friend."

—*Booklist*

"While the vintage Down Under settings might make this debut, which was short-listed for the Commonwealth Writers' Prize Best First Book, comparable to Kerry Fisher's Melbourne-based Phryne Fisher 1920s mysteries, Gentill works in historical events that add verisimilitude to her story. There are more political machinations going on here than Phryne could ever contemplate. VERDICT: Thanks to Poisoned Pen Press for bringing another award-winning Australian crime writer to U.S. shores. Her witty hero will delight traditional mystery buffs."

—*Library Journal*

Gentlemen Formerly Dressed

Books by Sulari Gentill

The Rowland Sinclair Series
A Few Right Thinking Men
A Decline in Prophets
Miles off Course
Paving the New Road
Gentlemen Formerly Dressed
A Murder Unmentioned
Give the Devil His Due

The Hero Trilogy
Chasing Odysseus
Trying War
The Blood of Wolves

Gentlemen Formerly Dressed

A Rowland Sinclair Mystery

Sulari Gentill

Poisoned Pen Press

Poisoned Pen Press

First Edition 2018

10 9 8 7 6 5 4 3 2 1

Library of Congress Control Number: 2017954235

ISBN: 9781464206931 Hardcover
9781464206955 Trade Paperback

Poisoned Pen Press
4014 N. Goldwater Boulevard, #201
Scottsdale, Arizona 85251
www.poisonedpenpress.com
info@poisonedpenpress.com

Printed in the United States of America

Chapter One

Meals Aloft

AIRWAY CATERING
Sumptuous Repasts

By Garnsey Potts

Before starting an aerial trip from London to Paris in one of the small pioneer machines of 1919, passengers often provided themselves with sandwiches. More often than not the sandwiches remained uneaten. The cabins of the two-seater machines were mere boxes, the engine roared only a few feet away, and the whole procedure of air travel in those days was such a breath-taking, exciting adventure that few developed appetites in mid-air.

With the advent of the three-engine air liner of the Hercules and Argosy types it became possible, for the first time, for a steward to serve refreshments from a small buffet at the rear of the saloon.

Six-course meals aloft. In the British air liners regularly flying between London and the Continent more than 500 people a week now enjoy, while up in the air, five and six-course meals which are equal in every respect to those provided in the most fashionable West End restaurants...

> Beverages not overlooked. In addition to the subject of food, the equally important question of beverages is not overlooked by the airway caterer. A comprehensive list of wines is available for passengers, and there has been developed a special airway cocktail, known as The Silver Wing Special.
>
> —*The Sunday Mail, Brisbane*, 1933

"He's going to hang himself...." Edna gasped as the knot was pulled tight, then reefed violently apart once more. The sculptress bit her lower lip nervously as she watched the process begin again.

"Looks that way." Clyde had folded his brawny arms as he leaned against the doorjamb. The faint smile on his lips was given away by the curve of the lines at the edges of his eyes.

Milton Isaacs poured tea from the silver service before him. "We'll get involved if he turns blue," he promised her. Rowland Sinclair would ask for help if and when he wanted it. In the meantime, Milton could not resist a poetic commentary. "There is in this no Gordian knot which one might not undo without a sabre." He flourished the cake knife like a sword.

"Poe," Rowland muttered just loud enough for them all to overhear through the bedroom's open door. It was possibly less than gracious to point out that Milton's poetry was not actually his, but the game of appropriation and attribution had become something of a tradition between the two men. Elias Isaacs had gained both the moniker "Milton" and his reputation as poet by virtue of his ability to quote the English bards at will. And, until he had taken up residence in Rowland's Woollahra mansion, few with whom he kept company had possessed either the education or interest to make the acknowledgement he so conveniently omitted.

Milton smiled, neither chastised nor offended. He handed Edna a cup of tea as they settled upon the chaise lounge to observe as Rowland struggled with his necktie, hampered by the fact that his right arm was encased in plaster beyond the elbow.

It had been reset and cast just the day before, and Rowland was still becoming accustomed to the restriction it inflicted.

Cursing as he realised the tie was again too short, Rowland pulled it off for a third time, frustrated. Movement had been painful in the rudimentary splint they had fashioned for their escape from Germany, but it had been possible.

Ever helpful, Milton suggested Rowland adopt the cravat, which the poet himself favoured. Their friendship was such that even Rowland Sinclair did not feel the need to respond politely.

"Give up and tie a four-in-hand, Rowly," Clyde called, checking his watch.

Although mumbled, Rowland's reply made clear what he thought of the knot Clyde advocated. He hadn't used a four-in-hand since he was a schoolboy.

Unable to watch him struggle any longer, Edna intervened. He protested, of course, but she ignored him, slapping his hand away and knotting the tie with the full Windsor she'd always known him to wear. She slipped the ends beneath the sling which supported the cast and turned down his collar.

He looked down, a little surprised that the length was perfect. "Thank you, Ed."

She reached up to brush the dark hair off his forehead. A barber had come to the hotel suite that morning, but Rowland's hair never stayed in place for long. "You really are ridiculous sometimes," she said, smiling into the intense blue of his eyes. "Come and have some tea before we go."

Rowland nodded. He could sense that his companions were anxious to depart, to put oceans between themselves and Germany. As much as Paris seemed a world removed from the dark, ordered insanity from which they'd fled, the fact that they were probably wanted for murder in Munich made the protection of a single border fragile. Even here in the Hôtel de Crillon on Place de la Concorde, it seemed that Nazi officialdom was a presence—on leave or business—recognisable by language and manner, though they were not in uniform.

The four Australians had been in Paris for three days and had, in that time, kept to themselves. All their meals had been taken in the privacy of the suite. They had visited the war cemetery in Ypres where one of Rowland's brothers was buried, but such pilgrimages were nothing out of the ordinary and they'd been careful to draw as little attention as possible. And yet they were uneasy.

Eager to be on home soil as soon as possible, Rowland had booked their passages on Imperial Airways' silver service between Le Bourget and the Croydon Aerodrome in Surrey. They would cross the Channel and land on the coast of Surrey in under three hours start to finish, and sail for Sydney thereafter.

They had little luggage. What clothes they now possessed had been purchased in Paris, for they had left Germany with barely more than what they'd been wearing. The new bags were, in fact, half empty—containing only basic and quickly acquired wardrobes.

Rowland drained the cup Milton had handed him. The poet wore a jacket of orange velvet which he had purchased from a street vendor near the hotel. In Paris it did not seem so odd, and Milton's tastes had always been flamboyant.

Rowland slipped his arm out of the sling to pull on his own jacket, easing the sleeve over the cast with Edna's help. The fabric was strained around the extra thickness, but at least it wasn't orange.

Clyde grabbed their bags, refusing to let Rowland help or call the bellboy. "It'll be quicker to take them ourselves," he insisted, handing Edna's Gladstone bag to Milton. "We don't want to miss that flight."

And so they made their way down to the hotel's gilded foyer. They found it uncommonly crowded. Not accustomed to anything but instantaneous and obsequious service, the guests who waited in the foyer were noticeably irritable and indignant.

"I'll settle the account," Rowland said quietly. "You chaps get the doorman to hail a taxi. I'll be as quick as I can."

Clyde nodded, glancing at his watch. They were cutting it fine.

Rowland joined the queue at the reception desk. There were several people ahead of him waiting impatiently. It seemed there was a problem at the head of the line. At the counter, a fair, thickset gentleman made demands of the manager. He spoke French haltingly with a German accent. He was accompanied by two gendarmes and a particularly fat man who compulsively mopped the perspiration from his brow with a large handkerchief. It was the presence of this fat man that alarmed Rowland. He knew him—Rousseau—the sweaty rotund doctor who had cast his arm and treated the burns on his chest.

The manager signalled the concierge, and they conferred before he turned back to the German. "Monsieur Sinclair's party has neither checked out nor called for a bellboy, Monsieur. I expect he is still in his suite." He took a key from the rack behind him. "I shall take you up myself."

For a moment Rowland was panicked, certain Rousseau would notice him in the crowd. As soon as the men left the service desk, the guests who had been waiting surged towards it, demanding to be attended. Rowland went with them, keeping his head down and his back turned. The concertina doors of the lift closed. Quietly then, without hurrying, Rowland walked out of the hotel.

Clyde waved him over to their taxi and Rowland slipped into the vacant front seat. The others were already inside.

"We're late, Monsieur—would you hurry, please?" he asked, slipping easily into French. He said nothing to his companions. There was a chance the taxi driver understood English and Rowland was uncertain of what extradition arrangements existed between France and Germany. They had already made one mistake.

When they reached the aéroport, he asked the driver to wait. "We are just seeing our friends off, and then we shall need to return to the hotel." He handed over a generous enticement and the driver agreed readily.

Edna, who understood French, cast a questioning glance in his direction but uttered nothing to contradict his story. It was not until they were within the aéroport building that Rowland told his friends what had happened.

Milton cursed the doctor. "Fat underhanded pig! I knew he was too interested in how you'd been injured."

"The cigarette burns," Clyde said grimly. "He must have realised we'd had trouble with Nazis."

"But this is Paris," Edna protested. "Surely the Germans can't..."

"We can't take the risk, Ed. We're wanted for murder, remember?"

"So what do we do?" Edna glanced uneasily at the customs officials.

"I'm hoping the French police won't have put out a general alert for us simply because Rousseau reported some unusual injuries...not yet, anyway." Rowland looked out at the double-winged Argosy, ready on the runway. Passengers had begun to board. He made a decision. "Wait until I've gone through. If there are no problems, follow." He took a pocketbook of money from inside his jacket and handed it to Clyde. "If they stop me, get back into that taxi and get out of here."

"We can't just leave you," Edna protested.

"There's not a lot of point in all of us being arrested." Rowland smiled reassuringly at her. "I didn't check out. With any luck, Rousseau and company will assume we stepped out to see the sights...they are probably still waiting for us at the Hôtel de Crillon."

Edna shook her head, unconvinced.

"We haven't time to argue, Ed." He grabbed one of the bags. "I'll be fine."

The customs official who took his passport paused, inspecting the photograph closely and then lifting his eyes to the sling which supported Rowland Sinclair's right arm.

"You've had some trouble, Monsieur Sinclair?"

Rowland shrugged. "Cycling accident—wasn't keeping a proper lookout, I'm afraid...rather embarrassing really."

The official shook his head. "You do not fool me, Monsieur Sinclair!" He pointed sternly at Rowland.

Rowland tensed, ready.

"Your eyes, they were on the mademoiselles and not the road!" The official laughed now as he handed back the passport and called for someone to take the Australian's bag. "It is always the way with young men like you. We remember your countrymen from the Great War...always chasing the mademoiselles!"

Rowland smiled. "You have found me out, Monsieur."

Rowland made his way slowly down the aisle between the seats. Having last flown in the rudimentary comforts, or lack thereof, afforded by the *Southern Cross*, he was more than a little impressed with the civility of the *City of Glasgow*'s cabin. Accommodating twenty passengers, it was not entirely spacious, but the appointments were tasteful and clearly designed to make the crossing as comfortable as possible. On either side of the aisle ran a single row of leather armchairs. The walls were panelled and the fittings, brass, in a style reminiscent of first-class train carriages.

Rowland took his seat, glancing back to see if his friends had boarded.

Edna waved from the rear of the plane. Rowland smiled, relieved, and she blew him a kiss.

"That is a very beautiful lady who blows you a kiss." The young man in the seat across the aisle spoke to him in English. The accent was European definitely, German possibly. "She is a friend of yours? Perhaps she would like to exchange seats with me...?"

"That won't be necessary." Rowland remained wary. "But thank you. I don't really know her."

"And yet she blows you the kiss."

"Yes, highly improper." Rowland tried to look disapproving. "Where I come from, women are not so forward."

The man laughed. "You must not be so strict, my friend. You are a lucky man then to catch the eye of so beautiful a stranger." He sighed and pressed his palm sadly to his heart. "It is only the flat-faced, toothless girls who smile at poor Arnold Deutsch." He chuckled at his own misfortune. "I would shake your hand, sir, but I see that doing so would cause you some difficulty."

"Rowland Sinclair. Pleased to make your acquaintance, Mr. Deutsch." The *City of Glasgow* had started to coast down the runway, gathering speed as she prepared to leave the tarmac. A bump, a sensation of heaviness, and she was airborne. Rowland relaxed now.

"Are you German, Mr. Deutsch?"

Deutsch laughed. "No, do not be fooled by the name. I have been recently in Berlin, but I am Czechoslovakian. Now I go to your Great Britain to study."

Rowland chose not to correct Deutsch's assumption that he was English. There was probably no reason to be suspicious of the man, but he had also thought that about Rousseau.

A uniformed steward walked down the aisle, distributing hot towels to each passenger. He had scarcely collected the used towels when he returned with an extensive luncheon traymobile, stopping to fuss over how Rowland would manage the buffet with the use of only one hand—his left, at that. Despite Rowland's assurances that he could feed himself quite adequately, the enthusiastic steward insisted on cutting his roast beef into manageable pieces before seeing to the other passengers.

Deutsch grinned. "The Imperial Airline is just a little bit too much first class, I think."

"Quite," Rowland muttered, ignoring his meal and resorting instead to the concoction of gin and vermouth he'd been told was a silver wing special.

The flight over the English Channel was blessed on this day with fair skies and gentle winds. Notwithstanding his initial caution, Rowland found Deutsch rather pleasant company. The Czechoslovakian, who it seemed intended to study psychology at the University of London, was friendly, and though he talked at length, he did not require too much by way of contribution from Rowland.

Still, Rowland was relieved when the English coastline came into view and the *City of Glasgow* finally touched down at the Croydon Aerodrome in Surrey.

One of the last passengers to disembark, he found his companions already waiting for him as their luggage was unloaded. Edna hugged him euphorically, whispering in his ear. "We're here, Rowly! I was beginning to fear that nightmare would never end."

Deutsch paused as he walked past. "She is unstoppable, this improper young woman that you do not know." He winked at Rowland and tipped his hat at Edna.

Rowland laughed as Edna stared after the Czechoslovakian, affronted. "Who was that?"

"Arnold Deutsch...he's some kind of scholar, I believe."

Chapter Two

The Trouser Craze

In a recent letter from London, a correspondent says:

At first we were inclined to treat the Dietrich-trouser craze reports emanating from America as the result of somebody's highly coloured imagination—but since photographic proof of ordinary women wearing them out shopping and so on has begun arriving, that's rather a different matter. Although no one supposes for a moment that the habit of wearing men's lounge suits will catch on among Englishwomen, there are designers who are determined to sponsor the mode. At a dress show the other day a mannequin caused quite a flutter among the feminine audience by strolling forth attired in a perfectly tailored men's lounge suit, cut from brown suiting cloth, and carrying a brown beret. Though the severity of the suit was somewhat softened by the rose-beige blouse which accompanied it, the mannequin seemed ill at ease in this essentially unfeminine attire!

On the other hand, we have the distinctly frilly frivolities of such designers as Norman Hartnell, to whose show at Claridge's Hotel I went along yesterday. His moods are quite Edwardian—and among reminders of other days, he shows chiffon frocks for Ascot with high boned collars!

While on the subject of fashion, you may be interested to hear that monkey fur has suddenly become the vogue. A few weeks ago these skins fetched only about 3d. or 4d. a skin in the market—but with the sudden demand prices have now risen to over 5d. Just another little instance of how fashion rules the intricacies of supply and demand.

—*Albany Advertiser*, 1933

The penthouse suites of Claridge's on Brook Street in London's Mayfair had fallen vacant unexpectedly when the fortunes of its long-term residents had finally succumbed to the Depression which gripped London as tightly as it held the rest of the world. Lord and Lady Abernethy had been moved out discreetly and quickly, and all signs of their existence at Claridge's removed. In certain polite circles their fall from grace caused a minor scandal; but, given the times, it was not unusual enough a story to be worth comment for long—and an unpaid account at Claridge's was at least a better class of debt. Of course, Rowland Sinclair had no idea who had occupied the top floor of the hotel before his own party. He had been mildly surprised that the penthouses were both available when the rest of the hotel was fully occupied. But then the penthouse apartments carried a rate that would have made most pocketbooks quail. Perhaps even the wealthy clientele of Claridge's was exercising fiscal restraint.

Rowland and his companions had taken a motor car from the airport directly to the Mayfair branch of Lloyd's Bank, where Rowland had presented his passport to the manager and arranged appropriate lines of credit. The Sinclair fortune was quite conveniently not confined to the Antipodes, and the manager was accustomed to accommodating the financially embarrassed traveller.

Thus having ensured that they would not find themselves vagrants, the Australians retreated to the traditional but uncompromising luxury of the Mayfair hotel.

It was not until later that evening, as they waited for Edna to finish dressing for dinner, that Milton noticed the article in the evening paper.

"Rowly," he said, holding the paper up to the light, "take a look at this."

Rowland peered over Milton's shoulder and then, startled, took the *Manchester Guardian* from the poet.

"What is it?" Clyde asked as he poured drinks.

"Wilfred."

"What? Your brother?" Clyde put down the decanter and strode over to scrutinise the paper. They had left Wilfred Sinclair in Sydney when they'd embarked for Germany in April.

"I think so." Rowland squinted at the newsprint. The article concerned some international economic conference being held in London. The accompanying photograph was of Ramsay MacDonald, the British Prime Minister, with an American delegate. A figure stood in the background, half-turned and somewhat out of focus, but Rowland was sure it was Wilfred.

"Did he say he was coming to London?" Milton retrieved the drinks Clyde had abandoned.

Rowland shook his head. "No." He looked at the picture again. "What the devil's he doing here?"

Clyde and Milton exchanged a glance. It was entirely conceivable that Wilfred Sinclair had come to London anticipating a need to rescue his younger brother, but that was not a notion that would please Rowland. So, they didn't mention it.

But clearly Rowland's mind had already moved in that direction. Irritated, he tossed the paper onto the couch. That he had very nearly needed rescue did not make Wilfred's interference any less annoying. He was twenty-eight, for God's sake!

Edna stepped out of her bedroom, in a simple navy evening dress which skimmed gently over the curves of her figure. Her dark copper tresses were caught in a coil at the base of her neck. She smiled.

Rowland forgot about Wilfred.

"Where did Mr. Beresford go?" Edna was looking about for the butler who had come with the suite.

"I believe he's checking on our reservations for dinner," Rowland said. "It might be difficult to keep him occupied." Beresford had already cleaned and pressed their suits, polished their shoes and mixed pre-dinner cocktails with extraordinary and yet unobtrusive efficiency.

"Well, you might have asked him to help you with your tie," Edna said, sitting on the arm of Rowland's chair.

Milton cleared his throat disapprovingly. The poet considered it a matter of Colonial evolution that the Australian gentleman dressed himself.

Sighing, Edna leaned down to deal with the bow tie which hung loosely around Rowland's neck.

"I thought I'd attend to it myself," he murmured, as her fingers worked deftly at his throat.

Clyde laughed. "I can barely tie a bow with the use of two hands."

"There." Edna considered Rowland critically. "How ever did you manage your cuff link?"

He grimaced. "I used my teeth, actually."

She smoothed his lapel. "Poor Rowly. You may have to start dressing more casually."

"Casually?" Rowland was clearly unenthused.

"I'm not suggesting you go out in pyjamas…We could get you one of those polo shirts."

"I don't intend to play polo," Rowland said firmly.

"Oh, don't be so stuffy, Rowly. They're all the rage and they'll be entirely adequate while we're on the boat, at least. The cast will be ready to come off by the time we reach Sydney and you can go back to your suits."

Rowland elected to leave the sculptress' fashion advice alone for the moment. "Actually, I was thinking I wouldn't go home just yet."

Milton and Clyde both looked up, surprised.

"Why ever not?" Edna demanded.

After what he'd been through, they had all expected Rowland would be keener than any of them to go home.

"I think I should speak to someone about what we saw—what's happening in Germany."

"Speak to whom?"

"I'm not sure." Rowland reached over to retrieve the *Guardian* from the table on which he'd discarded it. "Surely someone in His Majesty's government will be interested in what their German neighbours are up to."

"How do you propose to get an audience with a Member of Parliament?" Clyde was sceptical. The Sinclairs wielded influence in Australia, but Britain was another thing altogether.

"No idea." Rowland handed the paper to Edna and pointed out the photo they had been discussing before she'd entered the room. "Perhaps Wil will know someone."

Rowland stood to answer the door, but Beresford reached it before him. The caller was a gentleman, dressed for dinner in white tie and tails. His fair hair was thinning slightly but not one strand of it was out of place. Wire-rimmed glasses did nothing to lessen the intensity of the dark blue eyes which were common to all the Sinclair men. He addressed the butler politely but impatiently.

Beresford turned to Rowland who was now standing beside him, and announced, "A Mr. Wilfred Sinclair, sir."

"Yes, thank you, I can see that. Hello, Wil."

At first Wilfred moved to shake his brother's hand, breaking off as he noticed the sling. "Rowly...what in God's name?"

"What are you doing here, Wil?" Rowland asked as Wilfred strode into the room.

"I was told some chap called Sinclair was making enquiries as to where I might be lodging..." He looked again at Rowland's injured arm. "I expect we have rather a lot to talk about."

Rowland showed his brother into the suite's sitting room. "We'd better have a drink."

Aside from Beresford, they were alone in the suite. The others had already gone down to dinner. Rowland had planned to join them once he'd made a few more telephone calls to ascertain where his brother was staying in London. Apparently the news that he was here, and making such enquiries, had reached Wilfred first.

It was not until Beresford had served drinks and withdrawn that Wilfred began to interrogate his brother.

"You drew on the Deutsche Bank account."

Rowland nodded. The simple fact that he'd needed to call upon private funds would have told Wilfred that the Old Guard had abandoned him and his companions, and that they were friendless in Germany. He had no doubt that his brother had been preparing to go into Germany after him. He hesitated, unsure where to start.

Wilfred waited, tapping his fingers restlessly on the scrolled armrest of his chair.

Rowland began with their arrival in Munich as reluctant agents of the Old Guard, the clandestine organisation of which Wilfred was part. He gave an account of everything they'd been asked to do, and everything they'd done, to stop Eric Campbell—the commander-in-chief of the Australian New Guard from establishing links with the Nazis.

Wilfred listened silently as Rowland told him about camps in which "enemies of the State" were imprisoned, of the book-burnings, and the brutal oppression of dissent. He smiled faintly when Rowland recounted how they had finally panicked Campbell into leaving Germany by convincing him that his deputy, Francis de Groot, was mounting a coup to depose him as leader of the Australian Fascist movement.

Wilfred looked disapprovingly at the sling. "You still haven't explained what you did to yourself."

"Oh...yes." Rowland paused, surprised by how much he didn't want to talk about what had happened to him, how awkward and humiliating he found it.

"Rowly..." Wilfred prompted.

Rowland spoke quietly—without lingering on detail. He recounted the night when the Nazi SA came for him, how they'd broken his arm as a punishment of sorts for a picture he'd painted, beaten him senseless, and left him for dead. How he'd regained consciousness only to face another attacker and had been saved by the German girl whose portrait had brought him to the attention of Ernst Röhm and his Stormtroopers in the first place.

Wilfred stared at him, shocked, appalled, and furious. He took a cigarette from the gold case in his pocket and lit it. Rowland waited for him to say something.

"Dammit, Rowly! You and your obscene bloody paintings. Why is it that every time I let you out of my sight you try to get yourself killed?"

Rowland bristled. "For God's sake, I wasn't—"

"What possessed you to—?"

"Sod off, Wil!" Rowland sat back angrily.

Wilfred stopped. "Are you all right?"

Rowland let it go. It was as close as his brother would ever come to an apology.

"You've seen a doctor?"

"Yes, in Paris…though that was probably a mistake."

"Why?"

"Dr. Rousseau returned with the police and some Germans. We were lucky they arrived just as we were leaving."

"You told this doctor that you were wanted by the Nazis?" Wilfred flared again, exasperated that his brother could have been so reckless.

"No, of course not. He just deduced…"

"How would he just deduce such a thing, Rowly? You, or one of those hangers-on you insist on dragging with you, must have said something…Was it Isaacs? That blasted Commie never could keep his mouth shut…"

Rowland snapped. "It was nothing any of us said!" He pulled his bow tie undone and released the first few studs of his shirt to reveal the livid scarring on his chest.

Silence. Then Wilfred swore. The area around the swastika of cigarette burns was clearly still tender and so red that it seemed the Nazi flag itself had been grotesquely emblazoned on Rowland's body. He had been quite deliberately and brutally branded.

Wilfred stood, crushing his cigarette out on the smoker's stand. Involuntarily, Rowland flinched. He fumbled to refasten his shirt. The smell of the cigarette against his flesh came back to him suddenly and he felt ill.

"Bastards!" Wilfred began to pace. "They won't get away with this..."

"I'm afraid the Stormtroopers do what they want, Wil."

"I was talking about my esteemed colleagues who left you there to rot! They sent you to Munich against my express wishes; they should have bloody well seen that you got out." He shook his head, incensed with himself as much as anyone. "I was a damned fool to let you go. What the hell was I thinking?"

"I don't recall that there was a lot you could have done to stop me." Rowland shrugged. "For what it's worth, I think it worked, on the whole. Campbell's going home with scarcely more than a few German postcards."

Wilfred did not seem consoled. "I'll speak to our man in Paris. At the very least we can smooth things over with the French police...have that doctor, Rousseau, discredited somehow and make it plain that Rowland Sinclair has no connection whatsoever with the man the Nazis want for murder." He removed his spectacles, polishing them absently as he regarded his brother. "And I'll arrange another doctor to have a look at you."

"Rousseau has already—"

"Aside from the fact that he turned you in, he's a bloody Frenchman!"

Rowland smiled, vaguely aware that calling for doctors was his brother's way of expressing concern.

"How did you get out?"

Rowland told his brother then what his friends had done, the risks they had taken to get him out of Germany. Wilfred continued to pace.

Rowland changed the subject. "What are you doing in England, Wil?"

"I was asked at the last minute to come as a delegate to the London Economic Conference. There are a few matters to which I need to attend, and Kate wanted to take the boys to see her family over here. We sailed about a week after you left."

"Kate and the boys are here?"

As always, Wilfred's voice warmed when he spoke of his wife and sons. "Yes. Ewan's a trifle young to understand, of course, but Kate wouldn't hear of leaving him. And it's good for Ernie to see England before he goes away to school. He'll be pleased to see you, I expect."

Rowland nodded. He hesitated. "Is Mother…?"

"Mother's at Oaklea. She's no better, but there's no need to worry."

Need or not, Rowland was uneasy. Elisabeth Sinclair had for some time been suffering from a frailty of memory. And she had come to rely on the presence of her sons: Wilfred for himself, and Rowland because she believed he was his brother Aubrey, the son she'd lost in the Great War. Wilfred and Rowland had rarely been out of the country at the same time since Aubrey had died.

"Do you remember Arthur Sinclair?"

Rowland frowned. "Yes. Of course."

Arthur Sinclair was their first cousin, a year or so younger than Wilfred—the son of their father's brother, Edward. For reasons that Rowland could not completely remember, Arthur had been disowned and cut off when still a young man. Edward Sinclair had passed away a couple of years later, before the rift could be repaired. Rowland had seen nothing of Arthur since, though he was aware that Wilfred had tried to find their disinherited cousin after their own father had died.

"Arthur's been abroad for the past decade or so, but he'd write every now and then. I'm afraid he's become a solicitor, but considering the circumstances in which he found himself, we shouldn't condemn him on that account. He made a visit to Oaklea in April. Mother was clearly overjoyed to see him."

"She remembered Arthur?" Rowland's voice bore only the slightest hint of bitterness—a fleeting moment of unguarded hurt. For years now, his mother had failed to know him, insisting he was Aubrey, as if her youngest son had never existed.

Wilfred's eyes were sympathetic, but he was honest. "Yes, she recognised Arthur. It seems she was close to his mother, and rather fond of him."

"I see."

"Arthur very kindly agreed to remain at Oaklea whilst I was abroad…to keep an eye on Mother and relay any urgent matters from the managers to me."

"Oh." Rowland decided now was as good a time as any to ask an indelicate question. "Why was he…?"

"Disowned? An inappropriate liaison that he refused to relinquish, I believe," Wilfred said gravely. "Not something you are in any position to hold against him, Rowly."

Rowland smiled, conceding. "Indeed. We black sheep should probably stick together…form our own flock."

"Good man. I did always feel Arthur was a little hard done by. We'll organise your passages home tomorrow."

"Actually, I'd prefer not to go home just yet."

Wilfred sighed heavily. "Why?"

Rowland explained. "I think I should speak to someone about what's going on in Germany, Wil. The Nazis are not your run-of-the-mill conservative government."

"We are all aware of that, Rowly."

"I'm not so sure."

"You're not the first man to express misgivings about Mr. Hitler's Germany, Rowly," Wilfred said wearily. "Why should they listen to you?"

"I thought that perhaps you could have a word, Wil. Perhaps they'd take me seriously if you—"

"You overestimate my influence."

"Please, Wil. I can't just go home without trying."

Wilfred's brow furrowed. He reached for another cigarette and then thought better of it. It was more than just the burns, the broken arm. There was a change in his brother's eyes...a kind of controlled panic. It had been a long time since Rowland had actually asked for his help. Wilfred relented cautiously. "Perhaps I could arrange for you to talk to Pierrepont...he at least has some sway with that fool Chamberlain. I'll look into it. But, Rowly," Wilfred leaned forward, "you'll learn in time that there is only so much you can do."

Chapter Three

A Bystander's Notebook

POINTED PARS AND PITHY POINTS TO KEEP IT GOING

> The most exclusive "gentlemen's" club in the world is the Carlton Club, London, to gain membership of which a "gentleman" otherwise eligible may have to wait twenty years. But, as some of the exclusive members lately have found it hard to pay up, the exclusiveness has been relaxed to the extent of letting in a score of new members ready to enter and willing to pay the fees. The day, perhaps, is only a few years off when a "gentleman club man" may be classified among human beings.
>
> —*The Worker*, 1932

Wilfred Sinclair was not a member of the small but exclusive gentlemen's club, Watts, in London, nor was he ever likely to be invited to join. Although the Sinclairs had long been counted among the Colonial elite, the Bunyip aristocracy was not the stuff of Watts. Even so, the elderly steward was polite and helpful.

"Shall I reserve three places for luncheon, sir?" he asked, glancing into the dining room. Most of the places around the long table, which ran down its centre, were already occupied with men in white tie and tails, all speaking with unnecessary volume. The boisterous, all-male gathering reminded Rowland of boarding school dinners. Having no particular wish to revisit those years, he had never appreciated the attraction of gentlemen's clubs.

"No, thank you, George," Wilfred said, raising his eyebrows as a dinner roll was flung across a table to hoots of laughter. One of the diners began to crow like a cockerel and the others clucked in reply. "Lord Pierrepont is expecting us, but we don't plan to stay long."

"Very good, sir. Perhaps you'd like to take a refreshment while I call for someone to take you up to the suite."

"That won't be necessary, George. We'll go up ourselves directly."

"Certainly, sir."

Wilfred motioned his brother towards the sweeping staircase that led to the upper floors.

"Pierrepont can be a slippery sod," he warned quietly as they made their way to the second-floor suites that were reserved for members. "He's a self-important egotist, in desperate debt, but he is well-connected and, what's more, his first wife was German. He'll be very happy to think the worst of them."

Rowland nodded.

"Avoid mentioning those friends of yours," Wilfred went on. "Pierrepont's a Tory...he has no time for socialist sentimentality and he'll have no time for the crowd you insist on moving with. It will, quite understandably, cause him to distrust you. Do not mention that you think you're some kind of artist."

"Very well," Rowland said tersely.

Wilfred looked sharply at him. "Pierrepont cares very little about what happens to German Communists, so don't go bleating about how they're being badly treated. He won't give a toss. Your best hope is to demonstrate that the Nazis are not restricting their attacks to the leftist rabble...to show him what could happen to one of us."

Rowland's eyes darkened.

Wilfred stopped. "Rowly, if you are to have any slim hope of achieving anything, convincing anyone, you must curb your temper. This, dear brother, is the politics of diplomacy. Despite appearances, it is not necessarily a team sport."

Rowland rubbed his hand through his hair. He exhaled. "Fine. Let's get this over with."

"Rowly..."

"Really. I'll be charming..."

"See that you are." Wilfred rapped his knuckles on the door to Pierrepont's suite.

There was no answer.

Checking his pocket watch, Wilfred knocked again.

This seemed to prompt a response. The female voice was noticeably agitated. "No...No...don't come in...Oh, my God! My God!"

Both Sinclairs hesitated.

"Are you sure this is the right suite?" Rowland asked.

"I called on him here yesterday."

"Could he be...?"

Wilfred shook his head, disgusted. "Quite possibly." He turned to go.

But there was something about the woman's voice. Rowland tapped again.

"Madam, are you all right?" he called through the door.

Sobbing. Hysterical screaming wails.

Immediately Rowland tried the handle and, finding the door unlocked, pushed it open.

The sitting room seemed undisturbed. There was a crystal tumbler half-filled with brandy perched on the plush arm of a club seat and the secretaire was open, but otherwise the room was ordered and neat.

Rowland waited for his brother's lead. Wilfred gathered himself grimly, and they followed the wailing through to the adjoining bedroom.

Barely through the doorway, they faltered.

"Bloody hell!" Rowland murmured.

They stared speechless. A man lay on the bed. Rowland could tell it was a man only because the frilled nightdress was pulled up above his waist to reveal those parts of him that were unmistakably male. His face, frozen in some final grimace, was made up like a woman's, and a curly wig sat askew on his head. Whatever the original colour of the lace on the nightdress, it was now red—blood-soaked. One of the man's hands was clawed around a sword, which had impaled him to the bed, as if he had been trying to remove it before he died.

A young woman, who seemed barely out of adolescence, stood by the body. She screamed when she saw the Sinclairs, clasping her cut and bloodied hands to her breast and recoiling in terror.

Rowland waited for his brother's lead.

Wilfred spoke evenly, sternly. "Miss Dawe," he said, "it's Wilfred Sinclair...we met yesterday. This is my brother Rowland."

The young woman stopped screaming and, once reminded, she seemed to recognise Wilfred. "How do you do?" she choked before she crumpled by the bed, crying.

Wilfred let her be. He motioned Rowland aside. "I'm going to fetch help. Lock the door behind me and admit no one till I return."

"What?"

"Rowly, this is Alfred Dawe, Viscount Pierrepont. That he is dead is difficult enough without the rest of this getting out."

"But..."

"Just stay here and keep Miss Dawe calm, if you can. Give her some brandy. I shouldn't be long."

Given no other choice, Rowland did as his brother asked, though he did wonder fleetingly if he'd just bolted himself in with a murderess. He poured a generous brandy for the young woman whom he coaxed into the sitting room. He put down the glass so that he could retrieve a handkerchief from his pocket.

He noted uneasily the bloody handprints on the bodice of her dress. "We will have to find you a doctor."

She wrapped the monogrammed square of cloth around her right hand, which was the more seriously cut.

"How did you hurt yourself?" he asked gently.

"How did you?" she snapped, then seemed almost immediately regretful. "I was trying to get the sword out…so I could cover him up. I didn't want anyone to see him like that." She laughed harshly. "The man in the negligee and lipstick is my uncle."

At a loss as to how to comfort the girl, Rowland passed her the glass of brandy. She grasped it in two hands, both shaking, and lifting the tumbler to her lips, she downed the fortifying liquid in a single swig.

There was knocking on the door and a shout through the keyhole. "I say, is everything all right in there? The chaps and I heard the most frightful racket…Bunky? Are you all right, old bean?"

Rowland pulled his arm out of the sling, struggling out of his jacket to place it around the shaking girl's shoulders. He poured her another brandy, ignoring the shouts of, "Hold on, Bunky, we're coming!" and the feeble thumps and groans as someone tried to force the door open.

"Are you Bunky?" Rowland asked the young woman, hoping Wilfred would hurry.

"Gosh, good heavens, no…Bunky is in there," she added pointing at the bedroom. "I'm Allie…Allie Dawe."

"Rowland Sinclair, Miss Dawe. My condolences."

"Yes." Her eyes welled again. "Oh, my God!"

"Can you tell me what happened?" He glanced anxiously at the suite door which seemed to be taking a battering now.

"I came in this morning to start work…"

"Work?"

"Uncle Alfred was kind enough to provide me with gainful and respectable employment as his private secretary when my father passed away. I came in through the tradesmen's entrance because the club doesn't allow women, you see. I let myself in and I found…oh, my God!"

Another commotion at the door. This time it was Wilfred's voice. "Rowly, open the door."

Rowland did so, relieved. A crowd had assembled in the hallway: Wilfred; the steward, George; two uniformed policemen, another two in plainclothes; and half-a-dozen inebriated aristocrats who had risked life and lunch to come up from the dining room, one of whom looked distinctly unwell after having repeatedly charged the door.

Wilfred led in the policemen and the steward, and shut out the club's esteemed but intemperate members. The plainclothes men introduced themselves as Asquith and Entwhistle. Entwhistle was from Scotland Yard. Asquith did not say in what capacity he attended the crime scene, but Rowland guessed he was with the civil service in some role to which Scotland Yard deferred.

While the uniformed constables seemed shocked by the scene of Lord Pierrepont's demise, Entwhistle merely sighed, licked the lead of his pencil and took notes. Asquith looked irritated and weary. They conferred occasionally with Wilfred but generally ignored both Rowland and the steward.

Allie Dawe drank a third and then a fourth glass of brandy, after which she was less-than-coherent.

"Rowly, would you escort Miss Dawe home?" Wilfred asked when the young woman began to sing mournfully. "I suspect she is…tired."

"Don't you need—?" Rowland began.

"We have your details," Entwhistle said as Allie Dawe broke into a rendition of "Just a Closer Walk with Thee." "Best get the young lady home, if you don't mind, sir."

"Not at all." Rowland grabbed his hat from the mantel.

"There's a motor car waiting for you. Just tell the driver who you are," Wilfred added.

"Would you mind using the rear entrance, sir?" asked the steward. "I wouldn't want to upset the members. We're very strict about ladies being on the club's premises."

"One of your members has just been impaled in a frilly nightie," Rowland replied. "I would have thought, in the circumstances—"

The steward shook his head firmly. "Regardless, 'tis club rules, sir."

"Rowly," Wilfred warned.

Rowland relented. George was, after all, just doing his job. He offered his uninjured arm to the bereaved Miss Dawe, who took it, giggling, as she belted out "Onward, Christian Soldiers." As they left the suite, she lowered her voice to a hum, tiptoeing towards the back stairs, though she stumbled often enough to render any stealth useless. Rowland was beginning to quite like Allie Dawe.

A gleaming black Rolls Royce waited near the police cars, as Wilfred had promised. The portly chauffeur conveyed them discreetly away without so much as an improperly curious glance at, let alone a question about, the young lady with bloody hands leaving the scene of a crime.

Allie lived with her mother and several small fluffy dogs in a terrace in Belgravia. The Hon. Mrs. John Dawe, widow of the late Viscount Pierrepont's younger brother, was, at Rowland's guess, in her forties, a marginally faded beauty with a refined constitution. She took one look at her daughter's bloodied hands and promptly fainted. Fortunately, there was a housekeeper about—a stout, calm, and capable matron who said little but acted swiftly. She dutifully assisted Rowland who, one armed, was ill-equipped to hold up both women.

He settled Allie on the chaise while smelling salts were fetched for her mother. Once her mistress had been revived, the housekeeper attended to Allie's injured hands with iodine and tight-lipped disapproval. Rowland introduced himself then.

"I do beg your pardon, Mr. Sinclair," The Hon. Mrs. John Dawe said frostily, glaring at her daughter. "It is not my habit to faint, but I am not accustomed to strange men bringing my daughter home intoxicated and bleeding in full view of the neighbours! Whatever will your uncle say, Allison? I demand to know the meaning of this!"

Allie started to cry again, and so Rowland found himself left to explain that Alfred Dawe, Viscount Pierrepont, was dead and that Allie had cut her hands trying to remove the sword from his lifeless body.

The Hon. Mrs. John Dawe fainted again.

The housekeeper threw up her hands and glowered at Rowland. She retrieved the smelling salts muttering.

"How are your hands?" he asked Allie quietly as her mother was revived for a second time.

She showed him. The cuts were long but not as deep as he'd first thought. "I don't need this anymore," she slurred, handing him his very bloody handkerchief. "So thank you very much… you've been most kind." She looked up at him with smiling glassy eyes. "You're really rather handsome, Mr. Sinclair…I don't know why I didn't notice before."

Rowland smiled. "I suspect most people look significantly better after you've had a few stiff drinks."

She sighed. "Do you want to go dancing sometime?"

Rowland laughed. He handed her his calling card. "I'm staying at Claridge's if you need to contact me. I should probably go."

His gaze moved briefly to the lady of the house who was just coming out of her faint, murmuring, "Bunky…dear Bunky… whatever shall we do without you?"

"I am sorry I wasn't more tactful with your mother."

Allie giggled. "You wait till I tell her that Uncle Alfred was wearing her nightie!"

Chapter Four

Luke Among the Prophets

> It appears highly probable that Lord Luke, a director of the Australian Mercantile, Land, and Finance Company, also a director of Bovril Ltd., is one of the cautious persons behind the proposal that a chartered company, free from all restrictions by industrial awards and "the tyranny of union labour," should be given many other concessions also, and be permitted to build up treasures on earth in the North Australian territory. Obviously this chartered company development proposal was fostered and encouraged by S. M. Bruce, Resident Commonwealth Minister in London, for better or worse, for Australia, but certainly for the expected benefit of some of his London associates in "gentlemen's clubs" and other exclusive places wherein the Oxford bleat and the Cambridge "haw" provide the hallmark of social somebodyism.
>
> —*The Worker*, 1933

Rowland Sinclair returned quite thankfully to the sanctuary of Claridge's to discover that his friends had stepped out. The summer afternoon was particularly warm and airless. He began to loosen his tie, and then, realising he would struggle to reinstate the knot, thought better of it.

"Perhaps you would care to change your attire, sir?" Beresford suggested as he brought him a drink.

"Change? Why?" Rowland asked, wondering if there was some engagement he had forgotten.

"I could have your suit cleaned and pressed before the stain sets, sir."

Rowland looked down and observed that there were indeed dry brown smears of blood on his jacket and a partial handprint on his shirt. He presumed they had come from the hands of Allie Dawe. At various points in their fleeting association, she had grabbed him to keep from stumbling.

Rowland slung back his gin and stood. "You're right—I should clean myself up. Thank you, Beresford." He felt a self-conscious need to explain himself to the butler. He might indeed have done so if Beresford had not spoken first.

"May I suggest your grey suit, sir, with the blue tie and onyx cuff links if you are dining in your suite tonight? Otherwise, I could lay out your dinner suit. I'm afraid you don't have many other options at present."

"Just the grey, I think," Rowland said, somewhat startled that the man had taken such careful stock of the contents of his wardrobe.

"Shall I draw you a bath, sir?"

"No, thank you, Beresford. I shall manage." Rowland resisted an impulse to back away.

The butler's face was, as always, impassive. "If you'll forgive my saying, sir, I've noticed that you and the other gentlemen are travelling very sparely in terms of attire. I know of a reputable tailor who has rendered his services in a most timely manner to Claridge's guests in the past. Perhaps…"

"Yes, an excellent idea, Beresford," Rowland said, grateful for the suggestion but rather uncomfortable nonetheless. He had the distinct impression that Beresford found them a little wanting. "Would you make the arrangements as soon as possible, please?"

Beresford inclined his head. "My pleasure, sir. I'm sure Mr. Ambrose will be able to measure you and the other gentlemen this evening, if that would be convenient?"

"Yes, tremendous, Beresford...thank you."

"Very good, sir."

It was as the butler retreated to make these arrangements that Edna, Clyde, and Milton returned. They noticed the blood on his suit immediately.

"Struth, Rowly," Clyde said, looking him over for new injuries. "What have you done to yourself this time?"

"Me? Nothing." Rowland recounted the rather extraordinary events of the morning at Watts.

"What kind of nightie?" Clyde asked aghast.

"How would I know? One of those short lacy things."

"A baby-doll," Edna said with authority. "What colour was it?"

"Well and truly red by the time Wil and I got there. Why does that matter?"

The sculptress screwed up her face. "I was just trying to fix an image in my mind."

Rowland shook his head. "I'm trying to expunge the image from mine. Remind me to die in a suit."

Edna pulled off her gloves and flopped onto the settee beside him. "Do you believe poor Lord Pierrepont was wearing the... nightie of his own accord?"

A moment of awkward silence.

"I've an uncle who likes to wear silk stockings and women's shoes," Milton volunteered. "Sadly, he and my aunt don't wear the same size."

"Oh, yes, I remember him," Edna laughed. She and Milton had known each other since childhood. "I recall he wore heels rather well."

"That's him," Milton's voice held a note of admiration. "Actually, his legs weren't bad at all. If they hadn't been so hairy—"

"You don't suppose the girl did him in, do you, Rowly?" Clyde was desperate to change the subject.

"Who, Allie?" Rowland dismissed the idea. "She's just a slip of a girl. I can't see it."

"But he expired in her mother's nightie, you say?" Milton rubbed his chin thoughtfully.

"That's what she said." Rowland frowned. It did seem odd, unless Lord Pierrepont was on intimate terms with his brother's widow.

"Did Miss Dawe have any idea who might have wanted to kill her uncle?"

"I didn't have a chance to ask her. After the brandy she was a trifle indisposed, to be honest."

"We'll have to ask her when she's sobered up," Milton decided.

"We?" Clyde tensed. "Since when did this become *our* concern?"

Milton puffed. "This is the concern of every man who ever coveted a frilly nightie or pretty heels. Every young boy who ever wore a frock..." The poet paused, grinning in a manner that was quite evil.

Clyde glared at him.

Months ago, when he'd had far too much to drink, Clyde had admitted that he'd spent the first five years of his life dressed exclusively in hand-me-downs from his cousin, Charlie, more formally known as Charlotte. So that it would not look too odd, Mrs. Watson Jones had allowed Clyde's hair to grow long and tied it up with ribbons. The idea that the burly, weather-beaten, no-nonsense Clyde had started life in bloomers amused the poet no end, and while Milton could be surprisingly discreet, he was not always so.

Rowland laughed and diplomatically moved the conversation away. "I'll check on Allie in a day or two, just to make sure she's holding up..."

Clyde snorted. To his mind, Rowland Sinclair was too easily distracted by every corpse that fell across his path. He might have expressed that sentiment if Beresford had not come in to announce that the tailor had arrived. The butler's tone made it clear that it was not, in his opinion, a moment too soon.

Rowland alighted from the Rolls Royce at the steps of the South Kensington terrace. The rotund chauffeur came wheezing around the motor car's elongated bonnet. His face fell as he realised his passenger had managed to open the door himself.

"Sorry." Rowland stepped aside so the man could close the door behind him. Wilfred had sent the car for them. Rowland was aware that his habit of getting in and out of cars of his own accord was considered by some a sign of poor breeding. And he expected that protocol here would be somewhat particular.

"No 'arm done, sir," the chauffeur gasped, though it seemed the unnecessary exertion could yet finish him off.

Rowland opened the back door for Edna who stepped out of the motor car with her eyes wide and fixed upon the four-storey Victorian terrace to which they'd been delivered. Its doorway and windows were arched and framed with columns and finials. The stucco walls were white and it looked out on the park known as Ennismore Gardens.

"So, is Mr. Bruce Australia's High Commissioner now?" Edna whispered. "How should we address him?"

"M'lord should suffice," Milton murmured. The poet had no love for the erstwhile Prime Minister of the Commonwealth of Australia, whose conservative government had built its platform on breaking strikes.

Rowland smiled. "Technically speaking, I understand he's a special minister without portfolio…but to be honest I'm not sure what the protocol is. Wil calls him Spats."

Edna giggled. "Really? To his face?"

The Australian press delighted in poking fun at Bruce's fondness for spats—as either a symbol of the politician's patrician affectations or a dreadful folly of fashion. Edna had always imagined that Stanley Melbourne Bruce would take it as the slight it was intended to be.

"They're old chums." Rowland's brow furrowed slightly. He had, admittedly, been surprised when they were all invited to the home of the Bruces. Wilfred had never hidden his opinion of the set with which his brother chose to move. In the past he had, at most, tolerated them under sufferance. But then, Wilfred's young wife, Kate, had always enjoyed Rowland's friends. It was to her that they most probably owed the invitation.

Edna was, as usual, undaunted, entwining her arm in Rowland's uninjured one, and exclaiming at the beauty of the expansive terrace and the English rose gardens which surrounded it.

They were admitted by a maid in a traditional aproned uniform.

"Uncle Rowly!" Ernest Sinclair squeezed past the servant. "Why, hello, Uncle Rowly." The six-year-old extended and then dropped his right hand as he stared at the sling. "Hell's bells, Uncle Rowly, what's happened to your arm?" he blurted before clapping his hands over his mouth.

Rowland tousled the child's dark curls. "Don't let your mother catch you talking like that, Ernie, or we'll both be in trouble."

"Oh, I'd tell her it wasn't your fault," Ernest said solemnly. "A man's got to take responsibility for his own actions."

Rowland peered through the open door into the empty hallway. "But since your mother's not here," he whispered, "I trust there's no need to confess."

Ernest nodded emphatically. He paused to greet Clyde, Milton, and Edna before asking again, "What happened to your arm, Uncle Rowly?"

"I broke it."

"When you were in Germany?"

"Yes."

Ernest nodded in a way that made Rowland wonder exactly how much his nephew knew about what he had been doing in Germany. Wilfred's elder son rarely missed a thing.

Ernest was as curious as he was concerned. "Does it hurt?"

"Not anymore."

"I'm so glad." Ernest turned to the maid. "This is my Uncle Rowly and his Leninist friends. You can let them in…they're very nice."

The maid's eyes grew wide and she stepped back reflexively.

Ernest smiled.

Milton laughed. "That's the way, Ernie, mate…there's no point pretending."

The young woman composed herself and bobbed deferentially. "Very good, Master Ernest. Mr. Sinclair is expecting you, sir. I'm to take you in to the library and the rest of your…party…to Madam and Mrs. Sinclair in the drawing room."

Ernest took Rowland's hand. "I'll show him, Mabel. This way, Uncle Rowly."

The maid looked a little nonplussed, but Ernest was already dragging Rowland into the house leaving her to deal with the Leninists alone.

The library was on the ground floor. Its high, intricately detailed ceilings lent a gravity of scale to the walls of books in their thousands. Paintings of the ten Australian prime ministers since Federation adorned the walls in the spaces between the bookshelves. The furniture was substantial and modern—leather club chairs with conveniently placed smoker's stands in chrome and Bakelite.

Two men sat on either side of a scrolled oak desk, smoking. Wilfred Sinclair smiled when he saw his son. "What are you doing, you scamp?"

"Uncle Rowly's here, Daddy."

"I can see that. Now you run along and tell your mother that we'll join them all shortly…go on now."

Ernest released his uncle's hand and ran into the hallway.

Wilfred then introduced the Honourable Stanley Melbourne Bruce, Member of the House of Representatives, Companion of Honour, who was, it seemed, playing host to the Wilfred's family while they were in London. The Australian politician was tall, and though he must have been nearly fifty, he bore himself with an aristocratic confidence.

Bruce addressed him as "Rowland" from the first. Still unsure of the man's title, Rowland resorted to "Sir."

"Your brother has been telling me of the unpleasantness yesterday. A nasty business and quite distressing, I should imagine."

"It was certainly unexpected," Rowland replied.

Bruce directed him to a seat. "You understand, Rowland, that this is a matter of some delicacy."

"Oh?"

"What do you know about the London Economic Conference?"

Wilfred grunted. "He could probably paint you a picture of the venue."

"Nothing specific." Rowland glanced irritably at his brother. "I presume you gentlemen are trying to save the world with trade agreements or some such thing."

Bruce nodded. "Some such thing. If everything goes as planned, the free world will be saved, as you say, by an international currency agreement."

"Well, that's capital news." Rowland hoped he wasn't about to be subjected to a lecture on world finance.

"It is," Bruce agreed, "or rather it will be if it goes ahead. The agreement is tripartite and requires the participation of America as well as France and Britain. Regrettably, President Roosevelt has some doubts on the value of the agreement. There are those in the United States who seek to devalue the dollar instead of fix it at a reasonable level, as this agreement would do." Bruce then outlined what he saw as the effects the stabilisation of currencies would have on confidence, growth, and trade.

Rowland considered the minister. Bruce had an interesting face—strong brows flared sharply up above shrewd close-set eyes, a nose that pulled away from his mouth as if there were an unpleasant odour about, and a chin that sat proudly out from a pouting lower lip. They combined to give the man a permanently disdainful look. Rowland sat back mulling the composition of the portrait he was constructing in his mind: a full figure, he thought, to bring out the height and athleticism of Bruce's build as well as the self-conscious distinction in his bearing....

"Rowly!" Wilfred jarred him out of his contemplation.

It was only then Rowland realised that Bruce had stopped talking…and he had no idea what the minister had said.

"As Spats was saying," Wilfred said pointedly, "Lord Pierrepont's death could cause a scandal that would permanently derail the conference."

"Yes…why?"

"Because it seems the last person to see him alive was Cordell Hull, the American Secretary of State."

Rowland was confused. "Are you suggesting the American Secretary of State killed Lord Pierrepont?"

"No, of course not." Bruce drew on his cigar. "But the Americans may see any investigation of their delegates as hostile, diplomatically speaking." He shook his head. "Don't let their obsession with freedom of speech fool you — Americans are rather sensitive."

"I see." Actually, Rowland didn't see. He had no idea why Bruce was telling him this.

"Of course, one can't just ignore the murder of a peer," Bruce went on. "Scotland Yard will handle the affair as quietly and unobtrusively as possible, but I did want to impress upon you, Rowland, the importance of being discreet. Particularly with the more salacious aspects of Lord Pierrepont's demise."

Rowland smiled. "You mean the nightie."

"Yes, quite. It would probably be best if you did not mention that rather perplexing detail to anyone. In fact, the less said about Lord Pierrepont, the better."

"Surely there will be an investigation?" Rowland asked, vaguely disturbed by the manner in which murder was being treated as a political inconvenience.

"My dear man, of course! In fact I believe the Yard has already found a suspect."

"There are one or two reporters sniffing about," Wilfred said. "They're asking questions and we wanted to make sure that you don't give them a headline sensational enough to scuttle any hope of an agreement."

"How could they possibly even know to ask me?"

Wilfred frowned. "We gave our names to Samuel Playfair."

"Who's Samuel Playfair?"

"The steward."

"I thought his name was George."

"They call all the servants George at Watts…it's easier for the members to remember that way."

Rowland thought back to the rowdy luncheon at the gentlemen's club. He supposed Playfair could count himself lucky the members didn't want to call him "Bunky" or something equally absurd.

"What do you know about the new government of Germany, Minister Bruce?" Rowland asked.

Bruce looked at him, startled.

"Rowly…we are talking about—" Wilfred began.

"Yes, yes, I won't tell anyone about the nightie," Rowland promised impatiently. Then he asked his question again.

Wilfred cleared his throat. "I've told Spats about your experiences in Germany, Rowly."

Bruce shook his head. "A terrible business. The SA could potentially thrust Germany into civil war. Rest assured, Rowland, the governments of Europe have been vocal in their condemnation of the excesses of Röhm and his Stormtroopers."

"I don't think you understand—"

"I think you'll find I do."

"This is not simply about SA thuggery. The Nazi government is on an aggressive path."

Bruce regarded him sternly. "The Germans are at this conference in the spirit of co-operation, Rowland. They have territorial interests, yes, but I believe you'll find they are restricted to the Saarland and other traditionally German regions." He sighed. "I'm afraid talk of German expansionism is premature and generated by a few warmongers and conspiracy theorists." He looked Rowland up and down. "How old are you, if you don't mind my asking? I don't suppose you saw service."

"No, sir, I didn't," Rowland said tightly. War service was the trump card which the men of his brother's age liked to play against others—a kind of imprimatur which gave them the right to decide all matters thenceforth.

"Well, I saw a great deal." Bruce rubbed his knee. "I served at Gallipoli and now I deal with the Turks in an international spirit of co-operation and mutual respect." He pointed at Rowland with his cigar. "I can tell you the biggest threat to Australia at the moment is not German theatrics but the American Agriculture Bill which will have a devastating impact on our exports."

Rowland dragged his hand back through his hair, frustrated.

Wilfred intervened, "I do feel, in this instance, Rowly might offer some insight into the mood in Germany."

Rowland looked sharply at his brother, surprised by his support.

"Perhaps," Wilfred continued cautiously, "if you were to provide Rowly with a letter of introduction to one or two people who are interested in these matters...maybe someone close to Ramsay MacDonald. You never know, Rowly may be able to give some perspective to his dogged insistence upon disarmament."

Bruce frowned, his eyes narrowing as he considered the suggestion. "I fear it will be a waste of time, Wil."

"Even so."

"Very well." He turned back to Rowland. "You keep Lord Pierrepont's peculiar penchant under your hat, and I'll see what I can do."

Chapter Five

Table Manners

Points of Etiquette

At meals ladies always should be served first, even when there are men guests present. In no circumstances are bad manners more noticeable than when displayed at the table. To eat badly is to commit one of the greatest offences against the laws of politeness. Innate refinement will sometimes protect a woman in this direction, but unless girls have been subjected to proper home training in table manners they grow up usually with habits as vulgar as those of men whose home upbringing has been neglected.

A few points in training children that may be helpful to mothers are as follows:— The soup plate should be tilted away from the edge of the table, and soup should be taken from the side of the large spoon provided. Bread should not be crumbled into the soup, but broken with the fingers from a thick piece placed at the left hand. If special fish knives are not provided, fish should be eaten with two forks, or a fork and a piece of bread. When one is eating a dish that requires the use of a fork in the right hand, the fork may be held with the tines turned up; otherwise it is not correct to do this. Rissoles, mince and similar made dishes should be eaten with a fork only. All sweets, where possible, should be eaten with a fork alone. A spoon and fork may be used for fruit tarts, stewed fruit or other dishes of syrupy nature. Either the spoon or the fork should be raised to the mouth for the purpose of receiving fruit stones. In the case of plums and other fruit with large stones, it is better to separate the stone with the spoon and fork before putting the fruit in the mouth. When a course is finished the knife and fork or spoon and fork should be placed close together.

It is a bad plan always to give children the least attractive parts of a dish, that being apt to make them greedy for dainties when they are visiting. The knife should never be used to convey food to the mouth, and the special knife for butter should always be used, likewise the sugar spoon in the bowl, instead of individual teaspoons. When one is using knife and fork, the elbows should be kept close to the sides. If a plate is sent for a second helping, the knife and fork should be placed close together, as much to the side of the plate as possible. Nothing except fruit pips, stones, or skin, should be taken from the mouth with the fingers. Pieces of bone, gristle, etc., should be taken from the mouth with the fork and quietly placed on the side of the plate. Always leave the spoon in the saucer, and when it is necessary to do so, stir tea, coffee, or cocoa as quietly and unobtrusively as possible. The mouth should never be filled too full, and undue haste in eating should be avoided. No one should leave a meal table until everyone has finished. A guest should not fold the table napkin, but leave it on the table more or less crumpled.

—*The West Australian*, 1933

Mrs. Wilfred Sinclair was genuinely glad to see her brother-in-law's entirely unacceptable friends. Kate had always liked the bohemian entourage—something which her husband claimed was due to her too kind and persuadable heart. She knew of course that they lived at Woodlands House under Rowland's patronage and what seemed an ever-present cloud of scandal. Wilfred maintained that they were exploiting his brother's generosity, using Rowland while they turned the Sinclairs' grand Woollahra residence into some kind of artists' commune.

It was not in Kate's nature to contradict her husband and accordingly she'd never mentioned her fondness for her disreputable brother-in-law's set in Wilfred's presence. Indeed, she'd been surprised that he'd not objected to her suggestion that they be included in the invitation to luncheon. Perhaps this newfound tolerance had something to do with whatever had happened in Germany. Wilfred had returned from Claridge's angry and distressed. He had fired off several telegrams back to Australia, but had said nothing more to Kate than that Rowland had found trouble and that his useless unemployed friends had at least stuck by him.

And so she had not been expecting the plaster cast and sling.

"What have you done to yourself, Rowly?" Kate enquired as he kissed her cheek. "Wil didn't say you'd hurt yourself."

Rowland had no time to reply before their hostess intervened.

"Oh, my Lord," Ethel Bruce exclaimed. "This simply won't do...Why, we're serving crown roast!" The matronly wife of Australia's eighth Prime Minister looked at the cast in horror. "It'll have to be a consommé...there's nothing else for it!"

"Uncle Rowly broke his arm in Germany," Ernest announced solemnly.

"Yes, well, that explains it!" Ethel said, walking towards the door. "You must excuse me...I should speak to Cook."

Rowland wasn't quite sure what it explained.

Lunch with the Bruces was quite the gracious affair: elegant and formal. Clyde visibly paled as he beheld the numerous pieces of gleaming cutlery which rippled outwards from the fine china plates at each place setting. He had never become accustomed to the complexity of dining with the upper classes and, for a moment, he envied Rowland his injury. As it was, the rest of them would have to work out how and when to use the various utensils with some sort of proficiency and decorum.

"My goodness, Mrs. Bruce," Milton said winking at their hostess, "it must have taken you a while to polish all these."

She laughed. "Great Caesars! Go on!" She flapped her hand at the poet. "You are a card, Mr. Isaacs."

With a smile and a flourish, Milton offered their hostess his arm and escorted her to the table.

The conversation at luncheon was mostly light and inconsequential, until Ethel Bruce herself raised the subject of Lord Pierrepont.

"Stanley dear, did you hear that poor Bunky Pierrepont has died? Tragic…so very tragic." She turned to Kate. "You would have simply adored Bunky, Katie dear. Quite the old rogue, but charming in his way."

Bruce and Wilfred said nothing. Rowland broke the silence. "I say, did you know this chap Pierrepont particularly well, Mrs. Bruce?"

"I wouldn't say well. He was more of a robust acquaintance. Stanley played golf with him at St. Andrews on and off, and I'm sure we've had him for dinner once or twice, haven't we, Stanley darling?"

Bruce finished chewing before he replied. "I can't say I recall, my dear."

Milton shook his head gravely, despite the mischievous gleam in his eye. "It was an unfortunate way to go."

"Unfortunate?"

"Most people would, I imagine, consider being murdered in one's own bed somewhat unfortunate."

"Murdered?" Ethel Bruce's eyes widened, and her hand splayed against the base of her throat. "But however do you know that, Mr. Isaacs?"

"You must have read it in the paper, Milt," Rowland said pointedly as his eyes met the poet's.

Wilfred glared at them both.

Their hostess thought for a moment. "No, I'm sure it didn't mention anything about murder, merely that Lord Pierrepont died in tragic circumstances. I suppose it would be difficult to die in a manner that wasn't tragic...but murder? Why that's simply dreadful! Are you sure, Mr. Isaacs?"

"Um...perhaps not..." Milton rubbed his forehead, clearly having caught the message in Rowland's gaze and the hostility in Wilfred's.

Edna and Clyde watched curiously and said nothing.

Mrs. Bruce turned back to her husband. "Do you recall the article, Stanley?"

Again Bruce took his time, chewing and swallowing before he replied. "I'm afraid I barely glanced at the paper this morning, Ethel. But I understand there may have been something suspicious about Pierrepont's demise. Better leave it to the constabulary, don't you think, my dear? This new cook you've taken on is excellent." He nodded at Rowland. "What a gastronomic shame you must confine yourself to consommé, young man. The roast is undeniably superb."

"Incidentally, Rowly," Wilfred said following Bruce's lead in dissipating the topic of conversation. "I've organised a doctor to call on you at Claridge's this afternoon. Lord only knows if that French chap managed to set the correct arm!"

"I expect I might know if he hadn't, Wil," Rowland replied. Clearly, neither Bruce nor Wilfred wanted to pursue further discussion of Pierrepont.

Ethel Bruce was, however, not so easily diverted, and quite eager to discuss the recently departed man. From her they learned that Pierrepont was a wonderful dancer, a dab hand at bridge, and had once rowed for Cambridge. He'd been a notorious and committed flirt, which Ethel had found charming after a fashion, but which was not always proper.

"Oh, dear, you don't suppose he was shot by a jealous husband?" She cupped a hand over her mouth as the thought occurred to her.

"He wasn't shot," Bruce stated wearily, without looking up from his meal.

"Well, how would we know?" Ethel said, her voice quivering with excitement. "The newspapers didn't say. Bunky might have been shot!" She turned to Kate. "You mustn't be frightened, my dear, I'm sure no one would have any cause to shoot Wilfred."

Rowland smiled.

Wilfred cleared his throat.

"Stanley," Ethel said, "you simply must see what you can find out."

"Whatever for?"

"I'll need to send our condolences."

"Which only requires you to know that Pierrepont is dead."

Ethel Bruce smiled sweetly. "Of course, my dear, I don't know what I was thinking."

With that retreat, the conversation moved to matters less scandalous. Ethel and Milton found they had a common admiration for the works of Conan Doyle and Christie, and were soon immersed in a discussion of little grey cells and intellect. Bruce debated the implications of the Ottawa Agreement with Wilfred and spoke of his hopes for the League of Nations to which he was Australia's representative.

Clyde listened as Kate chatted about the exploits of Ernest and young Ewan, responding with the details of some country balm for teething when she mentioned that the youngest Sinclair had been fractious.

"You're quiet, Rowly," Edna whispered.

He smiled. "Just contemplating six weeks of soup." He glanced enviously at the generous portions of roast which had been placed before every other person at the table.

Edna laughed, though she rubbed his arm sympathetically. "Poor Rowly…you've had such a miserable time of it. Perhaps this doctor of Wilfred's will be able to help you."

"To use a knife and fork?" Rowland asked, bemused.

"No…but maybe he can give you something to help you sleep."

Rowland looked up sharply, startled that she knew he was having trouble sleeping.

"Clyde mentioned that you're still having nightmares," she said. "He's worried about you."

"There's no need to be." Rowland had not slept soundly since the night they'd fled the house on Schellingstrasse where the SA had left him for dead. He'd tried not to allow his friends to know, but, on occasion, Clyde had found him trying to read or simply drinking in the early hours of the morning. They'd played cards without mention of why either would choose pre-dawn poker over sleep. "I'm just getting used to sleeping with this cast," Rowland lied, vaguely embarrassed.

"Of course," Edna said gently. "Perhaps Wil's doctor will be able to give you something for that."

And so the meal was passed and, for the gentlemen, finished with cigars and brandy while the ladies retired to the drawing room for coffee. Ethel Bruce waited until the serving maid had left the room before she said, "There's more to Bunky's death than meets the eye, I'll warrant." She crossed her arms indignantly. "Stanley's so considerate of my delicate sensibilities, he won't tell me anything!"

"Perhaps there's nothing to tell, Ethel," Kate ventured.

"Poppycock! I haven't listened to Stanley drone on endlessly about his men, money, and markets, just to be kept in the dark when something interesting finally happens. Of course, it's very tragic...but it is more interesting than Stanley's blessed tariffs!"

Kate looked distinctly uncomfortable but Edna warmed all the more to Ethel Bruce.

"I'm having tea with the ladies of the Dominions this week," Ethel continued, nodding determinedly. "I'll discover more then...it's the only reliable source of information in the Empire. Why, the wife of the High Commissioner to Ceylon is always a mine of knowledge."

Edna really wanted to tell Ethel Bruce what she knew.

"Don't you worry, ladies." Ethel raised her cup of coffee. "Whatever I don't bully out of Stanley, I will gather from the wives of His Majesty's men. Now…" She changed the subject abruptly. "Edna, you don't mind if I call you Edna, do you, my dear? You must call me Ethel. What exactly happened to young Mr. Sinclair in Germany?"

Edna was caught unprepared. She hesitated, glancing uncertainly at Kate. "Rowly came to the attention of the Brownshirts when we were in Munich." She paused, unsure of how to phrase the brutality of it. "They found him…they hurt him."

Kate gasped, shocked, realising suddenly the reason behind Wilfred's fury. "They broke his arm? Intentionally?"

Edna nodded, placing her cup down and folding her arms tightly across her chest. "They nearly killed him, Kate."

"No wonder Wil was so…" Kate started, her face stricken with horror. "But why? Why would they?"

"Mostly because of a painting." Edna thought wistfully of the delicate blue nude in which Rowland had managed to capture the fragile essence of a young photographic assistant. "It was beautiful…revolutionary. They broke his arm for it." She told the two women about the state Rowland had been in when they'd found him, and how they'd all been given shelter by an underground of men considered enemies of Germany, before they eventually escaped to Paris with the help of an Australian journalist.

By the time Edna finished her story, Kate was near tears and Ethel was unusually speechless.

At this point, the gentlemen joined them again.

"You ladies look far too serious," Clyde said as they walked into silence.

"Perhaps you, too, have been discussing the importance of fixing the pound against the gold standard," Milton muttered miserably.

"Oh, Stanley!" Ethel gathered herself and addressed her husband. "You haven't been boring our guests again, have you? Honestly, it's a wonder anyone visits us at all!"

Bruce's brow rose, as if the concept that he could bore anyone was unexpected and somewhat silly.

"Not at all, Ethel," Wilfred said in Bruce's defence. "I'm sure Rowly and his friends appreciate the value of your husband's wisdom on these fiscal matters."

Milton sighed. "And money, that most pure imagination, gleams only through the dawn of its creation."

"Why Mr. Isaacs!" Ethel exclaimed. "That's very clever."

"Byron often was," Rowland said as Milton, unrepentant, accepted the accolade.

"Perhaps you should sit down, Rowly," Kate urged anxiously, her eyes still bright with distress. "Would you care for a drink?"

"Yes…Actually I'd best not, but thank you, Kate." Rowland was unsettled by her sudden need to fuss over him. "We really should be going…"

"But you must wait till the children return," Kate protested. "They'll be back in a minute and Ernest will be terribly disappointed if you're not here when he returns!"

Again Rowland was surprised by the emotion in Kate's plea. He shrugged. "Of course. We'll stay till the boys get back."

"Actually, Rowly, I wouldn't mind a word whilst you wait." Wilfred motioned towards the tiled balcony off the sitting room. "Shall we step outside for a moment?"

Edna looked at Rowland in alarm. In her experience, Wilfred requested these quiet words so that he could dress down his brother privately. She wondered now if she should have spoken of Germany.

Rowland did not seem to share her concern. Returning her glance with a wink, he followed Wilfred onto the balcony which overlooked the park below.

The rose beds of Ennismore Gardens were in full bloom, adding ordered colour to the sweeping paths which wound between the trees. Elegant couples strolled among the shrubberies and smartly dressed children played polite cricket and skipped on the lawns. Rowland waved as he spotted Ernest running ahead of his nanny, who was pushing Ewan in a large pram.

Wilfred lit a cigarette.

Rowland waited.

"I couldn't help but overhear your conversation with Miss Higgins, Rowly."

"What conversation?"

"As highly inappropriate as it is for her to know such a fact, Miss Higgins seems to be of the opinion that you're not sleeping."

Rowland studied his brother, not sure what he was getting at. Wilfred's disapproval of Edna was long-standing, but he was bewildered as to why it would warrant particular mention now. He tensed, preparing himself for an old and bitter argument.

"Is it true?" Wilfred demanded.

"Is what true?"

"That you're not sleeping."

Rowland relaxed. "I'm all right, Wil."

Wilfred smoked wordlessly for a while. "You know, Rowly, after the war, there were a few...several...chaps who stopped sleeping."

Rowland said nothing, surprised, not by what Wilfred said but by the fact that he'd said it. This was closer than his brother had ever before come to talking to him of the war. Fifteen years after the armistice, and Rowland still knew almost nothing about Wilfred's years in France—what he'd done, how he'd felt. It had always been a silence between them.

Wilfred met his eye. "Don't drink."

"I beg your pardon?"

"If you can't sleep...when you find yourself alone and awake in the middle of the night...read, take up smoking, learn to knit, if you have to. Just don't drink...not alone."

Rowland shifted uncomfortably. He dragged his good hand through his hair. He had taken the edge off with gin more than once. It all seemed so ridiculous in the light of day, but he understood what Wilfred was saying. "Very well, Wil, I'll knit you some socks."

Chapter Six

Madame Tussaud's Waxworks

Hitler's Figure Painted Red
TWO YOUTHS ARRESTED

London, Friday

> Three green-shirted youths entered Madame Tussaud's and smeared red paint on the wax figure of Herr Hitler and labelled it "Hitler, the murderer." They were later arrested.
>
> —*Border Watch*, 1933

The day was warm; possibly hot, by English standards. For the Australians, it was pleasant. They had set out on foot for the waxworks museum on Marylebone Road. Edna's interest was professional. She often worked in wax when creating a piece for casting in bronze, and the lifelike figures created by the sculptors of Madame Tussaud's both intrigued and impressed her. Clyde and Rowland, being painters, were less interested in the sculptures as examples of technical excellence than as contemporary curiosities. Milton was willing to go anywhere, as long as it did not involve another conversation about economics.

Rowland had been to the famous wax museum before, a number of times, in fact, during the eight years he was educated in England. The popular exhibitions had changed, with new celebrities taking the place of the silent film stars of the twenties. Nevertheless, there was something quite macabre about the museum: the statues were at once so lifelike and lifeless that they seemed to be parodies of the originals. It was not hard to believe that the museum's founder had refined her craft making the death masks of decapitated French nobles during the revolution.

Beyond the Chamber of Horrors, populated by monsters and celebrity criminals, stood the royal family.

"That's bloody disturbing." Clyde gave Princess Elizabeth, King George V's two-year-old granddaughter, a wide berth.

Rowland nodded. There was something a great deal eerier about a small girl frozen in wax than anything else they'd seen. Perhaps the stiffness, the lack of movement and sound, felt particularly stark in the depiction of a child.

Somewhere between Jack the Ripper and the newly unveiled statue of Adolf Hitler, Edna seemed to vanish. The men weren't particularly alarmed at first, for the sculptress had a way of becoming distracted and wandering off, and the museum was crowded with visitors. It was only after several minutes of searching that they began to be concerned. At that point, Edna reappeared.

She grabbed Rowland's hand, beckoning to Milton and Clyde to follow. "Come with me. I want to introduce you to someone."

She took them through a barely detectable black door in the black wall. It led to what looked like a series of studios behind the main exhibit hall. Rows of disembodied heads sat on overburdened shelves. Random body parts awaited attachment to twisted torsos on tables beside boxes of glass eyes and wigs.

Among the partially assembled figures of wax stood a few men of flesh, fitting limbs, inserting hair, or working with moulds. An old man, with a head so bald and shiny it might have been mistaken for wax, stood inspecting feet and shouting at a clearly harassed apprentice whenever he found a flaw in the toes. He berated the younger man for his carelessness, waving what appeared to be a hook as he ranted. As they came closer, Rowland realised that the hook was all that existed where the man's right hand should have been. When the man saw Edna, he stopped shouting and beamed. "Edna, my dear, you found your companions, then?"

Edna pulled Rowland forward. "Rowly, you remember Mr. Marriott Spencer?"

In truth, Rowland had no recollection of the man whatsoever, but he did recall Edna speaking of a hook-handed sculpture teacher from their days at the Ashton School of Art. It had to be him. How many hook-handed men could Edna possibly know?

"From Ashton's," Rowland said. "Of course. It's a pleasure to see you again, Mr. Spencer. You will excuse me if I don't offer you my hand."

"I am ill-equipped to accept it, son." Spencer held up his hook.

"Marriott is Madame Tussaud's chief artist now," Edna said proudly.

Spencer shook his head. "Ach...the Depression, you know. One must find work when commissions are scarce. When times get better, I will return to making art. Until then, I make mannequins."

"They're so much more than mannequins, Marriott," Edna protested.

"You are too kind, Edna." He smiled, looking at her over half-moon glasses. "You were my most talented student, you know. I expect great things from you. Promise me you will not follow in my footsteps; that you will not waste your unique gift creating novelties for the unwashed masses."

Edna laughed. "You are melodramatic, Marriott! You work with the most famous people in the Empire, unwashed or not!"

"I work *on* the most famous people, my dear. I work *with* wax. I have become a maker of giant wickless candles!"

Milton picked up a bust of Theodore Roosevelt. "Still, you do it well."

Spencer beamed, suddenly mollified. "Come, let me show you how we create the figures. Sadly, it is not art...but it is not an uninteresting livelihood."

He led them on a tour of the back studios where the figures were created, then dressed and posed. He showed them large sheets on which were recorded the hundreds of measurements taken to create a likeness. He explained the process from clay-sculpting, to mould-making, to wax casting.

"Our subjects sit for us like models," he said, "but it is more intrusive. We measure and measure and measure—every proportion, every wrinkle, every blemish—and then we sculpt."

"And people are willing to be so closely scrutinised and quantified?" Rowland asked. It seemed brutally mechanical to reduce a face to measurements, however precise.

"Of course...it is a great honour to be recreated in Madame Tussaud's. Some people sit for us many times."

"Why?"

"Alas," Spencer lamented, "wax does not age but the flesh decays." He pointed out the statue of a young Winston Churchill. "Originally cast in 1908, to take advantage of the public interest in his nuptials, but no longer a true copy of the original. I will be measuring Mr. Churchill next month. You can see he required much less wax back then."

But Rowland was not looking at the British politician's statue, his eyes fixed instead upon the bust and torso of a man among a collection of unfinished figures in the corner.

"Mr. Spencer, is that Lord Pierrepont?"

Marriott Spencer walked up to the figure and peered at it, adjusting the bifocals on the bridge of his nose. He lifted the wig and inspected the lettering on the skull. "Yes, that's what it says. Are you acquainted with him?"

"Briefly acquainted...yes, you could say that." Rowland frowned. "Why would Madame Tussaud's be sculpting Pierrepont?" he asked. "Was he famous in some way?"

Spencer shrugged. "I couldn't tell you...this is one of Francis' pieces. He is not in today."

Edna tilted her head as she studied the aristocratic waxen figure and Rowland guessed she was trying to picture it adorned in a frilly nightie. He glanced at his watch—they had lost track of time.

The bell in the main gallery rang to warn visitors that the museum was about to close.

"You must come back and visit poor Marriott again." Spencer took Edna's hand in his unhooked one and kissed it emphatically. "You can talk to Francis about your friend, if you like."

"Oh, Marriott, of course we'll visit again," Edna said, smiling at the old man. She looked longingly about the studio. "I haven't been able to work on anything in a while. I miss this."

"I am pleased to hear it!" He smiled thoughtfully. "Perhaps I will be able to find something for you to work on. Would you like that, my dear?"

"I would," Edna nodded. "Very much."

"It is settled then—you will return. I will send your gentlemen to talk with Francis and you will be my beautiful protégée again!"

"What on Earth is this?" Clyde picked up the large tin which had been left on the dressing table, as Rowland proceeded to get dressed again.

Rowland smiled. "Horlicks. I believe it's a malted milk powder. Pennyworth left it."

The doctor despatched by Wilfred had been waiting for him when they'd returned to Claridge's. Thorough, if a little dour, the English physician had established beyond any doubt that his French colleague had in fact set the correct limb and done so in a manner he deemed satisfactory. That done, he'd lectured Rowland on the dangers of infection as he treated the burns with iodine and petroleum jelly.

Milton took the tin from Clyde and read the label suspiciously. "What's it for?"

"I think it's supposed to keep me from becoming an alcoholic." Rowland took a fresh shirt from the wardrobe. "He also recommends I take up smoking cigarettes to calm my nerves."

Milton laughed. "Nerves? Since when do men have nerves?"

Edna pushed open the door. "Dr. Pennyworth said he'll come back in a couple of days to check the dressings," she said, walking in and sitting on the bed.

Rowland's eyes moved down to the gauze patch on his chest. That he no longer had to look at the swastika was an improvement, at least.

"Rowly's got a drinking problem," Milton announced, holding up the tin of Horlicks.

"Nonsense."

"No, really. They're medicating him with malted milk."

Edna reached over and took the tin. "I do love malted milk," she said. "Shall we ask Mr. Beresford to make some now?"

Milton grinned. "I suppose it mightn't be so bad with a good measure of brandy."

Rowland grabbed a tie and slung it awkwardly around his neck. "Ed, would you mind?"

"Of course not," she said, standing and reaching up to tie it. Rowland had become less stubborn about accepting help in this respect. "It might improve your sleep," she said quietly.

"I'll try it tonight," he promised. At the very least, heating milk would give him something to do in the long hours before dawn when closing his eyes took his mind too easily back to that night in Munich.

Beresford came to the door. His brow creased just slightly as he observed Edna adjusting Rowland's tie and affixing his cuff links. He cleared his throat. "There's a young lady asking for you in the foyer, sir…a Miss Dawe. Shall I ask the concierge to accompany her up?"

"Miss Dawe?" Rowland was clearly surprised. "Yes, of course."

He had just enough time to struggle into his jacket before Beresford admitted Allie Dawe into the penthouse.

"Oh, my," she said, looking about the apartment. "What super rooms, Mr. Sinclair."

Sober and composed, Allie looked rather different. Not quite pretty, she had, nevertheless, a pleasant face. Her dark hair was coiffed into some kind of elaborate twist and she wore a skirt suit which seemed at least a size too large. "I trust you don't mind my calling on you like this, Mr. Sinclair, but as you invited me to get in touch…oh." She stopped, her face falling quite dramatically as Edna walked out of the bedroom. When Milton and Clyde followed, however, Allie seemed to brighten a little.

Rowland introduced his companions.

Allie exhaled. "Thank goodness. I thought for a moment you might be married."

Rowland wasn't quite sure how to respond. "And how are your hands, Miss Dawe?"

She removed her gloves and attached them to a clasp on her handbag, before extending her hands for his inspection. The palms were lightly bandaged but she wiggled her fingers freely. "They are much recovered, thank you." She took the seat that Rowland offered her. "I've called to thank you for your consideration the other day, Mr. Sinclair. You were very gallant and I was not at my best."

"You are most welcome, Miss Dawe."

Allie beamed. "My mother sends her regards, Mr. Sinclair, and hopes that you will visit us again when she is in a less distraught frame of mind."

Rowland paused to ask Beresford to serve tea—having already concluded, on the basis of past experience, that it was not wise to offer the girl anything stronger.

"How are you and your mother coping?" Edna asked kindly. "It must have been a terrible shock to lose your uncle like that."

"Well, that's what I came to tell Mr. Sinclair." Allie bounced excitedly in her seat. She pulled a flyer advertising an hotel staff dance from her purse and handed it to Rowland. "See there… the last name listed under the other acts."

"It says Sarah Dabinett."

"That's me!" Allie squealed. "That's my stage name…Allie Dawe is so dull, don't you think? But Sarah Dabinett has flair!"

"I see."

"I'm a singer, you know," Allie went on. "Or at least I have always wanted to be. Uncle Alfred wouldn't hear of it when he was alive, but now I can pursue my dreams."

She was so obviously delighted that Rowland could not help but smile. "This seems like an excellent start to your new career, Miss Dawe."

"Oh, it is!" She closed her eyes and pressed her palms over her heart. "It's ironic really. Lord Erroll came to the house to express his condolences—he's a dear old friend of Uncle Alfred's. He heard me singing at the piano and asked if I would like to perform at a private club he knew. One of the singers had fallen ill, you see, and they were short an act—that's what they call the singers—*acts*."

"A private club?" Rowland's brow rose.

"It's perfectly respectable, I assure you!" Allie was quickly adamant. "Lord Erroll said Uncle Alfred regularly attended. Of course, he won't be there tonight, being dead. Anyway, he wouldn't have approved. He could be a dreadful hypocrite where I was concerned!"

"Does your mother know about this, Miss Dawe?"

"My mother's in mourning, Mr. Sinclair."

Rowland glanced at Edna uneasily. It all seemed dubious, at best.

"Do you know much about Lord Erroll, Miss Dawe?" Edna asked.

"I hadn't met him till he came to the house," Allie admitted, "but Uncle Alfred had often spoken of him. Why, Lord Erroll is one of his closest chums! My mother says he's from a very fine and well-connected family, and he was most kind and attentive."

Rowland perused the flyer again. The staff dance did not start till eleven in the evening.

"I came to ask if you'd care to come and hear me sing, Mr. Sinclair." Allie gazed as adoringly at him now as she had under the influence of several brandies.

Milton chuckled.

"You're all invited of course," Allie added quickly.

Rowland looked at Allie Dawe. She was holding her breath as she waited for his answer. The last thing Rowland wanted to do was to encourage her infatuation, but the situation worried him. Allie seemed barely more than a child, naïve in the extreme. He wondered what kind of man would call on a girl who had just lost her uncle, and means of support, to make such a proposal. "Yes, of course. We'd be delighted."

Chapter Seven

"Bad Blackguard"

THE EARL OF ERROLL JUDGE'S DENUNCIATION

(Australian Press Association)

LONDON, June 18

Mr. Justice Hill, pronouncing a decree nisi in favour of Major Hill, with £3000 damages, described the Earl of Erroll (the co-respondent) as a very bad blackguard.

The Earl met the respondent in Kenya. The judge said that the respondent previously had committed adultery with the petitioner, so she was a woman of easy virtue. Thus, it was a hateful thing to assess damages, as they must not be punitive. It was obvious that the wife was a person of the lowest character, and a liar, but that may largely have been the Earl's influence. There were no children. He had to consider that the wife had independent means, but she left bills of £2000 when she left Kenya, which her husband had discharged. "If I add another £1000," he said, "it will meet the case."

—*The Brisbane Courier,* 1928

That girl's set her cap for you, Rowly," Clyde said after Allie Dawe finally left.

"One-thoughted, never-wandering, guileless love," Milton added.

"Keats." Rowland didn't bother to deny it. Allie had made the fact amply clear.

"Are you sure you want to encourage her?" Clyde asked sternly.

Rowland grimaced. "For God's sake, Clyde, she's barely more than a schoolgirl!" He shook his head. "I just don't like the sound of this Lord Erroll and his private club. I fear Miss Dawe may be walking into trouble."

Clyde groaned.

"Rowly's right." Edna balanced on the arm of the settee. "We can't just let her wander in unchaperoned. The poor girl doesn't understand what she's getting into."

"But she's going to assume, Rowly—"

"Being disappointed by Rowland Sinclair is not the worst thing that could happen to her, Clyde," Edna said firmly.

Clyde sighed. "Yes, I know. We should go. I just have a bad feeling about this."

Rowland said nothing. Clyde had always been a bit of an old woman, but Rowland couldn't help but feel he was, in this case, right.

"What do you suppose we wear to this private club?" Milton asked, checking the flyer Allie had left behind for a stipulated dress code. There was none mentioned.

"I find there are very few occasions for which a dinner suit is not acceptable."

Clyde chuckled. "Clearly you are invited to a better calibre of occasion than am I, Rowly old mate."

They called for Allie Dawe in a motor taxi. Her mother, it seemed, was indisposed, still convalescing following the shock of Lord Pierrepont's death.

Allie wore a deep teal evening gown and an ermine stole. Several feathers had been twisted into her hair so that they fanned out around her face. Rowland thought she looked rather like a frightened peacock, but he told her she looked lovely. Allie blushed and held her knuckles up to his face. It was a couple of moments before he realised she wished him to kiss her hand. As Mrs. Dawe would not leave her bed, he promised the housekeeper that he would see Allie, or Sarah Dabinett—as she now insisted he call her—home safely.

The address on the flyer took them to a large house in Soho. Cars and taxis congested the narrow street outside. Rowland offered Allie his arm. "Are you ready, Miss Dabinett?"

She nodded, though she seemed mute with terror.

"You don't have to go through with this," Rowland whispered. "I'll explain to Lord Erroll, if you like."

Allie shook her head. She swallowed. "Tonight, Sarah Dabinett is born!"

"Right, then."

The entrance into the house had been made more imposing by a red carpet which led into the ballroom. Footmen and a line of maids flanked the doors. A man met them on the threshold. He held out his hands to Allie. "My star has arrived!"

Allie took his hands and introduced Josslyn Hay, the twenty-second Earl of Erroll.

Rowland was a little surprised. He had been expecting a man of Pierrepont's age, but Erroll was not a great deal older than he, slim and fair with feminine lips and a weak chin.

"Lord Erroll, how do you do?"

"Not bad at all, Sinclair." He paused to shake the hands of Clyde and Milton, and to place a lingering kiss on Edna's. "I say, you're Colonials," he said as Rowland's faint inflection was confirmed by the broader accents of his friends. "Just returned from Kenya myself. Rather looking forward to getting back, in fact. I'd forgotten how repressed it was over here in general. I daresay you know of what I'm speaking." He tapped the side of his nose.

Rowland had no idea what Erroll was talking about and he chose not to enquire further.

Erroll turned back to Allie. "I'd better show you to your dressing room, Miss Dabinett." He smiled. "I'm afraid you'll have to leave your charming Colonial gentlemen here—we can all get together afterwards to celebrate your success properly." He grinned and winked at Rowland.

Allie looked panicked.

"Perhaps I'd better…" Rowland began.

"Oh, may I come along with you?" Edna directed the question at Allie. "I've never been backstage before. Nobody will mind will they, Lord Erroll?" The sculptress blinked innocently at the peer.

Erroll seemed less than happy, but Allie consented immediately. "Yes, of course, if you'd like. You can help me get ready. That's not inappropriate, is it, Lord Erroll?"

"No…no…I suppose it isn't."

Gratefully, Rowland glanced at Edna. She met his eyes with such a smile that for a moment he forgot everything else. He didn't see Allie frown.

"You keep looking at Ed like that and little Miss Dawe might just claw her eyes out, mate," Milton muttered as Erroll led the ladies into the house.

"So what do we do now?" Clyde asked.

"We go in and wait for Sarah Dabinett to make her debut, I suppose."

They walked in past the footmen and the lines of maids who curtsied deeply.

"Is that normal?" Milton said under his breath.

"If you're the king." Rowland was genuinely perplexed by the pantomime. There was something odd about the maids—even without the curtseying. Many of them were unusually tall.

The ballroom had been set out like one of London's better nightclubs with linen-draped, candlelit tables arranged around a dance floor and a spotlit stage. The band played a sultry swing number and a haze of cigarette smoke further softened the lighting.

Other dance patrons had begun to arrive and the venue was filling fast with elaborately attired women and men in dinner suits of various styles.

"Rowly, have you noticed—?" Milton began.

"Yes, I have."

Clyde stared. "Holy mother of God."

"Why, hello, you're new!" The man removed his top hat as he sat down at their table. He tapped Rowland's arm with the carved silver handle of his walking stick. "What have you done to yourself, my lovely?"

"A misadventure." Rowland regarded the man curiously. He introduced himself and his companions.

"Cecil F. Buchan, at your service, my dear. I host these intimate soirées for a few hundred close friends and like-minded souls." Buchan handed each of the Australians a gilt-edged calling card. "But you boys can call me Countess." He raised a plucked brow. "Now I know you're not the Old Bill, or else you'd be in frocks...so what are you gentlemen doing here?"

"We have come to see Miss Dabinett perform," Rowland said uneasily. Couples had taken to the dance floor and, though some wore gowns, he could see now that there were no women in the ballroom. Clyde looked terrified and Milton amused.

Buchan gasped and clutched his hands to his breast. "Oh, dear heart, you didn't know what kind of party this was, did you?"

Rowland shook his head. "No. We most certainly didn't."

Now Buchan giggled. "And the three of you are such pretty lads...a crying shame." He looked about him at the increasingly crowded room. "I may have to stay with you tonight..." He flourished his walking stick like a sword. "Beat off the others. You see, no one actually comes here for the show—well, not the one on the stage."

Milton started to laugh. Clyde's lips were pressed tightly together, but Rowland could see the Lord's Prayer in his eyes. "That's very kind of you, Mr. Buchan, but we wouldn't want to keep you from your own enjoyment."

Buchan pulled a lacy white handkerchief from his pocket and dabbed at the thick line of kohl around his eyes. "Alas, alas, there will be no enjoyment for me. Do you see that magnificent creature over there?" He pointed his stick at what at first glance appeared to be a six-foot woman in a green chiffon gown. She danced with a young man in a mess jacket whose face was buried in the broad hard expanse of her chest. "I had an affair with that beautiful boy last week. I've adored him ever since—been unable to eat or drink, except for the odd meal and bottle of wine. Oh, how I've lain in bed obsessed with the thought of seeing him again. But passion, my dears, is a fickle friend and tonight the object of my ardour has eyes only for that inappropriately dressed fool. I understand that nautical dress is very fashionable right now, but a mess jacket…really!"

"I'm sorry to hear of your…disappointment, Mr. Buchan."

"Are you, Mr. Sinclair?" Buchan leaned in and gazed into his eyes. "Are you truly? It's good of you to say, even if you aren't truly sorry. It's well-mannered—a testament to gentle breeding. I think I might pass the time with you and your charming friends."

Clyde tensed, panicked.

Buchan reached across and patted his hand. "Relax, poppet. I know…I do. I'm not in the mood for love tonight and if you do intend to stay to see this girl, Dabinett, sing, you will need the Countess to keep less understanding suitors back."

"In that case," Milton rose, clearly unfazed, "I'd better fetch us some drinks." Rowland fumbled in his jacket and handed the poet his pocketbook, guessing that the cost of refreshments would be extortionate.

"A splendid notion," Buchan chirped. "I'd best accompany you, though. The *maids* at the bar can be forward." He turned back to Rowland and Clyde. "If anyone bothers you, my darlings, you say you're with the Countess."

"Clyde, old boy, are you all right?" Rowland whispered as Buchan sauntered off with Milton. "You look a trifle unwell."

"Of course I do." Clyde shook his head. "Why don't you?"

"I was at Oxford." Rowland shrugged. "Englishmen, you know. I'm sorry, mate, I should have realised this was not an ordinary dance."

"Rowly," Clyde said, convinced his friend was taking the situation far too lightly, "we are surrounded…surrounded by men in evening gowns and makeup. We have to get the hell out of here!"

Rowland grinned. "We'll leave as soon as Miss Dawe has finished her act." He nudged Clyde encouragingly. "Don't panic, mate. Just don't ask anyone to dance."

Clyde glowered at him and Rowland laughed.

Milton and Buchan returned with a tray of colourful cocktails.

"What in God's name are these?" Clyde demanded, staring at the selection of frothy concoctions, garnished with chunks of fruit and sprigs of mint. He was justifiably suspicious of everything now.

"Funny you should mention the good Lord, poppet." Buchan considered the selection with theatrical poise. "This divine creation is called an Angel's Wing!" He handed Clyde a carefully constructed drink of layered brandy topped with cream. "Mr. Isaacs quite excellently chose the Black Velvet, and for Mr. Sinclair, an Americano. And this," he said raising a glass himself, "is for me." He took a sip and a puckered approving. "Ahhh, Between the Sheets."

The first act took to the stage—a male crooner in petticoats and bows who sang favourites from the twenties. Some sang along, others danced.

The event did not seem to suffer from the inhibitions that stifled more conventional affairs. Men who had not been formally introduced flirted and cavorted and jostled to speak with the mysterious Australians whom only Cecil Buchan seemed to know. But Buchan was true to his word. He drove back every hopeful suitor with flamboyant threats, crying, "These are the Countess' men. They are not for the likes of you!" For this, even Clyde came to regard the man with something akin to gratitude.

Over a third round of cocktails, Rowland thought to ask Buchan about Lord Erroll.

"Oh, Joss," Buchan flapped his hand at Rowland. "He used to come by with Pierrepont on occasions, but his interest is financial. These are quite lucrative events, you know."

"Financial...and here I thought your lot objected to actually earning a crust?" Milton poked Rowland. As much as Wilfred accused his brother of being idle, the Sinclairs would never have allowed him to be engaged in conventional employment. That sort of thing was for the aptly named working classes, of which the Sinclairs were not members.

"Investment, sweet boy," Buchan corrected. "I'm not suggesting the Earl of Erroll is my employee!" He beckoned them closer and confided. "Sadly for Joss, his titles were frightfully hollow and came with very little, in terms of assets or private income. He finds himself in the sorry position of having to procure an honest living—though he is not so particular about the honest part—at least between seductions."

"I beg your pardon?"

"Joss has preferred to raise funds by marrying fortunes. Unhappily, his second wife is not as comfortably off as the one he divorced, which is possibly why he's back in London."

"He's married?"

"Yes, though Edith can rarely be persuaded to leave Kenya, even for a short while. By Joss' accounts, the Muthaiga Country Club makes these shenanigans rather look like high tea with Great Aunt Mavis and the Embroiderers' Guild!"

It was about one in the morning when Sarah Dabinett finally appeared in the spotlight. Rowland could see Edna standing offstage with the Earl of Erroll. Allie was clearly nervous. She began her song hoarsely and noticeably off-key but under the gaze of a ballroom of men she seemed to gather strength and musicality and was soon belting out, "Just a Closer Walk with Thee."

"She can't sing hymns here," Clyde whispered, appalled.

But perhaps the gentlemen in the ballroom were churchgoers, or possibly fallen clergymen, for it proved to be quite a popular waltz. Rowland could not help but be struck by the glorious absurdity of it all.

On impulse, fuelled by cocktails, Milton took to the dance floor with a middle-aged man in tartan frills and a blond wig. The poet was an excellent dancer. He led his partner on a twirling tour of the floor finishing with a somewhat ostentatious and unnecessary dip.

Of course, this resulted in a reinvigoration of unwelcome attentions, against which their only protection was Buchan.

"What the hell are you doing?" Clyde demanded when Milton returned to the table.

Milton laughed. "You wait till I tell them at Trades Hall that I dipped a member of the House of Lords." He put his arm companionably about Clyde's shoulders. "Actually, he followed a lead better than most girls in Sydney, and he was rather light on his feet."

"Dear Lord," Clyde groaned.

"I wouldn't call him *dear*, old mate…it was just one dance, after all…but he was a lord."

Edna slipped away from Erroll's side and came over to join them. "Oh, I wish I had knees like that," she said, glancing wistfully at a long-legged gentleman in a daringly split skirt and fishnet stockings.

Rowland smiled. There was not a woman, let alone a man, that the sculptress had just cause to envy.

"Allie's doing rather well, don't you agree?" Edna tried Rowland's cocktail and then Milton's to compare.

And then, suddenly, just as Sarah Dabinett began to sing "All Things Bright and Beautiful," it began—the sirens outside, the whistles shrill, and a deluge of constables into the ballroom. The exits were barred. Couples sprang apart and ran for it. Others fought and still others tried to negotiate.

Buchan sighed. "It's a police raid," he said, shaking his head. "Get out of here if you can, gentlemen, for we are all about to be arrested for public indecency."

Rowland cursed. "We'd better find Allie."

Milton grabbed his shoulder. "I'll find her, Rowly—you go!"

"What? Not a chance."

Milton dragged him aside as a fight erupted at the next table. "Listen to me, mate, you get arrested here, you can forget about anyone in a position of authority listening to what you have to say about Germany." He motioned to Clyde. "Get Rowly out of here."

Rowland began to protest again.

"Trust me, Rowly, I'll look after Allie. It'll be no use the three of you getting arrested, too, and, frankly, my reputation is already beyond salvation. If by some slim chance you manage to get away, at least you'll be able to bail us."

Buchan fell in with the poet. "Go," he advised. "I'll help Mr. Isaacs. I have nothing to fear from exposure—my affairs have already been aired in the press after the last raid. If you need your reputation for anything at all, get out of here, Mr. Sinclair."

"I brought you here," Rowland said to Milton. "I said I'd—"

Milton reacted angrily now. "Look, you bloody fool, you're the only one of us with any influence. I've been arrested before, Rowly. I'm happy to spend a few hours in an English gaol, if it means you might be able to help those poor blighters in Germany. This is England—the police are not going to harm us. Now get the hell out of here or I'll break your other arm!"

Rowland stared at him, startled.

Clyde took charge. "Where will they take you?" he asked Buchan.

"Brixton Bailey, most probably."

"Right, we'll meet you there with a solicitor."

Buchan led them to a narrow stairwell. "The stairs take you to the bedrooms on the second floor. Your best chance is to climb out onto the roof and down a trellis." He regarded Rowland's arm with some consternation, and embraced him suddenly. "Farewell, dear heart—try not to fall."

Milton laughed. He slapped Rowland on the shoulder. A truce. "Go on, mate. Good luck."

Chapter Eight

Malted Milk

English Company's Plans

Mr. Peter Horlick, a director of Horlick's Malted Milk Company, who arrived by the R.M.S. *Maunganui* on Saturday, stated that, although there were no definite plans, it was possible that his company would consider manufacturing malted milk in Australia. Malted Milk was drunk in practically every country in the world, and if a factory was established here it would probably supply all countries of the East.

The United States was the best customer for malted milk, said Mr. Horlick. The partial abolition of prohibition had not affected the consumption there.

—*The Sydney Morning Herald*, 1933

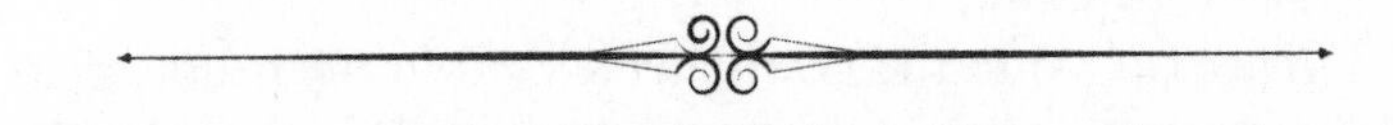

"What in…?" Rowland slammed the bedroom door shut.

"What's in there?" Clyde demanded as he tried the door himself.

There was a scream and several naked men ran past them into the hallway. Clyde glared at Rowland, speechless.

The corridor at the top of the stairs was long and wide, a dimly lit avenue of doors that were meant to be closed. The floor was littered with fox stoles and paste tiaras discarded in mid-flight. Dozens of men in dinner suits or evening gowns or now, nothing at all, ran into the bedrooms. Clearly this escape route was no secret.

Clyde crossed himself and led them to the room at the far end of the hallway into which the naked men had, among others, fled. The two windows which had been opened were congested with hysterical escapees.

"This way!" Clyde tried a third window, which, it seemed, had been bypassed in the panic. It was heavy and the sash sticky but, determined to avoid jostling for space at the other windows, Clyde persisted. Finally he succeeded in shaking loose the counterweights and he forced the window up. "You first, Ed." He glanced down at her pretty heels. "Better take off your shoes."

Edna did so, stuffing them into the pockets of Clyde's dinner jacket. In stockinged feet, she climbed carefully out onto the slate roof. Clyde motioned Rowland out next and then followed himself. It had rained while they had been inside and the steeply pitched roof was treacherous.

Rowland cast his eyes towards the lawn below, which now teemed with police and Black Marias ready to convey prisoners to the station. Then one of their fellow escapees slipped, sliding down the slope of the roof, collecting several men on the way. Tangled and grasping, the men tumbled in a frenzied clamour of arms and legs and lacy skirts, all screaming like hairy banshees.

Edna gasped as they disappeared over the edge.

Clyde craned his neck to see. "It's all right, Ed. The box hedge has broken their fall."

Bobbies surged to the newly made dent in the hedge, grappling to separate and then restrain the conglomeration of bodies. Rowland saw their chance.

"Over here," he said heading towards the other side of the roof. "Let's get down while they're arresting those poor chaps."

The rose trellis was within easy reach but it was, as one would expect in late summer, covered with the barbed growth of a rambler. Edna was wearing gloves but Clyde and Rowland were not. Still there was nothing for it but to grit their teeth and climb down.

Clyde went first, cursing as the rose thorns ripped and embedded in his bare hands. Edna climbed down with less damage by placing her gloved grip where his had already been. With only one hand to support his weight, Rowland's descent was the most awkward and unpleasant but, in the end, they were all on the ground.

"Dammit!" Clyde swabbed his torn palms with a handkerchief. He returned Edna's shoes and placed his hands in his pockets. "We're just going to saunter out of here," he said. "If the police stop us, we say we were at a dinner party with Australia's delegates at the economic conference, and came across to see what the commotion was about."

"Do you think they'll believe that?" Edna was sceptical.

"You have the distinction in this crowd of being a real woman, Ed—so, yes, I believe they will."

Rowland followed Clyde's lead and thrust his hand into his pocket. Edna slipped her arm through his and they walked casually towards the gate.

Beresford stepped into the room, rolled his eyes and retreated. The Australian had once again answered the door himself. The butler could do nothing more. Surely he could not be expected to educate ill-bred Colonials on matters of propriety.

"Wil, come in," Rowland said, relieved.

Wilfred pushed past him. "This had better be important." His eyes slowed upon the scratches on Rowland's face and hands. "What the blazes have you been doing, Rowly?"

"Good evening, Mr. Sinclair," Edna said, looking up briefly, before she returned to Clyde's hands from which she was extracting thorns and splinters with tweezers.

"Miss Higgins, Mr. Watson Jones." Wilfred nodded curtly.

Edna stood. "I believe there's a stock of iodine in the bathroom. Come on." She smiled at Wilfred as she pushed Clyde ahead of her. "Don't let the screaming bother you, Mr. Sinclair. Painters, you know, they have such sensitive hands…and Clyde can be a terrible baby."

Wilfred stared after her.

"Wil, I need a solicitor," Rowland said the moment they were alone.

"A solicitor? What on earth for?"

"Milt's been arrested. I need to secure his release."

"Arrested…when?"

Rowland checked his watch. "About two hours ago."

Wilfred reared. "If that Communist troublemaker has broken His Majesty's laws, then I don't see why you should—"

"Bloody hell, Wil, just help me find a solicitor!"

Even with Edna out of the room, Wilfred did not swear at his brother, though it was clear he wanted to. "What exactly has Mr. Isaacs done to get himself arrested?"

"He was at a dance in Soho."

"And…?"

"And nothing, he was arrested for being at the dance."

"What? Why?"

"It was a dance for gentlemen…*only* gentlemen."

Wilfred stopped. "I knew it! Bloody cravats and poetry," he muttered furiously. "I knew your so-called friends would—"

"None of us knew what kind of dance it was," Rowland said tightly.

"None of you?" Wilfred's eyes narrowed. "My God, Rowly, are you telling me that you were there, too? Are you out of your mind? Do you have no concept of respectability?"

"Miss Dawe invited us to come hear her sing. We didn't know that it was anything other than a dance."

"I would have thought it'd be bleeding obvious!" Wilfred stepped closer, suspiciously, accusingly. "Had you been drinking?"

"For pity's sake, Wil!"

"If your drinking has deteriorated to such a sorry state that you can't tell—"

"I promise you, Wil, I have never been that intoxicated that I can't tell the difference between a man and a woman! Besides, I was cold sober when I walked into that dance."

"Tremendous!" Wilfred rubbed his face wearily. "Inebriation would have at least been a reason! You're just an idiot!"

Now Rowland really wanted a drink. "Look, Wil, just help me find a half-decent solicitor…please."

"Rowly, you cannot afford to be associated with—"

"It was my idea to attend, in the first place," Rowland said angrily. "Milt stayed with Miss Dawe so that I could get out and protect my flaming reputation."

Wilfred sat down and removed his glasses. "And why was Miss Dawe performing at this so-called dance?"

"She quite desperately wants to be a singer. Some chap who calls himself the Earl of Erroll arranged it."

Wilfred looked up sharply. "Josslyn Hay?"

Rowland nodded. "He was a chum of Pierrepont's, apparently."

Wilfred seemed about to say something but decided against it. "I presume this need to rescue your long-haired hanger-on cannot wait till morning."

"No, it can't."

Wilfred stood, shaking his head. "I'd better make some calls." He regarded Rowland sternly. "But once this is sorted, you and your idle Bolshie friends are on the first ship to Sydney!"

Rowland flared. "I am not a child, Wil. The days when you could pack me off out of the country are long gone."

Wilfred smiled coldly. "Don't count on it, Rowly."

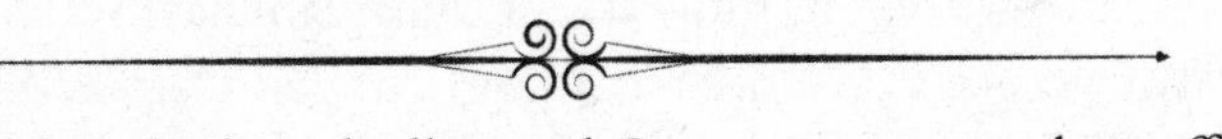

The Sinclairs had used Allen and Overy to manage their affairs in Britain and France for the past two years. And though the learned gentlemen were not often called to act on criminal matters, they performed admirably to secure the release of Mr. Elias Isaacs and Miss Allison Dawe from the Brixton court.

The task had been made arguably more difficult by the fact that Mr. Isaacs—outraged at having his cheeks rubbed with blotting paper to test for rouge—had taken the opportunity to speak out against capitalist oppression and nearly incited a riot among his fellow detainees. As such, the constabulary was not inclined to be lenient.

George Allen gave the matter his personal attention, impressing all and sundry with his extraordinary command of legal maxims in their original Latin. He made representations to a variety of people and, eventually, the poet was released. As a special favour to the younger Mr. Sinclair, Allen also secured the release of a certain Cecil F. Buchan. Resigned to the follies and indiscretions of young men, and financially invested in retaining the business of both Sinclair brothers, the wily lawyer mentioned nothing of Buchan to Wilfred.

Having been formally charged, Milton was required to present before the courts the following month. Rowland would not hear of returning to Sydney without him, no matter what Wilfred directed or threatened. And so the Sinclair brothers were at odds, but that was not unusual.

The sun had risen by the time Rowland finally escorted Allie Dawe to her Belgravia residence. On the doorstep she'd started to cry. "It's all ruined," she wept. "My career is in tatters and you'll never speak to me again for inviting you to such a place. First Uncle Alfred and now this…Whatever must you think of me, Mr. Sinclair? Do you hate me for inviting you to that den of iniquity and vice?"

"To be honest, Miss Dawe, I was having rather a good time until the constabulary arrived," Rowland said kindly and quite sincerely. "But I do think that chap Erroll might have warned you."

"You've been so understanding, Mr. Sinclair." Allie took the handkerchief he offered her and wiped her eyes. "I've been quite frightened since Uncle Alfred died. I'm not sure what to do. I thought if I could sing, I'd be able to look after mother and myself even without Uncle Alfred's help." She broke down again. "I'm not sure how things could be any worse."

Rowland wasn't entirely sure what to do himself. He'd run out of handkerchiefs.

Allie clutched his arm. "Will I ever see you again, Mr. Sinclair? I could not blame you for wanting to leave me and my troubles to whatever cruel fate has in store!"

Rowland smiled. Despite what he sensed was a genuine panic, Allie Dawe had quite a flair for the melodramatic. "I'd better come in and explain to your mother, don't you think?"

The housekeeper opened the door and, overjoyed to see Allie, shouted for the lady of the house. Mrs. Dawe came slowly down the stairs wearing a sky blue matinee jacket of chiffon and feathers over a matching floor-length nightgown. Briefly, Rowland wondered if Lord Pierrepont had ever tried on this particular ensemble—it was at least, as far as nightgowns went, more appropriate for a man of his age than the revealing negligee in which he'd been killed.

Mrs. Dawe paused mid-stair, threw back her head and placed her hand limply against her forehead. She held the pose for several seconds before she resumed her descent.

"Allie darling," she said, allowing the girl to kiss her offered cheek. "I haven't slept a wink worrying about you. I have the most dreadful headache. Oh, where have you been? I expected you home hours ago."

Rowland waited as Allie explained. Quite predictably, Mrs. Dawe gasped, stumbled towards a convenient chaise lounge, and fainted.

"Drink this." Edna handed Rowland a steaming cup from the tray that Beresford had placed on the sideboard.

Rowland was less than enthusiastic. He wasn't sure he liked malted milk. Still, he drank it obediently.

Edna curled up on the settee beside him.

Milton was already stretched out asleep on the other couch, and Clyde snored softly in an armchair. Their dinner jackets had been tossed carelessly over the back of a chair, their ties removed and the collar studs undone, but that was as much preparation for sleep as they could manage. Rowland had dozed off for a few minutes but had woken soon after into a sharp and familiar terror.

"What are your dreams about, Rowly?" Edna rested her head drowsily against his shoulder. She'd been awake to notice the manner in which he'd jolted back to consciousness.

"It's all a bit muddled," he said. "Mostly Germany. I can't seem to get away from that moment when my arm snapped or when that boy fired." Rowland smiled ruefully. "You'd think that since I know how it turns out..." The clarity of his mind's eye had always served him as an artist by casting memory to vibrant detail, but now it forced him to relive those moments of agony and panic, night after night.

"I used to have nightmares after my mother died," Edna said quietly. "I found her, you see."

Rowland placed his uninjured arm around the sculptress. Marguerite Higgins had taken her own life when her daughter was just a child. He'd known the fact for only a short while, and so it staggered him still.

"She used a shotgun, you know."

Rowland shook his head and held Edna close to him, sickened by the thought of what she would have found after the shotgun had done its grisly work.

Edna's voice was quiet and sad. "There was so much blood, Rowly, more than seemed possible. Papa had the walls papered because the blood would show through, no matter how many times we painted...but we couldn't paper the ceiling." She shuddered.

"My God, Ed, I'm sorry...I wish I could..."

She looked up at him. "I'm all right, Rowly. It was a long time ago. Dear Papa...he stayed by my bed, holding my hand every night for a year. It kept away the nightmares." She pulled Rowland's arm gently off her shoulder and took his hand. "Why don't you try to sleep now, Rowly?"

"I'm a grown man, Ed."

"You look so tired, darling," she said, frowning. "Just try."

Rowland couldn't deny he was tired. A kind of agitated exhaustion.

Smiling suddenly, Edna stood and fetched the book which lay facedown and open on Milton's chest. She wriggled back into a comfortable position beside Rowland and slipped her hand back into his.

"What are you doing?" Rowland asked, aware of the familiar rose scent of Edna's closeness.

"This will help you sleep," she promised opening the volume of John Milton's *Paradise Lost.* "I remember studying it at school; it'd knock me out in seconds." She laughed, leaning her head back on his shoulder as she did so. "And you may as well brush up—I suspect that Milt will be stealing from his namesake very soon."

Rowland smiled. He'd always kept note of what Milton was reading. It helped him decipher who exactly the poet was plagiarising. Clearly, the connection had not escaped Edna either.

She read then, her voice languid and drowsy. Perhaps it was that, or the malted milk, or the fact that the sculptress was curled into his side, but Rowland did sleep, and for a time, a short time, it was undisturbed.

Chapter Nine

Foreign News

London Economic Conference

June, 1933

> Sixty-six nations took their places last week at the long pew-like desks of the London Geological Museum, all ranged alphabetically, in French, by tactful Alfred the Seater so that Cordell Hull of Tennessee (Etats Unis) sat at the end of the row, before, not next to, the kinky-polled delegates from Addis Ababa (Ethiopie). The League of Nations organizing committee invited 67 nations, but Panama was too poor to accept.
>
> —*Time Magazine*

Beresford presented the letter on a silver tray. Rowland opened it quickly with scant regard for the gold-leaf embossing and wax seal on the envelope. Scanning the meticulous copperplate on the scallop-edged sheet within, he frowned.

"Problem, Rowly?" Clyde asked.

"A familial summons."

"From Wilfred?"

"No...one of the local Sinclairs—my cousin."

"There are local Sinclairs?" Edna moved to perch on the arm of his chair.

Rowland nodded. "One or two. Wilfred had Quex keep an eye on me when I was at school in England."

"Quex?"

"Admiral Sir Hugh Sinclair. God knows why they call him Quex."

"Ahh...*The Gay Lord Quex*, a comedy in four acts," Milton said. "Perhaps your cousin was a thespian."

Rowland smiled. "It probably wouldn't be wise to accuse Quex of that."

"Well, it's lovely that he wants to see you." Edna peered curiously at the note. "Were you close?"

"Not at all."

"Why not?"

Rowland smiled. Edna had always been rather direct.

"I was fifteen when I was sent over here to school," he said. "Quex is about twenty years older than Wil, and was busy doing whatever it is that admirals do. I really only saw him when I was in some kind of trouble."

"You don't suppose he knows that you were in Soho last night, do you?" Milton pointed at *The Daily Mail* which lay open on the card table. The paper carried a lurid account of the gentlemen's dance.

Rowland shook his head. Milton alone had taken the fall for their presence at the event. The poet's name had been listed along with Buchan's, in what was claimed to be the public interest. The dance was decried across the media as an example of the lax morality and decadent perversion of the upper classes.

For the most part, Milton seemed to regard the incident as a grand joke, though every now and then he was moved to quote Wilde.

"Wilfred may have mentioned it to him," Clyde speculated. The summons was surely too coincidental.

"I doubt it," Rowland said. "Wil is usually discreet about my indiscretions." He sighed as he dropped the letter back onto the tray. "But he may well have let Quex know I'm in London."

"So, you'll have to go see him?" Edna watched Rowland carefully.

"Yes, eventually." Rowland checked his watch. Wilfred was sending a car at ten to take him to the Geological Museum, the venue of the London Economic Conference. He was not entirely sure why he was being sent for, but he assumed—hoped—it meant that Stanley Melbourne Bruce had found someone who would give him a hearing.

"We'd best set off." He grabbed his hat from the stand by the door and waited for Edna to pull on her gloves.

Ethel Bruce had invited the sculptress to join her and Kate for luncheon. Edna was sure that the minister's wife had discovered some tantalising gossip about the late Lord Pierrepont through her networks among the Empire wives. She did, in any case, rather like Mrs. Bruce.

And so they left Clyde and Milton to their own devices.

The black Rolls Royce took them first to the Bruces' terrace in Ennismore Gardens, where Edna alighted to join the ladies and both Bruce and Wilfred climbed in.

Stanley Melbourne Bruce was dressed in the impeccably conservative and elegant style with which Australian caricature artists made him synonymous. He made no mention of the previous night's affair. Rowland's eyes moved to Bruce's feet, checking for spats. Bruce noticed.

He shook his head. "For pity's sake, man, it's the middle of summer!"

"I beg your pardon, sir?"

"The attire for which you are so obviously looking, which the gullible Antipodean media have convinced hoi polloi I never step outdoors without, is actually an item which is sensibly worn in the winter—helps with chilblains."

"I see."

"I'm meeting with Chamberlain today. If the opportunity so arises, I shall introduce you, but I'm afraid that's the best I can do. You'll just have to be on hand on the off-chance that I can convince him to have a drink with you."

"Thank you."

"You can watch from the public gallery. You might even find it interesting."

Rowland nodded politely, though he very much doubted it.

The hall, in which the conference was being held, had been arranged with pew-like desks at which representatives of the sixty-six participating nations took their places in an order determined alphabetically and in French. Wilfred sat with the Australian delegation in the first pew. Bruce sat with his fellow gentlemen of the League of Nations who had organised the conference.

From the vantage of the elevated public gallery, Rowland watched with the gathering of London press and a scribbling gaggle of foreign correspondents who followed the proceedings with a zealous attention. In this company, he felt the need to at least feign some sort of appreciation for the importance of the men below, and so he consciously set his face to look engaged.

It was of some consolation that the conference hall was at least visually interesting: the dark-skinned delegates from African nations, the representatives of the subcontinent and, of course, the delegations from Europe. Cordell Hull, the American Secretary of State, stood by his chair in conversation with Daladier, the French delegate. The Frenchman's hands moved expansively and vigorously as he spoke. The American stood with his thumbs hooked in the pockets of his waistcoat, rocking slightly on his heels.

An enthusiastic member of the British contingent opened with an impassioned presentation on currency exchange. One by one the delegates rose to speak on the subject. Some spoke through interpreters, or with heavy accents. By the sixth delegate, Rowland was restless and becoming desperate for distraction. He had counted the ceiling roses, imagined wives for each delegate, and mentally raced the Spanish translator.

He pulled the artist's notebook from his breast pocket and attempted to clamp it open between his thumb and the cast. Inevitably it slipped from this awkward grasp and fell between the two seats in front of him.

The occupant of one of those seats turned sharply. It was an old man, small and dumpy with penetrating eyes beneath thick, untidy eyebrows that sloped down in a way that made him seem both enquiring and melancholy. His moustache was wide and thick and he, too, had a notebook.

He reached down to retrieve what Rowland had dropped. The battered leather book had fallen open. Clearing his throat, he paused to take the liberty of leafing through it. Sketches of naked women, as one would expect in the notebook of a young man, and darker drawings of people gathered under Nazi banners, soldiers—strutting, assured—and civilians with their faces turned away. The edges of the pages were stained a dark brown. The notebook had at some time been splattered with blood. All this seemed to pique the old man's interest. He returned the notebook and introduced himself.

"Herbert Wells," he said in a piping voice. "I say, did you draw these?"

"Rowland Sinclair, Mr. Wells…yes."

"Not bad, my boy—jolly good, in fact. I've been known to pen the odd picshua myself."

Rowland slipped the notebook back into his jacket. "I'm afraid I find penning anything rather tricky at present," he said ruefully. Though he'd only been in the cast for a few days, it felt like an age. He nodded towards Wells' notebook. "Are you…?"

"Sketching the conference? In a manner of speaking, my boy. You're an Australian, are you?" He scrutinised Rowland as if he could see nationality in his features. "Your countrymen among the delegates have been honing my ear for the Australian inflection. I have been looking in vain for inspiration for my latest book."

It was only then that Rowland realised that he was talking to the renowned novelist and futurist, H.G. Wells. Clearly it showed on his face, for Wells smiled.

"I am not entirely unknown in the Antipodes, then?"

"Not entirely," Rowland replied. "An honour to make your acquaintance, Mr. Wells. I hope I haven't interrupted your... research."

"Not at all, my boy. I had wished for a chapter on vision and hope, but I fear I shall have to write instead about petty bickering and self-interested posturing! Even the Soviets are entirely unimpressive."

Wells beckoned Rowland to the seat beside him.

"The world is in debt, Sinclair, but most of that debt is owed to the Americans." He pointed to Cordell Hull. "That gentleman there holds the financial future of the civilised planet in his hands. If the Americans can bring themselves to act in the interests of the world as a whole, then perhaps there is a chance, but I would not wager more than a shilling upon it."

For some reason Rowland recalled then that Cordell Hull was the last person to have seen Pierrepont alive. He wondered what the American Secretary of State thought of the peer's strange demise, if he had indeed been told it was anything out of the ordinary.

"Are they actually making any decisions here?" Rowland was not particularly well versed on the processes of international politics, but he presumed that in this arena, as in business, all the actual negotiation was done beforehand at the Masonic Temple or other such venue.

Wells nodded. "You have a valid point, Sinclair, but a good businessman keeps his word. A good politician doesn't give the same weight to his promises." He pointed out MacDonald, Prime Minister of Britain, Daladier of France, and Cordell Hull. "Those gentlemen believe they have an agreement, a way forward, and that, after this conference, mankind will hail them all as heroes."

"Are they wrong to believe this?"

Wells shrugged. "Hull has, in the finest American tradition, reminded us of the piety of his nation. With grave and splendid words he has called on the rest of the world to abandon such sins as selfishness. He has called on his God to forbid, and the delegates to resist, the temptation of the serpent that carries local interest in her belly...but to ask that of his own president is perhaps even more than his God could expect."

"I see." Rowland was a little surprised by Wells' cynicism. The streets outside were be-flagged and celebratory. Expectations that the conference would achieve some kind of salvation for the failing economies of the world were great.

Apparently pleased to have someone receive his learned commentary, Wells set about to educate the young Australian on the games of power being played out before them. He pointed out delegates, commenting on their influence, intelligence, and allegiances. "Do you see that chap with our lot? The fellow with the rather large mouth?"

Rowland stretched to see whom he meant. There was, indeed, a man with an extraordinarily wide mouth. "A delegate?"

"No. Keynes is an advisor. Friend of mine—brilliant chap—an economist. He has some rather interesting theories on government investment in public programs to stimulate recovery—quite revolutionary. The Germans have taken it on, but Britain is far too democratic to take decisive action!"

Rowland nodded, hoping that Wells wouldn't feel the need to explain Keynes' theories in any more detail.

Perhaps Wells sensed his alarm. He smiled. "I digress. My point is that John Keynes' solution will work for all of us, but politics is a game of petty segregations, while the only true nationality is mankind."

"I don't suppose you remember a chap called Pierrepont?" Rowland asked. Wells had clearly been watching the conference since it opened, and Rowland was unwilling to risk the conversation returning to economic theory, however revolutionary. "Alfred Dawe, Viscount Pierrepont. He would have been a member of the British delegation."

Wells nodded. "He died, you know." He wiggled his moustache as he pondered. "There was, from what I've observed, something odd about it."

"How do you mean?"

"All too quiet...no speeches about his great service to the nation and the world, no pledges to fix the currencies in his posthumous honour. A news report or two that he was dead, a new man in his chair, and that was all." Wells looked hard at Rowland, his drooping eyebrows furrowed. "Why do you ask about Pierrepont? He was not a major player by any means."

"I'm acquainted with his niece, Miss Dawe."

"Oh yes...skinny young thing in ill-fitting clothes. He brought her once, ordered her to sit in the public gallery to bear witness to his importance."

"I take it you didn't exactly like Lord Pierrepont?"

"Pompous irrelevant man, an unrepentant hypocrite."

"Was that the general opinion of his character?" Rowland enquired as casually as he could.

Both Wells' gaze and the angle of his brows sharpened. "You wonder if Pierrepont has been the victim of foul play?" the writer accused. "It seems, Mr. Sinclair, you prefer the literary work of Madam Christie to that of H.G. Wells!"

Rowland wasn't quite sure how to respond, uncertain of what professional jealousies existed between Wells and the famous mystery writer. To his relief, Wells smiled. "Actually, I wondered about that myself." He leaned his elbows on the balustrade and looked down on the conference delegates below. "It's just hard to know which side would have wanted to kill Pierrepont the most."

"I beg your pardon?"

"There are two schools of economic thought below us," Wells said quietly. "Those who recognise that collective action—world co-operation—is the only way forward, and those who would profit by the world remaining an undisciplined herd of selfish nation states. The British are ostensibly for world co-operation, so perhaps Pierrepont was eliminated by the opponents of sane action. On the other hand, I have been privy to rumours that he was breaking ranks, advocating isolationism surreptitiously...in which case perhaps it was the gentlemen who wish to ensure a global solution who acted."

"I see." Rowland said not entirely positive that he did. It all seemed a bit convoluted and dramatic for an economic conference.

"Of course, it might not have had anything to do with the conference. Pierrepont moved in some, let me say, rather unsavoury circles," Wells continued.

"Really? What circles?"

"He was a peer, my boy! Here in Britain we give our oppressors titles." Wells tapped his nose. "Come the revolution, it'll make them easy to identify."

"Do you know of a Lord Erroll?" Rowland asked on impulse.

"A failed diplomat with a penchant for other men's wives, I believe." Wells did not hide his disdain.

"He's a diplomat?"

"Was a diplomat. Appointed by pedigree rather than merit. Left the service under somewhat of a dark cloud. Why do you want to know about Erroll?"

"I met him the other evening. I wasn't quite sure what to make of him."

Wells seemed to accept this, and though Rowland was convinced the novelist knew there was more to it, he did not ask. Instead he chatted amiably about all manner of things. Rowland found himself being drawn into the possibilities of Wells' conversations, the extraordinary speculative ideas that the writer made plausible.

"Tell me, Mr. Sinclair," Wells said at the close of a detailed postulation on the potential good of a world government, "what are *you* doing here? You don't appear to have a particular knowledge or interest in the subject of economics. What could possibly entice a young man to pass the entire day here?"

That very question had occurred to Rowland in the course of the last three hours. Bruce hadn't left the hall. Wilfred had glanced up at the gallery every now and then, possibly to check that his brother was still where he'd left him. "There was someone I was hoping to meet."

"I take it you don't mean me?"

Rowland smiled. "No, that was just good luck." It had been. Without Wells' company the morning would have passed slowly indeed.

Around midday, most of the reporters left to write up their stories and meet publication deadlines. Wells, too, bid his new acquaintance farewell and went on his way.

Facing an afternoon of economic theses and deliberations, Rowland began to look quite earnestly for an escape.

And then the empty seats in the public gallery were claimed. Nearly a score of men in black shirts filed in to take them. Rowland stiffened, as he recognised the infamous uniform of Oswald Mosley's British Union of Fascists.

Chapter Ten

British Fascists Now Anti-Jewish

Party Comes Into Open at Last
("Mail" Special Representative)

LONDON, Saturday

Mr. William Joyce, an official Mosley speaker, declared early in 1934: "I do not regard Jews as a class but as a privileged misfortune. The flower—or weed—of Israel shall never grow in ground fertilised by British blood."
—*The Mail, 1934*

The conference fell into silence as the delegates looked up. The Soviets were clearly offended and mutinous. The Blackshirts remained, claiming their right to sit in the citizens' gallery.

For a moment it seemed their mere presence might derail the conference, but then the British delegate took the floor once more, determined to continue. The Fascists sat with their legs apart and their hands fisted upon their knees, almost as if they were assembled for a team photograph.

Rowland could sense Wilfred's eyes upon him. He returned the glance and nodded. There was no need for Wilfred to be concerned. These were British Fascists, the bored sons of lords who practised revolution between spots of tennis. They were not Nazis, and Britain was yet a democracy.

After several moments the shock subsided, and the delegates returned to the business of currency and debt.

Then a single Blackshirt stood. Two others closed the doors to the public gallery, barring both entry and exit, and Rowland was effectively trapped.

If the Blackshirts noticed him, they gave no indication of it. Their purpose was clearly prearranged, their action rehearsed. The man who stood, and who now interrupted the proceedings, was pale and thin and spoke the King's English with the inflection of the privileged and the intensity of a crusader. He called on the men below to restore the world, to make Britain great once again. He demanded they expel the Soviets and take arms against the economic dictatorship of Communist Jews. He praised Germany for being the only nation strong enough to meet the Jewish threat with necessary force.

"How dare you!" Rowland knew he was acting rashly, unwisely. He was, after all, alone and there were at least twenty Blackshirts, but the rage which took hold of him was not predisposed to caution, or even good sense. He stood, and though his voice was low, it was somehow made audible by the force of the fury behind it. "Sit down you stupid, vile little man."

The stupid, vile little man turned to scrutinise the challenger. A curved scar which ran from earlobe to lip seemed to glow white against the red flush of his skin. He held up his hand—a signal to keep his Blackshirts at bay.

"The gentleman takes issue," he said loudly. "Perhaps he has something to fear from a new world order...perhaps he is a Communist or worse—one of those fetid, hypocritical, traitorous apologists for the outrages of Jewry."

Someone in the conference hall shouted for security. A grapple began at the door. Several Blackshirts heaved to keep it closed as it was sieged from without.

Rowland's eyes blazed. "You, sir, are an imbecile in the costume of a moron!"

The Fascist threw the first punch, but Rowland was far from turning the other cheek. It did not begin as a brawl because Rowland was, after all, just a single man, but the doors soon gave way to admit uniformed constables and public servants eager to help. And then it was on.

Some members of the entourage of Fascists smashed chairs and then used the fragments as weapons. Fists flailed wildly in every direction. The Blackshirt leader, whose oratory Rowland had interrupted, marked the Australian as his own, attacking him with no quarter given to the broken arm. Rowland, too, gave no concession to his injury. In truth, it was not the first time he'd fought one-handed and so he was not as handicapped as he might have been. Sparring with an arm secured behind his back had been part of the training when he'd boxed years before. The memory of it came back to him now. He landed several staggering blows with his left fist. His opponent reeled, swearing and spitting blood.

The Blackshirt responded with intense rage, unleashing a vitriolic assault that pinned Rowland against the wall, giving blow after blow to his ribcage. Against this, the plaster cast became something of a shield and Rowland exploded out of the clinch with a series of shattering jabs.

A stream of constables forced their way onto the gallery. Soon there were two or three for every Fascist, and by sheer force of numbers, the troublemakers were gradually subdued. Even when all the other rioters were controlled, the officers found it necessary to restrain both Rowland and the Blackshirt, to keep them from each other's throats.

Rowland was not, to be honest, sure how he escaped being arrested alongside Mosley's agitators. Perhaps it was simply because he alone was not in Fascist costume. The Blackshirts were outraged. Immediately they decried the partisan, Communist-riddled police force and promised to seek justice outside the corrupt legal system of Britain.

"Just you worry about your own arrest, Mr. Joyce," warned the captain as he handcuffed the Blackshirt orator.

Joyce glared at Rowland with the eye that was not swollen shut. "For the sake of the record, just what do you call yourself, sir?"

"Sinclair, Rowland Sinclair." Rowland had no intention of backing away in any respect. He was quite happy to put his name to his opposition of this man, Joyce, and his principles.

"Well, Sinclair, I'll remember your Jew-loving face. You've made an enemy of William Joyce. I'll come for you, lad, I'll come for you."

"Make sure you bring your friends, Joyce. You'll need them."

A constable pushed Joyce out before the exchange could escalate and Rowland was delivered to his brother like an errant child. Wilfred was none too pleased.

"Are you completely insane?" he demanded. "What did you think you were doing?"

"What else could I do, Wil?"

"You might have just waited for security to throw them out. But, no! You have to step in and incite a brawl!"

"Someone needed to belt that idiot. I was the only one within reach willing to do it!"

Wilfred took a deep breath. "Dammit, Rowly, don't you have enough enemies?"

Rowland glanced at the ceiling exasperated. "I'm sure Joyce threatens every second person he meets…he won't remember my name tomorrow."

"I wouldn't count on it. From what I know about the man, he bears a grudge."

"Well, I don't think we were ever going to be chums anyway."

Wilfred removed his spectacles and polished them furiously. "All you have managed to do with your little stand is stop the conference!"

Rowland paused as the truth of Wilfred's words hit him. He cursed, realising suddenly that he had, however unintentionally, contributed to the Fascist cause. "I'm sorry," he said. "I lost my temper." He tried to explain himself. "I've seen where this kind of vicious rhetoric is leading in Germany, Wil…but I shouldn't have lost my rag like that. I was just so angry."

For a moment it appeared Wilfred would launch into one of his customary tirades, but for some reason he seemed to think better of it. "Understand me, Rowly, I have no sympathy for the idiotic convictions of William Joyce and his kind, but you can't simply cry havoc at every turn. It just won't work."

Rowland pushed the hair out of his face, wincing as his hand made contact with his right brow. It was sticky and tender. He vaguely remembered Joyce belting him with the leg of a bentwood chair.

"Go and get yourself cleaned up." Wilfred sighed. "I'll have the car brought around. It can take you back to Ennismore Gardens, and come back for Spats and me later."

Once again, Ernest Sinclair burst past the maid to meet his uncle at the door. "Where's Daddy, Uncle Rowly? Did he come with you?"

"I'm afraid not, Ernie. He had to stay a while longer."

"Why are you back then?"

"I'm a little tired."

Ernest nodded as if he understood. "Have you been staying up late?"

"I suppose I have."

Ernest sighed and shook his head. "When will you learn, Uncle Rowly?"

Rowland laughed, allowing his nephew to take his hand as they followed the maid into the parlour. Ernest would one day assume control of the Sinclair fortune. It seemed the boy was born to the role.

Edna was teaching Ethel Bruce and Kate to play poker.

"Rowly, what are you doing back?" Edna said putting down her cards as she stood. "Is the conference over already?" She looked closely at his face. "Good Lord, what did they do to you?"

Rowland sat down at the card table. "There was a spot of trouble."

Kate paled. "Is Wil—"

"Wil's fine," Rowland said quickly. "There's no need to worry. He and Minister Bruce will be back later."

Edna touched the abrasion on his brow tentatively. "Does it hurt?"

"I've got a thumping headache, but the conference speeches might have been responsible for that."

"My poor Mr. Sinclair," Ethel Bruce said, quite enthusiastically. "You must have a drink and tell us all about it." She poured Pimms and lemonade from an etched-glass pitcher and handed the tumbler to Rowland, nodding expectantly for him to complete his part of the bargain.

So he recounted the events of the day: the Blackshirts, William Joyce, and the unpleasantness which followed.

"A brawl?" Ethel exclaimed. "There was a brawl at Stanley's conference?" There was just the slightest hint of delight in her voice.

Rowland nodded.

"You fought him with one arm?" Kate said, horrified.

"Once it all started, I had little choice, Kate." Rowland was aware that he was being slightly disingenuous. He had quite willingly entered the fray.

Ethel Bruce came to his aid. "Of course you didn't, Mr. Sinclair. That Joyce is a thug, an uncivilised, Irish thug! He is said to be a wonderful orator, but his reputation for violence is appalling—claims that Jewish Communists slashed his face as if that's some excuse for his behaviour. Disgraceful! I do hope you walloped him hard!"

Rowland smiled. "I did. A few times, in fact."

Ethel clapped her hands. "Well done, Mr. Sinclair. We cannot have Mosley thinking he'll have it all his own way!" She leaned over to top up his glass. "I've just been telling Edna what the wife of the High Commissioner to Ceylon told me."

"Indeed."

"Now don't look like that, Mr. Sinclair. Some people may call Bertha a gossip, but I have found her information invariably reliable."

"I see."

"Just a minute, Ethel." Kate turned to her son who was sitting quietly with pricked ears. "Ernie darling, would you mind seeing if Nanny has attended to Ewan yet."

"But…Do I have to?"

"Ernie…"

Rowland whispered to Kate and then beckoned his nephew. "How would you like to come to Madame Tussaud's with us tomorrow, Ernie?"

Ernest looked sharply at Rowland, clearly aware he was being bribed. "Who's Madame Two Swords?"

"Tussaud. She was a sculptor, like Miss Higgins. She made people out of wax."

Ernest sighed. "Very well, Uncle Rowly, I'm going, though I think you should know that I am very discreet."

Rowland nodded gravely. "I'll keep that in mind, Ernie."

And so Ernest left the room with all the dignity it was possible for a six-year-old to muster, and Ethel Bruce was able to safely return to the intelligence she had garnered from the High Commissioner's wife. She lowered her voice nonetheless. "It seems that our Bunky married The Honourable Euphemia Thistlewaite that was."

"I'm afraid I've never—"

"Yes, of course, you wouldn't be acquainted. Euphemia is the youngest child of Lord and Lady Harcourt."

"Harcourt?" Edna's brow creased. "I thought you said her name was Thistlewaite."

"It is dear," Ethel explained. "Harcourt is the title, Thistlewaite the name. Euphemia's father is Henry Thistlewaite, Baron Harcourt."

"Oh. How long had she and Lord Pierrepont been married?"

"When he died? Barely a month."

Rowland shrugged, unsure why this was scandalous enough to be whispered among the ladies of the Dominions. "Lord Pierrepont was free to marry, and he wouldn't be the first man to fall in love with a beautiful younger woman." He winked at Kate who was sixteen years Wilfred's junior.

His brother's wife blushed.

"Oh, Euphemia isn't beautiful, Mr. Sinclair. The poor thing has rather too many teeth to be beautiful or even handsome, I'm afraid. And she isn't all that young. She's an odd girl really, quite bookish and peculiar."

"Even so," Rowland said. Who knew what a man in a nightie would find desirable?

"But there's more, you see. Some of the other wives have heard—and this is a rumour, mind you, and not something to which Bertha would attach her reputation, though I do think there may be something to it—that Bunky was carrying on with an American."

Rowland waited.

"An American," Ethel repeated.

"Which American?" he asked, trying to respond enthusiastically.

"That's the strange thing, nobody seems to know. Bunky has never been so circumspect in the past. I've known him to introduce his dalliances to each other. It's rather mysterious."

"But that was before he was married."

Ethel's face fell. "Oh dear, that is true. The marriage could explain it." She sighed. "Mr. Isaacs will be less than impressed with my efforts at sleuthing, I'm sure."

"Not at all, Ethel," Edna protested. "After all, perhaps the new Lady Pierrepont discovered Lord Pierrepont's inconstancy and killed him!"

"So, we are all agreed that Bunky was murdered?" Ethel smiled triumphantly.

Edna stopped, realising that the fact was not supposed to be common knowledge even in Stanley Melbourne Bruce's own home. She looked to Rowland hesitantly.

"What does Minister Bruce say on the matter?" Rowland asked carefully.

"He said he rather likes my new hat, as he always does when he wants to change the subject and convince me to leave it to the police!" Ethel glanced at the portrait of her husband over the mantel and rolled her eyes, exhaling fiercely.

Rowland smiled. He did wonder how regularly Mrs. Stanley Melbourne Bruce came upon matters that her husband thought were best left to the police. He said, "Sadly, the police do not have the wives of the Empire's diplomats at their disposal."

"Indeed, Mr. Sinclair, they do not."

Chapter Eleven

Madame Tussaud's

Additions to Australian Group

LONDON, March 7

Messrs W. M. Woodfull, W. M. Hughes, S. M. Bruce and J. T. Lang have been included in the Australian group at Madame Tussaud's waxworks. The secretary told a press representative that Don Bradman had been removed, following complaints by enthusiasts that his hair was incorrect and his batting position was faulty. "So many people are asking, 'Where is Bradman?' that we are hoping to obtain accurate details enabling his restoration."

—*Townsville Daily Bulletin*, 1933

Milton was quite unashamedly envious that Rowland Sinclair had found H.G. Wells at the Geological Museum, and more so that he had managed to exchange fisticuffs with Fascists in the same afternoon. It seemed to the poet that Rowland did not fully appreciate either encounter as he should.

He was almost inconsolable when Rowland informed him of the other literary luminaries who had also been in the public gallery that morning.

"You met them?"

"Not at all. They just waved at Wells and sat down. He told me who they were."

"Don't you think it's odd to find so many illustrious figures in one place?"

"Not really. In my experience illustrious people seem to know one another. As far as I can tell, they all seem to be part of a set. It's probably not surprising that they step out together from time to time, though why they'd choose to do so at an economic conference is beyond me entirely!"

While Rowland had been at the conference, Milton and Clyde had set out from Claridge's for Hyde Park, where Clyde had hoped to capture the famous English stroll in pencil and wash. Milton had taken *Paradise Lost.* Their intention had been to pass the day in these tranquil pursuits. As it happened, however, they'd found themselves in that part of Hyde Park known as Speakers' Corner where public discussion was at least tolerated, if not encouraged.

The forum had its equivalent in Sydney's Domain and perhaps it was a sense of familiarity that drew the Australians towards it. They had seen many impassioned speakers state their particular cause and case on the grassy lawns before the National Art Gallery back home—Milton had often mounted the soapbox himself, moved by either the Party or poetry.

"At first it was just crackpots proclaiming the end of the world," Clyde explained. "But eventually the Communists turned up, so we hung about for a bit and introduced ourselves to the local faithful."

"Ended up at a pub listening to speeches about the Fascists," Milton sighed. He pointed at Rowland. "You should have told us you were going to brawl!"

Rowland laughed. "If only I'd known. I could well have used a hand..." He trailed off as the butler emerged with a tray of drinks. "I say, where's Beresford?" The man bearing the tray was new.

"Mr. Beresford has been assigned to another guest, sir. I'm Menzies. I'll be looking after you for the remainder of your stay at Claridge's."

Fleetingly, Rowland wondered if they had offended Beresford somehow. He was aware that the butler found them wanting in many respects but he hadn't thought their transgressions of protocol that objectionable.

Whatever may have caused Beresford's departure, it seemed he had taken the time to instruct Menzies on the subject of Horlicks. Rowland stared at the cup of steaming malted milk which Menzies set before him. "I believe this is your beverage of choice, sir."

Milton laughed. "For he on honey-dew hath fed, and drunk the milk of paradise," he said raising his glass of sherry in toast.

"Coleridge," Rowland said miserably. He very much doubted the milk of paradise would be flavoured with Horlicks powder.

Ernest Sinclair was waiting eagerly when they called for him at Ennismore Gardens. The six-year-old was obviously looking forward to an outing in the company of his uncle. Wilfred and Stanley Bruce had already left for the day's business. Kate gave her elder son last-minute instructions for manners and behaviour.

"Heavens, Kate, I'm not taking him to church!" Rowland said as she fussed over the sharp slick of Ernest's hair. "You mustn't worry—we'll look after him," he assured his sister-in-law, who he thought predisposed to be unnecessarily anxious. "Though you're welcome to come, too, if you'd care to."

Kate shook her head. "Ethel and I are going to the ballet this afternoon when Nanny takes Ewan for a nap. I was planning to take Ernie, but he'd doubtless prefer the waxworks."

Rowland looked at Ernest, grimacing. "The ballet! Good Lord, a narrow escape!"

"I'll say, Uncle Rowly."

"Ernest!" Kate scolded her son because she could not admonish his uncle.

"We'll have him back in a few hours then," Rowland said hastily before she could change her mind. "Come on Ernie, run!"

Ernest did so without hesitation, leaving Rowland to say farewell for them both. Kate smiled as she watched her son run giggling into Clyde's brawny arms and be thrown into the back of the motor car as if they were fleeing mortal danger.

And so once again, Rowland and his companions wandered through the waxwork exhibition. Edna disappeared through the black door to find Marriott Spencer, as arranged. The gentlemen took their time, allowing Ernest to examine each figure in his solemn, thoughtful way.

The boy gasped and pointed occasionally, and reached for Rowland's hand in the Chamber of Horrors. Milton "enhanced" each statue with amateur ventriloquism and potted biographies that were more creative than accurate. Under his tutelage, the Prince of Wales became a famous shoe salesman, Lord Nelson a bloodthirsty pirate, and Winston Churchill the man who invented the Arrowroot biscuit. Neither Rowland nor Clyde bothered to correct him or disillusion Ernest, who was rapt in attention.

In this manner they spent most of the morning.

As Big Ben struck one o'clock, Clyde hoisted Ernest onto his shoulders and they ventured into the crowded streets of central London to find an eatery of some sort. The presence of Rowland's nephew made them a little more discerning with respect to the venue, and they bypassed public houses and the bohemian haunts—to which they were usually drawn—in search of more respectable establishments.

Ernest gazed at the lines of hungry men outside the Salvation Army soup kitchen as they walked past. Rowland gave him a guinea to drop into the collection box, and Clyde told him stories of the days when he had walked the wallaby track in search of work, when he, too, had relied on charity to eat.

"Why didn't you get a job, Mr. Watson Jones?"

"There weren't any to be had, Ernie."

"Couldn't your mother and father have helped you?" the child persisted. Ernest could not yet comprehend a problem that his own father could not solve.

"My mum and dad could barely feed themselves, Ernie."

Ernest slipped off Clyde's shoulder, silent and clearly troubled. The child was aptly named. Rowland took the boy's hand. The refined, sheltered world in which he and Ernest had been raised was rarely touched by the day-to-day realities of the Depression. Only through his friends had Rowland become aware of the struggles of the unemployed and the families that relied upon them. In Sydney, he did what he could with quiet anonymous donations. But the problem was not confined to any one city or nation. For the first time he began to wonder what Wilfred's economic conference might achieve.

After that, dining seemed less important. In the end they found a restaurant that sold battered fish and chipped potatoes. The meal was one that Rowland could manage one-handed without fuss or embarrassment, and so it was particularly enjoyed, despite its simplicity.

By the time they returned to the waxwork museum, Edna had quite happily spent most of the day immersed in the art of Marriott Spencer. They found her using what looked like surgical instruments to whittle refinements into the facial features of a wax-cast head under the guidance of the hook-handed sculptor.

"Gentlemen!" Spencer exclaimed. "You have come to take my protégée so soon. We are not finished!"

Rowland checked his watch. It was getting late.

"You must speak with Francis about your friend the aristocrat! He is in the next room…Go! Edna and I are busy."

Edna laughed. "Go on," she said quietly to Rowland. "I'll wash up while you speak with Frankie."

Francis Pocock had worked at the wax museum since before the war. He was an immense man. His jowls expanded down to his shoulders in a way that made him look like a squat melting candle. Rowland could not help but wonder if the years of working with wax had caused the man's flesh to behave like his material. Pocock did not look up from his work.

Rowland introduced himself and his friends and eventually the wax sculptor extended a pudgy hand in greeting. "I'm busy. What do you want?"

"We were wondering about the statue of Lord Pierrepont, Mr. Pocock."

"What about it?"

"For what kind of display do you intend it?"

"What's it to you?"

"I'm a friend of Lord Pierrepont's family," Rowland said, knowing the claim was at best a gross exaggeration and more accurately an outright falsehood. "I thought it might comfort them to know he was going to be remembered at Madame Tussaud's."

Pocock grunted. "He won't be." He looked at Rowland fiercely. "Friend of the family, eh? Well, you tell Lady Pierrepont that unless she settles the account as agreed, I'll be melting him down to wax the floors!"

"Lady?" Rowland remembered then the intelligence of the wife of the British High Commissioner to Ceylon. "Euphemia is paying for the statue?" he asked, feigning familiarity with the new Lady Pierrepont. "I say, she didn't tell me that!"

"She hasn't paid a single penny for anything yet!" Pocock was clearly irate. "I risk my job to take on a private commission and then, when I've already cast the head, she decides a statue would be ghoulish just because he's dead!"

"I see. That is bad luck," Rowland said, glaring at Milton who was grinning openly.

Pocock sighed. He stepped over to where the unfinished statue of Pierrepont had been leant against a wall and, with a measure of twisting and grunting, removed the head. He gave it to Rowland. "Here, for Lady Pierrepont, with my condolences. She will at least be able to tell the baby what its late father looked like. If she pays her account, I will make the rest of him!"

Rowland looked down at the waxen head which Pocock had thrust at him. It was, as far as he could tell, a startling likeness, though admittedly he had last seen Pierrepont in less than ideal circumstances.

Clyde, who was standing behind Pocock, was signalling wildly for Rowland to give the head back. Milton was trying not to laugh, and, thankfully, Ernest had stopped with Edna and Spencer.

"I'll see that Lady Pierrepont—Euphemia, gets it—him," Rowland said. Clyde groaned audibly. "I'm sure she'll be grateful."

Pocock grunted and waved for them to go. "Tell her to pay!"

Rowland tried to carry the head discreetly, but it was not really possible to do so. As it had no handle of any sort, he was forced to bundle it under his uninjured arm like a ball.

"I don't suppose you could wrap this up in something for me, Mr. Spencer?" he asked when they rejoined the sculptress and her tutor.

"Do we get to keep that?" Ernest stared at the head in awe. The glass eyes looked blankly out from the crook of Rowland's arm.

"Afraid not, Ernie, we're just delivering it to someone for Mr. Pocock."

The boy was clearly disappointed. Milton seemed so, too.

Obligingly, and without question, Spencer had Pierrepont's head wrapped in brown paper and twine, tying an extra loop to act as a handle. He swung the package on his hook a couple of times to test the knots were secure and, so satisfied, returned it to Rowland.

They thanked and farewelled Marriott Spencer then, and took Ernest to the souvenir shop in the vain search for something as desirable to a small boy as a wax head.

Exhausted by the day's adventures, Ernest fell asleep on the drive back to Ennismore Gardens. Clyde carried him into the terrace and they stayed for a while to drink tea with Kate and Ethel Bruce. They had a perfectly civilised conversation without once mentioning the head of Lord Pierrepont.

It was not until they'd returned to the privacy of their suites at Claridge's that Clyde spoke his mind.

"What the Dickens were you thinking, Rowly?" he demanded. "Why would you agree to take Lord Muck's ugly mug home with us?"

Rowland glanced at the head, which Milton had unwrapped and placed prominently on the sideboard. "It didn't seem like I could politely refuse."

"For God's sake, he gave you a head, not his flaming dance card!"

"I trust your judgement, Rowly," Milton said as he poured drinks. "You've got a good head on your shoulders...and another on the sideboard."

Rowland smiled. "I'll take it to the recently widowed Lady Pierrepont. I'm more than a little intrigued to meet her, to be honest."

"Meet her? Doesn't it alarm you that she would want a wax replica of her husband?"

"Alarm me? No—not excessively."

"Why not?"

Rowland shrugged. "I was at Oxford."

"What's that supposed to mean?" Clyde asked.

Rowland sat down. "I shared digs once with a chap called Rutherford, son of an Earl. Nice fellow, liked horses. He had every nag he ever owned stuffed and mounted when it died... kept a taxidermist on staff and the horses in his ballroom. Had his first pony moved into our rooms at Oxford—a moth-eaten Shetland called Cloppy."

Clyde stared at Rowland for a moment, unsure whether he was joking. "Right, then," he said uncertainly. "You're saying the English are mad?"

"The ones with titles can be eccentric." Rowland rubbed the back of his neck where the weight of the sling was concentrated. "It's a wax head, Clyde—a little odd, I'll grant you, but probably not all that different from commissioning a painting of your husband."

Clyde gave up. "Very well, then. Go ahead and call on a grieving widow with her husband's head under your arm, but mate, don't be surprised if she calls the police."

Chapter Twelve

Hence Insanity

A medical man, who has travelled extensively for the purpose of studying human development, asserts that two of the greatest evils in the world are over-indulgence in alcohol and tobacco. "I am not speaking as a moralist, but as a physician," he said. "The strain of modern life is leading more and more to its victims flying for relief to alcohol and tobacco, and I believe that these are tremendous factors in bringing about conditions favourable to insanity. I have seen cases of lunacy directly caused by excessive cigarette smoking, and the insanity born of alcoholism is well known to doctors. It is not the pressure of modern life that breaks us down. It is the drugs and stimulants we take to mitigate its effect."

—*Camperdown Chronicle, 1933*

The light of the summer moon was almost bright as it streamed in through the open window. Rowland looked out onto Brook Street, reorienting himself after a brief and troubled sleep. Cursing, he wiped the cold sweat off his brow, his heart still beating rapidly and his breath ragged. Blow Wilfred and his advice… he needed a drink.

He didn't bother with a dressing-gown—the night was warm enough—making his way towards the sitting room and its ample drinks cabinet.

"What the hell…?" It took him just a moment to realise that it was the waxen head that glared at him like some apparition from the sideboard. The moonlight gave Pierrepont's face an ethereal luminosity; the shadows gave it a kind of sinister life.

"Good evening, Lord Pierrepont," Rowland said quietly, smiling at his own reaction. "I gather you, too, are unable to sleep." How could he have forgotten, even for a moment, that there was a head on the sideboard?

He poured himself a brandy and took the armchair opposite. The glassy eyes—baleful, resentful—of Pierrepont's effigy seemed to follow his every move.

"I'm not sure what you expect me to do, old boy," Rowland muttered flinching under the strange gaze. "It seems to me that you were determined to end badly. Someone was bound to take issue with your shenanigans eventually."

It was fatigue, of course, but for a moment Rowland thought the head sighed.

"I do wonder, though," Rowland went on, setting down his brandy without taking a sip, "exactly how the murderer managed to get into your rooms at that club of yours, without anyone raising an alarm. He might have used the tradesmen's entrance, I suppose, which means he was familiar with the club…"

Rowland sat back tapping his cast thoughtfully. For some reason, Pierrepont's glass eyes seemed less hostile now.

"The authorities don't seem too interested in who killed you, do they, old boy?" Rowland pointed sternly at the head. "That's what you get for dying in a frilly nightie. But I hear what you're saying…perhaps I could make some enquiries on your behalf."

"Rowly?" Clyde stumbled into the sitting room, crashing into the couch as he came. "Are you talking to a ball of wax?"

"Clyde…sorry…I didn't mean to wake you."

"Were you talking to Pierrepont?" Clyde repeated the question, incredulous.

"Yes."

"Do you think that perhaps you are losing your mind?"

"He didn't reply, so no." Rowland smiled. "When he begins to talk back, by all means, have me committed."

"Rowly…"

"I was just thinking out loud, Clyde."

Clyde stopped on the couch. "You still can't sleep?"

Rowland said nothing, aware that his ongoing insomnia was beginning to worry his friends.

Clyde noted the glass of brandy. "I thought Wilfred told you *not* to drink."

"He said don't drink *alone*," Rowland replied. "You're here now…not to mention my good friend Pierrepont."

Clyde laughed despite himself. "Fair enough." He stood and poured himself a whisky, raising his glass to the wax head before he sat down again. "I expect Lady Pierrepont is glad she got old Bunky here to the altar before he was no longer able to make an honest woman of her."

Rowland nodded. He, too, had concluded that the marriage was one of necessity. "Poor girl seems to have swapped one scandal for another."

"She may not welcome you."

"No doubt." Rowland swirled the brandy in its glass. "But as fond as I have become of Pierrepont's sparkling conversation, he does not belong to us. I'll have to at least try to return him to his widow."

Rowland read the letter without flinching. Penned in flowing ink on superior paper it nevertheless was a vitriolic diatribe of threats. Declaring him a race traitor, and a Bolshevik, among other things more crude and profane, it explained in detail what he could expect when he fell into the hands of right-thinking men. It was the third such letter he'd received since the incident at the economic conference with Mosley's Blackshirts.

"What is it, Rowly?"

Rowland handed Milton the page. The poet read silently. His jaw hardened and he cursed quietly. "Just let them try," he snarled. "Just let them try."

Rowland nodded. He had no intention of paying any attention to the missives. There were more important things to deal with than the schoolyard threats of the British Fascists.

Upon making enquiries through Menzies, Rowland discovered that Lady Pierrepont, formerly The Honourable Euphemia Thistlewaite, had retreated in her grief to the house of her godmother, who lived in the town of Bletchley.

"Where on Earth is Bletchley?" Edna asked.

"It's my understanding that it's somewhere between Oxford and Cambridge." Rowland frowned. He hadn't anticipated roaming the countryside with a wax head. This was turning out to be an utter nuisance.

The telephone rang before the logistics of the head's return could be further considered.

"A Miss Dawe for you, sir." Menzies, who was clearly spryer than Beresford, had reached the telephone first.

Rowland stepped into the small library off the sitting room to take the call. He returned just a minute later, fuming as he searched for his hat.

Edna looked up, alarmed. "What's happened?"

"Apparently some idiot has decided that Allie is the principal suspect for the murder of Pierrepont. They've been interrogating her most of the night. The poor girl is beside herself."

Edna gasped. "That's outrageous! They can't do that!"

"I've called Allen and Overy. I'm going to meet George Allen at Allie's house to see if there is anything we can do legally to make them see sense."

Edna was already pulling on her gloves. Rowland didn't try to dissuade her. In his experience the sculptress was a lot better with tears than he, and while their conversation had been brief, he had ascertained that Allie was in tears.

Milton tossed him his hat. "Call if there's anything we can do, Rowly, especially if you're thinking of hitting anyone."

Clyde rolled his eyes. "Tell Allie to keep her chin up, mate."

Edna and Rowland took the motor taxi Menzies had arranged directly to Allie Dawe's residence in Belgravia.

"Is that a police car?" Edna asked as they pulled up behind the two-toned grey sedan.

"An Armstrong Siddeley?" Rowland said, shaking his head. "I doubt it." He paid the driver and offered Edna his hand as she alighted.

It wasn't till the motor taxi had pulled away that all four doors of the Armstrong Siddeley were flung open. A man emerged from behind each. They wore suits, tailored to a level of excellence that spoke of the public service rather than the constabulary.

Rowland tipped his hat as he and Edna moved to step past. "Gentlemen, if you'll excuse us."

The men stood four abreast, barring their path. Only one spoke or responded in any way. "Mr. Sinclair, if you wouldn't mind coming with us?"

Rowland moved Edna behind him. "I do mind, actually. Have we met, sir?"

"I'm afraid we must insist."

"You can insist all you want."

"We require you to accompany us, Sinclair."

"How dare you?" Edna said angrily. "I'll scream!"

The man nearest moved swiftly and efficiently, seizing the sculptress and clamping his large hand over her mouth.

Rowland reacted furiously, launching himself at Edna's assailant and prompting the other three men into action. They dragged him off and pinned him against the trunk of the Armstrong Siddeley.

Rowland glanced at Edna, struggling against the iron grip which held and silenced her. He had no hope of even trying to protect her with one arm in a wretched cast.

"Let the lady go and I will come with you," he said. He repeated it in German.

Now Edna looked terrified.

The same man spoke again. "We are not interested in your young lady, Sinclair. Get into the car."

Slowly, with his eyes fixed on Edna, Rowland complied.

"Madam," the man addressed the sculptress now, "my colleague will release you directly. Bear in mind that Mr. Sinclair will be accompanying us, and we will be in earshot for at least a couple of minutes."

Edna nodded with the hand still suffocatingly firm across her face. She understood the threat.

And so, when they released her, she watched helplessly as the car doors were slammed shut and the Armstrong Siddeley pulled sharply away. She waited in desperate torn horror, until the vehicle turned and disappeared from sight before she screamed.

Allie Dawe had anticipated the arrival of no one but Rowland Sinclair, yet it seemed that everyone but him converged upon her home.

Edna was first.

"Allie, I need to telephone the police."

"Whatever for? I don't ever want to see the frightful police again!"

"Allie, please...they've taken Rowly...Mr. Sinclair."

"The police have arrested Mr. Sinclair?"

It took Edna several moments to make Allie understand that Rowland had been abducted by people who had nothing to do with the girl's present troubles. Allie took her then to a neighbour who had the telephone connected.

Edna telephoned the police, then Claridge's, and then Ennismore Gardens. She broke down in panic when speaking with Clyde but gathered herself a little before she told Wilfred what had happened. By the time they returned to Allie's home, the Sinclairs' solicitor, Allen, had arrived as arranged. Soon the small house was crammed with police, Rowland's friends, his brother and Stanley Melbourne Bruce, all asking questions with increasing urgency and volume. The Hon. Mrs. John Dawe fainted.

Wilfred, in his way, took charge. First he demanded silence, and though he did not raise his voice or make any threat, he got it. The constables who had been sent to take Edna's statement stood by sheepishly as Wilfred directed the housekeeper to make the distraught young woman a cup of tea. Then quietly, firmly, he asked the sculptress to tell him precisely what had happened.

She did so.

"What did these men look like?"

Edna buried her face in her hands, trying to think. "Big, they were big and clean-cut. But otherwise nothing in particular… no—the one who put his hand over my mouth had a mermaid tattooed on his wrist."

"How long ago was this, in your estimation, Miss Higgins?"

"Half an hour at least." Edna left the tea—she felt shaky, unable to manage the fine hand-painted china.

"Did these men say who they were?"

"No. They just demanded that Rowly go with them."

"What about Rowly? What did he say?"

"He didn't know them…at least at first. He asked if they'd met before." Edna stopped, suddenly cold as she remembered. "German! In the end, he spoke to them in German!"

Wilfred tensed, and Milton swallowed a profanity.

"Surely they wouldn't dare…" Clyde began.

"My God, they'll kill him," Edna whispered.

Wilfred sat opposite her, and looked directly into her face. "Think, Miss Higgins, did they seem German to you?"

Edna hesitated. "Only one of them spoke," she said, swallowing. "And he didn't sound German, but perhaps he was…" Edna wiped the single tear which had made its way past her resolve not to cry in front of Wilfred. "Who else would take Rowly, Mr. Sinclair?"

Wilfred took the handkerchief from his breast pocket and handed it to the sculptress. "In my experience, Miss Higgins, Rowly acquires enemies the way you ladies acquire hats."

Edna studied him. "I know you're worried, Mr. Sinclair," she whispered. "Rowly obviously thought they were German."

Wilfred stood. "We'll leave you to talk to the police, Miss Higgins." He replaced his hat and tipped it at the sculptress before stalking away with grim purpose and Stanley Melbourne Bruce.

Rowland sat wedged firmly and uncomfortably between two men in the back of the Armstrong Siddeley. They didn't speak to or even look at him. Neither did they utter a word to each other.

He tried to focus on his options, such as they were; to guess how they would get him back to Germany—was there an aeroplane waiting somewhere to return him forcibly to face trial…or worse? The man on Rowland's left took a pewter cigarette case from his pocket. He extracted and lit four cigarettes one after the other, handing a stick to each of his companions before drawing deeply on his own. Rowland's fist clenched as he struggled not to panic. With four men smoking within the cabin, the air was becoming thick and pungent.

The Armstrong Siddeley did not pull up at the remote airstrip that Rowland expected, but at a mansion in St. James's in what was clearly a better part of London.

"Come on, Ed." Milton took Edna's hand. "Let's get out of here."

The sculptress nodded. The policemen—an elderly half-deaf constable and another who was barely literate—had taken her statement and departed to canvass neighbours for any witness accounts. Allie had retired to her bedroom in tears—whether for Rowland or for her own predicament, was hard to tell. Clyde was already outside. They walked silently at first, as if speaking of what had happened might endanger Rowland further somehow.

Finally Milton spoke. "Prussia House is somewhere near here, I believe."

"What's Prussia House?"

"It once housed the Embassy of the Weimar Republic. Now it's where one would find the Embassy of the Third Reich."

"You think they might have taken Rowly there?" Clyde followed Milton's thinking.

"Technically speaking, I believe the Embassy property is Germany."

Clyde removed his hat and looked up at a patch of blue between the buildings. He could not help but miss the broad Australian sky. "We'd better put Ed in a taxi back to Claridge's and go have a look."

"You're not putting Ed anywhere!" the sculptress said, angrily shoving Clyde. "Aside from the fact that I'll do as I please, I'm the only one of us who can recognise the men who took Rowly!" For a moment the assertion was met with only silence.

"She's right, Clyde," Milton said eventually. He frowned. "They'll also recognise her, I suppose."

Clyde sighed. "Let's go," he decided. "If we see an Armstrong Siddeley in the driveway, we'll have Wilfred declare war."

Chapter Thirteen

Oxford Shocks Britain!

The Union Goes Pacifist

(By R. J. Foster)

LONDON, February 16

THE young bloods—or should it be the young bloodlesses?—of Oxford have been and gone and done it! Assembled in the Oxford Union, which is the University's debating society, 275 of them against 153 have carried a motion: "That this House will in no circumstances fight for its King and country."

Let King George and the British Empire take notice. If they will insist on getting mixed up in a war, they mustn't look to Oxford to win it for them. They will just have to muddle along as best they can! It does not matter whether it is a war of aggression, or a war waged in self-defence, or in fulfilment of treaty obligations. In no circumstances—no circumstances, mind you—will the Oxford Union fight. So there!

...In the drawing-rooms of Mayfair, in the clubs of St. James' and Piccadilly, in all the places where Old Boys congregate to lament the decadence of the new generation, the disloyal declaration of the Oxford Union has been heard, with indignation and pain. Oxford, they are

> saying, has gone Red—or Yellow. And they are not only saying it: they are writing it, in purple letters to the press.
>
> ...The letter-writers are not being allowed to have it their own way. The leader writers, too, are busy. Thus the, "Daily Express":
>
> "The woozy-minded pacifists, the practical jokers, and the sexual indeterminates of Oxford have scored a great success in the publicity that has followed their victory at the Oxford Union. Even the plea of immaturity or the irresistible passion of the undergraduate for posing cannot excuse such a contemptible and indecent action as the passing of that resolution."
>
> —*The Daily News,* 1933

Rowland stared, rendered speechless by fury and disbelief.

The rear admiral stood and extended his hand. "Rowland! Delighted to see you again, my boy!"

Rowland cursed. "Quex...what the hell—?"

"Now, now, calm down, there's a good chap. I did issue an invitation previously. Unfortunately, it was to no avail."

"You had me abducted from the streets, you flaming lunatic!"

Hugh Sinclair sighed, and slapped Rowland companionably on the shoulder. "There's really no need to get upset, sport, I simply sent a car for you."

"You sent four thugs to take me by force. For God's sake, I thought..." He stopped. "Ed will have called the police by now."

Clearly the police did not concern Rear Admiral Sinclair. Instead, he chose that moment to introduce the thugs who had come for Rowland—all naval officers of considerable rank. And then he dismissed them.

Rowland watched, fuming and incredulous. He had neither seen nor corresponded with his second cousin since before he'd left Pembroke House, and even then their relationship had been barely more than administrative.

Hugh Sinclair hummed as he poured two generous glasses of pre-war scotch. He motioned Rowland to the captain's chair by his desk and set the whisky before him. Rowland left the glass untouched. Even if he had been predisposed to drink with his abductor, he hated whisky.

"I must say, Rowland, I'm a little hurt that you have not called on me earlier."

"What do you want, Quex? Surely you didn't kidnap me to remind me of my social obligations."

"Social obligations?" Hugh shook his head sadly. "Surely more than that. I was like a father to you, Rowland."

"I wouldn't say that."

Hugh paused. "No, I suppose I should be relieved."

Rowland bristled.

Hugh continued. "I remember that you and Henry were not always friends. I hoped that when Wilfred sent you abroad, and entrusted you into my care, that we at least could be friends."

"I don't mean to sound ungrateful, Quex, but I don't recall seeing you very often back then…unless I was about to be expelled."

Hugh Sinclair smiled. "Well, that was often enough."

Rowland rubbed his face. This was ridiculous. "What do you want from me, Quex?"

"I'm a little concerned about the company you're keeping, sport. You do realise that Mr. Isaacs is a Communist?"

Rowland stood. "Since this isn't an abduction, I assume I'm free to go."

For a moment there was silence and then Hugh laughed. "Have a drink with me Rowland, for old time's sake."

Rowland turned to leave.

"You know, your namesake, my dear late cousin Rowland, would often have a drink with me when he was in London. Very fond of my aged malt…and equally fond of you. I can't tell you how often we discussed you and your brother till the wee hours." Hugh raised his glass in a kind of salute. "I miss old Rowland."

Rowland stopped. His favourite uncle—another Rowland Sinclair—had been dead for well over a year. He'd loved the old man but even from beyond the grave his namesake was capable of causing trouble. Rowland turned back to meet the rear admiral's eye, trying to determine exactly which family secret Hugh Sinclair was using against him.

Hugh Sinclair held his gaze. Reluctantly Rowland sat down. "What is it you want, Quex?" he asked wearily.

"I don't want us to be at odds, Rowland…there is no need. I've organised for a spot of luncheon. I suggest we take our drinks to the dining room and talk over Cook's very fine roast duck."

Rowland cursed openly, but he could see that he had little choice. "Could you at least telephone Claridge's and tell them where I am?"

Hugh smiled. "Of course. It would be my pleasure." He picked up the receiver immediately, and left a message with the concierge that Rowland Sinclair was perfectly well and would return soon.

And so Rowland stopped to dine with the second cousin he barely knew, but who seemed to know a great deal about him. If he hadn't been brought forcibly into Hugh Sinclair's company, he might have found the admiral affable and his manner warm and charming. The food and wine at Quex's table were excellent and the conversation thoughtful. It was only the manner in which he seemed to acquire his guests that was less-than-impeccable.

"Look, Rowland," Hugh said as the soup was served, "I apologise for not having made more time when you were in England. The job was demanding all of my attention—blasted Communists everywhere—but you had just lost your father in quite horrendous circumstances. I was remiss and I regret it."

Rowland shifted uncomfortably. In truth, he had neither sought nor missed Hugh Sinclair's attention back then. He doubted very much whether his cousin would have reached him with a few kind words and the odd day out.

"I should have at least taken you to the waxworks…boys love the waxwork museum. And I hear you are still very fond of our Madame Tussaud's."

Rowland regarded the admiral warily. Was Hugh Sinclair having him followed?

"I called on Wilfred at Stanley Bruce's last evening," Hugh explained. "That delightful young scamp Ernest was full of his day at Tussaud's with his Uncle Rowly."

"Did you tell Wil you were planning to kidnap me?"

"Let's not fall out over that again. Shall we talk of happier things? Your recent travels? I believe you were in Germany just lately?"

"I was."

"And you had an accident of some sort?" Hugh gestured at the sling.

Rowland made a decision then as to how much he wanted Hugh Sinclair to know. "It wasn't an accident, Quex. Mr. Hitler's Stormtroopers broke my arm as a kind of art lesson."

Hugh showed no sign of surprise. "Tell me," he said.

Rowland recounted the final days of their stay in Germany, mentioning nothing about why they had been sent to Munich in the first place. As much as the Old Guard had abandoned him, he would not betray them to the British admiral.

Quex shook his head. "You'll be happy to know that Herr Hitler is under significant international pressure to do something about Röhm and his brown-shirted rabble. I believe he will have no choice but to act soon."

"That's not the point," Rowland said, frustrated. "The Nazi regime is dangerous with or without the likes of Ernst Röhm!" He told Hugh of Dachau, where socialists were imprisoned en masse. Cautiously and without any detail which might identify or endanger them, he spoke of the men of the German Underground who lived like rats and in hiding. "The Nazis have eradicated the Communists, the unions, and any other organisation that might have opposed them."

"I personally wouldn't waste sympathy on the Communists, Rowland." Hugh sat back as the duck was served. It had been deboned and prepared in a manner that Rowland could manage, despite the sling and plaster cast.

"Oh, for pity's sake, the Communists seem to be the only ones concerned with stopping Hitler!"

Hugh Sinclair shook his head. "It appears every young man nowadays has sympathy for the Communist cause, even within the better social circles. Lord knows it's no longer an impediment to progress in the public service to have flirted with Communism in one's university days." The admiral stabbed aggressively at his meal. "Why, apparently, Oxford men no longer consider themselves British! Traitorous privileged brats!"

Rowland's brow rose. "Oxford men?"

"Oh, yes…you're an Oxford man, too, I recall. Well, I'm afraid standards have changed since your time, my boy! Only months ago, that blasted Oxford Debating Union passed a motion that it would not fight for King and country. Can you imagine that? The wastrels of the present generation will not fight!"

"The Debating Union?" Rowland laughed. The debaters he remembered had taken pride in their capacity to argue the absurd. "I distinctly recall the Oxford Debating Union also passed a motion for the creation of a Doctorate in Lager. I wouldn't take their motions too seriously, Quex."

The admiral paused and placed his knife and fork neatly on his plate. "I'm concerned about the company you're keeping, Rowland."

"Don't be."

"Wilfred tells me you've been more or less drifting since you returned to Australia. Perhaps I could find something for you."

Rowland shrugged. "I appreciate your concern, Quex, but I rather like drifting."

To Rowland's surprise, Hugh Sinclair did not argue with him. Instead the admiral refilled his reluctant guest's wineglass. "Just remember, I'm here to help, if you change your mind. We're family…and you can trust me. Your life could well amount to something, Rowland. It's not too late."

The three Australians who loitered outside Prussia House were dismissed as inquisitive tourists; their interest in the diplomatic vehicles a natural consequence of the universal high regard in which German engineering was held. It was only as he ran his eyes over the rows of parked Mercedes-Benz motor cars that it occurred to Clyde that they were on the wrong track.

"Are you sure they were driving an Armstrong Siddeley, Ed?"

"I wouldn't have a clue, but Rowly said it was an Armstrong Siddeley."

Clyde frowned. "Rowly would know." He glanced at Milton. "No self-respecting German would drive a Siddeley."

Milton rubbed his face. "Maybe Rowly was wrong."

"About the car? Not a chance. Rowly knows his motors."

"Not that...about the blokes who took him. The only reason we've concluded they were German is because he spoke to them in German. Maybe he was wrong."

"But who else would take him?" Edna asked.

Milton cursed as he remembered the succession of threatening letters from within the membership of the British Union of Fascists. Rowland hadn't taken them seriously. "The B.U.F., the flaming B.U.F.!" he said. "They've had it in for him since he took on that cretin Joyce."

Edna nodded, eager for any reason to believe that Rowland was not in the hands of the Nazis.

But Milton was no happier with this conclusion. He had seen the letters. "We'd better find him quickly."

"But how?"

"We'll find Joyce and choke it out of the bastard!"

Clyde groaned. They were guessing—pulling at vague straws in the hope that one would hold. Perhaps it was the B.U.F., but in truth they still had no idea what had become of the Siddeley or Rowland Sinclair.

When Rowland was returned to Claridge's he found the suite in uproar and somewhat crowded—his companions, his brother, Menzies, and two police officers had all gathered there. He walked in just as Milton demanded of Wilfred, "What do you mean it was a hoax?"

"Not a hoax, a misunderstanding, Mr. Isaacs."

"Rowly!" Edna threw herself at him. "Are you all right? Where have you been?"

The room fell silent then roared again as questions and demands were hurled in every direction. Milton and Clyde joined Edna in relief, greeting Rowland with a familiarity which Wilfred was bound to find improper.

Eventually some sense was extracted from the melee and, after establishing that Rowland had had nothing to do with his own supposed abduction, the police officers departed.

Rowland sat down. "Did you know anything about this, Wil?"

"Of course not. If I'd wanted you to have lunch with Quex, I would simply have insisted you do so." Wilfred retrieved his hat from the sideboard. "When Miss Higgins mentioned the tattoo, I wondered. Midshipmen were always decorating each other. I telephoned Quex. By then you were both eating pudding!"

Rowland remembered that Hugh had, indeed, stepped out to take a phone call during dessert.

Wilfred went on emphatically. "I sent men to find your somewhat excitable companions and bring them back here so that I might inform them that there was no need to hurl accusations at every man in London!"

"What?"

"Milt wanted to storm the office of the B.U.F.," Edna whispered.

Wilfred opened his pocket watch, and checked the time. "I must get back. Rowly, for pity's sake, try and leave a couple of days before the next crisis!"

"That's it?" Rowland said, outraged. "That lunatic abducts me for lunch and you want *me* to stay out of trouble?"

"He said he had asked you to come see him."

"I am not one of his crew. I don't have to drop everything just because Admiral Hugh flaming Sinclair shouts!"

Wilfred stepped towards the door and waited impatiently while the butler opened it to let him out. "I'll deal with Quex.

However, I suggest that next time our cousin wants to see you, you just jolly well go."

As the door closed after Wilfred, Rowland slipped his arm out of the sling and rubbed the back of his neck, both annoyed and embarrassed by the morning's events.

Edna sat on the arm of his chair and brushed the hair away from his face. "I'm glad it was your cousin," she said. "It was frightening, but at least that's all it was."

Milton put a glass of gin down in front of him. "What was he after, Rowly, this cousin of yours?"

"I'm not entirely sure. I think he wanted me to come work for him."

"He wanted you to join up? It's all a trifle high-handed, isn't it?"

"He's taking his knighthood a little seriously, I suppose."

"He's been knighted?"

"His Majesty knighted most of his admirals after the war."

"Nothing like a cape and a funny hat to keep you loyal to the status quo."

Rowland smiled: if any man could be seduced by a cape, it was probably Milton.

"Rowly, did you talk about Germany?" Edna asked earnestly. "Your cousin sounds like he may be an important man. Perhaps…?"

"Yes, I did, actually." Rowland frowned. "He seems to believe the Nazis are not nearly as dangerous as either the Communists or the Oxford Debating Union."

Chapter Fourteen

Terrible Despotism

LONDON, July 8

"There is the most absolute, terrible despotism conceivable in Germany," said Herr Rudolph Breitscheid, former leader of the Social Democrats in the Reichstag, who was banished by the Nazis, when addressing the National Peace Conference at Oxford. He added, "There are hundreds of separate local dictatorships. The anti-Semitic feeling is due to the hatred of doctors, lawyers and business men to their more successful Jewish colleagues. We are bitterly disappointed by the lack of sympathy from Britain and Italy. Hitler is pacifist because he cannot be otherwise. Europe should act accordingly and institute the strictest international control of armaments."

—*The Central Queensland Herald*, 1933

Menzies brought *The Guardian* in on a silver tray and enquired if the gentlemen would be requiring tea. The manservant assiduously avoided any mention or acknowledgement of the wax head which sat conspicuously on the sideboard.

"No, thank you, Menzies."

Rowland checked his watch as Milton took the paper. They had still an hour before they were expected in Belgravia for the meeting that had been aborted the day before.

"There is a gentleman waiting to call on you in the foyer, sir. Are you at home?"

"What gentleman?"

"The Honourable Archibald Murcott, sir. He claims to be an old friend of yours."

Rowland's brow arched. He was sure he didn't know anyone called Murcott. "Yes, I'm at home. Have them send him up. Oh, perhaps you had better serve that tea, after all."

"Very good, sir."

The butler answered the door to a young man, well-dressed, and clearly well-fed. The buttons of his waistcoat stretched over the rounded expanse of his torso and his bowler sat at a jaunty angle.

"Sinclair!" he boomed by way of greeting. "How fabulous to see you again, old chap!"

Rowland stared. He knew this man but not by the name Murcott. "Lesley?"

"Not anymore, I'm afraid. Oh, I say, I can't even shake your hand." He slapped Rowland on the back instead. "It turns out another heir emerged. Who knew the old man was such a rogue? I lost the title...so I'm simply The Honourable Archibald Murcott now!"

"I see." Rowland was unsure if he should be expressing condolences. He had known Murcott at Oxford in the twenties as the young Lord Lesley, an arrogant, condescending member of the entitled classes with a fondness for Regency dress and cards. The portly, congenial man before him was quite stark in contrast. Rowland introduced Clyde and Milton.

"Delighted to make your acquaintance, gentlemen," Murcott said enthusiastically, shaking what hands he could.

He started as his eye caught the wax head on the sideboard. "By George, is that Pierrepont?"

"Yes."

"Shall I take your hat, sir?" The butler broke the awkward silence which followed as they all simply looked at Pierrepont.

Murcott held up his forefinger. "No...no, that's perfectly all right." He strode over to the sideboard, placed his bowler on the wax head and adjusted it until the angle pleased. "Bunky here will hold it for me. Now, Sinclair, are you ever going to ask me to sit down?"

"Please." Rowland motioned to a chair.

"I don't suppose your man can make a decent martini?"

Rowland looked questioningly at the butler who inclined his head and said, "And the rest of you gentlemen?"

The Australians elected for tea, though Milton visibly wavered.

"Good heavens, Sinclair, what's happened to you?" Murcott demanded, learning he would be drinking alone.

"It's barely ten in the morning."

"Letting the side down, Sinclair, letting the side down." Murcott sighed. "I heard you were back in London and I couldn't pass up the chance to drop in and enquire after *my* car."

"She's well. The Australian climate suits her."

Shortly before he'd returned to Australia, Rowland had won his beloved 1927 Mercedes S-Class from the then Lord Lesley in a gruelling, twelve-hour game of poker. Though he'd known the German automobile would raise both eyebrows and ire in post-war Australia, he'd had her shipped home.

"It took me a long time to stop hating you for taking my car," Murcott admitted.

"I believe I won her."

"Oh, yes, yes, old man. Fair and square. It was more wounded pride than anything else, to be honest...you being a Colonial and all. Losing the title to my father's youthful indiscretion put it all into perspective."

"It must have been a blow," Rowland ventured.

"A frightful scandal, but you know it all turned out rather well in the end. The new Lord Lesley is actually not such a bad chap, settled on me quite generously, really, and I'll no longer have to live in that draughty gothic mausoleum that came with the title!"

"So you're living in London now?"

"Not especially. I have my club here, of course, but my dear sister Ivy and I have moved back to Oxford." He pulled out a calling card and handed it to Rowland. "Purchased a quaint little place called Bloomington Manor. You really must come and stay…Do you gentlemen shoot?" He looked at Rowland. "I suppose we'll have to count you out, Sinclair, what with your being winged and all, but no matter, Ivy will be delighted to see you." He leaned over to Clyde and Milton. "My sister did always consider Sinclair rather dashing—part of the reason I wanted to give him a damn good thrashing, I suppose." He laughed. "Of course, I knew my limitations—I don't expect Sinclair's told you gentlemen that he boxed at Oxford: Antipodean savagery kept in check by the Queensbury rules." Murcott tapped his temple. "I thought I'd defeat him with my superior British intellect, but sadly, you Colonials play poker rather well, too." He shook his head forlornly. "I should have challenged him to a footrace around the quadrangle instead. I was quite swift in those days."

Rowland sat back, bemused. He had no recollection of meeting Ivy Murcott, and he hadn't realised there was anything more to the high-stakes poker game than cards.

"But that's all water under the bridge," Murcott said, raising his martini glass. "You chaps really must visit Bloomington. Oxford is so dull this time of year—I'm simply desperate for some civilised distraction."

At this juncture, Edna walked in through the door that connected the penthouse suites. "Rowly…Oh, hello."

The gentlemen stood, and Rowland introduced Murcott.

"I am very glad to hear Sinclair introduce you as Miss Higgins, dear lady. If he had introduced you as *Mrs. Sinclair*, I'm afraid I would have been forced to hate him again."

Edna laughed. She had always enjoyed meeting Rowland's university chums. For men so privileged and educated, they were invariably idiots. Thoroughly pleasant, but idiots.

"If you and your charming friends don't come to Bloomington, Sinclair, you may consider our families at war!" Murcott declared. "I may no longer be a lord, but I could raise an army of sorts. I'm sure Mummy would fight if I asked her..."

Rowland laughed now. Losing the peerage suited Murcott. He was a great deal more agreeable than he had ever been as Lord Lesley.

Murcott stood. "I should go. It would be frightfully rude to stay longer since I have come unannounced, and I do have an appointment for billiards at my club. Perhaps we could chalk a cue at Bloomington, Sinclair? We might even wager a little something on the outcome to make it interesting."

Murcott shook Milton and Clyde's hands and kissed Edna's. "I know, my dear," he said as he did so. "A dreadful French affectation, but you must forgive me for I am but a man enslaved."

Once again, Edna laughed at him.

"Remember, Sinclair," Murcott warned as he retrieved his hat from the wax head and stepped towards the door. "Visit or it will be war!"

"Good Lord!" Clyde groaned as Menzies closed the door behind Murcott.

Edna smiled. "I quite liked him. Were you good friends, Rowly?"

"Not at all. He was insufferable, but he does seem to have mellowed somewhat. If he'd been like this back then, I wouldn't have taken his car."

"Perhaps he's hoping you'll give it back," Milton suggested.

"Not a chance of that," Rowland said firmly, vaguely glad his Mercedes was safely garaged at Woodlands House.

"Shall we accept his invitation?" Edna uncurled her legs and sat up.

"To Bloomington?" Rowland looked a little alarmed. "You're bound to find Oxford rather dull after London."

Clyde snorted. "That's not what I've heard, mate. Your time there seems to have prepared you for every bizarre perversion under the British sun!" He nodded towards the head on the sideboard.

"A change of scenery might be just what the doctor ordered," Edna said as she noted the weariness around Rowland's eyes.

"No…I'm sure he said I should drink Horlicks and smoke."

Edna continued undeterred. "I think Mr. Murcott is rather fun and it's quite obvious that Wilfred doesn't want you anywhere near his conference."

The last was certainly true. While Rowland Sinclair had not been arrested for the incident with Mosley's Blackshirts, it had been made amply clear that he was no longer welcome at the Geological Museum. Wilfred had renewed his demands that his brother return to Sydney.

Milton glanced up from his paper. "You haven't any indiscretions buried at Oxford that you don't want us to discover, do you, Rowly?"

Rowland laughed. "I don't remember burying any of them."

"We could return Lord Pierrepont to Lady Pierrepont on the way…or the way back." Edna looked over to the head. "Though I have become rather attached to him, to be honest. It really is a friendly face, once you become used to it."

"Bletchley is not actually on the way to Oxford," Rowland objected.

"This is England." Milton was not unconcerned by the geography. "The place is so flaming small, everything's on the way."

Despite his exasperation with Rowland's more recent conduct, Wilfred did, over the next week, manage to secure appointments with two separate senior advisors to Ramsay MacDonald's government. Rowland left both meetings frustrated to the point of despair.

Unable to reveal what exactly he was doing in Germany, the young Australian was dismissed as some art-loving dilettante who had offended the Nazis with reckless and tactless liberalism.

"It is important to be culturally sensitive, Mr. Sinclair. Not every country is as tolerant as England."

His broken arm was discounted as the unfortunate result of a too zealous, but legal, restraint.

"It's not unusual in these volatile situations for some unintentional injury to occur. In most cases the authorities are justified."

The incarceration and abuse of dissidents in the Dachau concentration camp was scorned as left-wing propaganda.

"You didn't actually enter the camp, did you, Mr. Sinclair? I think you'll find that reports of mistreatment are vastly exaggerated. Our delegations to Germany have come back with only praise for the order of German society. Certainly your own countryman, Colonel Eric Campbell, has just returned from a tour of Germany—to sell soap, I believe. He is perfectly satisfied that Jews, in particular, are being well treated."

Even the burning of books was rationalised and excused.

"The Germans are as entitled as we to censor in the interests of public morality, Mr. Sinclair. As I said, it's imperative that the modern traveller exercise a little cultural sensitivity."

Appeasement, it seemed, was the policy of the day and what influence Wilfred and Bruce had exerted in procuring Rowland audiences with these men of the Civil Service only went so far. Everybody was sympathetic, of course, but really it was a bit much to expect that his personal misadventure would influence the course of nations.

Humiliated and disgusted, Rowland had begun to consider Archibald Murcott's repeated invitation to visit.

Wilfred had encouraged him to venture out of London—to clear his head and get some sleep before he tried again. His companions had agreed. For one thing, the wax head was still on the sideboard at Claridge's and they had all begun to talk to it.

"You'd better get rid of it soon, Rowly," Clyde grumbled. "They won't let us have it at the asylum."

Adding irritation to Rowland's frustration, the threatening letters had not ceased. Although he was scornful of what he called the letter-writing arm of the B.U.F., the vitriolic correspondence contributed to his weariness of London.

And so, Rowland accepted the invitation to Bloomington Manor. Exhausted and discouraged, he even welcomed the idea of a few days' distraction. He had, after all, promised a wax head that he would make enquiries into the murder of Pierrepont. Where better to start than with the late lord's widow?

The Oxford train pulled into Kings Cross Station emerging through a cloud of steam and a herald of screaming whistles. Edna rose onto her toes trying to see through the press of bodies.

Wilfred lifted Ernest in his arms. "I'll see you in a few days then, Rowly. Try to stay out of trouble."

Rowland winked at his nephew.

Ernest giggled.

The porter took their trunks aboard and secured the luggage onto a rack above the seats in their first-class compartment. If he noticed that the contents of the hatbox were particularly heavy, he did not mention it.

When Edna had first produced the hatbox, it seemed an insensitive and rather undignified manner in which to transport the head of a peer. But, after due consideration, it was decided that the silk-lined box was the most sensible option. They couldn't very well travel with the wax likeness tucked under their arms.

Rowland opened the window and summoned the magazine vendor who spruiked his wares up and down the platform. They all hung out of the window choosing reading material with the enthusiasm and debate of children. The vendor ran beside the train to hand over the last newspaper and they eventually retreated into the compartment.

Clyde alone did not disappear behind a newspaper or magazine, using the time instead to finish a letter to his sweetheart,

Rosalina. Beside him lay open Milton's copy of *Paradise Lost* from which Clyde was carefully transcribing.

Rosalina Martinelli had once been an artist's model. It was when she'd posed for Rowland that she had met Clyde. Now Rowland happily used the fact that Clyde was stepping out with the young woman to refuse to use her again. He called it a courtesy to his friend, but the decision had more to do with the fact that, while beautiful, Rosalina did not have the temperament he required of a model. She was shy, and fidgety, and predisposed to tears. He'd found painting her a trial of the worst kind.

The letter Clyde was writing was already several pages long, as it seemed Rosalina insisted upon long protestations of adoration. Taxed beyond measure by the literary demands of love, Clyde had turned to his friends for help. Milton had suggested he insert vast tracts of poetry, prefaced with, "In the words of so-and-so, my love…" He assured Clyde it would work. Rowland simply expressed surprise that Milton was advocating attribution rather than barefaced plagiarism. And so Clyde was transcribing from *Paradise Lost.*

"I'm sorry, mate," Rowland said quietly as he watched Clyde work diligently with his pen. "You must be desperate to get back to Miss Martinelli, and I'm keeping us here…"

Clyde looked up. "Rubbish. You'd put me on a ship back today if I asked. I haven't asked."

"I do wonder why not. God knows how long it will take me to get someone to listen…and Miss Martinelli would be glad to see you."

Clyde shook his head. "Rosie's family emigrated from Italy to Australia to escape the Fascisti," he said, pulling a handkerchief from his pocket to mop his forehead. "Her father was a trade unionist when Mussolini came to power. She understands why I'm here, mate, and it may make her father hate me less."

Rowland smiled. He'd gathered that Rosalina's father considered Clyde unsuitable. "I'm not sure how much of what we did in Germany you'll be able to tell him," he said regretfully.

They had, after all, gone there as spies and left being wanted for murder.

Clyde sighed. "There is that. Still..." he glanced at the hatbox which sat on the rack above Edna, "we can't very well leave without seeing Pierrepont safely home. Now that he's become your confidant and all."

Rowland laughed. "If you change your mind, Clyde, just say. I'll organise something."

Clyde grunted and returned to transcribing. "Did you and that solicitor bloke sort Allie out?" He changed the subject.

"As far as possible. Allen's let the police know that he's acting for Allie, but really there's not much more he can do legally." Rowland frowned. The constabulary's focus on Allie concerned him for a number of reasons. The notion that she had murdered Pierrepont was ridiculous, of course, but if the official scrutiny of Allie reached the papers, she would be socially ruined regardless.

"What motive could Allie possibly have to kill her uncle?" Clyde asked. "Wasn't he looking after her and her mother financially?"

Milton turned. "There's a lot more that goes on within families than that which meets the world's eye. One can't help but wonder how Pierrepont got hold of his sister-in-law's nightie. If she didn't keep fainting we might have asked her by now whether she actually gave him her night attire or whether Bunky was a snowdropper!"

As indelicately as the poet had chosen to put it, Rowland had to agree. Not that he thought Allie was guilty, or intentionally keeping things from them. It was merely that there were questions that they had not yet thought to pose.

Chapter Fifteen

"Nonsense"

No Degeneracy
OXFORD AND CAMBRIDGE

More nonsense has been talked in the last year of the relative degeneracy of Oxford as compared with Cambridge than any similar topic has excited since I first began to know and understand the University (writes Lord Birkenhead, High Steward of Oxford University, in the London *Daily Telegraph*).

It may perhaps be premised that the principal object of a university is still to produce men of learning, research and cultivation; highly equipped scholars, resourceful and up-to-date scientists, erudite theologians. It has not, so far as I know, even been pretended, in any one of these matters, that Oxford lags behind any university in the world. Some of us, indeed, who particularly love this venerable home of learning, would put the matter considerably higher. But the argument does not require it.

—*Northern Star*, 1930

They disembarked among crowds of students and professors returning from weekends in London—young men in blazers and straw hats, older men with academic gowns billowing about them in the late summer breeze.

Murcott emerged from the first of two waiting Bentleys and waved excitedly. "I say, Sinclair, over here." He clapped his hands to encourage the chauffeurs who ran out to meet the Australians and take the trunks.

"I'll take that for you, sir." The young driver reached for the hatbox.

It was perhaps that the chauffeur was too eager, or that, reluctant to hand the contents of the hatbox to the keeping of another, Rowland was slow to release his grip. The result was that both fumbled and the hatbox was dropped. The lid fell open, Lord Pierrepont's head tumbled out and rolled onto the platform. One man and two women fainted and several screamed.

Milton acted quickly, scooping up the head before it could roll onto the track. Someone shouted for the police and Rowland cursed as several railway officials headed towards them.

"Quickly, into the motors," Murcott cried, waving them in.

They hesitated for only a second as the passengers who had seen Pierrepont fall out of the hatbox became still more agitated. Rowland and Edna rode in the first vehicle with Murcott, while Milton and Clyde took the second. Despite the shouts from the platform and the red-faced official rapping on the windscreen, Archibald Murcott instructed his chauffeur to "Drive on."

"I'll telephone and explain later," he promised. "I don't fancy waiting to answer a lot of hysterical facile questions and, after all these years, Ivy is most anxious to see you again, Sinclair. What do you think of my new motors, old boy? The latest Bentleys—every modern convenience, but still I miss that Mercedes you won from me. I hope you're treating her as a gentleman should..."

Rowland sat back as Murcott played tour guide to a delighted Edna, pointing out the areas of the various Oxford colleges within the centre.

"That's Bath Place," Murcott said as they passed a cluster of stone cottages. "Lodged there myself in the day…passed it on to my cousin when I left Merton…and just beyond is the Bridge of Sighs."

"Oh, how lovely," Edna gasped as they drove beneath the small covered bridge which spanned the road. "Why is it called the Bridge of Sighs, Mr. Murcott?"

"I'm not sure, dear lady," Murcott admitted. "I presume it's something to do with lovesick students…" He gazed at her and smiled. "I must say I feel rather like sighing myself."

Rowland grimaced and Edna laughed.

Bloomington Manor stood at the centre of a large estate south-west of the university city. It was an early Victorian jewel of extraordinary proportions, vast and white with multiple rows of Palladian windows overlooking lush manicured lawns and Italianate gardens tended by a small army of groundsmen.

The house servants stood in a formal receiving line at the foot of the entrance stairs. A young woman stood at the top. From a distance, she cut a striking figure in a slim-fitting skirt and bolero jacket. Her hat, set at an angle, was a vibrant red.

Ivy Murcott was small, pale, and bird-like in her features and movements. To Rowland she seemed to flutter and dart, directing servants to attend to luggage and others to make tea. She flushed deeply as Rowland shook her hand. "It's a pleasure to see you again, Mr. Sinclair. It seems like just yesterday when we last spoke."

"Likewise, Miss Murcott," Rowland replied, though he could still not recall ever being introduced to the sister of Murcott—or Lesley, as he was then. He found it puzzling—a little unsettling. Rarely did he forget a face, and Ivy had the kind of face he was likely to remember. It was not beautiful, by any means, but interesting. There was a kind of anxious mystery to the girl, a quiet, sharp observance. Her nose was narrow, her eyes small and dark, but her lips were generous and voluptuous, a surprise on her otherwise unremarkable face.

The Murcotts took their guests on a tour of the manor and its immediate grounds. There were two separate stables on the property. One housed Murcott's beloved motor cars, of which he seemed to own six. The other, more conventionally, kept horses—excellent animals which were apparently Ivy's great passion.

"I have never yet been able to reach a kill before Ivy," Murcott boasted for his sister. "I venture there is no man or woman in England who could best her in the hunt!"

"Archie, stop," Ivy pleaded. "It's not me," she said, stroking the nose of a black Arabian gelding. "It's Duke. You were born for the hunt, weren't you, darling?"

Rowland reached out to pat the horse.

"Careful, Sinclair," Murcott warned. "He's a bad-tempered beast…bitten me twice, nearly took my fingers last week!"

With Ivy present, however, the horse seemed no longer a man-eater and tolerated Rowland's hand without blood being drawn.

They returned to the manor for a luncheon of cold roast pheasant served with piccalilli and spiced quail eggs.

"You must watch out for the buckshot," Ivy Murcott warned her guests. "Archie shot this one."

Among the Australians, only Rowland did not seem confused.

"I say, that's uncalled for, old girl!" Murcott protested.

Ivy rolled her eyes. "Archie is a terrible shot. If he actually manages to bring down a bird, you can assume there will be buckshot scattered through it." She removed a fragment of lead shot from between her teeth and placed it on the side of her plate in demonstration of her point.

Murcott sighed. "I'm afraid, unlike Ivy, I can never seem to take the head off cleanly. Make sure you don't chew too vigorously…you're quite likely to break a tooth."

Conversation became a little subdued as the men chewed tentatively and with great concentration thereafter. Edna decided to abandon the pheasant entirely and stay with the quail eggs and piccalilli. It was not a great deprivation, as the pheasant had been preceded by a course of soup and then fish.

Rowland asked Murcott if he knew Lady Pierrepont. "She was The Honourable Euphemia Thistlewaite before her marriage, I believe."

"Good Lord…Euphemia married? Did you hear that, Ivy? I can't believe we weren't invited!"

"You know Lady Pierrepont?"

"Well, I thought we did! But clearly we're not good enough for Lady Pierrepont anymore!" Murcott said indignantly. He shook his head sadly. "You know, Sinclair, I have come to realise—since my demotion—that people can be very stuck up!"

"Apparently, the wedding was small and a little rushed," Milton said soothingly. "I wouldn't feel overly offended."

"Oh…? Oh!" Murcott gaped in realisation. "I say, that's too bad! Euphemia was such a mouse of a thing. Who would have thought?"

Rowland explained then about Pierrepont's head and the charge he'd been given by the waxworker to return it to the lord's widow. If the Murcotts thought Lady Pierrepont's desire to have a wax replica of her husband odd, they did not mention it. "We believe she's staying in Bletchley somewhere," Rowland finished.

"That would be with Lady Leon," Ivy said confidently. "At Bletchley Park. She's Euphemia's godmother."

Rowland made a mental note of the address and the name of Lady Leon. "We'll take the long way back to London and drop it off on the way."

"I will not hear of it!" Murcott declared. "You must take one of my cars. Lord knows you'll probably win a couple from me before the night is out…I say, shall we play cards?"

"Yes, if you'd like." Rowland was still a little unaccustomed to the manner in which Murcott became routinely distracted by tangents of conversation.

"Splendid! Viggers…" Murcott summoned his butler and asked him to prepare the library for cards. He ate quickly, despite the dangers presented by the buckshot, and waited impatiently for his guests to finish, ushering them into the library the moment decorum would allow.

"Your old chum seems rather fond of cards," Clyde observed quietly.

Rowland nodded. Murcott was clearly eager to play.

The library had been set up for a long game, the card table readied with several decks of cards and poker chips, a traymobile of drinks within reach. Clearly, Murcott took his poker seriously.

The game began affably enough, but soon, despite Rowland's best efforts, the stakes began to rise alarmingly. Clyde and Edna folded out very quickly. Milton played for a while longer until he, too, became unwilling to wager money that was not his. Ivy told her brother he was being ridiculous and refused to continue.

"Shall we call it a day and take a stroll?" Rowland suggested, realising that Murcott was gambling compulsively now. He had no desire to take so much money from his host.

"Just one more hand," Murcott pleaded. "I've nearly got you figured out, Sinclair! After all these years, I'm sure I finally know how to read you."

Rowland shrugged. "One more hand then."

Edna shuffled and dealt for him. Almost immediately Murcott raised the stakes exorbitantly. Rowland did not flinch. He could afford to lose and he doubted he would. Murcott's left eyelid twitched involuntarily whenever his hand was good. It was currently still. The paucity of the Englishman's cards was only confirmed by the faint increase in the pitch of his voice when he bluffed. Rowland dragged his hand through his hair, knowing that Murcott thought the action a tell.

Murcott smiled slightly.

Clyde shook his head and groaned. They were watching a financial bloodbath. He and Milton had played enough with Rowland to know it.

Murcott slammed down his cards triumphantly. Rowland opened his hand almost apologetically.

"Oh, I s-say," Murcott stuttered. "B-but I thought..."

"It was a lucky hand," Rowland lied. "What say we go into Oxford? I haven't been back in years."

"Yes, let's do that," Ivy said, glaring sternly at her brother, "before Archie loses the house!"

Subdued now, Murcott agreed.

They drove back into Oxford and spent the late afternoon wandering through the narrow cobbled streets of the university town, browsing through bookshops and museums, exclaiming at the magnificence of every building. Edna was fascinated by the gargoyles, mesmerised by the dark individuality of every demonic face, and delighted at each discovery of yet another stone guardian.

Rowland pointed out Oxford Castle, which now served as a prison. Its rough bleached walls were stark against the elaborate architecture which surrounded it. Still, it undeniably belonged, like an echo of Oxford's beginnings.

Curious about Rowland Sinclair's life before he'd met any of them, Edna asked after the college he'd attended. And so they found themselves strolling about the Mob quad—an extensive, grassed quadrangle around which loomed the gothic structures of Merton College. As it happened, both Murcott and Rowland were Mertonians.

"I don't suppose you'd consider that footrace, Sinclair?" Murcott asked, assessing the length and breadth of the quad. "Give me a chance to regain my dignity."

"No, I wouldn't," Rowland said flatly. "Believe me, Murcott, tearing around the quadrangle will do nothing for your dignity, whether or not you win."

The Englishman sighed. "Yes, I suppose you're right. What about croquet? I was a dab hand…Oh, dear…I suppose you're not really in any condition to play croquet."

"How about we play chess later this evening?" Rowland offered. He was pretty sure he could convincingly throw a game of chess, and clearly Murcott would not leave him alone until he'd beaten him at something.

"I say, really? That's a perfectly splendid idea! Be warned though, Sinclair, we Englishmen have been defending our monarchs and castles for hundreds of years!"

"I'm willing to chance it."

Thus mollified, Murcott took more interest in the sightseeing. "I say, Sinclair…we're alumni now. What say we borrow the key to the belltower?"

"Why?" Rowland asked suspiciously. Did Murcott want to race him to the belfry?

"To take in the view, of course! We'll be able to see right across Oxford."

Rowland nodded, relieved. "Jolly good idea. I've always wondered what you could see from up there."

"You haven't been up before?" Edna asked, surprised.

Rowland had spent four years at Merton College and it seemed to the sculptress that the multi-spired and crenulated belltower beckoned seductively to all who looked up from the quad.

"Undergraduates are not permitted to have the key under any circumstances," Rowland explained.

"Why ever not?"

Rowland smiled. "They're considered too emotionally unstable…always falling in love and such. I believe the fear is that they'll leap from the battlements and create a terrible mess in the quadrangle."

"But once you've graduated…"

"Well, then you have an Oxford degree. It wards off the extremes of passion. So you can safely borrow the key."

Milton laughed. "Yes, of course. I can see that."

It took them about an hour to locate the keeper of the key and prove their status as alumni. By then the sun was sinking towards the western horizon. Murcott unlocked the door and they took the stone steps quickly, coming out onto an open viewing gallery.

Edna inhaled. The towers and spires of Oxford were cast in violet. From here, the university city seemed not quite real, a myth, a Camelot.

Rowland watched Edna as she leaned out as far as she could, drawing in the vista with more than her eyes. Against the golden bloom of dusk she was undiminished, a creature as beautiful as the sunset. His fingers twitched for a pencil, every part of him ached to catch that moment, to commit the glory of it to line and shade.

Clyde stood next to him, observing the frustration in his friend's eyes. He followed Rowland's gaze to Edna stretching out over the crenulated wall. "Now that would make a nice picture."

"Yes, it would." Rowland's voice was strained, tired.

Clyde said nothing more, but he was thoughtful.

And so they watched until darkness descended upon the dreaming spires of the learned town.

Chapter Sixteen

On Introductions

A point of etiquette that often troubles people who have not had a great deal of experience in social intercourse is how and in what form introductions should be made. The great question as a rule is "whom to introduce to whom?"

Now, the laws of etiquette rest on the old foundation that the lady is the superior of the gentleman, and that her wishes are paramount. Therefore, before making an introduction, or when making an introduction, you ask permission in the words, "May I introduce Mr. So-and-so, Miss Brown?" thus introducing the gentleman to the lady. In introducing two ladies you introduce the younger to the elder, the single to the married—a married lady takes precedence whatever her age. The same in the introduction of two men—the younger to the elder of the two.

The form of introduction which says: "Meet Mrs. Brown," is incorrect, and is never used by people who wish to be considered "good style." It was introduced to Australia from America.

—*The Brisbane Courier*, 1933

Edna inspected the head of Pierrepont under the light. There was a minor dent in the peer's nose, an injury sustained during his roll on the platform.

"What's your assessment, Ed?" Rowland kept his eyes clear of the glass gaze, which seemed to reproach him for his carelessness.

"It's not too bad, Rowly. Barely noticeable, really. I could try to smooth it out a bit, but I'm afraid anything more would risk disaster."

"Whatever you think best, Ed." Rowland was happy to defer to the sculptress' expertise on the matter. "I say, where is everybody?" He and Edna were alone at breakfast.

"I'm not sure." Edna placed the head on the sideboard beside various covered dishes of eggs, bacon, wild mushrooms, kidneys, and kedgeree. "Perhaps they're all still asleep."

The previous evening's game of chess had turned into something of a tournament, during which Rowland quite skillfully and subtly allowed his host to win back most of the money he'd lost through poker.

Rowland pulled out Edna's chair as the sculptress returned to the table with her plate. "I thought we might head out to Bletchley Park today," he said. "Murcott's happy to allow us to borrow one of his motor cars and we should probably return Lord Pierrepont's head before we damage it further."

"Perhaps Mr. Murcott and Ivy should come with us," Edna suggested, watching as Rowland managed breakfast quite adeptly with a single hand. "They seem to be well-acquainted with Lady Pierrepont and her godmother. It might make the delivery a little less awkward."

Rowland smiled. "I don't know what you mean. What could possibly be awkward about delivering the wax head of a dead man to his widow?"

Edna sighed. "You know, Rowly, Mr. Murcott has been so kind and generous." She lowered her voice. "It's difficult to imagine that you weren't friends when you knew each other first."

"He was different and so was I, I suppose." Rowland spread a slice of toast with butter. "And we moved in rather different circles. Being de-titled has, to my thinking, improved him, no end."

"You don't remember Ivy Murcott whatsoever, do you, Rowly?" Edna asked, still whispering.

Rowland grimaced. "Was it obvious?"

"Not at all. I'm sure even Milt and Clyde are fooled...but I do wonder why you don't remember her."

"I don't remember Marriott Spencer, either," Rowland confessed before Edna read something more sinister into what appeared to be his failing memory.

"You might not have ever met Marriott," Edna said. "You were a painter, after all. Marriott came to Ashton's to teach sculpture and only for a little while." The sculptress frowned, puzzled, contemplative. "You don't usually forget faces, Rowly—I've never known anyone to capture likenesses from memory after a single meeting the way you do."

Rowland knew that Edna had a point. Ivy Murcott's countenance was artistically interesting. Even back then, he was sure he would have noticed her, thought about drawing her. And yet he had not even the vaguest recognition of the girl.

"Well, perhaps nobody introduced us," he said finally. "Lord Lesley was adamant back then that Colonials were merely criminal stock. I was probably not the kind of acquaintance he would have allowed his sister to make."

"And yet she seems to know you."

"She knows *of* me."

"No, Rowly—when we were in town yesterday she showed me where the boxers would train, told me about some of the fights... said you stopped just when you started winning nearly every bout."

"How could she possibly know that?" Rowland was a little alarmed. He'd never known women to attend boxing matches—not then, at least.

"She knew that you hate whisky!" Edna offered as final proof.

"Miss Murcott told you all this?"

"Well, Clyde, Milt, and me, collectively, but in separate conversations." Edna mentally added the various snippets. "Milt first mentioned that Miss Murcott seemed rather curious about you, and we compared notes while you were playing chess." She sipped her tea. "Milt's convinced she's romantically obsessed with you."

"But you think that's unlikely?"

Edna smiled. She looked at him almost tenderly. "It's nothing to do with whether you are worthy of obsession, Rowly darling. It's just that Ivy seems far too sensible for such things."

"Oh." He frowned, shaking his head. "I really can't remember her at all."

"It is odd, don't you think?"

"Yes, but what, since we arrived in England, *hasn't* been odd?"

Edna laughed. "Perhaps Ivy did simply admire you from afar. I'm sure she wasn't alone."

They had only just risen from breakfast when the others returned. Noticeably excited, Murcott rushed in to intercept Rowland. "We have the most wonderful surprise, old boy. It'll help you get over the drubbing I gave you last evening—quick sticks!"

Clyde and Milton came in carrying between them several brown-paper parcels, which they dropped thankfully in front of Rowland.

"What's this?" Rowland asked.

Murcott's footman then dragged in the largest package.

Edna didn't wait, opening the box before Rowland could ask anything more. "It's an easel!" she said.

"Your chums are convinced that you're pining for your studio, old boy, so I thought, why not set one up here? I knew of a little shop in Oxford which deals in paints and brushes and whatnot—and Ivy's always wanted to learn to draw. Perhaps you could show her how it's done?"

Rowland looked at Clyde and Milton, expecting to see in their faces evidence that this was just some mad whim of Murcott's. But they were, by all appearances, at least complicit.

Clyde rolled up his sleeves. "Archie's happy for us to set up in the conservatory," he said. "It's got good light," he added, as if that would be Rowland's only concern.

"Ivy and I will go find some servants to move the furniture out of the way," Murcott said decisively. "If you gentlemen wouldn't mind bringing the boxes..."

Clyde waited till Murcott and his sister had left before he tried to explain. "I realised when we were on the belltower what's wrong with you, Rowly—why you can't sleep. You haven't drawn anything since they broke your arm. It's driving you insane."

"I've tried...I can't..."

"You can draw as well with your left hand as your right—you just can't hold that notebook of yours at the same time...which is why we found you an easel."

"But..."

"It's not the same as your notebook, I know, but it's got to be better than nothing."

Rowland shook his head.

Milton and Clyde exchanged a glance. The poet picked up a box. "Come on, Ed. We'll go give the Murcotts a hand."

Edna nodded. Clyde was a painter. For years now, he and Rowland had shared pigments and ideas and inspiration. They would leave Rowland's reluctance to him.

"You know, Rowly," Clyde said, when they were alone, "I wouldn't push if I couldn't see that not working was hurting you."

"Hurting me?"

"I know you too well, mate—you work things out with a brush. You've just got to get over whatever's stopping you..."

"I would have thought that what's stopping me is pretty obvious." Rowland lifted the cast at Clyde.

"You've been using your left hand on and off to paint for years, Rowly. The bloody cast isn't stopping you. You've just got to get over this fear—"

"Fear?" Rowland flared, affronted. "You think I'm afraid to paint? That's preposterous!"

Clyde moved to stand beside Rowland, shoulder to shoulder rather than face to face. He spoke calmly. "I think the last time you painted, someone broke your arm for it. They burned a swastika into your chest, for good measure. I don't know what it's like to believe you're going to die, mate…to really think that the next breath will be your last. You came that close twice that night. And still you pulled yourself together and got Eva out of there. But, Rowly, you wouldn't be human if you didn't think twice about ever painting again."

Rowland said nothing.

"For some blokes," Clyde continued, "that would be all right…for you, it's not going to work. Not painting is driving you crazy."

"I'm not crazy, Clyde," Rowland said wearily.

"Not yet," Clyde conceded. "But how long can you go without sleeping or working? Wilfred, as much as he disapproves of what you do, bless him, can see it. It's why he's so worried you'll start drinking to numb it all."

Rowland stared at the H-frame easel, the packages of pencils and brushes and paint. Some part of him knew that Clyde was right. Not drawing, not putting the images in his head onto paper or canvas, had been building into an almost unbearable frustration. But he could have procured an easel days ago if he'd wanted to. He'd thought about it, and then avoided thinking about it.

"Just try it, Rowly. Start painting again and things will work themselves out. You'll work them out."

Edna and Milton returned then to collect more boxes. They looked cautiously at Clyde, hopefully at Rowland.

Rowland picked up a brush, rubbing the sable bristles between his fingers as he studied the sturdy easel. "I thought we'd go to Bletchley Park today," he said glancing back at the wax head which Edna had left on the sideboard.

"We'll go tomorrow," Milton shrugged. "It'll provide us a chance to give Pierrepont a proper send-off."

They set up a makeshift studio in the conservatory which looked out towards the spires of the university city over meadows of wildflowers. Clyde had thought of everything that Rowland might need.

"Don't be too grateful," Milton warned. "They'll be sending *you* the account for this paraphernalia."

Clyde suggested, in fact insisted, that they play croquet, and by this promise of competition, lured Murcott away. Rowland was left with peace and solitude to paint. For a while he just gazed at the easel, and then he began, though his hand shook and he felt sick.

After the first tentative strokes, images seemed to explode onto the heavy sheets of cartridge: dark works in charcoal and wash, and splashes of vermilion. The compositions were raw and confronting. Rowland cast the images onto the sheet as if by doing so he could expel them from his mind. Visions of Germany: the Stormtroopers in line, a wall of brooding malice; the Königsplatz decked out in the banners of the Nazis; the inmates of Dachau, some broken, some defiant; a bonfire around which children danced while books were burned; and violence, pain, fear…his own attack.

Finally Rowland paused; his hair was damp with perspiration and his breathing heavy. There were over a dozen wet sheets strewn across the conservatory floor. It was barely midday.

Edna and Milton returned first. Apparently both had been banished from the game of croquet: Edna for cheating and Milton for making such a fuss about it. Still bickering about whether or not the sculptress had moved her ball illegally, they walked into the conservatory and stopped. The paintings still lay on the floor. Rowland was endeavouring to clean his brushes. There was vermilion in his hair and on his waistcoat. He looked exhausted.

Edna studied each painting in turn. "Oh, Rowly," she said quietly. "This was in your head? No wonder you couldn't sleep." She stepped closer and took the brushes from him. "I'll do this."

Rowland smiled slightly. He felt strangely relaxed now, and drowsy.

Milton squatted over the painting of an adolescent—a fair-haired youth in Brownshirt uniform. He guessed it was the boy who'd been ordered to shoot Rowland as he lay tortured on the ground. There was a kind of desperate terror in the eyes of the young Stormtrooper, a creeping realisation of the fact that he was about to kill a man. The perspective was unusual, the gun large, dominant, the boy receding. Milton turned back to Rowland. "You look knackered, mate," he said. "Go get some sleep."

"It's the middle of the day," Rowland protested half-heartedly.

"Go, Rowly. We'll make your excuses…and see that your paintings don't scare our hosts."

Rowland was unconscious to the sunset, but he woke early enough to see the following dawn. He had stirred not once in the last fifteen hours and if he dreamed, he did not remember it. For a while he lay still, enjoying the feeling of having slept. He shook his head. After weeks of Horlicks and counting sheep, all he'd needed was to paint.

He bathed and dressed, stuffing a tie into his pocket for Edna to see to later.

Quietly, he slipped downstairs to the conservatory. Not even the servants were about yet, but Rowland had always preferred the softness of the light at this time.

"Pierrepont," he greeted the sculpted head, which sat on a small circular table. A glass of whisky had been placed beside it like some offering to a wax idol. Rowland smiled. Perhaps this was the send-off Milton had promised the murdered peer.

The pictures he had completed the day before had been neatly stacked beside the easel. He didn't stop to go through them, clipping a clean sheet of cartridge to the board. He rummaged until he found a box of artists pencils among the packages of brushes and tubes of paint.

Rowland worked more calmly than he had the previous day, taking time with detail. He was not sure his demons had been exorcised completely but at least now he knew how to deal with them. He drew from memory again, but a more recent image. Edna on the belltower, leaning out as if she could at any moment take wing and fly. The lines of the sculptress' face were familiar and, to his mind, perfect. He didn't want his work to become permanently dark. To prevent that, there was Edna.

"Mr. Sinclair, there you are! Cook said she thought you were up and about."

"Miss Murcott…Good morning. I do hope I didn't disturb you." Rowland had been so engrossed in what he was doing, he had not noticed Ivy's entrance. She leaned against the door jamb, wearing a closely tailored riding habit, brandishing a crop in one hand and a cigarette in the other.

"Not at all, Mr. Sinclair. I'm a creature of custom, and wretched without my morning ride." She walked slowly over to the easel. "Do you have everything you need?"

"Yes, thank you. You've been most kind to tolerate this mess."

"Not at all. I was quite intrigued by your paintings. You are rather talented, Mr. Sinclair."

"Thank you…" Rowland put down his pencil. It was obvious that Ivy was not going to allow him to go back to work.

"Tell me, for how long have you known your fascinating troop of chums, Mr. Sinclair?"

"A few years now."

"Where did you meet them all?"

"I met Ed…Miss Higgins…at Ashton's—an art school in Sydney. She introduced me to Mr. Isaacs, who in turn introduced me to Mr. Watson Jones."

"How wonderful! And how did they all know each other?"

"Miss Higgins and Mr. Isaacs have been acquainted since childhood; Mr. Isaacs and Mr. Watson Jones have similar political interests."

Ivy smiled knowingly. "They're Commos aren't they? It's perfectly all right, Mr. Sinclair. England is very tolerant and liberal now. Why, there are simply legions of Communists in our set… Oxford was always full of them and I hear Cambridge is worse!"

Rowland retrieved his pencil. "Would you mind if I drew you, Miss Murcott?"

She glanced at the pencil sketch Rowland was making of Edna. "Why not? Why not, I say!" She stepped closer and looked up at Rowland. "How would you most like me, Mr. Sinclair?" she asked huskily.

Rowland's brow arched. "Just make yourself comfortable somewhere, Miss Murcott."

"Oh, I'm comfortable right here, Mr. Sinclair."

Rowland smiled. He couldn't deny he had a good view of her face, but he wasn't accustomed to having to reach around his model to find the easel. He let her be and moved the easel instead.

Clipping a fresh sheet of cartridge to the board he began, working with the flat of the lead to pull out the shape of her face before he defined her features with the point.

The Honourable Ivy Murcott stood with one hand on her hip and the other holding her cigarette. Her conversation had the appearance of being light, though she asked many questions: about Rowland's friends, his interests, his travels. Every now and then she would drop into the conversation a phrase that may well have been taken as flirtatious or even improper.

Fleetingly, Rowland thought about kissing her, not because he particularly wanted to, but to see how she'd react. There was something rehearsed about her manner, a pretence at the femme fatale. He was sure that for some reason Ivy Murcott was feigning a romantic interest in him. He just couldn't, for the life of him, comprehend why.

"I say, what are you two up to?" Murcott wandered in wearing plus-fours and a tweed golfing cap. There was just the slightest note of accusation to his voice.

"Go away, Archie," Ivy said irritably. "Can't you see Mr. Sinclair is working on me? I expect he would prefer to do so in private."

"Actually, I've finished," Rowland said hastily. "Come and tell me if I've done your sister justice, Murcott."

Ivy rolled her eyes, drawing impatiently on her cigarette, as Murcott approached the easel.

"I say, you've made the old girl look quite lovely!" He shook his head. "Who would have thought? It's really quite remarkable."

An unmistakably volatile silence followed as Ivy seethed and Murcott grinned at his barbed wit. Finally, inevitably, Ivy turned on her brother. "What would you know about art, you fat buffoon?"

"I know that Sinclair is a very gifted propagandist!" Murcott threw back. "He should be in advertising. Imagine what he could do for cabbages—I hear nobody's buying cabbages anymore...."

Ivy almost hissed, before stamping out of the conservatory.

Murcott laughed as he watched her go. "She has a temper, my dear sister. You may want to take note, Sinclair."

"Good Lord, is that the time?" Rowland said, glancing at his watch. He picked up the wax head. "I'd better polish Pierrepont for his homecoming...he seems to be developing something of a patina."

"Oh, yes, you were going to Bletchley today, weren't you, old boy?"

"Yes, would you care to...?"

"Sadly, I have another engagement today—Ivy, too. You must take one of our motors, though...I will not hear of you taking the train."

"Thank you, Murcott. That's extremely kind."

"Not at all, old boy. Just wander over to the stables when you're ready and take your pick. They're all very sporting vehicles. It's a shame I can't come along, really...we might have raced...."

Chapter Seventeen

Secrets of a Luxury Hotel Detective

Surprising Number of Eccentrics

Among the wealthy there are a surprising percentage of eccentrics, perhaps because they have the means to indulge in all their whims. Hotels, as a rule, do not serve such people, but if such guests have money and high connections, it is not always policy to refuse them accommodation. We detectives bear the brunt of their presence. The line between eccentricity and insanity in many cases is a slender one, and for that reason careful watch has to be kept on eccentric residents.

—*The Queenslander*, 1938

Bletchley Park was, to put it politely, architecturally interesting. It seemed to Rowland that the mansion had repeatedly fallen victim to fashionable renovation at all costs. Either that, or the original architect was mad. The result was a massive, eclectic conglomeration of Victorian Gothic, Tudor, and Dutch Baroque with features that could only be described as baronial and

Neo-Jacobean, and other elements that seemed more whimsy than anything else. It stood like a vast monument to asymmetrical inconsistency. Though the overt gaucheness of the structure should have been enough to offend an artistic sensibility, Rowland found the mansion more amusing than ugly. It was like a precocious child playing in its mother's clothes—ludicrous but somehow endearing for its folly.

Clyde brought Murcott's Vauxhall to a stop in the sweeping driveway, and they disembarked. Milton carried the hatbox containing Pierrepont's head.

The first challenge was to choose a point of entry, for the mansion had several porticos. They opted for the largest, in the hope that the doors it housed were the appropriate entrance. It seemed they were.

Murcott had kindly provided them with a letter of introduction to both Lady Leon and Euphemia Thistlewaite, now Lady Pierrepont, and Rowland duly presented it to the manservant who answered the door. They waited while he took it in to "her Ladyship".

He returned minutes later. "Lady Leon and Lady Pierrepont will receive you in the lounge hall, sir. If you'd care to follow me."

Inside, Bletchley Park was similarly mismatched.

Entering through the vaulted Gothic-style porch, they found themselves in a dark entrance passage with panelled walls and ceiling. The lounge hall was approached through a three-bay arcade of polygonal columns in grey marble. The room had no windows but its roof was made of painted glass. The furniture was Victorian and arranged about an elaborate stone and marble chimneypiece.

Lady Leon stood to receive them, an operatic figure of regal carriage, despite her advancing years. In the chair beside hers was a woman who might have been thirty, whose teeth seemed unable to fit in the confines of her mouth and whose expanding waistline was obvious at first glance—Lady Euphemia Pierrepont. Rowland introduced himself and his companions, expressed his condolences at the recent passing of Lord Pierrepont, and conveyed the regards of the Murcotts.

At this last communication, Euphemia seemed delighted. "Oh, I haven't seen Archie and Ivy in ever so long. We must invite them to visit. May I, Godmama? I am ever so in need of distraction."

"You shall have quite enough to distract you soon, my dear," Lady Leon said sternly. "Now Mr. Sinclair, I believe you are making a delivery of some sort."

"Yes..." Rowland said tentatively, beginning to rethink the wisdom of what he'd come to do. Nevertheless, he continued. "I believe, Lady Pierrepont, that you are acquainted with a Mr. Francis Pocock, who you commissioned to create a sculpture of the late Lord Pierrepont."

"Oh, yes," Euphemia displayed an extraordinary number of teeth in what may have been a smile. "I thought it would be fun to have a statue of Bunky to play tricks on people! I was going to stand it in the hallway and laugh as callers got a fright. But now that Psychopompos has taken my Bunky to the Underworld, Theo thought it would be improper."

"Your brother shows discerning judgement," Lady Leon said curtly. "What a silly notion!"

"It seems Mr. Pocock had already begun work on the sculpture when Lady Pierrepont cancelled her commission," Rowland said.

"Well, I can hardly be held responsible for that," Euphemia exclaimed. "I'm bereaved!"

Rowland took a breath. "Mr. Pocock thought you might like the...bust...he completed before Lord Pierrepont's passing... as a gift."

"Really, for nothing? Why that's simply marvellous!" Euphemia clapped her hands. "Can I see? Can I see? Is that it?"

"Lady Pierrepont, I should warn you..." Rowland started.

But Euphemia had already launched out of her chair and snatched up the hatbox. She threw open its lid and squealed in delight. "Look, it's Bunky!" She laughed, scooping out the head and tossing it like a ball. "Look at this, Godmama! I could hang it from the ceiling with my bats. And I didn't have to part with a penny for it!" She kissed the waxen lips, exalted.

"Bats?" Clyde asked.

Rowland glanced at his companions, unsure what to do. Euphemia was tossing Pierrepont higher and higher. She stopped suddenly and sat with her elbows resting upon the head in her lap. "Do you know where Lord Pierrepont and I were introduced, Mr. Sinclair?"

"I can't say that I do, Lady Pierrepont."

"Theo, my brother Theo, introduced us at a meeting of the Eugenics Society. It was very romantic—all that talk of selective breeding."

Lady Leon gasped, mortified. "That's enough, Euphemia!"

"Do you know a great deal about eugenics, Mr. Sinclair?"

"More than I'd care to, madam."

"Oh, you don't approve of eugenics," she said, smiling sadly. "Natural selection is all very well for wild beasts, but surely, Mr. Sinclair, the human race can aspire to more than that?"

"Euphemia!" Lady Leon said sharply. "I don't approve—"

Euphemia jumped up abruptly. "I say, catch!" she cried, throwing the head in Rowland's direction. Milton reacted quickly, intercepting the toss in a rather spectacular dive.

"Stop this at once!" Lady Leon said furiously. "What is the meaning of this? Mr. Sinclair, that is not a bust. That is a head! You will take it back to your Mr. Pocock with the message that his gift is declined!"

"No!" Euphemia said, stamping her foot. "It's mine!"

"Euphemia, that is enough! I forbid you to accept that...that thing. It is indecent!"

Lady Pierrepont glared at her godmother.

Milton put the head back in the hatbox and closed the lid.

Slowly, Euphemia turned to Rowland. "Godmama says I may not have the head. You may have it, if you like..." She burst into tears suddenly. "It's not fair," she called back to her godmother as she ran from the room. "It's not fair!"

And so they were left with Lady Leon.

"My goddaughter is, as you can understand, not herself," Lady Leon said. "I'm sorry that you have had a wasted trip, Mr. Sinclair."

Clearly they were being dismissed. Rowland apologised for any disturbance their coming may have caused and they left… with the wax head.

They sat wordlessly in the car for a few minutes.

Then Clyde asked, "What in God's name was that?"

"Hundreds of years of selective breeding." Milton engaged the Vauxhall's start button.

Rowland shook his head. "Do you suppose that was grief?"

"No."

"Didn't Mrs. Bruce say that Euphemia was odd? Perhaps this is what she meant," Edna ventured. She patted the hatbox, comforting the wax head within after its ordeal at the hands of Lady Pierrepont.

"What was it she said about bats?" Clyde asked.

"Do you suppose she's mad enough to have killed Pierrepont?" Milton said as he swung the car out of the drive.

"Possibly," Rowland conceded, "but I don't see her walking quietly out of the club afterwards."

"Unless the dread of something after death—the undiscovered country, from whose bourn no traveller returns—is what pushed her over the edge…"

"What do you mean by that?" Clyde demanded of the poet.

"Shakespeare meant guilt, I believe," Rowland murmured. "God only knows what Milt meant."

"What if it's an act?" Edna said, leaning her head against Rowland's shoulder in the back seat, and closing her eyes. "Surely, Lady Leon would not have allowed Euphemia to receive guests if she's like that all the time."

"Ed's got a point," Clyde said after a moment. "Lady Leon seemed reasonably sensible…and formidable, to be honest. Why would she allow Euphemia to talk to anyone if she thought she was insane?" He turned back to look at Rowland. "Don't your lot refer to that as 'indisposed'?"

Rowland flinched almost imperceptibly. His own mother had often been indisposed. "Yes," he said glancing down at Edna. The sculptress seemed to have fallen asleep.

"What now?" Milton asked.

"I'm famished," Edna said, without opening her eyes.

The Crown Inn in the hamlet of Shenley Brook End, a couple of miles from Bletchley, was as typical as its name. The Edwardian simplicity of its brick and tile construction was something of a visual relief after Bletchley Park. As the day was warm and clear, they sat outside to enjoy a hearty ploughman's luncheon.

"This is the most scrumptious relish," Edna said, piling piccalilli onto her smoked ham. "We don't have it at home."

Rowland smiled, making a mental note to have a crate of piccalilli shipped back to the larder of Woodlands House. He loved the sculptress' ability to take such delight in the smallest of things.

Clyde looked back at the Vauxhall where they had left the wax head. "So what do we do with Pierrepont?"

Rowland shrugged. "We return it to Pocock, I suppose."

Milton waved his fork as a thought occurred. "The murder weapon—the sword that killed our mate Pierrepont...did you get a good look at it, Rowly?"

"Not really, to be honest. Why?"

"Well, it seems to me that either the killer brought the sword with him—a difficult item to carry down the street unnoticed—or it was already in Pierrepont's suite, in which case the mortal act may have been impulsive, a crime of passion. Two different types of murder altogether."

Rowland nodded. Milton's logic was inescapable. He groaned. Why hadn't he taken a closer look at the sword? "Surely, if it was emblazoned with a coat of arms, or some such feature, they would have arrested someone by now?"

Milton nodded. "That makes sense. We should check anyway. Presumably the police will still have the sword, it being the murder weapon."

"Yes, but they're hardly going to hand it over to us!" Clyde spread a thick slab of bread with freshly churned butter.

"Perhaps Wil will remember more about it," Rowland suggested. "He spoke at length to the detectives. I was mostly trying to keep Allie calm."

"Did you notice anything else in the room, Rowly?" Milton prodded.

Clyde rolled his eyes. "Don't tell me...you've been reading Agatha Christie again." Detective fiction was, in his opinion, a bad idea where the poet was concerned.

Milton ignored him. "Anything at all, Rowly."

Rowland closed his eyes for a moment as he tried to recall. "One dirty drink glass on the armchair...the secretaire was open...dead man in the bed...that's about it."

"Did you inspect the empty glass? Could his drink have been drugged?"

Rowland nearly laughed. "How would I know, Milt? Even if I'd thought to check the dregs in the glass? I couldn't possibly know if it had been poisoned unless I drank it myself!"

Milton sighed, clearly exasperated with Rowland's lack of commitment.

"I have the card of that chap, Entwhistle, who's leading the investigation," Rowland offered. "We'll go see him when we get back to London. He may have some light to shed. Perhaps he tasted the drink."

They headed back to Bloomington Manor soon after lunch, as Murcott was expecting them for supper. The dining room was being prepared in the most lofty style when they arrived back in the late afternoon. Clearly they would be dressing for dinner.

"So, who are you expecting this evening?" Rowland asked as Murcott made martinis to see them through the afternoon.

"I'm not at liberty to say. It's a surprise," Murcott said, beaming. "It was Ivy's idea...and rather brilliant, I can tell you."

Reclined on the chaise lounge, Ivy sipped her martini serenely. Apparently, brother and sister had mended their earlier spat.

Murcott patted the wax head which had found its way back to the sideboard. "I say, weren't you going to leave this with Euphemia?"

"Unfortunately, Lady Leon would not allow it." Rowland recounted what had transpired.

"Oh, my gosh, that's too bad!"

"Was Lady Pierrepont always so…unorthodox?" Edna asked.

"Euphemia was born eccentric," Ivy declared. "But no more so than many people."

"A great deal more so, my dear," Murcott corrected. "I'm quite fond of Euphemia, but she is undeniably odd! Why, last time we saw her she wanted to leave the ball to wander about looking for bats! She was most unreasonable about it."

"Euphemia is very interested in the biological sciences," Ivy explained, regarding her brother reproachfully. "Bats are her particular passion. She's very clever, really—might have gone to Oxford if her family had allowed it, but they're tiresomely old-fashioned. I presume that's why she's staying at Bletchley Park."

"I've not seen poor Euphemia in nearly two years," Murcott said, now repentant. "We really should visit. Perhaps Lady Leon will be less strict if Ivy and I accompany you."

"I'm afraid we won't have time to call on Lady Pierrepont again—we're returning to London in the morning." Rowland broke the news that he and his companions had agreed upon on the journey back from Bletchley.

Murcott seemed genuinely dismayed. "But you only just got here!"

"Regrettably we're in the middle of something in London," Rowland apologised. "We had only intended a short visit, and we really must get back."

"Yes, you did say, but I had hoped to persuade you all to stay a while longer. If Evelyn hears that we don't have anyone staying with us, he'll move in!" Murcott groaned.

"Archie, how could you?" Ivy demanded. "You've spoiled the surprise!"

"Evelyn…" Rowland frowned. "Do you mean Waugh?"

"The same."

"But I thought you and Waugh were chums. Weren't you a Hypocrite?"

"Rowly!" Edna was shocked that he would be so rude.

"It's a drinking club, Ed."

"I say, that's a bit unfair, old boy. The Hypocrites were much more than a drinking club."

"I beg your pardon," Milton interrupted. "Do you mean *the* Evelyn Waugh, the writer?"

"Yes, he put out quite a successful novel a couple of years back."

"*Vile Bodies*?"

"That's it. One of those dreadful murder mysteries, I suppose."

Milton stared at Murcott for a moment. "Am I to gather by the fact that your sister looks ready to cut your throat that Mr. Waugh is your surprise guest this evening?"

"Oh dear, the cat really is out of the bag, isn't it?" Murcott grimaced at his sister. "Ivy ran into him in the village. Evelyn was very intrigued that we had Australians visiting. He has a dear friend there and was wondering if you might have run into the gentleman, and so Ivy invited him to dinner." He beamed at Rowland now. "I thought you might find it fun to see Evelyn again."

Rowland smiled politely.

"So, why will he move into Bloomington Manor if we aren't here?" Milton asked, doggedly trying to follow the random tangents of the conversation.

"Well, you see, Evelyn has no fixed abode presently. He's become something of a serial house guest."

"And you wouldn't welcome that?"

"Lord, no! Evelyn's amusing enough, but one dinner will suffice!"

"Well, what say we don't mention that we're going tomorrow?" Edna suggested.

"I couldn't possibly ask you to lie, but if you were to do so of your own accord I'd consider it a very great kindness, dear lady."

Chapter Eighteen

Lord Beauchamp

Sydney, May 15

When at Albany, Lord Beauchamp's private secretary handed the press the following message from the Governor to the people of New South Wales. It is in verse, being an adaptation of a verse of Rudyard Kipling's "The Song of the Cities":

Greeting! Your birthstain have you turned to good
Forcing strong wills perverse to steadfastness
The first flush of the tropics in your blood
And at your feet success

—*Beauchamp*

The message has occasioned much talk. The "birthstain" is an unfortunate reference in the case of New South Wales.

—*Chronicle*, 1899

"Come in," Rowland called as he rummaged for cuff links in his travelling case.

Edna stepped into the bedroom, resplendent in the elegant black velvet gown she'd purchased at a boutique in Mayfair not long after they'd arrived in London. The neckline was beaded on the fitted bodice and the skirt tailored to the subtle rise and fall of her hips. "I thought you might need help with your tie," she said, smiling.

Rowland said nothing, admiring the manner in which the darkness of the gown highlighted the cream of the sculptress' skin. Ink, he thought, to capture the dramatic nature of the contrast and the exquisite movement in the smooth curving lines of her body.

She smiled knowingly. "It's nice to have you paint me again, Rowly, if only in your head." She twirled so he could see the dress complete. "This is the most divine fabric," she said, stroking the velvet. "It's almost furry. I feel rather like a cat!"

Rowland laughed. "Well, you look beautiful," he said quietly. He handed her the tie and waited as she knotted it into the perfect bow.

"I take it you don't particularly care for Mr. Waugh," Edna whispered, as she folded back Rowland's cuff and secured the cuff link.

Rowland sighed. "He left Oxford about a year after I arrived, so I didn't know him all that well. He always seemed to be inebriated, which sadly was probably the most pleasant aspect of his character."

"That bad?"

"Yes, but to be fair," Rowland admitted, "I abhorred Murcott once. Perhaps Waugh, too, has with the passing of time become more palatable."

"Well, it's only one evening," Edna said, fiddling with the sling so it didn't crush his collar unduly.

"Rowly have you seen…?" Clyde walked into the room with a tie in his hand. "Ed, there you are! Would you mind? I can't seem to get the wings even slightly even!"

Edna took the strip of cloth and within moments Clyde, too, was completely dressed. She surveyed her work. "You know," she said with satisfaction, "there's nothing quite as pleasing as a man formally dressed. If I had my way, I wouldn't let you wear anything else."

At that, Clyde responded quite bluntly and less than enthusiastically.

They walked down to take drinks in the drawing room while they waited for Ivy's eminent guest to arrive.

The writer came late and duly apologised, though he gave no reason for his delay. He greeted Murcott exuberantly, throwing open his arms and calling him "Pixie." Murcott introduced Rowland.

Physically, Waugh was as Rowland remembered him: intense, piercing eyes that seemed to glare at the world as a matter of course. His features were fine and the natural curve of his mouth could be mistaken for a sneer. Waugh was, as far as Rowland could tell, sober.

"Sinclair...Rowland Sinclair...Ivy tells me you are a Mertonian, but I cannot seem to recall your face."

"Sinclair's the Australian chap who won my Mercedes at cards, Evelyn. After you'd left Oxford, but surely you heard about it."

"Is that so? I believe someone may have mentioned it. Good show, Sinclair...your birthstain you have turned to good!"

Rowland's eyes flashed. "Indeed."

Waugh smiled—a passing, perfunctory stretching of his lips. "I jest, my good man! I suppose I should have learned from the inadvertent folly of Earl Beauchamp when he sought to praise your people, and met with the ire of a colony desperate to deny its dubious roots."

The first of many awkward silences followed.

Ivy intervened hastily to introduce Rowland's companions.

Already Waugh looked a little bored. "How clever of you to surround yourself with like minds, Sinclair," he said after the formalities had been seen to. "I can't imagine anything more pleasant than simple undemanding conversation at the end of the day."

Rowland smiled tightly. "Really? And here I thought the imagination of a novelist would be extraordinary indeed."

Waugh stopped and then laughed so softly that there was no actual sound.

In what may have been an attempt to diffuse the tension, Ivy suggested they go in to supper.

Waugh offered their hostess his arm and Murcott escorted Edna.

The dining hall had been readied for the most formal and elegant occasion. The seating arrangement was carefully drawn. The menu was extravagant, course after course of exquisitely constructed dishes, exotic salads, game meat, and soufflés, with generous garnishes of caviar and buttery sauces. There was a separate wine for each course, fruit and cognac to follow, and in a salute to their days at Oxford, cigars and snuff.

The conversation was mostly Waugh's. Recently converted to Catholicism, he delivered polemic after polemic on the failings of the world, the decadence of modern society and the bumblings of government. Murcott fought admirably to keep the evening from disintegrating.

Only Edna was unperturbed by the manner of the writer. She seemed to find Evelyn Waugh amusing, and for this he began to direct much of his conversation in her direction. Perhaps he believed that Edna alone amongst the Colonial dullards understood and appreciated his wit. In truth, the sculptress simply found him ridiculous.

"Mr. Sinclair and his companions visited the recently bereaved Lady Pierrepont today." Ivy opened a conversation. "You know, Evelyn, Euphemia Thistlewaite that was."

"Oh, yes, Euphemia. Homely and quite graceless, but not as dull-witted as those moronic brothers of hers. What were their names? Whole family was christened in line with some facile classical affectation, if I recall."

"Theophrastus and Diogenes," Ivy said with authority.

"Were you aware Euphemia married Alfred Dawe, the Viscount of Pierrepont?" Edna asked suddenly.

Waugh nodded. "Alfred Dawe, Viscount Pierrepont," he corrected. "A marriage of tedious convenience."

"I'm not sure I know what you mean, Mr. Waugh."

"Pierrepont had a mildly worthwhile title, and yet he was, I am told, poor as a church mouse. He lost most of what capital he had financing Joss Hay on some scheme to grow tea in Kenya. Euphemia has no money in her own right, and very little charm, but her boorish brothers are wealthy enough. A sufficiency and deficiency that is both complementary and convenient, I would say."

"These brothers of Lady Pierrepont's—Theophrastus and Diogenes," Rowland asked, "are they in London?"

"Yes, I believe the younger one is a civil servant or something equally tawdry." Waugh digressed then into a condemnation of the lack of any real intellect in Britain's civil service.

When he began on the scourge of Communism, Milton was the first to bite back.

Waugh was scathing in reply. "Communism, like homosexuality, is a phase tolerated in young men at university, as long as it goes no further. A harmless, perhaps necessary, passing experimentation on the way to adulthood. Even if you were a man of letters, Mr. Isaacs—which I doubt—you and I are too old to expect further forbearance in the face of such folly."

For a moment it looked like Milton might ask the novelist to step outside.

"Come now, Evelyn," Murcott said a little nervously. "You're quarrelling with the only man here who has read your books." He kept talking, desperate to get through the moment without fisticuffs, enquiring after the other Hypocrites from whom it seemed he had not heard since the loss of his title.

After a heavy pause, Waugh recounted at length what he knew: who had married and become respectable, who had published, and who were living dissolute lives abroad in a flagrant disregard of the teachings of the Roman Church, or any other.

"Hypocrite is bloody right," Milton muttered for Rowland's hearing. Despite being a Catholic, Clyde did not seem inclined to disagree.

"Now, Sinclair," Waugh began as the final course was served. "You must not suppose that I am one of those fools who assumes that simply because you hail from New South Wales that you would be acquainted with the Earl of Beauchamp. It's just that I remember that you boxed."

"I thought you didn't recall my face," Rowland said curtly.

"That's so. I don't recall your face...just that you boxed."

"Yes, I did." Rowland wondered what this had to do with Earl Beauchamp who had been governor of New South Wales years before he was born.

"Perhaps in your amateur boxing career you were fortunate to come across another devotee of that brutish pastime by the name of Lygon...Hugh Lygon?"

"I remember Lygon," Rowland said carefully. Hugh Lygon, too, had been a Hypocrite and had insisted on carrying a teddy bear about with him—some bizarre fad among the aesthetes. Rowland recalled having, not unreasonably, underestimated Lygon because of the stuffed toy which sat in his corner. Hugh Lygon had turned out to be quite a formidable boxer—when he was sober.

"Well, as it happens, Hugh's the son of Earl Beauchamp, and has travelled to the Antipodes to be with his father in his exile."

It was not necessary for Waugh to elaborate as to why Lygon's father was in exile. Beauchamp had been in Australia when the scandal broke and the revelations about the sodomite Earl and his merry footmen were made public in a spectacular international fall from grace.

Waugh continued. "Earl Beauchamp has, it seems, become the Australian President of your national boxing association, or some such endeavour, but I'd hoped you'd know that and have some friendly news of Hugh."

"I haven't boxed since well before I left Oxford, I'm afraid, and we have all of us been abroad since April."

Waugh sighed. "Pity. My thoughts turn to Hugh now that I'm no longer abroad." He gazed in his intense, wide-eyed way at Rowland. "We're losing men like him, you know. Bit by bit the grubby ambition of the aspirant bourgeoisie is dismantling the great and worthy traditions that built the Empire."

"Evelyn Waugh may be a renowned novelist, mate," Milton said as he watched Edna help Rowland remove his cuff links, "but he's also a pompous git."

Rowland made no move to defend his old acquaintance. It would have been disingenuous to do so. Waugh practised a kind of intellectual thuggery that Rowland had always found more tiresome than amusing.

Edna placed the cuff links into Rowland's hand and patted it fondly. Her brow arched mischievously. "So...you lived in the midst of all that for four years?"

"I wasn't in the midst of all that." Rowland frowned. "As much as the Hypocrites like to believe that theirs was the only Oxford, that wasn't the case. While they were carrying on like insane delinquent children, the rest of us just got on with it!"

Edna giggled. "Oh, Rowly, you sound like Wilfred."

Rowland stopped. He grimaced. "Good Lord, you're right." He hadn't realised how much Waugh had gotten under his skin.

Milton laughed. "A week ago you might have hit him, mate."

"That much is true," Rowland conceded. Sleep had had a containing effect on his temper. Still, as much as it had disrupted the economic conference and brought him the enmity of the B.U.F., he wasn't sorry he'd hit Joyce.

"So...Waugh knocked about with old Beauchamp's son... it's a small world," Milton mused.

"You know Beauchamp?" Rowland asked, surprised.

"Friend of a mate. He's not a bad bloke when you get used to him. Completely queer, of course, and obsessed with embroidery, but otherwise..."

"You didn't mention it at dinner."

"Waugh asked you if you were acquainted with Beauchamp, not me..." Milton grinned. "It would probably disturb Mr. Waugh to know that we of the proletariat have the odd connection...and in the case of Beauchamp, quite odd."

"Where's Clyde?" Edna asked. "Is he still cross?"

Rowland winced. "Possibly."

They had abandoned Clyde to a theological conversation with Waugh...or rather a theological lecture by Waugh. It was Milton who had carelessly revealed their friend's Catholicism. Waugh, having declared that he was most comfortable talking to adherents of the Roman Church, had decided to demonstrate the preference by engaging Clyde in a rather one-sided discussion about the nature of grace. Rowland and the others had tried to rescue Clyde, to no avail. Rowland, at least, felt bad about it.

"Did you notice Mr. Waugh say that Joss Hay was involved in Lord Pierrepont's financial woes?" Edna asked.

Milton nodded. "It makes you wonder if Earl Erroll might also have had reason to do away with his old chum, Bunky. Running a man through with a sword does seem like a rather aristocratic way of despatching a problem."

"We need a little more than dinner table conversation to make an accusation." Rowland removed the sling and rubbed the back of his neck. It was surprising how heavy the cast seemed by the end of the day.

"Pierrepont must have an accountant or a solicitor, someone who manages his affairs," Milton suggested.

"Wouldn't Allie know?" Edna asked. "Wasn't she his private secretary?"

"Yes, she was." Rowland realised the sculptress was right. "I'm not sure what exactly her duties were, but Allie could well hold the key to all this."

Chapter Nineteen

Art of the Theatre

FILMS AND IMAGINATION
ENGLISH PLAYERS' VISIT

> Of the English stage at the moment Mr. Hannen takes an optimistic view. A number of really big successes were now running in London, he said. One was the historical play "Richard of Bordeaux," put on by John Gielgud, one of the younger lights of the stage.
>
> —*The West Australian*, 1933

Clyde sat by the easel in the conservatory, smoking. The moon bequeathed enough light to define the ferns and pick out the petals of orchids in bloom. Evelyn Waugh had finally gone. Everybody else, as far as he knew, had retired, exhausted by the rigours of being civil. Now that he thought about it, Clyde was inclined to feel a little sorry for the Murcotts. Hosting that dinner party must have been like negotiating a minefield protected only by wine and caviar blinis.

"Clyde…hello…I thought you'd gone to bed." Rowland stepped into the conservatory. He was without his tie or jacket, and though he still wore his dress shirt, the sleeve of his left arm had been folded to the elbow.

Clyde smiled. "I needed a cigarette. I feel a bit like I've been to mass. It's frightening."

"Waugh doesn't seem to do anything by halves," Rowland agreed.

"What are you doing down here, Rowly?" Clyde asked.

"I thought I'd work for a bit."

"Really? Now?" Clyde tapped his watch.

Rowland shrugged. "Our train back to London isn't till midday."

Clyde stepped away from the easel. Rowland found a pencil, removed the study of Edna on the belltower and attached a clean sheet of cartridge. He drew with loose strokes: the thin upswept brows, the almost manic eyes, and a strained sarcastic smile.

Clyde watched the likeness develop. He laughed. "Waugh! I thought you'd have had enough of him."

Rowland smiled. "He's got quite an interesting face, don't you think? I might have asked him to sit for me if I could think of a way to shut him up. I wanted to get the wretch down on paper before I forgot...or tried to forget."

Clyde smiled, observing both the artist and his sketch. Rowland had a very physical way of working—he almost attacked the paper. "What made you give up boxing, Rowly?"

Rowland paused. "I got thoroughly thrashed in the ring by a chap called Eddie Eagan. He was a Rhodes Scholar from America."

Clyde recognised the name of the Olympic boxing gold medallist. "Eddie Eagan...for pity's sake, Rowly, there's no shame in being beaten by Eagan!"

"Oh, I wasn't worried by the loss." Rowland smudged the graphite with the side of his palm to create shadows. He shook his head and admitted, "Actually, I might have been put out, if I'd been conscious."

Clyde blanched.

"It was a few weeks before I could go back into the ring," Rowland explained. "I started drawing to pass the time, and then I didn't really want to fight anymore."

"Just like that?"

"Basically. I used to draw boxers for a while and then it occurred to me that I could draw women instead."

"Bloody glad to hear it."

And so they continued for a while, Rowland drawing, Clyde making suggestions on shade or form, or talking about other things. The pencil portrait was nearly complete when Clyde noticed the missing paintings.

"What have you done with your paintings of Germany?" he asked, casting his eyes about the conservatory.

"They should be there somewhere," Rowland murmured without looking up.

Clyde rummaged for a while. "They're not here, Rowly."

Rowland put down his pencil and helped his friend search. They found the sketch of Ivy that Murcott had called propaganda, but all the paintings of Germany were gone.

"Perhaps one of the servants packed them away somewhere," Rowland suggested.

"Strange that they'd put those away and not the others."

"Not really," Rowland countered thoughtfully. "Those paintings are pretty grim. I'll ask Murcott about it in the morning. They've got to be somewhere."

They closed up the conservatory and padded softly up the staircase, cognisant of the hour and the fact that most of the household was asleep. Halfway up to the guestrooms they heard a whisper on the floor below.

Both Rowland and Clyde looked down over the balustrade.

Murcott came out of a door, leaving it open. The dim light from the bedroom backlit Ivy in her nightgown at the doorway. Rowland turned away. It was Clyde's gasp that drew his gaze back. Murcott had seized his sister in a passionate kiss. For a moment the Australians froze, shocked, doubting their own eyes. Ivy dragged Murcott back into the room and the door was closed.

"Jesus, Mary, and Joseph." Clyde was immobilised by shock.

Rowland said nothing. This was something he definitely hadn't seen before at Oxford.

They didn't speak of it that night. Neither wanted to. They retired to their own guestrooms with their own thoughts and horror. By morning, each was beginning to doubt what they had seen. Surely…

At breakfast, Murcott and Ivy bickered and otherwise carried on in a manner one would expect from siblings. Rowland enquired after the missing paintings.

"My goodness, what could have happened to them?" Ivy scowled and called the housekeeper and the butler. The staff were questioned, the house was searched, but the whereabouts of the paintings were not uncovered.

Rowland was puzzled but he did not labour the disappearance. He had committed the images to cartridge in an attempt to expel them from his mind and his thoughts. He didn't really want to keep them.

They farewelled both Murcott and Ivy on the platform and boarded the train to London a little before midday.

It was in the privacy of the first-class compartment that the subject of the Murcotts was eventually raised.

"Clyde, you're not still cross with Rowly, are you? He tried very valiantly to rescue you from Mr. Waugh." Edna stood with her hands on her hips.

"I'm not cross with Rowly." Clyde laughed. "Waugh's a convert—they're all desperate to prove they're better Catholics than the rest of us. It's best just to shut up and nod."

"You and Rowly have barely said a word to each other since last night."

Rowland glanced at Clyde. Both flinched.

"What?" Milton demanded.

Rowland told them what they'd seen.

Clyde shook his head as if he were trying to dislodge the memory.

Milton groaned.

Edna regarded her companions, her lips pressed together in contemplation. "Well, that makes sense."

"What!"

"Ed, I don't think you understand…"

"That pervert is having an affair with his sister…it's—"

"I think it's more likely that Ivy is not Mr. Murcott's sister," Edna said calmly. "Think about it, Rowly. You freely admit you've no recollection of Ivy and she knows of things about you that generally only men would discover…or even be interested in." She recited the list. "Boxing games, the excellence of your left hook, what you drink, or don't drink. Mr. Murcott must have told her."

"They're called bouts or matches, not games," Rowland pointed out, "and I doubt Murcott knows any of that!"

"And Waugh knew Ivy as Murcott's sister!" Milton argued.

"No. Mr. Waugh knew Ivy and knew she lived with Mr. Murcott. He didn't say anything about them being siblings. Remember she insisted that we should all call her Ivy before the dinner party…perhaps it was to ensure Mr. Waugh didn't hear us calling her *Miss* Murcott."

"But why? Why would she pretend to be Murcott's sister?"

"To us at least," Milton added.

Edna shrugged. "It could be they're not married and they were worried we'd deem it improper."

"Hardly."

"Well then, I don't know. But I do believe it's more likely that Ivy is simply not Archibald Murcott's sister. She must be his lover or his wife."

"But she spent the whole weekend flirting with Rowly," Milton argued. "And Murcott with you!"

Edna folded her arms, frowning as she considered the bewildering behaviour of the Murcotts. "Your Uncle Seth used to like to pretend he was the landlord and *call in* on your aunt in the middle of the day for the rent," she said. "Don't you recall? We were playing hide and seek when he…stopped by. Maybe it was one of *those games*."

Milton grimaced. "I remember Seth gave me one hell of a hiding when we jumped out from behind the couch. But you're right."

Rowland stared at the poet. He was beginning to wonder about Milton's relatives. "Are you suggesting the Murcotts were using Ed and me to add some kind of interest to their conjugal relations?"

"Conjugal relations? For God's sake Rowly, where did you learn to speak? But yes." Milton grinned now. "They might have invited you to participate more actively if we'd stayed longer. Good Lord, they might have wanted us all to join in!"

Edna giggled. "Now that would have been funny."

Clyde had his hands over his ears.

Rowland shook his head. A thwarted orgy was to his mind a more palatable explanation than the alternative. Either way, he was glad they were returning to London.

They were back at Claridge's by the mid-afternoon.

The easel and other equipment had already been delivered from Kings Cross Station. Menzies greeted them with drinks and the messages received in their absence.

Rowland frowned as he flicked through a number of messages from Allen and Overy, as well as another from Mrs. Anthony Dawe, who he presumed was Allie's mother. He slipped into the library and called Mrs. Dawe first. The housekeeper answered, informing him curtly that Madam was indisposed and Miss Dawe away.

Rowland phoned through to George Allen, already uneasy.

"Rowly?" Edna poked her head into the library when she heard him cursing. "Whatever's the matter?"

He apologised for his language.

She took his hand and asked him again. "What's wrong?"

"Allie's been arrested for the murder of Lord Pierrepont," he said angrily. "Apparently there was nothing Allen could do to prevent it. The poor girl tried to telephone me but…"

"Oh, Rowly, you weren't to know. Is she—?"

"In prison? Yes, she's been remanded in Holloway. Allen is going to arrange a visit, but he can't do so any earlier than tomorrow."

"God, poor Allie! Why have they arrested her now?"

"I'm not sure. Allen will explain, I suppose."

"Will Allie have to stay in prison? Can't we bail her?"

"Allen thinks not," Rowland said, pacing. "It's a capital offence, and Pierrepont was a peer."

Milton and Clyde came in, curious as to what was keeping Rowland, and now Edna, in the library—they were reasonably sure it wasn't a book. The news of Allie's arrest and incarceration left them dumbfounded and then outraged. It seemed so obvious a travesty.

"So, what are we going to do?" Milton said. "We can't just leave her there."

"We can't break her out, Milt."

"No, I suppose not."

"But we will do something," Rowland promised. "Allie didn't kill anybody."

Rowland arrived unannounced at the terrace in Ennismore Gardens to be told that his brother and sister-in-law had gone to the theatre with the Bruces. The children were in their pyjamas, about to be put to bed. His arrival caused an excitement that clearly exasperated the nanny.

"I'll wait in the nursery," Rowland offered, a little at a loss. His head had been full of Allie and his need to speak to Wilfred. "Perhaps I can read to the boys."

Nanny Gray did not seem to think it such a good idea—the children needed their sleep—but Rowland promised he would ensure they were asleep by eight, and Ernest begged to be allowed this special treat promising angelic behaviour for the rest of his life. Clearly unsure of whether she had the authority to refuse Rowland, the young nanny conceded. The boys were, after all, fond of their uncle. His presence would give her a little unexpected time to herself.

The nursery was a large room which looked out over the gardens. Despite the fact that the Bruces had no children, it had been thoughtfully stocked with rocking horses and trains and an entire bookcase of books.

Rowland grabbed one-year-old Ewan in his good arm and took the large winged-back chair which Ernest called the reading chair.

"Choose a book, would you, Ernie? You might have to turn the pages for me."

Ernest returned from the bookcase and solemnly presented Rowland with a beautifully bound copy of *Tom Brown's Schooldays* by Thomas Hughes.

"Good Lord, mate, where did you get this?"

"Mr. Bruce gave it to me. He said it would help prepare me for school. I'm going away to school next year, you know, Uncle Rowly."

Rowland did not open the novel. He'd read it years ago and, though it had been written in the middle of the last century, there were aspects of his own schooling experience that were not so far removed from Tom Brown's. Still he wasn't going to scare Ernest witless by reading it to him. "Are you worried about going away to school, Ernie?"

"I'm not frightened at all," Ernest said quickly, "but Ewan doesn't want me to go."

Rowland winced as his godson bounced against his chest and babbled an incomprehensible response.

"I'm sure he doesn't."

Ernest whispered now, his dark blue eyes wide. "Rupert McIntyre says the masters all have canes and so do the bigger boys and everybody hits you for everything and if you're really naughty you get called into the headmaster's office and you never ever come out!"

Rowland's brow rose. Rupert McIntyre wasn't completely off the mark. "I was called to the headmaster's office a few times,

Ernie, and I came out." He pulled Ernest onto his lap beside Ewan. It occurred to him that his young nephew would get a bit of a shock when he started at Tudor House, where all the Sinclair boys had been pupils. Wilfred adored his sons and was an unexpectedly gentle father. Ernest—unlike his uncle—would be quite unprepared for the various brutalities of boarding school... aside from the advice of Rupert McIntyre, of course. Still, *Tom Brown's Schooldays* was going a bit far.

"Were you in trouble a lot, Uncle Rowly?"

Rowland smiled. "School isn't so bad, Ernie. Nobody much likes it at first, but you'll make friends and the term will go quickly."

"Rupert says I'll have to learn to fight."

"I suppose we all have to learn to fight sometime," Rowland said more to himself than his nephew.

"Oh." Ernest looked terrified and Rowland regretted his words.

"When I get this cast off, I could show you how to box a bit, if you like."

Ernest nodded vigorously.

"It's a promise then. You haven't a Tom Swift book on that shelf have you? I always liked Tom Swift."

As it turned out *Tom Swift and his Photo Telephone* was indeed among the books the Bruces had acquired for their young guests. Rowland spent the next hour reading aloud the adventures of the fictional inventor's preposterous process for sending photographs by telephone.

Mr. and Mrs. Wilfred Sinclair and the Bruces were quite late. Rowland might have given up and left if he hadn't fallen asleep in the chair, with his nephews both sprawled on top of him.

And so, Wilfred and Kate returned to find the young nanny in a nervous quandary as to whether she should wake Rowland Sinclair and insist her young charges were put in bed, as they should have been hours ago. Wilfred rolled his eyes. He had no time for inexperienced staff. Kate had employed the girl when the children's usual nanny had been unable to travel with them.

Miss Gray was simply too young and too timid to deal with two high-spirited boys, let alone Rowland.

"Thank you, Nanny Gray, I'll see to the children. But in future they are to go to bed regardless of what my brother has in mind."

Rowland woke up as Kate took Ewan off his chest. She put a gloved finger to her lips as her youngest son snuggled into the fur of her stole. She kissed Ewan's head softly and put him in his cot. Wilfred had already taken Ernest to bed. Quietly, Rowland retrieved *Tom Swift and his Photo Telephone* from the floor, returned it to the bookcase, and followed Wilfred out of the nursery.

"Rowly, what are you doing here?"

"Sorry." Rowland tried to rub the crick out of his neck. "I was waiting for you…must have dozed off."

"That I can see." Wilfred sighed. "You'd better come down and tell me what's on your mind."

Wilfred had intended to take Rowland directly and discreetly to the sanctuary of Stanley Bruce's library. They were, however, intercepted by Ethel Bruce, who pounced at the foot of the stairs.

"Mr. Sinclair!" she said linking her arm through his. "You must come and sit down…"

"Rowly just needs to have a word—" Wilfred began.

"Yes, but the poor man's been entertaining the children all this time…he must be parched!"

"I'm sure he must," Stanley Bruce said as he walked out of the drawing room. "We'll all join you ladies for a nightcap shortly. You might also ask Cook to prepare some refreshments, my dear…I'm famished." He gazed sternly at his wife. "Unhand the boy, Ethel."

Sheepishly, Ethel Bruce released Rowland's arm and stood by, frustrated and clearly vexed, as her husband ushered Rowland towards the library.

"You're here about Miss Dawe, no doubt." Bruce closed the door.

"You're aware she's been arrested?"

"Yes, I was informed."

"Well, what are you going to do about it?"

"Miss Dawe, as you are well aware, is not an Australian, Rowland," Bruce said calmly. "Her predicament is not a matter in which I can become involved."

Rowland turned to Wilfred. "She didn't kill anybody—Wil, you were there."

Wilfred frowned. "I would have thought it unlikely, Rowly, but her hands were covered in blood, not to mention the fact that she tried to keep us out of the room initially."

"Why would she want to kill Pierrepont?" Rowland demanded.

"Apparently he was in the process of amending his last will and testament. I am advised the new deed would have disinherited Miss Dawe and her mother."

"And Allie knew this?"

"That is the allegation, I believe."

"This is ludicrous—where would she have got a sword?"

"It seems," Bruce said, "the sword in question was normally displayed in the billiards room of the Watts Gentlemen's Club."

"Wil..."

"For pity's sake, Rowly, you've already retained George Allen on her behalf. What more can we do?"

"Could you arrange an appointment with this chap Entwhistle...the detective? Perhaps if I talk to him."

Wilfred glanced at Bruce.

The minister exhaled. "I'll see what I can arrange, provided you continue to maintain your discretion on the more sordid details of Lord Pierrepont's passing."

"Yes. Thank you."

When the gentlemen joined them, Kate Sinclair and Ethel Bruce were discussing the production of *Richard of Bordeaux* they had just seen in London. The playwright had been billed as Gordon Daviot, the mystery writer, who Ethel had on good authority—from a source amongst the Commonwealth wives, no doubt—was in fact a Scotswoman named Elisabeth MacKintosh.

That aside, Mrs. Bruce had particularly admired the performance of a young actor by the name of Gielgud who had played the king, and was saying so in a manner that left Kate blushing.

Bruce snorted, muttering that the fruit bowl featured in the set was woefully anachronistic. "Whoever heard of pineapples before Queen Anne!"

Rowland told them about Oxford, Bletchley Park, and—with certain delicate details omitted—Lady Pierrepont.

Wilfred was less than pleased that his brother had felt the need to deliver a wax head for some "corrupt circus sculptor".

"My hat!" Ethel Bruce exclaimed. "Does Euphemia have any thoughts on who killed her husband?"

"Speaking of your hat, Ethel dear," Stanley Bruce interrupted, "you might think about purchasing a new one for the theatre. The gentleman seated behind you seemed a little put out."

"Oh, Stanley, he was a very short man. I would need to be headless for that poor little fellow to see!"

"I should be going," Rowland said, standing. He gathered Ethel Bruce wanted to speak to him, but he couldn't see that they'd have the opportunity to do so alone. "I am sorry I interrupted your evening."

"At least you got some sleep." Wilfred handed Rowland his hat. He considered his brother critically. "You're looking well, Rowly…rested."

"Just a moment, Mr. Sinclair," Ethel said, rushing to the small writing desk in the corner of the drawing room. "I must send a note to Miss Higgins. Perhaps you'd be so kind as to take it for me."

"Of course." Rowland waited as she opened the desk and scribbled onto a sheet of crested stationery. She slipped the leaf into an envelope and handed it to him as he took his leave.

Although Rowland suspected the note was for him, he waited, returning to Claridge's with it unopened. The sculptress was still up playing cards with Clyde, and Milton was reading the paper.

"Looks like things are going awry at Wilfred's conference," Milton said, showing him the article. "It seems Roosevelt has rejected the plan for stabilisation."

"The what?"

"It's what the conference has been about...Bruce explained it in lurid and exacting detail, if you remember."

"My mind might have been elsewhere."

"I wish all of me had been elsewhere."

Rowland smiled. "So, what does it mean? Is the conference over?"

"As far as I can gather, everybody's pretty cross at the Americans. This chap Cordell Hull looks like a bit of a fool but they're all going to press on and hope the Americans come around. Didn't Wilfred mention it?"

"He didn't have much of an opportunity, and it's not really the kind of thing he'd discuss with me."

"Did you talk to him about Allie?" Edna enquired anxiously.

Rowland nodded. "Bruce has agreed to arrange an audience with Entwhistle as soon as possible. In the meantime we'll try to glean as much as we can about who else may have had reason to kill Pierrepont."

"And we'll go see Allie tomorrow?"

"Of course." Rowland produced the envelope from his breast pocket and passed it to Edna. "From Mrs. Bruce."

Edna was clearly surprised. She extracted the deckled stationery, reading it quickly.

"What does it say?"

"It's about the American." Edna's eyes were still fixed on the page.

"What American?"

"The woman Lord Pierrepont was seeing—apparently her name is Mrs. Ernest Simpson."

Chapter Twenty

Spent Four Weeks In A Gaol

Feels Sorry For Prisoners
NOW LECTURES

For four weeks Miss Clara Codd, who is lecturing in the Theosophical Society's rooms, was merely "Number Nine" in Holloway Gaol. She was arrested during the memorable Suffragette raid on the House of Commons...

Prison Garments: Once in Holloway, I was ordered to remove my clothes and to don some extraordinary prison garments. The dress was of coarse material, and pleated so that it would fit any figure; thin women had to tie it round their waists. I was given a blue deck duster for my neck and another for my waist. That was to be used as a pocket handkerchief. Over my head I drew a three-cornered handkerchief, tied with strings.

On my first day I was put in solitary confinement in my 10 x 10 cell, alone with a Bible and a hymn book...

Monotonous Life: The monotony was the worst feature. We knew every day exactly what we were to eat and to do...Twice a week we had a long address from the prison chaplain. I remember that up in the gallery at the rear of the prison chapel was a red screen behind which a young woman, condemned to death, used to sit. I think she had murdered her baby. She was surrounded by wardresses, and we were never allowed to see her face. It was a pitiful reminder.

—*The Mail*, 1933

His Majesty's Prison Holloway was a foreboding structure; its grand turreted gateway, a gothic fortress built, not to keep the enemy out, but securely within. It had been constructed midway through the previous century, designed with all the menace that Victorian architecture could conjure. The prison's gallows were housed in a separate hanging shed while a new condemned suite was being built. It was in this place that Allie Dawe was being held.

George Allen accompanied them into the facility and demanded habeas corpus. They were duly processed and searched and then taken to a reception cell. Rowland noticed a look pass between one of the wardens and the solicitor. He assumed that rules were being bent to allow them all in to see Allie. Whether it was by virtue of Allen's reputation or some direct compensation, Rowland didn't know, or much care.

The women's prison was, to say the least, grim. It had been built at a time when punishment and deterrence were held above all things. Now age and wear added to the misery which rose with the damp in its walls. It smelled of decay, inadequate plumbing, and despair.

At first it seemed Allie would do nothing but cry. The prison uniform made her seem smaller and younger than ever. Rowland moved to comfort her but the guard reminded him that there was to be no physical contact with the prisoner, so they were forced to sit across the table and watch. After a time, when he could stand it no longer, Rowland reached across and grabbed her hand.

The guard started, but pulled back when Allen cleared his throat.

"Allie, listen to me," Rowland said. "We will help you. You mustn't lose hope."

Gradually Allie's manner became calmer, hiccoughing and wiping her face with the coarse fabric of her sleeve. Rowland handed her his handkerchief.

"Allie," Edna said gently, "do you know a great deal about your uncle's business affairs?"

"Yes...I think...I don't know what he didn't tell me."

"Were you aware he'd bequeathed his estate to you and your mother?"

"Yes. We were his only family."

"But there wasn't anything, was there?" Clyde said almost hopefully. If there was no estate, Allie had no motive. "Lord Pierrepont was in terrible debt."

Allie shook her head. "One of Uncle Alfred's investments came in not long before he died. He paid back everything. He and Lord Erroll were talking about a new venture in Kenya, and he'd just given a hundred guineas to the Sir Oswald."

"Sir Oswald...as in Mosley?"

Allie nodded.

"Pierrepont was a member of the B.U.F.?" Milton asked.

Allie looked away from the poet, her lip trembled. "Not officially..."

"But he made donations? He must have been sympathetic?" Milton persisted.

Allie nodded, crying again.

Rowland waited as she blew her nose.

"Allie, do you know from where, exactly, the money came?" Rowland asked.

"No, Uncle Alfred seemed to have money in so many ventures. I wasn't a lot of use to him really. He was just trying to keep me from a career on the stage...you know...singing."

"Did you know your uncle was in the process of changing his will?"

"He wasn't."

"Did you know he was married, Allie?"

Allie laughed, and then gasped, startled, by the sound which seemed so out of place in the cell. "Uncle Alfred? I don't think so, Mr. Sinclair. He didn't act like he was married."

The guard began to tap his watch. Rowland tried one last question. "Allie, do you know how he acquired the particular garment he was wearing when he died?"

"From Mother, I suppose." Her eyes welled again as she realised their time was nearly up. Edna defied the guard, walking around the table to embrace the terrified girl. "We'll get you out of here, Allie. You just be strong."

Allie clung to the sculptress until the surly guard removed her bodily; she wept inconsolably as he led her out.

Edna wiped her own eyes. "Rowly…"

"I know." He pulled Allen aside. "You do whatever you can for her while she's in this wretched place. I don't care what it costs."

The solicitor nodded. "I'll have a quiet word."

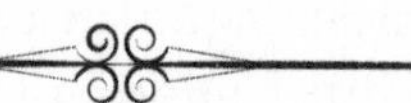

They left Holloway in a troubled and sombre mood.

Milton shook his head angrily. "She doesn't belong in there. Poor, daft kid."

"What now, Rowly?" Clyde asked.

Rowland checked his watch. The conference would have already resumed sitting, meaning Bruce and Wilfred would have left Ennismore Gardens. "Ed, why don't you and Clyde call on Ethel Bruce? Tell her what we know about Euphemia Thistlewaite and see what she can find out through the Dominion wives. Milt and I will meet you back at Claridge's."

"And where are you going?"

"To Watts. I want to talk to the steward—George. We need to find out more about this sword which Allie allegedly used to impale her uncle."

The gentlemen's club was quieter than Rowland remembered. Perhaps because it was too early for luncheon: the hijinks of dining aristocrats had not yet begun.

The steward remembered him. "Are you here as the guest of a member, sir?"

"No, Mr. Playfair, I came to speak with you."

Playfair seemed a little startled by Rowland's use of his actual name.

"I'm afraid I cannot admit you without the sponsorship of a member, Mr. Sinclair."

Rowland's tone hardened a little. "All things considered, I think you might make an exception in this case."

"Impossible, sir. Our membership values—"

"—discretion, I imagine," Rowland finished. "It's jolly good luck that the tawdry details of Lord Pierrepont's demise have not reached the newspapers, don't you think, Playfair?"

The steward studied him frostily, evidently assessing the risk. Rowland stared out his threat.

"What can I do for you gentlemen?" Playfair asked eventually.

"I'd like to see where the sword that was used to kill Lord Pierrepont was normally housed."

Playfair glanced at Milton. "I can make an exception for you, Mr. Sinclair, but I'm afraid your friend will have to wait here. The club rules are very strict."

"I don't care—"

"It's all right, Rowly." Milton placed a calming hand on his friend's shoulder. "I'm not sure I want to be seen inside one of these places…my reputation, you know. I'll wait for you here."

Playfair stopped to glare at the poet, before sniffing haughtily and motioning Rowland through the door which led to the establishment's inner sanctum.

The club was much larger than it seemed from the street. The billiards room housed three full-size tables and, along the far wall, what appeared to be a trophy cabinet full of artifacts and trinkets donated by Watts' illustrious members. The room was currently empty.

Over the yawning fireplace hung a sabre. Another bracket above it was empty. "The sword in question was identical to the one that remains," Playfair said curtly. "Donated by a member who served in the cavalry during the Great War."

"May I?" Rowland asked, pausing as he reached for the hilt.

Playfair inclined his head.

Rowland was tall but still he had to stretch to take the sword off the lower bracket. It was lighter than he expected.

"Sinclair, isn't it?" Josslyn Hay appeared suddenly in the doorway. "I say, I didn't realise you were a member."

"I'm not." Rowland did not hesitate. "Just contemplating joining. George here is giving me the tour."

Playfair looked panicked. Rowland replaced the sabre.

Hay looked questioningly at the steward, but did not challenge the claim.

"I take it you've heard about Miss Dawe's predicament?" Rowland watched Hay's face carefully.

Hay shrugged. "Dreadful, dreadful business. Who would have thought little Allie was Jack the Ripper in a frock!"

"You don't mean to say you believe she actually—?"

"I'd say you and I had a lucky escape, Sinclair. I presume the authorities have their reasons for arresting her." Hay cupped his hand round the side of his mouth in a theatrical whisper. "And you do know she's from bloody dubious stock?"

"You mean Pierrepont?"

"Good God, no! Pierrepont was a member of this establishment after all. The girl's mother was riffraff—some stage actress Pierrepont's younger brother got involved with. A few shelves below the top, if you know what I mean? You know, they say the girl will hang for certain. In fact, Nobby Dunlop Smythe at the club is running a book on the outcome. Rather tragic, but what can you do?"

"Yes, quite." Rowland was not so well rested that he didn't want to punch the Earl at that moment, but he reminded himself of his purpose and the fact that Allie Dawe's life depended on what he could find out. "I understand you and Pierrepont were embarking on a venture in Kenya," he said casually.

"I say, you're not looking for a sound investment are you, Sinclair? I'd be prepared to second your nomination for membership." Hay smiled slyly. "I think you might find joining rather difficult otherwise. Watts can be tediously particular."

"Perhaps." Rowland tried to look vaguely interested in the propositon. "I'll be in touch."

"You do that. Now I really must get on." He waved his hand at Playfair. "I'm sure George here will see you out."

Playfair escorted Rowland back to the reception. "If there's nothing else, sir?"

"There is, actually. I'd like a membership list."

"Absolutely not, sir. The privacy of our esteemed membership is guaranteed. To give it to you would be an act of betrayal and treachery. Why, I would not surrender the names of our members to King George himself!"

Rowland tried again, first to persuade and then to coerce the old steward into giving him the names of Watts' members. In both instances, he failed. Playfair would not be moved and was, in fact, outraged that anyone, particularly a non-member, would have the audacity to make such an appalling request.

"Leave the poor man be," Milton said, joining them at the counter. "Playfair here is just doing his job, Rowly."

Rowland stopped, realising that he was being unreasonable. Playfair was a servant, trying to keep the indulged membership of Watts happy at a time when jobs were scarce. "You're right, Milt." He turned back to the steward. "I apologise, Playfair. Thank you. You've been most helpful."

It wasn't until they were in a motor taxi back to Claridge's that Milton removed a sheaf of papers from his breast pocket and placed them in Rowland's lap.

"What's this?"

"The most recent ten pages or so from the guest book behind the counter. I tore them out while Playfair was showing you around." Milton grinned. "It's not a membership list, but it should give us a fair idea who's been coming in and out of the joint."

"How did you manage to do that without anyone noticing?" Rowland stared at the pages incredulously.

"There weren't many people in the foyer." Milton was clearly pleased with his own ingenuity. "I just pretended I was leaving you a note and couldn't find a pen. The security at that place isn't all that tight. I can tell you, I won't be joining!"

Ethel Bruce was delighted to see Edna and Clyde.

"Oh, I'd hoped you'd come," she said, sending for cake and tea as they sat down.

Kate stood suddenly. Clyde jumped up.

"I hope you won't think me rude," she said, "but I must go and attend to Ewan. I shouldn't be more than half an hour." She smiled warmly at Edna and Clyde, hoping they understood.

Edna did. Kate didn't want to hear anything that she'd have to conceal from Wilfred. She adored her husband and thought his judgement sound on all matters, but she knew Rowland and his friends had their own way of doing things.

Edna reached up and took Kate's hand. "We simply won't cut the cake till you're back."

With Kate gone, Edna informed Ethel Bruce of the arrest of Allie Dawe, the unfortunate niece of the late Lord Pierrepont.

"Oh, dear," Ethel said, shocked. "I've seen that sweet girl with Bunky from time to time. Why in heaven's name do they believe she's involved?"

Edna explained the circumstances of how and where Allie had found the body, omitting—in deference to Rowland's promise—any mention of the fact that Pierrepont had died in a woman's nightie.

"A sword, you say. Why, that's ridiculous! Decent girls don't know how to use swords!"

"So you see, Ethel, we need to know as much as we can about this American woman."

"Why?"

"To convince the police that Allie Dawe is not the only one who might have had reason to kill Lord Pierrepont."

"Oh, I see...we're flushing out suspects!"

"I suppose so."

"I'm not sure I understand why Bunky's American paramour would kill him."

"She might not have, but maybe she was cross because he married Euphemia, or perhaps her husband found out..."

"Oh, yes, I see." Ethel leaned forward and patted Edna's knee. "Leave it to me, dear. I shall invite the appropriate ladies to tea. I promise you I will let nothing stand between us and the truth!"

Chapter Twenty-one

England's Police Headquarters

> Scotland Yard got its name from the fact that it occupies the site of a place built for the reception of the Kings of Scotland when they visited London. The palace fell into ruin during Elizabeth's reign. The correct title is New Scotland Yard.
>
> —*The Queenslander*, 1933

Edna and Clyde had not yet returned to Claridge's. Rowland and Milton greeted the wax head of Pierrepont in what had become their custom and, bringing him in to the dining room to watch, they spread the torn pages of the visitor's book across the polished table. The record revealed that Watts was an interesting hub of social connexions.

"Lord Harcourt," Milton said putting his finger on the name. "Wasn't Lady Pierrepont a Harcourt or something of the sort?"

"Ethel Bruce mentioned that the Thistlewaites were the Lords Harcourt, I believe."

"So, the father of Euphemia Pierrepont, née Thistlewaite, is a member?"

"Unless he's passed away. In which case the current Lord Harcourt would be one of her brothers, I suppose."

"And the other brother would be a Thistlewaite?" Milton was weary of the strange naming and titling conventions of the English.

Rowland shrugged. "Possibly. People here always seem to have a few names from which to choose."

"Rowly—look at this."

Rowland glanced at the name which had caught Milton's eye: The Honourable Archibald Murcott.

"Seems strange he didn't mention that he was a member," Milton said quietly.

Rowland frowned. "We didn't talk of Watts..."

"But he knew we were wandering about with Pierrepont's head in a hatbox. Surely he would have mentioned that they shared a gentlemen's club, especially given that Pierrepont died in that very club?"

Rowland nodded. "You would think so."

There were other names too. Rowland expected the name of Josslyn Hay, Earl of Erroll, but not that of Cecil Buchan, their flamboyant protector from the gentlemen's ball at which Allie had sung, and who was apparently the Earl of Bishopthorpe.

"That explains how Buchan came to know Erroll," Rowland said thoughtfully.

"Perhaps the venerable members of Watts were keeping an eye on Allie. They might be able to help her now."

Rowland shook his head. "Hay, at least, seems to have concluded she's guilty." He told Milton of what Hay had said of the girl's parentage. "You know," he added "we should call on Mrs. Dawe. She must be beside herself about Allie, and we have yet to establish why Pierrepont was wearing her nightie."

The butler, Menzies, interrupted them to inform Rowland that he was wanted on the telephone.

Wilfred Sinclair was calling between meetings at the economic conference, and so he was particularly rushed and familiarly brusque. "Entwhistle has agreed to speak with you, Rowly.

Three o'clock at New Scotland Yard. Don't be late, do *not* take your friends." The phone clicked in Rowland's ear before he could say a word.

It was already half past two and so Rowland grabbed his hat and stuck his head into the dining room to tell Milton where he was going.

New Scotland Yard, located on what was known as the Thames Embankment, was the headquarters of the London Metropolitan Police. The building was another impressive, gothic structure, its upper storeys banded with red brick and white Portland stone and its base granite. Rowland walked through the iron gates to the reception. A solemn young constable took him up to Detective Inspector Entwhistle.

The office was cluttered. Paperwork was stacked in disordered piles on the desk…at least Rowland assumed it was a desk, as no part of it was actually visible beneath the layers of documents. A black Bakelite ashtray sat precariously on the top of one pile of reports and a half-eaten apple on another.

Initially, Entwhistle was friendly enough. He poured two glasses of Scotch and offered Rowland a drink. When Rowland declined, he poured the second glass into the first, and drank it himself.

"Detective Inspector Entwhistle," Rowland began, "I'm here about the arrest of a Miss Allie Dawe."

"Yes, the Pierrepont murder. I must thank you for your help that day. You rendered an invaluable service by removing the perpetrator so that we could examine the crime scene in her absence."

"No thanks necessary, Detective Inspector," Rowland said. "For one thing, I didn't remove the perpetrator at all—just the poor girl who found the body."

"Ahh, yes." Entwhistle tipped back in his chair, rocking gently to and fro. "I gather you believe we have arrested the wrong culprit."

"I'm not sure I understand how you can possibly be convinced of Miss Dawe's guilt."

Entwhistle laughed. "Because, Mr. Sinclair, it takes more than a come hither glance to make me dismiss the obvious. My mother raised me to look past a pretty face and shapely legs." The inspector counted off the facts on his stubby fingers. "Miss Dawe, the accused, was found with the body, her hands bore injuries from the same blade that killed the victim, she had access to that blade and the victim, and she had motive."

Determined to present as objective and reasonable, Rowland ignored the detective's condescension. "Miss Dawe injured her hands trying to remove the blade—the natural act of a niece who cares for her uncle. Surely if she had used the sword to kill him she would have held it by the hilt and not the blade?"

"People behave strangely under pressure, Mr. Sinclair. My old mum always said, 'Rotten bridges crumble under weight'—and, as is often the case, she's correct. Villains make mistakes. It's what allows us to catch them and bring them to justice."

"I've seen where that sword was kept, Detective Inspector. Miss Dawe could not possibly have reached it without the aid of a ladder or a chair."

Entwhistle shrugged. "So, she used a chair."

"The room is used exclusively for billiards. There are no chairs in it. With due respect, Inspector, you cannot suppose that she dragged a chair from another room to take down the sword in a gentlemen's club which did not allow women beyond its threshold."

"It was midday, Mr. Sinclair. The gentlemen of Watts were dining. The billiards room was empty. Miss Dawe, knowing the layout of the club, had ample opportunity to procure the sword—with or without a chair."

"She knew the trade entrance to the accommodation. She'd never been in the club proper."

"Now, how would you know that, Mr. Sinclair? Who knows what services she may have been providing to the gentlemen of Watts, aside from her uncle?"

Rowland's eyes darkened but he kept his voice calm, affable. "I suppose, Detective Inspector, you have already discovered that Lord Pierrepont was recently married."

"Indeed, Lady Pierrepont claimed the body this morning."

"The rumour is that Lord Pierrepont was also conducting an extramarital affair."

Entwhistle rolled his eyes. "For pity's sake, Mr. Sinclair, Pierrepont was a peer. I'd be bloody surprised if he was conducting only one extramarital affair!"

"But doesn't it indicate, sir, that there were others with motive to kill Lord Pierrepont?"

"Perhaps…but Miss Dawe had motive and opportunity. She is not the sweet little miss she seems, Sinclair. She's been arrested before, while she was using the rather ludicrous alias of Sarah Dabinett, no less. As my mother would tell you, innocent people do not have the need for aliases."

Rowland was beginning to wonder if Entwhistle's mother also worked for the Yard. "Sarah Dabinett is her stage name—the poor girl fancies herself a songstress!"

"Mr. Sinclair, do you have any actual evidence, aside from your faith in Miss Dawe and gossip?"

"You are looking into Lord Pierrepont's financial and political affairs?"

"My dear sir, this is Scotland Yard. Of course we're looking into his affairs, but I doubt anything we find there is going to lessen the case against your Miss Dawe."

Rowland took a deep breath. "I am concerned, Inspector Entwhistle, that the pressure to keep this murder out of the papers is superseding the vigorous pursuit of all potential suspects, to the very serious detriment of Miss Dawe. For God's sake, man, we are talking about a young woman's life!"

To Rowland's surprise, Entwhistle did not explode at the criticism. He sat back tapping his fingertips together thoughtfully. "You're not a solicitor are you, Mr. Sinclair?"

"Not at all."

"Pity…you can argue a good case, even with no case to argue. My old mum, bless her, would probably find your loyalty quite romantic. Tell you what, if you come across anything that you think might change my mind—and you haven't yet—I'll listen. I can't say fairer than that."

The butler informed Rowland that a Mrs. Stanley Bruce was in the foyer. "Are you home to visitors, sir?"

"Yes, of course." Rowland gathered up the stolen pages of Watts' visitors' book. They had been going over the names again with the fresh eyes of a new day.

Milton went down to escort Ethel Bruce up himself.

Rowland straightened his tie and asked the butler to make tea.

Ethel Bruce arrived on Milton's arm, quite plainly excited. Her face was flushed pink and she beamed broadly. Apart from a little strangled scream when she first saw Pierrepont's head gazing out from the sideboard, she barely waited to sit before she blurted out her news. "I've done it," she crowed. "By George, I've done it!"

"Have you discovered something, Ethel?" Edna asked, curling up on the settee beside her.

"Better, my dear, better!" She preened. "You and Mr. Sinclair are going to a party."

"I beg your pardon?"

Ethel Bruce looked Rowland up and down. "Do you have a tailcoat with you, Mr. Sinclair?"

Rowland nodded. "Yes." Beresford, the first valet, had very nearly insisted upon it.

"Splendid, there's no problem then."

"I'm not sure I understand you, Mrs. Bruce."

"I had tea today with Lady Vera Winslow-Scott, who is hosting a party this evening for her dear friends Mr. and Mrs. Ernest Simpson." She sat back triumphantly. "It turns out the Simpsons are about to take a tour of Germany and Norway."

"And Mrs. Simpson is the woman you believe Lord Pierrepont was seeing."

"Yes, yes. Now at first I thought to simply ask Vera about Mrs. Simpson's disposition, because one would expect that if there was any truth to the rumour about her and Lord Pierrepont, his passing would not have gone unmourned...but then I thought, wouldn't it be better to judge such things for ourselves?"

"Indeed," Rowland said cautiously.

"Lady Winslow-Scott is a perfectly pleasant woman but she does like to see herself as a bastion of modern taste—always talking about this play, or that poet, or this artist; intellectual this, symbolic that—all complete nonsense, of course!"

Ethel paused to take a breath.

"So...when I told Vera that I had met the most exciting young artist, she was mad with envy." Ethel smiled here at Rowland. "She asked where you'd hung and I told her all over Europe—I may have exaggerated a little but it was with a purpose. Vera was intrigued, as I knew she would be. Then I told her that an entire wing of the Australian National Gallery was dedicated to your work and that you'd recently returned from a very successful tour of Germany where you were lauded as the new Picasso."

"The current Picasso might be a little alarmed," Clyde murmured.

"Now, it must be said of Vera—even by her friends, of which I consider myself one—that she is an ardent admirer of scandal. Too dull to be part of one herself, mind you, but she does cherish the talent in others! Less understanding people might call her a gossip." Ethel looked a little nervous now. Her words took the tone of confession, hurried and apologetic. "I'm afraid I might have become a little carried away with my part in this investigation. You see the art itself wasn't enough. I was compelled to reveal that Rowland Sinclair was forced to flee to London after taking another man's wife as—and I hope you'll forgive me for this, dear—his *lover*. You see Vera considers lovers very European and sophisticated. Stanley is convinced her parties are just gatherings of cads and fallen women! He has a point, but one must be courageous in one's pursuit of justice…wouldn't you agree, Mr. Isaacs?"

"Where lies the truth? Has man in wisdom's creed a pitiable doom?" Milton sighed deeply.

"I could not have put it better myself, Mr. Isaacs."

"Nor Wordsworth." Rowland wondered fleetingly why the poet had not yet quoted Milton, before his thoughts returned to the elaborate fabrication of Ethel Bruce.

"There is just one other thing," Ethel added quite guiltily now. "I may have intimated that, though Australian, the woman now calling herself Edna Higgins was the wife of a very senior member of the Nazi government…though I refused to disclose his name."

For a moment nobody said anything, unsure what to make of Ethel Bruce's extraordinary tale. The wife of the former Australian Prime Minister extracted an exquisitely illuminated card from her handbag and presented it to Rowland.

He cast his eyes over the florid script: an invitation from Lady Winslow-Scott to Rowland Sinclair and his guest to a private soirée that evening, with an apology for the lack of notice. Apparently, Lady Winslow-Scott had only just been informed that he was in London and, being a great admirer of his work, she would be delighted if he'd attend. He handed it to Edna.

"Where exactly does Lady Winslow-Scott believe she's seen my work?"

"Oh, the Louvre. I told her everybody who knows anything about art will remember your revolutionary exhibition at the Louvre."

Edna took a deep breath. "Ethel, you are simply wonderful!" she said. She paused as an obstacle occurred to her. "Does Mr. Bruce know we'll be coming too?"

"Stanley? My hat, no! Stanley doesn't approve of Vera or her set. He could not, and would not, be seen at one of Vera's parties—they can be quite wild affairs." She looked sternly at Rowland. "You will need to guard Edna quite jealously, Mr.

Sinclair. If not for the fact that this woman, Simpson, will be in attendance, I would never suggest you go."

Edna laughed. "You mustn't be concerned, Ethel—we've all been to the odd wild affair. We've thrown one or two."

Ethel glowed happily. "I thought as much, dear."

Chapter Twenty-two

British Art

A Splendid Exhibition
EPSTEIN AND AUGUSTUS JOHN

Tile collection of pictures by British artists, which Mrs. Alleyne Zander has placed on view at Farmer's Blaxland Galleries, is intensely interesting and stimulating. It is definitely the most important exhibition of contemporary English work that has come to Australia.

Another eminent artist well represented is Richard Sickert. Time was when Sickert was considered appallingly subversive. Now he has been accepted into the Royal Academy, together with John, the two do much to instill life into that rather sombre institution. "Horses, Barnet Fair" is a particularly virile piece of work. It carries things through in forceful style, without bothering for a moment about conventional finish in detail.

—*The Sydney Morning Herald*, 1933

The Winslow-Scotts resided in one of the great houses on the northern side of Piccadilly—immense, elegant, and overtly fashionable. It had been built with an assumption that its inhabitants would entertain in a style and on a scale that was grand.

With its street façade set right against the pavement, there was no driveway to speak of and the street was congested with the vehicles of arriving guests. Rowland stepped out of the Bruces' Rolls-Royce and offered Edna his hand.

Once again, the sculptress wore her black velvet gown, with diamonds borrowed from Ethel Bruce, and a wrap of Chinese brocade. Her hair had been crimped and twisted into a knot at the nape of her neck.

She swung her legs out of the cabin first, unfurling and emerging like some beautiful exotic butterfly. Rowland smiled. Edna was already playing her part—the mysterious adulteress who had run away with her lover. His role would be easy, natural—a man bewitched.

He wore white tie and tails. The shirt was Milton's, as his own had acquired a smear of vermilion at some point. It was not something that would have normally bothered Rowland, but Ethel Bruce had impressed upon them the exacting style that would be expected at the Winslow-Scotts' soirée.

"Ready?" Rowland whispered.

Edna nodded. "Of course." She brushed down his lapel. "Shall we turn some heads, then?"

They were admitted into the house by a footman who announced their arrival, then ushered them to a receiving line at the anteroom adjoining the lavish ballroom. Footmen bearing silver trays laden with glasses of champagne wove among those who had already arrived, and a string-and-brass ensemble played from one of the internal balconies at least thirty feet above the parquetry floors. They were greeted by Lord Winslow-Scott, a tall, broad man with a waxed moustache, who informed Rowland that most people called him "Great Scott," and invited the Australian to do likewise. Lady Winslow-Scott fussed over Rowland like he was a dear friend of long-standing. She dragged him off to ask his opinion of a painting she had just acquired for the dining room, while her husband introduced Edna to other guests.

Rowland looked back to the sculptress, remembering Ethel Bruce's warning. Edna blew him a kiss.

The painting was a piece by Sickert—an urban landscape as opposed to the confronting nudes through which Rowland had come to know and love the artist's work. Still, the masterly handling of light and mood, the sense of moment, was very much Sickert.

Rowland was careful to appear unimpressed—polite but underwhelmed. His lack of enthusiasm only strengthened Lady Winslow-Scott's conviction that he was an artistic genius.

"I must say that I am delighted to have you here, Mr. Sinclair. Some people can be very high-handed about artists, but, as a patron of the arts, I like to consider myself rather more modern than that. I tell you I am determined to have one of your more recent pieces for my drawing room…but I suppose you're not painting a great deal at the moment." She put her hand gently on the sling. "How tremendously frustrating it must be for a man of your talent." Her voice dropped to a whisper. "It can be a dangerous exercise—rescuing a woman from a jealous brute." She rubbed his arm, setting the stage for a confidence.

A brief moment of awkwardness followed. Then Rowland realised that Vera Winslow-Scott had assumed he'd been injured in some kind of duel with Edna's fictional Nazi husband. As she was obviously enamoured of the romantic image, Rowland did not disillusion her. The party was not an intimate affair, and he would have to rely on his hostess to introduce him to Pierrepont's alleged mistress.

"In the end, madam, it was a question of which of us wanted her more. He was less than understanding, which was a pity. The subsequent unpleasantness was unnecessary."

"Oh, Mr. Sinclair," Lady Winslow-Scott gasped. "I couldn't agree more. In a modern world these differences can be dealt with politely, without recourse to incivility, let alone violence."

Lady Winslow-Scott engaged him then in a series of introductions, mostly to and of women—gay, practiced socialites who were intrigued by artists, if not art itself. In an attempt to avoid having to canvass too many untruths, Rowland maintained a courteous reserve which a few found arrogant, some appealing, and others both. It seemed he was making a reasonable impression, one way or another. Between conversations Lady Winslow-Scott would whisper some scandalous tidbit about the woman to whom he'd just been introduced.

When Rowland caught sight of Edna again, she was surrounded. He recognised the eager countenances of hopeful men. It was not an unusual sight where the sculptress was concerned. One man seemed particularly confident with his attentions, leaning in and whispering often in her ear.

Rowland excused himself from a conversation with the Baroness Von Flyte and joined them.

"Rowly, darling." Edna entwined her arm with his. "I thought you'd abandoned me."

Rowland smiled. "Never."

Edna introduced the gentlemen who had been keeping her company: a collection of young peers, wealthy industrialists, and His Royal Highness Prince George. The King's fourth son laughed as she fumbled with protocol, trying to recall who was a lord, who was honourable, and who was simply mister.

Rowland was a little surprised to encounter a prince of the realm mingling so informally, but perhaps Vera Winslow-Scott's parties were more exclusive than he had realised.

"It's a pleasure to make your acquaintance, Your Royal Highness," Rowland said, smiling briefly at Edna, who, he guessed, had no clue how to address a prince.

"Likewise, Mr. Sinclair. I wondered about the gentleman fortunate enough to claim the affections of this divine creature."

Edna turned to Rowland and pulled a face.

Prince George seemed in excellent humour, charming and conversational. Curious about Australia, he expressed a desire to explore the far reaches of the Empire. "What has brought you to London, Mr. Sinclair?"

"We were in Germany, actually, and found we had to leave rather suddenly."

"I see." The prince studied Edna in a way that led Rowland to suspect he had already heard of Ethel Bruce's fictional scandal. "How exceptionally lucky for London."

Prince George did not show any signs of moving to another conversation, and all but ignored the other gentlemen gathered, while he monopolised the Australians over the course of several drinks. He talked to Rowland about his art, of which their hostess had apparently waxed lyrical. Rowland accepted the accolades modestly, knowing Vera Winslow-Scott had never laid eyes on his work. For a time they discussed the burgeoning popularity of the Surrealist movement in a conversation that Rowland found surprisingly comfortable and engaging. The prince had a certain dignified flamboyance about him, as if he assumed they were being watched—which, of course, they were.

Rowland suspected that George, being a man as well as a prince, was as drawn to Edna as any sentient male would be. That in itself he did not mind; it was inevitable. What did irritate him, however, was the brazen manner in which the prince flirted. While Rowland did not consider himself prudish, there was, he believed, an accepted courtesy between gentlemen. He wondered if it was expected that he would simply step aside for the son of his King. Admittedly, the affair between him and Edna had been fabricated, but Rowland could not help feeling affronted by any man who would blatantly attempt to seduce the sculptress in his presence.

Initially, Edna accepted Prince George's attentions warmly and with good grace, although she occasionally seemed bewildered and at other times amused. She deflected his invitations and laughed off the more forward suggestions.

When finally he proposed a drive in the moonlight, Edna apparently decided enough was enough. "You do realise, sir, that Mr. Sinclair and I are very much in love! Your attentions are unwelcome!"

Rowland, unprepared for so direct a declaration, choked on his champagne.

The prince smiled and once again whispered in Edna's ear.

Rowland's face darkened. "Just a blasted minute..."

Edna reacted even more angrily and in a manner quite unanticipated. She shook off the forward royal, and pressing herself against Rowland, she reached up and kissed him, passionately and without reserve.

He responded unequivocally, despite wondering if the world had suddenly gone mad, and not much caring if it had. The sculptress' kiss was searing. In that moment she possessed him completely.

Edna paused the demonstration of her affections, only to take the champagne glass from his hand and give it to one of the hapless gaping lords who lingered still. Then she kissed Rowland once more—slowly, sensuously, and he forgot he was standing before a Prince of England in a ballroom full of people. Part of him knew there was some reason for her sudden ardour, but God, he wanted it to be real.

Too soon, she pulled away and turned back to Prince George. "I do trust that settles the matter to your satisfaction, sir," she said hotly. "Rowly, we should dance, don't you agree?"

If Rowland were ever able to refuse the sculptress anything, it was not now.

They joined the couples already on the dance floor. He held her unconventionally to get around the limitation imposed by the plaster cast, but they had always moved well together.

"Oh, Rowly," she whispered. "I'm so sorry I attacked you like that."

"Attacked me?"

"I couldn't think of any other way to show him we were together...and he just made me so furious!"

Rowland's jaw tensed—anger, sharpened by a vague, though not unexpected, disappointment. "What did he say to you, Ed? I should have punched him in the nose."

Edna smiled. "His Royal Highness? I suspect they would shoot you for that...and if they didn't, Wilfred might." She rested her cheek against his lapel as he led her into the turn. "He didn't say anything so terribly awful. Just that he didn't think you had any interest in me whatsoever."

"Did he, indeed? The man's obviously a flaming idiot."

Edna laughed as she looked up into his face. "What I did was inappropriate enough. You are not to hit a Prince of England!"

Rowland shook his head. "What is it we're doing here again?"

Edna sighed. "We're trying to find out if this Mrs. Simpson woman was having an affair with Lord Pierrepont, whether she might have been so scorned when he married Euphemia that she killed him."

"Hell hath no fury," Rowland mused. "Have you been introduced to Mrs. Simpson yet?"

Edna shook her head. "I'm not even sure who she is."

"This is going to be more difficult than I anticipated," Rowland said, noticing Prince George speaking earnestly to Lady Winslow-Scott.

Edna saw, too. She bit her lip nervously. "Oh, dear, perhaps he's dreadfully offended. Rowly, I'm so sorry. I'm afraid I might have landed us in terrible trouble."

Rowland laughed. "I understand the Tower of London is no longer in use, Ed. Let him be offended."

They danced together until the bracket had concluded, expecting at any moment to be asked to leave. As it was, they were not.

Taking advantage of the reprieve, they made a concerted effort to mingle with as many people as they could in an effort to happen upon Mrs. Simpson. The crowd seemed to be made up of the young elite of London: well-bred, well-educated, and very well-to-do. They were gay and loud and for the most part oblivious or indifferent to the troubles of the world. As the night wore on, guests became less concerned about appearances, or perhaps it was just that appearances were blurred by champagne and cocktails of various sorts. The tempo of the music increased and then became sultry as the ballroom lights were dimmed.

Lady Winslow-Scott appeared suddenly and quite intimately between Rowland and Edna, entwining her arms with theirs.

"Well, didn't you lovebirds make an impression on the prince! His Majesty has asked me to ensure you are both invited to one of our weekends."

"Really?" Edna was surprised.

"We host a few very special friends down to our house in the country for a wickedly fabulous and thoroughly indulgent weekend. You must promise me you'll come!"

A young woman with a champagne glass in each hand joined them. She took a sip from each glass. Lady Winslow-Scott introduced the Viscountess Thelma Furness.

"Oh, no, Vera, it is Thelma the Viscountess Furness. A subtle change in order to signify the viscount and I are now divorced!"

"Delighted to make your acquaintance, Lady Furness." Rowland took the lead so as to remind Edna of the protocol that went with the title of Viscountess, divorced or not.

Thelma Furness spoke with the gentle drawl of an American whose accent had been consciously mitigated. In her late twenties she was the epitome of fashionable style. Her figure was petite to the point of being too thin and shown to best advantage in a form-fitting sleeveless gown.

"You must excuse me," she said. "I'm a little tight."

She gave one of her glasses of champagne to Edna. "You certainly made a wonderful spectacle of yourself," she said, though not unkindly. "I must admit I felt a guilty thrill to see you defy all this stuffy, tiresome British protocol."

Edna smiled in reply, a little startled by what she had started. She reached for Rowland's hand.

"You mustn't be frightened that I would censure you, my dear," Thelma went on. "I know exactly what Georgie can be like." She brought her face a little too close to Edna's in a display of confidence. "The Prince of Wales has had the most worrying time with him. Georgie has a weakness for Americans, too, you see, but he's a terrible picker. The hijinks he got up to with that Preston woman! *Kiki,* for pity's sake! Did he really think his dear papa would countenance, let alone tolerate, a *Princess Kiki*?"

"Thelma and the Prince Edward are very intimate friends," Lady Winslow-Scott contributed. Then to Thelma, "I had hoped your being here would entice His Royal Highness to accept my invitation."

"I hoped so, too, but who knows what rules that might have broken." Lady Furness sighed. "It seems Ernest and Wallis have also stayed away."

"Oh, Ernest is here somewhere," Lady Winslow-Scott informed her. "Although he did come quite late. It seems Wallis became ill at the very last minute."

"Well, I must say, I'm awfully disappointed. Neither my sweet prince nor my dearest Wallis to keep me company!"

"I hope your friend is not too unwell," Edna ventured.

Lady Winslow-Scott frowned as she contemplated Wallis Simpson's health. "She has seemed a little out of sorts these past weeks. I do hope she isn't coming down with the dreaded influenza."

Thelma Furness gulped and giggled. "How *uncommonly discreet* of you, Vera." She held her hand up to her face and whispered loudly to Edna. "Wallis' lover died recently. She's quite at a loss, but, of course, she can't mourn him publicly. I suspect that's the cause of her current indisposition."

Edna nodded in a gesture of understanding. "And is Mr. Simpson aware of the reason for his wife not being well?"

"Who can say what Ernest knows," Lady Winslow-Scott interjected, unwilling to let the news of the scandal be delivered entirely by another. "He's devoted to Wallis." She looked from Edna to Rowland. "Devotion makes some men tolerant and others angry."

They were interrupted by Lord Winslow-Scott and an elderly gentleman who wore round spectacles and a showman's moustache, which he twirled like the villain of some silent picture. Winslow-Scott introduced Herr Von Kirsch, a member of the German delegation to the London Economic Conference.

Von Kirsch clicked his heels and bowed his head. "Have we met before, sir?" he asked, squinting intently at Rowland.

Rowland answered carefully, cognisant of the fact that the German must have seen him—albeit from a distance—the day the Blackshirts disrupted the conference. "My brother is one of the Australian delegates at the economic conference, Herr Von Kirsch. Perhaps you have noticed some fraternal similarity."

"Sinclair…yes, of course. I have spoken with your brother. He is a respected gentleman." He turned to Edna. "Will you do an old man a kindness and allow me to have this dance, Fraulein Higgins?" he said, holding out his hand.

Edna glanced at Rowland. If anyone would realise that she was not the runaway wife of a Nazi, it would be Von Kirsch. Yet, how could she refuse?

Rowland shook his head slightly.

"Just one dance, Fraulein," Von Kirsch persisted. "Surely, Herr Sinclair can spare you when he has the company of two such beautiful women," he added, acknowledging Thelma Furness and Lady Winslow-Scott.

Edna took the German's hand uncertainly.

Von Kirsch led her onto the dance floor.

Rowland made inconsequential conversation with the Winslow-Scotts and Lady Furness but his eyes remained fixed upon Edna and the man with whom she danced.

"Why, Mr. Sinclair," Thelma Furness laughed. "Shame on you. It's so terribly old-fashioned to be possessive."

Rowland could see that Von Kirsch was speaking to Edna and that the sculptress was startled. He excused himself, walking towards them. Then suddenly Edna stopped dancing and pulled away from the German. She walked off the dance floor to Rowland.

"Ed?" he said as she grabbed his arm. She was shaking. "What is it?"

"He knows, Rowly."

"That you're not married?"

"He knows we were in Munich. He was at the King Rupprecht's ball that night. He remembers me. He knows that we're wanted in Germany. We have to leave—now!"

Chapter Twenty-three

Prince George Robbed

> A message from Vancouver states that the Buenos Aires newspaper "Critica" says that the bedroom of Prince George, at the Embassy, was ransacked on the night of March 14, and personal jewellery of considerable value was stolen. Since the Prince of Wales and Prince George left for Brazil, the police have recovered the valuables and identified the thief. His name has not been divulged, but it is said that he is a prominent young man, who was so friendly with the Princes that his presence at the Embassy was not considered suspicious.
>
> —*Singleton Argus*, 1931

Von Kirsch beckoned for aid. Rowland didn't wait to see who would respond. He took Edna's hand and led her briskly towards the door. They stopped to thank the Winslow-Scotts for their hospitality, only because slipping past their hosts was near impossible.

Rowland explained that Edna had suddenly taken ill, an excuse corroborated by the sculptress' shaken pallor. In the far periphery of his vision Rowland could see Von Kirsch pointing them out…but to whom, he could not discern. A footman was sent to inform the Bruces' chauffeur that they were ready for the car.

"We might wait outside," Rowland told the Winslow-Scotts. "The fresh air may do Miss Higgins some good."

And, on that premise, they escaped the ballroom.

"Don't panic." Rowland squeezed Edna's hand as they stepped out into the portico. "We're in England."

Edna nodded.

"Mr. Sinclair!"

Rowland tensed, turning quickly.

Prince George strode over and stood beside them as they waited for the car. At first he said nothing, lighting a tailor-made cigarette and drawing deeply. He smiled. "What? Going so soon?"

"I'm afraid Miss Higgins is unwell."

"Jolly shame, I was hoping I could convince you both to take supper,"—he glanced at his watch—"or breakfast with me somewhere. I'm a little bored of Lady Winslow-Scott's usual collection of scandalous women."

"Thank you, sir, but perhaps another time," Rowland said, standing firm between the prince and Edna.

"I must say, you make a particularly handsome couple." George regarded Rowland intently, assessing, it seemed, the calibre of his rival. He smiled. "Perhaps we could—" The arrival of the Rolls-Royce cut short whatever proposition was on His Royal Highness' lips. "Oh, here's your vehicle…." He stood back as Rowland, deciding not to wait for the portly chauffeur to clamber out, opened the door for Edna.

Prince George slapped Rowland's shoulder warmly. "Well, Sinclair, I'll look forward to meeting you both again."

"Thank you, sir," Rowland said awkwardly. "Good evening, then."

He slid into the rear seat beside Edna, as the Prince waved them off.

Reluctant to disturb the entire Bruce household by calling in at the Ennismore Gardens terrace, Rowland telephoned Wilfred from Claridge's and had him come to the hotel.

As it was three in the morning, Wilfred was not in the best of moods when he arrived. Rowland told him about the encounter with Von Kirsch.

Wilfred questioned Edna closely. "And what exactly did he say, Miss Higgins? You and Rowly are a little too prone to see vengeful Germans around every corner."

"Herr Von Kirsch said that he remembered me from the Royal Ball in the palace of Rupprecht of Bavaria, a few weeks ago." Edna tried not to drop her gaze from Wilfred's accusing one. She felt like a child confessing some transgression. "The ball was held the very same night the SA attacked Rowly and Alois Richter died."

"Is that all?"

Edna shook her head. "Herr Von Kirsch said he knew Herr Richter well and was deeply saddened by his terrible death. He said he recognised Rowly as the man who caused all the trouble at the Geological Museum." She swallowed. "He said he was finally putting things together."

"Did you confirm any of his accusations?"

"No. I didn't…I…couldn't say anything."

"Good. All the fellow has is a belief he saw you at a ball. You will deny you were ever there. He won't have enough to pursue anything legally."

He turned to Rowland. "What were you doing at this party, anyway?"

On this point Rowland was evasive. "Lady Winslow-Scott invited us. She's acquainted with Mrs. Bruce."

"She invited you without ever having made your acquaintance?" Wilfred's scrutiny was piercing, suspicious.

"I can only presume she thought the good Mrs. Bruce's recommendation sufficient."

"Very well," Wilfred said, though it was clear that that was not at all what he meant. He'd been woken at three in the morning after all. "I'll see what I can do to head this latest embarrassment off at the pass. May I suggest, dear brother, that since you cannot attend any form of gathering without causing an international incident, from now on you avoid all parties, dances, or blasted soirées!"

For a few moments after Wilfred slammed the door and stormed out, no one said anything.

Then Milton broke the silence. "It was bloody fortunate you didn't tell him the whole story."

"I'm not afraid of Wil," Rowland muttered sullenly. "I just didn't wish to implicate Mrs. Bruce in this mess."

"Out with it, then," Clyde demanded. "We'd better have it, warts and all. What did you find out?"

And so Rowland and Edna relayed the events of that evening.

Milton hooted as Edna described the incident with Prince George. "You molested poor Rowly right in front of royalty! Good Lord, Ed! Couldn't you have just told the poor bloke to sod off? God knows you've sent men packing before."

"He was jolly persistent," Rowland said in Edna's defence. "In fact, he might have been a tolerable chap if he hadn't thought himself entitled to any woman in the flaming realm."

Edna looked at Rowland, surprised. "Oh, he wasn't trying to seduce me."

"What in heaven's name do you mean? Of course he was!" Rowland objected. "If he'd flirted any more intensely, he might well have hurt himself."

Edna's eyes glinted and she tried not to smile. "Darling, those invitations were intended for you. That's why *I* had to claim you with that kiss. You were being so polite that he—" She giggled. "Oh, dear…and you thought he was making advances towards me." Unable to suppress it any longer, Edna collapsed into laughter.

Rowland stared at her in stupefied horror. "Nonsense," he decided. "You're being ridiculous."

But now both Milton and Clyde joined the sculptress, clearly preferring her version of events.

"You know, Rowly," Clyde said wiping a tear from his eye, "I'm starting to wonder why the English haven't died out as a race."

Rowland pulled his bow tie undone, and ignored them. Perhaps it was the shock of Von Kirsch's recognition. Edna had obviously lost her mind.

When they'd had enough of laughing at him, Rowland told Milton and Clyde about the revelations of Thelma, Viscountess Furness.

"So, she confirmed that this Mrs. Simpson was having an affair?" Milton asked.

"She certainly seems to believe it to be the case, and that the affair ended recently, at which point Mrs. Simpson started becoming unwell—"

"To hide her grief," Milton finished triumphantly. "Or her guilt! She's got to be Pierrepont's mistress!"

"So, what do we do now?" Clyde asked.

Rowland groaned. "I suppose we try and find out where Mrs. Simpson was when Pierrepont was murdered."

"What about Mr. Simpson?" Edna said, removing the pins that held her hair in place and shaking her copper tresses loose.

For a moment Rowland could contemplate nothing but what it had been like to kiss her.

"Lady Winslow-Scott said he was devoted to his wife. Perhaps he found out," the sculptress prompted when he didn't respond.

"Yes...yes, you're quite right." Rowland forced his mind back to the matter at hand.

"I don't suppose he was a member at Watts?" Milton opened the sideboard drawer where they had stowed the stolen pages of the visitors' book.

"I doubt that somehow," Rowland said. "Watts is particularly exclusive. Simpson doesn't seem to have a title of any sort."

"Common as muck, really." Milton rolled his eyes.

The expression reminded Rowland of something Josslyn Hay had told him. "We should speak with Allie's mother. Pierrepont died in her nightie. She, too, might have had reason to kill him."

"But she was at the residence in Belgravia when he died," Clyde protested. "You saw her."

"I saw her when I escorted Allie home, hours afterwards."

"We'd better call on Ethel, too," Edna mused. "She'll want to know what happened, and if Herr Von Kirsch spoke to the Winslow-Scotts, we'll need to warn her that they might never speak to her again."

Rowland yawned. "I don't think that will be a problem, Ed. I suspect Lady Winslow-Scott might find it very modern to have had a suspected murderer at one of her soirées."

When Rowland stepped out of his bedroom the next morning he found Clyde already up, working on his correspondence.

"Do give the lovely Miss Martinelli my regards," he said as he collected the post from a silver tray on the sideboard. Another vitriolic letter from the Fascist acolytes of William Joyce. He tossed it back on the tray.

"I'm afraid Rosie is quite irrational where you're concerned, mate." Clyde sighed. "So, I might have to give your regards amiss, if you don't mind."

"Really?" Rowland chose not to mention that he thought Rosalina Martinelli was irrational about more than just him. "What have I done?"

"You saw her naked."

"She was my life model!"

"I know, Rowly. But she's decided."

Rowland left it. It wasn't necessary that Rosalina like him. It was enough that she loved Clyde, who obviously hadn't seen her naked. He helped himself to the coffee on the sideboard, moving the hot silver pot away from Pierrepont's head in case it melted him.

"Are you certain you don't want to go home straight away, Clyde? I feel miserable about keeping you and Miss Martinelli apart."

"Look, Rowly." Clyde put down his pen and rubbed his face. "It's probably best I stay away for the moment."

"Why?"

"Rosie wants me to marry her. As soon as I get back she's going to expect..." Clyde shrugged despondently.

Rowland placed his coffee cup on its saucer. "Good Lord!" Clyde had been courting Rosie for barely a month before they'd left Sydney. He contained his astonishment and asked, "Don't you want to?"

"It's not a matter of if I want to, Rowly. We all know I'm batting well above my average with Rosie. I just don't see how we can. I don't have work. If it weren't for you, I'd still be on the wallaby scraping hardly enough to feed myself. Even if I could get work, it would mean I'd have to give up painting and that might just kill me."

Rowland said nothing. He could help—and he dearly wanted to—but he knew Clyde too well to even suggest it. The Sinclair fortune was vast enough to keep them all, and generally it did. But there were limits—imposed, not by Rowland, but by the dignity of the friends who enjoyed his patronage.

Clyde sighed. "I'm hoping that by the time we get back to Sydney, Rosie may have given up this marriage notion...for the time being, at least. One day I'm going to have to return to the real world, but God forgive me, I'm not ready yet." He looked Rowland in the eye. "So what I'm saying, mate, is don't feel bad about Rosie and me. I'm quite happy to write letters for a while."

Rowland sat back. "Fair enough. Just tell me when that changes." He pushed his hair back from his face, wondering what he was going to do when his friends returned to their real world. He checked his watch. "Are Milt and Ed—?"

"Still asleep I think." Clyde noted the tie protruding from Rowland's pocket. "Shall I give them a hoy?"

Rowland shook his head. "Let them be. It's early."

"Are you all right, Rowly?" Clyde asked.

"Yes, why wouldn't I be?"

"I dunno...Ed?"

Rowland smiled wryly. "I wasn't fool enough to imagine... well, not for long."

Clyde winced. "If Ed knew what she was doing to you—"

"She'd leave, mate." Rowland's voice was quiet but he was resolved. "This, I can live with. That, I could not."

Clyde exhaled. There was no point telling Rowland not to love Edna.

Rowland changed the subject. "How do you suppose we prove Mrs. Simpson was having an affair with Pierrepont?"

Clyde glanced down at what he was writing. "Letters," he said. "Women hold onto them, I'm told."

"I don't like our chances of ever seeing what Mrs. Simpson's kept, but what about Pierrepont?" Rowland gazed thoughtfully at the wax head. "I don't suppose you were sentimental, were you, old boy?"

"You said the secretaire was ajar, perhaps he was sitting in his nightie composing a love letter when the killer arrived."

Rowland blanched as the image came too easily to mind. "I wonder what happened to the papers that were stowed in the secretaire?"

"Wouldn't the police have taken them?"

Rowland stood. "I'll place a call through to the solicitors. Allen might be able to find out."

"Can you understand a word that pompous old codger says?" Clyde asked, shaking his head. "Sounds very clever and legal, but it's bloody Greek to me!"

Rowland smiled. "Latin, actually. I remember enough to make an educated guess most of the time."

The solicitor came to the telephone immediately and, though he had no information about the documents in the secretaire, he agreed to look into the matter.

"I was just about to 'phone you myself, Mr. Sinclair."

"Indeed. Has there been some development, Mr. Allen?"

"Not as such. My information is *non constat* and would therefore be nullified in a court of law. I was enjoying a social drink last evening with a chap from Barlowe, Ferguson and Associates—a reasonably respectable firm who were the late Lord Pierrepont's solicitors. Naturally, I tactfully enquired about the alleged amendments to Pierrepont's last will and testament... whether he had, in fact, approached them with *animo testandi*."

"And had he?"

"Yes, of course. You see, the Viscount of Pierrepont married. Under the *lex communis* of England, his nuptials effectively revoked all previous testamentary acts. He was in the process of writing a new will to ensure he did not die *intestatus*...which, in fact, he did, because the new will was not executed."

"I see. What does that mean in terms of his estate?"

"Even without a will, Lady Pierrepont is *prima facie* his next of kin. Therefore she has *jus ad rem* to his estate...though it is a bit of a mess. Presumably, they'll wait for the outcome of Miss Dawe's trial before probate is granted. But it does seem, according to this colleague of mine, who is probably not as discreet as a member of the Bar should be, that the draft of the will, which Pierrepont did not get round to signing, would in fact have been *contra* to Lady Pierrepont's interests. But of course he passed and *mortis ominia solvit*."

"Really?" Rowland said surprised and hopeful. "Do you mean to say Lady Pierrepont had good reason to prevent this new will being executed—more, it seems, than Allie?"

"Unfortunately, the new will did not favour Miss Dawe either. Presuming she was unaware of the legal technicality which revoked the old will, she had as much reason as Lady Pierrepont to fear the signing of those documents. To that extent they are what we in the profession call *pari passu*."

"Damn!"

"Yes, quite."

"Who would have benefited under the provisions of this new will?"

"Cecil Frederick Buchan, Earl of Bishopthorpe."

Chapter Twenty-four

Fascists On Trial

Riotous Assembly
BRUTAL ATTACKS

LONDON, Thursday

Sir Oswald Mosley and three other Black Shirts, including William Joyce, "Director of Fascist Propaganda," and Captain Budd, "West Sussex district officer," were committed for trial to-day on charges of riotous assembly arising out of the Fascist meeting at Worthing on October 9. Yesterday an assault charge against Mosley, arising out of the same affair, was dismissed. All pleaded not guilty. Seventy witnesses were examined, and the case occupied five days.

The prosecution alleged that the Black Shirts, under the leadership of the defendants, brutally attacked a crowd which hooted and cheered when they departed from the pavilion in which Mosley had addressed his supporters.

"False Police Evidence"

Mosley, in evidence in the assault case, aroused a strong protest when he said the prosecution was the result of political influence and false police evidence.

Nine Black Shirts were charged variously with assault and damage, and inciting to committing a breach of the peace at Fascist meetings at Plymouth.

Free Fight.

The prosecution alleged that a meeting on October 5, which was addressed by Mosley, developed into a free fight, in which press cameras were smashed, also that during an open-air meeting on October 11, the crowd heckled the speaker, who signalled to his colleagues to attack them. The victims included an octogenarian and a cripple.

It was also alleged that the Fascists were wearing body protectors and that their knuckles were bound with tape.

—*The Advocate*, 1934

The Earl of Bishopthorpe lived in an exclusive mansion block in Hampstead Village, Inner London. Delighted to receive a telephone call from Rowland Sinclair, he was more than happy to be at home for a visit from the Australians.

His suite was quite exquisitely styled. The decorative details, both internal and external, were elegant and distinctive and the space was furnished with an eclectic flair. Egyptian artefacts sat beside Ming vases beneath crystal chandeliers. Japanese paper screens provided a backdrop for Victorian armchairs upon which slept an extraordinary number of ginger cats.

The artworks which adorned his walls evidenced the discerning eye of an experienced collector. Rowland stood admiringly before a live-sized nude by the French academic artist William-Adolphe Bouguereau, whose traditionalist work had, in the last decade or so, fallen out of favour. Rowland's own style was closer to the Impressionist School to which Bouguereau had been so staunchly opposed, but it did not prevent the Australian from seeing genius in the work before him.

Each wall seemed to display a painting of breathtaking quality by an artist currently deemed unfashionable. Of course, fashions would change. Rowland began to realise that Buchan was not merely a collector, but an astute investor.

Buchan welcomed them like old and dear friends, demanding to know why they hadn't called before. Shooing the cats off the chairs, he invited them to sit and shouted to someone for cakes.

Politely, but without delay, Rowland told him why they'd called.

Buchan seemed neither surprised nor moved by Lord Pierrepont's testamentary gesture.

"Bunky was setting his affairs in order, I expect," he explained as a burly manservant wheeled in a silver samovar upon a traymobile. Buchan took the teapot from atop the elaborate urn and poured each of his guests a cup of dark brew. It was only after each had been offered milk and sugar—or, interestingly, jam—to sweeten their tea that he continued. "Bunky and I are distantly related—third cousins on his father's line. He has no progeny of his own and the title and what remains of the estate must of course pass to a male heir."

"I don't understand, Mr...Lord...Count...Buchan," Edna said moving over to make room for an indignant cat. "Why did Lord Pierrepont suddenly wish to leave no provision for his niece and her mother?"

"Oh, he didn't. He adored little Allie. Poor Bunky knew full well I'd see the girl and her mother right. I daresay the will was about confirming that I was his heir. Perhaps he was concerned someone else would make a claim." Buchan crossed his legs and balanced his teacup on his knee. "I can only imagine the original will was made some years ago before Bunky knew I existed, when he thought the line would end and he could distribute his assets as he pleased."

"How long have you known Pierrepont, Lord Bishopthorpe?" Rowland asked, using the correct title for the elucidation of his companions.

Buchan pursed his lips. "I thought I asked you to call me *Countess*." He leaned across and rubbed Rowland's arm. "Try and remember, lovely. Lord Bishopthorpe sounds so morally foreboding. I've known Pierrepont for 'bout five years. We rubbed along tremendously well."

"Then why did he wait so long to make a will declaring you his heir?" Rowland persisted.

Buchan waited expectantly, motioning Rowland to keep talking.

"Er...Countess?" Rowland added.

"Better!" Buchan declared triumphantly. "I really can't say why he bothered at all. The entailment is set in law. He couldn't change it if he wanted to."

"And if Pierrepont were to have a child?" Milton posed carefully.

"You're alluding to the new Lady Pierrepont, I gather. I had heard—it seems Bunky was a bit of a dark horse. If she has managed to conceive already and the child is male, he will inherit the title and the estate, of course. But you mustn't worry about little Miss Dawe and her mother. I will look after them notwithstanding the anomalies of entitlement. I sent my solicitors as soon as I heard she'd been arrested, but I'm told dear Mr. Sinclair had already organised excellent representation. To be honest, I don't need Bunky's wealth, which was, I suspect, minimal, considering the fact that I was about to loan him quite a tidy sum to meet his obligations."

"And his title?" Clyde asked.

Buchan laughed. "Bless you, poppet. You have no idea, do you? It's really quite lovely in a way." He put his tea on the smoking stand beside him and rested his elbows on his knees gazing adoringly at Clyde. "Even if I were to care about such things, my own title is superior to Bunky's."

Clyde frowned. "So, if all of this is preordained, why was Pierrepont having a new will drafted at all?"

Buchan shrugged. "Perhaps it was just to avoid intestacy—penalties, that sort of bother."

"Is Allie—Miss Dawe, aware of all this?"

"One can never be sure, but I doubt it. Bunky didn't consider her particularly clever. I would be surprised if he discussed his affairs with her."

"You're a member at Watts," Milton said, remembering the entry in the stolen pages of the visitors' book.

"Oh, yes. I 'inherited' my membership with my title, so to speak. I rarely go there...dull little place, really."

"Do you know Lady Pierrepont's family? I believe Lord Harcourt is a member of Watts, too." Rowland absently stroked the cat that had settled into his lap.

"Good Lord, Fruity Harcourt? Yes, everyone knows him, though he keeps to his own set. A club within the club, so to speak—call themselves the 'Callow Cads' or some such juvenile title to announce how very witty they are." Buchan folded his arms and rolled his eyes. "Harcourt himself is a very proper sort of chap. I'm surprised he let his sister marry a rogue like Pierrepont."

Rowland frowned. This was all getting more murky and convoluted. "Lord Bish...*Countess*," he said, correcting himself, "do you have any idea who might have wanted to kill Lord Pierrepont?"

Buchan smiled happily and mouthed, "Oh, bless you," as he flapped a hand in Rowland's direction. Then he cupped his chin in his hand and screwed up his face, concentrating, contemplating. Seconds passed as they waited for his revelation.

"We've all wanted to kill Bunky from time to time," he said finally. "He could be quite vexing. Beyond that, I might as well draw a name from a hat!"

They had intended to stop only briefly at Claridge's to check for messages before going out again in pursuit of anything that might aid Allie Dawe's case. Circumstances, however, saw those plans abandoned.

The motor taxi stopped on the other side of Brook Street as the verge outside the hotel's entrance was congested.

"Wonder what that's about." Rowland and Clyde alighted first. Horns blared, traffic slowed and swerved to get past. Clearly, the parked vehicles were causing an obstruction.

Clyde shrugged. "Some toff who thinks he can park wherever he likes, I presume."

"Hurry up, Ed!" Milton held the car door open for the sculptress who had stopped to adjust her hat.

Rowland was paying the driver when the gang of Blackshirts emerged.

"Rowly," Clyde warned as they approached.

Rowland turned—about a dozen men, among them a man with a curved scar from lip to ear: Joyce.

Realising they'd been seen, the Blackshirts began to run towards the taxi, dodging through the oncoming traffic. Milton slammed the taxi door shut with Edna still inside.

"Go!" Rowland said, tossing his entire pocketbook at the driver. "Now!"

Seeing what was coming, the driver did not hesitate and screeched away before Edna had time to object.

Milton and Clyde stood with Rowland as the Blackshirts surrounded them.

"What is it you want, Joyce?" Rowland asked with frosty control and undisguised contempt.

"I did say I'd come for you," Joyce sneered. "And I am a man of my word."

"I received your letters," Rowland said disdainfully. "Sir Oswald must be very proud of your penmanship."

"We have unfinished business, Sinclair."

"The man can only use one arm, you Fascist coward!" Milton spat.

Joyce swore at the poet. "It behoves you to remember that you are the criminal refuse of Britain—thieves and murderers expelled to the most godforsaken end of the Earth in the hope of removing the stain of your birth from England's fair soils. Who do you think you are, dictating to Britons with your Bolshevik malcontent?"

Clyde was possibly less eloquent in response, but quite clear in his sentiments. He threatened to "behove" Joyce in the nose. It was, in fact, hard to know who struck the first physical blow. The confrontation just seemed to explode. Onlookers screamed and tyres squealed as the fighting fell back onto the road. The Australians were realistic—the odds were ugly and they expected to come out badly. Knowing Rowland was Joyce's target, both Clyde and Milton grappled and clawed through the fracas to keep within arm's-length of their friend. But the Fascists quickly succeeded in isolating each man. Rowland hit the ground after Milton had been felled. For a moment Rowland could see nothing but boots as he tried to protect his head. He twisted as a blow caught him in the ribs and then a boot came down on his chest. Instinctively he brought up his plastered arm to protect himself and it caught the full weight of the strike. He heard a crack. Winded, Rowland lay on the ground gagging, unable to move. Joyce stood over him, gloating. Rowland braced himself.

And then, it changed—the arrival of help—men in flat caps and braces, waving what appeared to be dismembered body parts. They ran headlong into the fray screaming like barbarian warriors caught up in some medieval charge into war. Rowland wondered if he was hallucinating.

Joyce reeled as he was slammed with a leg. A woman's scream. Edna's voice. Rowland rolled onto his front. Someone kicked him in the back and Joyce fell upon him again, only to be pelted once more by men wielding limbs. Some appendages shattered on impact, others bent. Nonetheless, they were heavy enough to force the Fascists back. Long before the first police constable arrived, the Blackshirts were in flight, abandoning the scene in their vehicles as heads were launched at their backs like surreal cannonballs.

Rowland sat up slowly, dazed and uncertain of what had happened. He wiped the blood off his lip and looked for his companions. The Fascists were gone, half-a-dozen dishevelled young men and a few boys in their place...all holding limbs. He might have stopped to wonder about it, if he hadn't then glimpsed Edna kneeling over the motionless body of Milton Isaacs.

Chapter Twenty-five

Fashion's Puppets

Lay Figures of Today

By Elizabeth George

The evolution of the contemporary mannequin from wax dolls which once used to pass from Paris to London to display the cut of a dandy's vest is one of the lesser triumphs of our day, but even more interesting, from a romantic point of view, is the modern lay figure. At the recent London Exhibition of Men's and Women's Fashions, the lay figures were quite as remarkable as the designs of the clothes themselves. Wooden and immobile, they yet contrived to look more expressive than the most alluring mannequin. Art, with its uncanny power of embodying abstract ideas, has given them the authentic air of modern youth—sophisticated, intelligent, and unexpectedly wistful.

Of another age again are those old fashioned blondes with diminutive waists which were once the pride of drapers' windows. Their bust measurements would fill a prima donna with envy, and their painted smiles have an unabashed coquetry which is almost alarming.

> Perhaps the type of the "New Woman" which "Punch" once delighted in, was a reaction from this ideal of the nation's shop window. Impossible to imagine them wearing shorts or displaying tennis frocks, these simpering and elegant damsels of plaster.
>
> —*The Advertiser*, 1933

Rowland scrambled to his feet. A boy of about fourteen helped him steady himself. "It's all right, sir," the boy assured him, pointing to the man now bending over Milton. "My uncle's a doctor."

"Rowly, what the hell?" Clyde, too, was battered and confused, but standing.

The police now arrived in force, summoned by Claridge's and panicked bystanders who feared they were witnessing the beginnings of another Blackshirt riot.

Milton was carried into Claridge's while Rowland and Clyde spoke to the police. Anxious to see after the poet, their statements were hurried and concise. Rowland volunteered the name of William Joyce, but he had recognised none of the others.

The men who had come to their aid began to collect up the broken limbs which littered Brook Street. And finally Rowland realised that their saviours had used mannequin parts as weapons—some plaster, some wax. The plaster arms and legs were shattered, the wax misshapen. In the midst of it all, Rowland recognised the tailor Beresford had found for them when they had first arrived in London.

"Mr. Ambrose?"

"Mr. Sinclair! Are you all right?"

"Yes, I believe so." Rowland was still not sure what to make of it all.

"Your suits will need some repair, I think," Ambrose said, dusting plaster off the torn shoulder of Rowland's jacket. "It's fortunate I was delivering another suit in the van."

He introduced his sons, six men and the boy whose name was Elliot. Two more youths were apparently his nephews. It seemed that, in addition to tailoring, the Ambroses conducted a business which produced mannequins for boutiques and clothing stores across London. They had been making their way to Harrods Department Store with a batch of mannequins for a large window display when the tailor had thought to drop off the additional shirts and suits he'd made for the Australians staying at Claridge's. And so it happened that they came across the brawl.

"We didn't know it was you, of course, Mr. Sinclair," Ambrose confided. "We saw black uniforms and knew immediately there would be someone in need of help."

Rowland thanked them all, sincerely and profusely. He offered to pay for the damage to their mannequins, but Ambrose would not hear of it. "I have run from Fascists once, but never again."

"Well, then you must all join us for a drink at least," Rowland insisted. "Please. Mr. Isaacs will want to thank you, too. God knows what might have happened if you hadn't intervened."

"We are not dressed for the bar at Claridge's," Ambrose said uncertainly.

"You're dressed well enough for my suite. I will have refreshments sent up."

Eventually Ambrose nodded. "Very well—I am also anxious to see that Mr. Isaacs is not badly hurt."

Ambrose, his sons and nephews stowed the salvageable limbs into a pair of Bedford vans with *Ambrose Bros. Shop Décor* emblazoned on their sides. Then, self-consciously dusting themselves off, they trooped behind Rowland and Clyde, into the chequerboard marble interior of Claridge's foyer.

If the hotel staff were at all alarmed by the bloodied state of their guests, or the men who accompanied them—some of whom were not even wearing ties—they showed no sign of it. They received them all as if they were the visiting dignitaries or travelling aristocrats who were Claridge's usual clientele.

Milton had been taken up to the suite already, under the care of Ambrose's brother, who, although now in the business of mannequins, had trained as a physician.

The poet had regained consciousness by the time they walked in. Ambrose, the doctor, was inserting a few small neat stitches into a gash near his temple.

Milton waved away their concern.

"You were knocked unconscious, Mr. Isaacs," Ambrose chided. "It is a serious thing."

"I didn't get knocked out," Milton said adamantly. "I fainted when I saw that a crazed lunatic had hacked off some poor bloke's arm and was using the limb to belt a Blackshirt!" He winced as Ambrose bandaged his head. "They're not going to believe this back at Trades Hall."

Edna—who'd alighted from the taxi as soon as she could persuade the driver to stop—had returned to Brook Street in time to witness Milton hit his head on the curb as he fell. She watched him now, pale and still shaken. "I thought they'd killed you, you idiot," she said, as if it were his fault.

Milton smiled weakly. "Die not, poor death, nor yet canst thou kill me."

"Donne," Rowland murmured, relieved.

"We are, we are indeed," the doctor declared as the suite's unflappable butler served refreshments. A waiter from the restaurant delivered several tiered silver trays of finger sandwiches and fancy cakes presented with such a delicate flair that one might have thought Rowland was entertaining the Queen Mother, as opposed to several burly men.

The tailor's sons gathered about the head of Pierrepont, admiring the skill of the sculptor. They did not appear to wonder at all what the Australians were doing with a wax head. The eldest of them confessed that he dreamed of working for Madame Tussaud's, and Edna told him of what she had learned from Marriott Spencer. She promised to mention the young man's name to Spencer when next she saw the sculptor.

With Milton seen to, Dr. Ambrose turned his attention to Clyde and Rowland. "Your cast is broken, Mr. Sinclair."

Rowland looked down and saw that the plaster had indeed cracked. He wiggled his fingertips—the arm itself seemed fine.

"It'll have to come off," Ambrose said, poking at the crack with his pen. "We can put on a new cast for you—something not quite so excessive."

"Excessive?"

"The physician who made this, I suspect, has invested heavily in plaster of Paris!" Ambrose tapped the cast with his knuckles. "We don't use this much plaster on the mannequins!"

Before Rowland could respond, Ambrose the tailor had sent his youngest son back to the vans to fetch bandages and plaster powder, both of which they apparently used to repair mannequins from time to time.

The doctor put his thumbs into the wide crack and, with a little grunting and leverage, broke the cast off Rowland's arm.

Rowland was able to flex his arm at the elbow, and scratch below it for the first time in over three weeks.

"Stop waving your arm about, Mr. Sinclair." Dr. Ambrose scowled. "The bones have knitted, yes; but the join will be weak and easily rebroken!"

Suitably chastised, Rowland sat meekly as he waited for Ambrose to begin.

"You'll have to remove your shirt, Mr. Sinclair."

Rowland was startled. "Is that really necessary?"

"I'm sure Miss Higgins will avert her eyes."

"No, that's not—"

"Remove your shirt, Mr. Sinclair. We are wasting the day!"

Uneasily, Rowland slipped his right arm—now free of the cast—out of its rolled sleeve. He left the rest of the shirt in place, cringingly aware that the swastika of burn scars would be revealed if he removed it entirely.

"I thought I asked you to…" Ambrose pulled at the shirt. He saw the scarring and stopped, staring. Rowland wasn't sure what to say. Ambrose swallowed, shook his head, and replaced the shirt to cover the scar before it was seen by anyone else. "Yes, that much will be fine…there is no reason for you to get cold." He clasped Rowland's shoulder but said nothing more about the Nazi brand.

Gently now, the mannequin-maker cleaned Rowland's arm and wrapped it with padding, before encasing the limb with bandages soaked in plaster of Paris. It seemed each of the near-dozen Ambroses had an opinion about how thick the new cast should be or how tightly bound. The discussion became quite heated at points. Rowland stayed out of it, deciding that he was qualified neither as a doctor nor as a mannequin-maker on the subject.

Ambrose the Tailor insisted that the cast taper at the wrist to have some chance of accommodating a cuff. Ambrose the Doctor was adamant that the old cast had been over-engineered and that a lighter version, which began below the elbow, encasing the palm but not the fingers, would be more than sufficient and not waste plaster.

Through this, Menzies continued to serve drinks and tea, and pass around the petits fours.

"If I may be so bold as to enquire," Ambrose the Tailor asked as they waited for the plaster to harden, "what business has the British Union of Fascists with you gentlemen?" He addressed the question particularly at Milton who, having been forbidden alcohol, was dulling his headache with tea.

Milton looked up. "It wasn't about me," he said. "Well, not directly. I'm sure they thought I was just a particularly handsome Protestant. The useless mongrels were after Rowly here."

Rowland explained briefly his encounter with the Blackshirts at the London Economic Conference.

The Ambrose brothers glanced at each other.

"We were German once," Ambrose the Tailor told them. "We came to London a year ago. Abel leaves his practice behind, I leave my factory. In Berlin you once had to wait many months to become a patient of Abel Ambrose." Clearly the tailor was proud of his brother.

"Do you have a surgery here, Dr. Ambrose?" Edna asked.

"No. Now I make mannequins."

"But why?"

Abel Ambrose smiled sadly. "We learned that some professions are more visible than others…and more dangerous. We are a cautious family."

Edna's eyes softened. They had heard stories of the persecution of Jewish doctors when they were in Munich. "But this is England," she said gently.

"I like to make mannequins. Nowhere else in England will you get such strong, lifelike figures!"

"Jolly lucky for us," Rowland said.

"We were pleased to assist." The doctor chuckled. "The looks on their faces when we came running with arms and legs…we will tell that story again." They talked of the battle, laughing and toasting the small victory in Brook Street.

"We must be going," Ambrose the Tailor sighed after a time, gathering up for repair all the jackets the Australians had been wearing. "There is still a window at Harrods that we must dress somehow."

Dr. Ambrose gave Rowland a card. "I am not licensed to practise here, but if you need any further plasterwork done, by all means, call by the factory."

Rowland and his companions remained in the hotel that evening. Their investigations could wait till the next morning when their heads would be clearer. Though Rowland suggested they call Pennyworth—the doctor Wilfred had sent them when they'd first arrived in London—for Milton as a precaution, the poet himself would not hear of it.

"Why would Ambrose wander about pretending to be a doctor? It's not as if he were trying to impress a girl."

"That's true, but he hasn't a licence to practise."

"Licences," Milton sniffed. "You know some people claim I'm not a poet simply because my genius is not documented. It's outrageous!"

"*They* say you're not a poet because you don't actually write anything," Clyde informed him. "And they have a bloody point!"

"Well, if Ambrose isn't really a doctor, he should be!" Milton declared. "And he's a damn fine plasterer. You'll be able to hold your notebook again, Rowly."

On that score, and probably the other, Rowland had to agree. He had much more movement with the refashioned cast, and it was a good deal less heavy. He barely required the sling now.

Clyde eased himself into an armchair, grimacing as his bruised body sank into the cushions. "We're getting too old for this," he muttered.

"I'm sorry," Rowland said. "I should have paid more attention to those letters. This is my fault."

"Don't be daft," Milton said with his eyes closed. "Who would have thought Joyce was so petty as to hunt you down? But then, those militant Fascist types have always been bloody obsessive."

"Ethel said something about his holding Communist Jews responsible for what happened to his face," Edna placed a cushion behind Milton's back.

"You don't suppose the Fascists had anything to do with Pierrepont's death, do you, Rowly?" Clyde asked, gazing thoughtfully at the wax head. "Perhaps this had nothing to do with his will or his women. It could be that this is all about the conference."

"It's possible," Rowland admitted, "but Joyce and his band of fools seem much more likely to have cornered Pierrepont in the street and beaten the living dickens out of him."

"Are there any Fascists among the members of Watts?"

"I'm sure there are several, but sadly there's no way to tell simply by virtue of an entry in the visitors' book."

"Allie said that Lord Pierrepont donated a hundred guineas to the B.U.F.," Edna reminded them. "Why would they want to kill him?"

Rowland nodded. Edna was right. The B.U.F. was just an annoying distraction.

"Do you think they'll come for you again?" she asked anxiously.

Rowland was about to dismiss her concern, when it occurred to him that ignoring the letters he'd received had not been the best idea. "They'll arrest Joyce, at least," he said eventually. Though he and Clyde had given the constables descriptions of some of the others, it was doubtful that anybody but Joyce would be charged. "And we'll just have to be careful."

"If you'll excuse me, sir," the butler interrupted, "perhaps I could show alternative routes by which you might enter or leave Claridge's in the future."

"Thank you, Menzies," Rowland said a little startled. The valet seemed to overhear everything...he was not yet used to it.

"It will ensure these gentlemen are not able to keep an eye on your comings and goings," Menzies continued. "We have used the routes in the past when we were looking after guests of particular celebrity."

"That's a terribly good idea, Menzies, old mate," Milton said with his eyes still closed.

"Very good, sir."

Edna sat on the coffee table, as Milton had commandeered the couch and refused to make room. "What are we going to do next, Rowly?"

Rowland frowned. He had been pondering that very question himself. Allie Dawe still languished in Holloway Prison and it seemed they were the only people who cared. His mind moved to the American woman who, according to Ethel Bruce's sources, had been embroiled in an affair with Pierrepont. "First thing tomorrow, we'll see what we can find out about the Simpsons."

Chapter Twenty-six

The Royal Supplement

With today's issue is published a special Royal supplement containing full details of all the arrangements connected with the visit to Australia of Prince Henry, Duke of Gloucester.

Life Story of the Duke

...On his first safari the Duke, who was attended by a party of only about 30, secured 36 kinds of various game in 17 days. One of his trophies was a magnificent specimen of an African lioness. It cost him a great deal of arduous toiling through the bush country and the kill was not without its thrill. The Duke and his equerry had stalked their quarry to a water hole and the lioness was about to spring when the Duke fired and killed her. An American paper describing this incident, in the typical picturesque journalese of the United States, told how the Duke had come within an ace of losing his Royal life in the hungry jaws of a "tiger." It said that he fired, at the last second, almost into the mouth of the "striped terror of the jungle." The Duke would be a very proud man indeed if he were able to say that he had brought down a tiger in Africa.

—*The Daily News*, 1934

The invitation was presented to Rowland at breakfast, with the information that the servant who delivered it was waiting for an answer.

"Who is it from, Rowly?" Milton asked, cutting into poached eggs.

"Theophrastus Thistlewaite, Baron Harcourt," Rowland said, reading through the handwritten note. The penmanship was neat and precise, the signature tight and small. "He'd like me to call by his house in London this morning, if it's at all convenient."

"Euphemia—Lady Pierrepont's brother?" Edna asked.

"He is, indeed."

Rowland sent a reply that he would be pleased to call upon Harcourt at about ten.

"One of us should go with you," Clyde said, passing the sugar bowl to Edna.

Rowland shook his head. "There's no need. You chaps visit Allie as we planned." He glanced over to the wax head, which presided over breakfast from the sideboard. "I'll take Pierrepont to keep me company."

"You're taking the head?"

"Euphemia might have changed her mind…and I'm curious as to what Harcourt might divulge with respect to his dear sister's mental state."

Clyde looked worried. "You be careful, mate. I have sisters. We brothers can be protective."

Rowland nodded. "Consider me forewarned."

Rowland departed Claridge's through the back corridors the butler had shown them. "Guests are not technically permitted to use these parts of the hotel, sir, so if you wouldn't mind being discreet."

"Of course…thank you, Menzies."

A motor taxi met him around the corner as arranged, and Rowland gave the driver the address of Harcourt's house in

Park Lane. Having decided that a man could not carry a hatbox through London without looking ridiculous, Rowland took Pierrepont in a Gladstone bag.

Arundel House stood among other mansions on the south-east corner of Hyde Park. A chic and highly desirable address which afforded views of the park and neighbours of a certain class. The house itself was a Tudor construction of a size and architecture that may have been remarkable in a less salubrious location. As it was, it did not seem in any way lesser than the houses that surrounded it, which was saying something indeed.

The footman who answered the door took Rowland into a cavernous hall, hung with the oil images of Harcourts past and the mounted heads of large game. Rowland walked through the room while he waited for Theophrastus Thistlewaite, studying the generations depicted on the high panelled walls. He read the brass plates on each gold-gilded frame, the various Barons of Harcourt and the Baronets of Salisbury, Asquith, and Merivale.

Arranged on an inlaid cabinet, was a collection of modern portraits, photographs of a girl at various stages of her life, from infancy to adulthood. Rowland recognised Euphemia Thistlewaite with her excessive teeth—as a small child holding kittens, dressed in hunting pinks astride a horse, and, intriguingly, in a fencing uniform with a foil in her hand. The only image not of her was a group portrait of several men etched on porcelain with the words "the Kalokagathia" inscribed below.

Rowland smiled, realising that the Kalokagathia was probably what Buchan meant by "the Callow Cads." Rowland's knowledge of ancient Greek was rudimentary, but he was sure the term translated roughly as "noble society"—a more likely, if less accurate, name for a gentlemen's drinking club, he supposed.

"Mr. Sinclair, I am so sorry to have kept you waiting. How do you do?" Lord Harcourt strode into the room and approached with his arm extended—he was a well-proportioned figure with a confident carriage and immaculate grooming.

Rowland took the proffered hand. The mannequin-maker's minimal cast enabled him to accept a handshake now. Indeed, he had discarded the sling that morning as the new cast felt so light.

"Oh, I say, you've been injured," Harcourt said as his palm made contact with the plaster.

"Yes. I apologise. My handshake is still a little awkward."

"Not at all. I broke a clavicle coming off a polo pony last season. Damned nuisance, I can tell you!"

Harcourt invited him to take one of the Victorian armchairs clustered around the skin of a zebra spread flat on the floor. Briefly, Rowland glanced around the room to see if the beast's head was mounted on a wall somewhere. It was.

Harcourt called for tea, though he offered his guest something stronger first. The Baron, it seemed, did not drink. Rowland declined, hoping that he would not regret the decision to forgo alcoholic fortification at some later point in the conversation. Thus far, his host seemed quite regular, even friendly.

Harcourt pointed out the African wildlife now decorating his walls, which he had apparently shot on safari in a party accompanying Prince Henry, now the Duke of Gloucester. He chatted amiably, enquiring about Australian game.

"We have plenty of rabbits," Rowland offered. "And snakes… but I can't think of anything else you'd want to shoot."

Harcourt laughed as he helped himself to bread and butter which had been served with multi-layered cake and a tray of boiled and garnished eggs. "I did hear somewhere that the bunnies were taking over the colony. Now, Mr. Sinclair, I suppose you are wondering on what business I asked you to visit me?"

Rowland nodded. "I presume it is to do with Pierrepont."

"Most certainly, yes! I understand you do not concur with the constabulary's opinion with respect to who murdered my beloved brother-in-law."

Rowland tensed, surprised that Harcourt would know such a thing.

The lord smiled. "Word gets around, old man! We are all subject to the relentless run of rumour."

"I do not believe Miss Dawe killed anyone," Rowland said carefully.

Harcourt leaned forward. "Well, who do you believe topped Pierrepont, Sinclair?"

"I don't know," Rowland admitted after a moment's pause, "but, unlike the police, I am determined to find out."

"Why do you think it could not be Miss Dawe?"

"What motive would she have to murder her only means of support? As far as I can tell, Pierrepont has been nothing but kind to Allie and her mother."

Harcourt bounced his head from side to side, as if he was weighing up Rowland's words.

Finally, he said, "I can see, Sinclair, that you are acting out of a genuine sense of justice and kindness, and for that reason I am going to allow you into a confidence. This is something I found out only recently through my poor sister."

"Go on."

"Lord Pierrepont—as you may well have discovered—had something of a playboy's reputation. As much as I hate to speak ill of the dead, I must say that before he met my sister, he was not a particularly moral man, and a slave to certain…appetites."

"I see."

"Poor Miss Dawe, dependent on him for the roof over her head, was at his mercy."

Rowland stared at him. "Are you saying…?"

"Yes, I am."

"That's abominable! My God, she's his niece!"

"You can understand the shame of the situation and her consequent desperation."

"You are suggesting Allie murdered Pierrepont to—"

"Avenge past outrages and prevent future ones. It was a desperate act of self-defence against a despicable incest."

For a time, Rowland sat silent, shocked by the revelation. Could Pierrepont have been so evil? He resisted believing it, for Allie's sake. "If that was the case, Lord Harcourt, why would Miss Dawe not have said so in her own defence?"

"Perhaps she will, perhaps she would prefer to hang than have the fact known."

Rowland shook his head. "No, that's insane. She's terrified. Lady Pierrepont told you this?"

"It seems the love of my sister reformed Lord Pierrepont and he regretted the contemptible crimes of his past. Of course, the burden of his confession has all but destroyed poor Euphemia."

Rowland studied his host. "I called on your sister at Bletchley Park."

"I know. You have clearly seen then what this horror has done to her emotional state."

"I have also seen her physical state, Lord Harcourt."

Harcourt bristled. "Euphemia is not worldly. She is an innocent, brilliant but naive." He paused, exhaling like an angry bull. "As I said, Pierrepont was not always a gentleman! He did, however, do the right thing by Euphemia in the end."

"Why are you telling me this, Lord Harcourt?"

"As you might have gathered, Mr. Sinclair, there are several scandals buried with Lord Pierrepont." Harcourt sat forward on the very edge of his seat. "It's probably best for all concerned if they remain buried."

"I doubt it's best for Miss Dawe."

"I feel sorry for the girl. I do. But she did kill a man, Sinclair. Revealing the circumstances will just make her more notorious, more reviled. And it will ruin my sister as well."

"What exactly are you asking, sir?"

"I'm asking you to leave these sordid matters well alone, to realise that your meddling will only make it worse—destroy two women instead of one." Harcourt looked him directly in the eye. "I love my sister, Sinclair. She has never been strong… my brother and I have protected her all our lives. If this comes out, it will ruin her and her unborn child, and I fear her mental health will never recover. I know you have some attachment to Miss Dawe, but I am given to understand that the Crown case against her is clear and robust. This is not a miscarriage of justice but a simply a sorry state of affairs." Harcourt put his cards on the table. "If you will leave this alone, I give you my word as a gentleman that I will use all my influence to ensure Miss Dawe's sentence is as lenient as the law will allow."

Rowland pulled back. "And if I don't?"

"Then two young women will be destroyed and one will probably hang. I'm not asking you to do anything illegal or immoral, Mr. Sinclair, simply to allow justice to run its natural course without dragging into public view shameful secrets that will have no impact whatsoever on the outcome of these tragic circumstances."

Rowland shook his head. "I don't believe Miss Dawe murdered Lord Pierrepont."

"Perhaps you underestimate the fairer sex, Mr. Sinclair. They are not so prone to overt displays of violence as we men, but, backed into a corner, they will fight as fiercely as any man."

Rowland hesitated. Edna had fired a gun in his defence. Of course, she had only managed to shoot him, but that was beside the point. And in Munich his life had been saved by the fact that a young woman had killed his attacker. Could he be sure what Allie would do, how far she would go, to defend herself?

"Consider it, Mr. Sinclair." Harcourt's voice was thick with emotion. "Let us work together to save both Miss Dawe and Euphemia."

"I shall think about your proposal, Lord Harcourt," Rowland said slowly. He stood and retrieved the Gladstone bag which he'd placed by his chair. It seemed heavier now—with the head of a monster rather than a victim.

"Thank you, sir," Harcourt said, grabbing Rowland's hand and pumping it warmly. "Thank you. We both want the best for all parties concerned. I'm sure you'll see that this is the only tolerable way forward."

Rowland declined Harcourt's offer to have him driven back to Claridge's. He headed instead into Hyde Park to walk and think. On this occasion he did not even pause to glance at the columned grandeur of the entrance to the park. Nor did he notice the first golds and pinks of impending Autumn which touched the birches and tall limes that lined formal avenues and whispered of an early winter. The encounter with Harcourt had not been what he'd expected, and the lord's revelations disturbed him deeply. Did it fit? Could the poor girl, abused and violated by her own uncle, have been driven to such desperate lengths?

It occurred to him that there'd been no signs of struggle in Pierrepont's suite at Watts. The viscount had possibly known his murderer well enough not to be alarmed…despite the fact he was wearing a woman's nightie. Could the murder have taken place in the throes of some illicit and unnatural liaison?

Rowland stopped by a colossal figure of Achilles—the Wellington Monument—to slip the coins in his pockets into the hands of those who begged in the statue's shade. He knew artists who now begged to survive, who would no longer talk to him for shame or because they had come to hate him for the inequity with which fate had treated them.

A thin, ragged man asked Rowland for a cigarette.

"I'm sorry, mate, I don't smoke."

At first the beggar seemed a little taken aback—perhaps by the fact that Rowland didn't smoke or because a gentleman had called him mate. Then he produced a stub from his pocket. "What about a light?"

Rowland put down the Gladstone bag as he retrieved the lighter he kept in his breast pocket.

The man moved quickly, snatching the bag and shouldering Rowland in the chest in the same explosive movement. Rowland fell backwards, hitting the ground hard as the thief ran into the park.

There were shouts of "Stop him!" and "Thief!"

One of the men to whom Rowland had just given a coin offered him a hand. "Are you hurt, sir?"

Rowland took the hand and pulled himself up. "No, not at all," he said, slapping the dirt off his trousers. "Thank you, Mr…?

"Brown. John Brown, sir."

"Rowland Sinclair, Mr. Brown."

Another man handed him his hat. "The blighter's long gone with your bag, sir."

Rowland scanned the parklands about the monument. It did indeed seem that way. "I don't suppose you gentlemen know who he was?"

Either the men didn't or they were unwilling to tell him.

Rowland smiled ruefully. The thief was going to get a fair shock when he opened the bag.

"Shall I get a constable?" Brown asked nervously.

Rowland shook his head. "No. There probably isn't much point." He rubbed his hand through his hair before replacing his hat.

"You should be more careful, sir," Brown said. "There are plenty of desperate men in Hyde Park."

Rowland nodded. He had been preoccupied and now he'd lost Pierrepont's head.

Brown and his companion shook Rowland's hand, refused to take any further gratuity in appreciation of their help, and left him to contemplate his course.

Despite the scuffle and the theft, Rowland's mind returned easily to his troubles. He could see that persisting with his enquiries could well be worse in the end for Allie...but only if she had in fact killed her uncle. If she hadn't, then he and his friends might be her only hope. He frowned, realising the decision was not rightfully his.

Turning back, Rowland made his way towards Hyde Park Corner, and hailed one of the black taxis which often dropped well-to-do tourists at the famous botanical park. He asked the driver to take him directly to Holloway Prison.

Chapter Twenty-seven

New Scheme

Scotland Yard
CRIME DETECTION

LONDON, October 25

The Home Office has decided to speed up the detection of crime by the establishment of a national detective force at Scotland Yard, according to the "News-Chronicle". At present Scotland Yard officers are unable to investigate a crime that is committed outside London unless they are specially requested to do so by the local authorities. The new scheme will permit an immediate investigation by Scotland Yard men anywhere.

—*The Courier Mail*, 1933

Visiting Allie Dawe proved difficult. The accused had already received visitors that day and the demands of Rowland Sinclair were most irregular. Rowland telephoned George Allen from the prison. An hour or so later—during which time Rowland presumed the solicitor was making calls, promises, and threats in the fine and age-old tradition of his profession—he was taken to the reception cell.

Rowland readied himself for the conversation he was about to have.

Allie embraced him, clinging desperately until the guard pulled her away and directed them to chairs on different sides of the wooden table. Rowland felt ill. He wasn't sure how he was going to ask the girl if what Harcourt had said was true.

"I knew you hadn't forgotten me, Mr. Sinclair!" Allie was already emotional. "When your friends came without you earlier, I wondered if you were staying away for the sake of your reputation…and I would have understood if you had. What people think of you is so important and I know I'm…but I'm so glad you came. I think not seeing you would be one deprivation more than I could bear."

Rowland rubbed his face as he listened to her ramble.

"Miss Dawe," he said. "I need to ask you something very personal and you must forgive me for asking. I wouldn't think of it if it weren't important. Whatever your answer, it will help me know what to do, how best to help you."

"You don't have to ask," she said quickly. "I love you! I do. I'll marry you."

Rowland stopped, unable at that moment to imagine how the situation could be any worse. "Miss Dawe…Allie, you barely know me. I know you're frightened but I won't abandon you…I promise. We don't have to be married for me to help you. However, I do have to ensure that what I'm doing is helping and not hurting your cause."

Allie flushed red, embarrassed and confused. "You don't want to...you weren't…oh."

"I called on Lord Harcourt this morning. His sister Euphemia married Lord Pierrepont shortly before he died."

"Tommy rot! That's not true. I would have known if Uncle Alfred had married."

"I'm afraid it is true." Rowland told her then what Harcourt had claimed. He spoke quickly but plainly, ashamed of asking and in dread of her response.

The colour drained from Allie's face, and her mouth moved soundlessly until she seemed a spectre of the excited girl who'd taken to the stage and sung hymns at the ball for men.

And then the sound came, raw and broken. "What precisely are you asking, Mr. Sinclair? If I killed my uncle or if I was his… his whore?" She stood and screamed. "Get out, get out, get out!"

The guard opened the door to the reception cell and called into the corridor for help.

Rowland stood. "Allie, please…I'm sorry."

She was crying now, hysterical. "Get out! I never want to see you again!" She lashed out trying to reach him over the table. The guard stepped decisively to restrain her and she fought him.

"Stop, don't hurt her," Rowland moved to her aid.

Another guard intervened to hold him back. "Just let us handle this, sir," he said as two more guards ran into the cell. One assisted his colleague to drag Allie away, sobbing and clawing, and the other helped keep the object of her fury from trying to defend her.

If Allen had not appeared, Rowland might well have been arrested. How the solicitor calmed the situation, Rowland knew not, except that there was a great deal of Latin involved.

Guilt-ridden now, Rowland explained himself.

George Allen shook his head sternly. "You really should have brought this information to me *ab initio*, Mr. Sinclair. *Nescit vox missa reverti*. Still, there was no *mala fides* on your part, so let us say no more about it."

"I need to see Miss Dawe again."

"I'm afraid she has worked herself up into quite a state. She won't see you. I recommend you give Miss Dawe a little time to calm down."

"Do you think it could be true, Mr. Allen?"

"Only Miss Dawe could tell you, Mr. Sinclair. Isn't that why you asked her?"

Rowland buried his face in his hands, frustrated. After all this he was still unsure. Was Allie's dismay indicative of the truth in Harcourt's claim or merely the fact that it was so appallingly insulting?

"Why don't you go, Mr. Sinclair?" Allen suggested. "I will see that Miss Dawe is not too distraught and let her know that you did not intend to offend."

"Tell her I'm sorry," Rowland said.

"I will, I will. If you come across any further information which may pertain to Miss Dawe's case, may I suggest you bring it to me before you confront anyone?"

"Yes, of course."

"As for Lord Harcourt's offer, his sister, as the victim's wife, may apply to the court for clemency, if it should come to that. But rest assured, Mr. Sinclair, *adhuc sub judice lis est* and I have not come to the conclusion that my client is guilty."

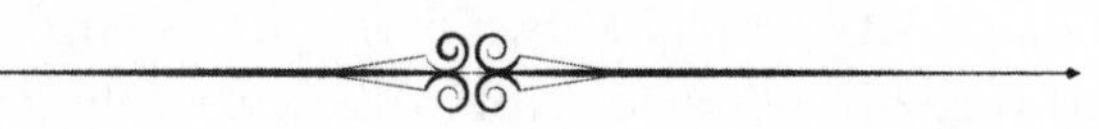

It was late afternoon by the time Rowland walked back into the suite, dishevelled and cross. The muscles in his arm, having become accustomed to the sling, ached.

"You're back," Edna said, relieved. "We were beginning to worry about you." She looked up into his eyes. "Rowly darling, whatever is the matter?"

Milton walked over to the drinks cabinet and poured Rowland a generous glass of gin. "Right, mate, sit down and tell us what's happened."

Rowland collapsed into an armchair and loosened his tie. He drank before he spoke.

They listened without interruption as he told them of Arundel House and recounted his conversation with Euphemia's brother, Theophrastus Thistlewaite—the Baron of Harcourt.

"He's lying!" Milton said flatly. "We have no other evidence that Pierrepont's relationship with Allie was anything other than uncle and niece!"

Rowland thought uncomfortably of the careless aspersions proffered by Entwhistle at Scotland Yard.

"So, you were at Arundel House with that awful man all this time," Edna said, perching on the arm of his chair.

"I don't know that he's that awful, Ed," Rowland said. "He's just trying to protect his sister. Apparently her mental health has diminished somewhat since Pierrepont died."

"Yes, I think we saw that," Clyde muttered.

"Lady Leon relented," Edna said.

"I beg your pardon?"

"You left the head with Lord Harcourt, so I assumed..."

Rowland groaned. For a moment he'd forgotten about the wax head. "I didn't leave it with Harcourt. I lost it."

"What? How could you lose it?"

"Some chap snatched it in Hyde Park."

"Someone stole the head?"

"The bag with the head in it."

"He didn't know?"

"Not then."

"So you've been trying to find this fellow who stole the bag?" Edna asked, sensing there was more.

Rowland wished that that was the case. "I went to Holloway...to see Allie." He confessed then to what he had done and how terribly wrong it had gone. "The poor girl didn't know where to turn...God, what was I thinking?"

Edna stroked the hair away from his face. "Oh, Rowly, you didn't mean to hurt her."

Milton poured him another drink.

"Did she deny it, Rowly?" Clyde asked.

"She was too distraught to deny or confirm anything. All I managed to do was make her hysterical."

"What do you think, Rowly?"

Rowland dropped his head back against the chair. "I don't know. If what Harcourt thinks is true, then I couldn't blame her for killing Pierrepont...but the only criticism she's ever made of her uncle was that he wouldn't let her sing."

Milton shrugged. "Perhaps she's a better actress than we're giving her credit for."

Rowland rubbed the back of his neck as he met the poet's eyes. "Do you really think so?"

"God, no!" Milton dropped into the couch with his own drink. "If it were some messy, impulsive shooting—maybe. But this was organised—tidy in a way. I hate to sound like old Murcott, but I'd put money on her having nothing to do with it."

Rowland and Clyde were alone at breakfast. Milton and Edna had left early for Holloway to check on Allie Dawe and to see if they could smooth things over a little.

"Rowly..." Clyde said as he picked up the paper and took in the cover, "I think they might have found that bag you lost."

He handed *The Times* to Rowland. The headline "Grisly Discovery at Station" appeared on the front page. Apparently, a Gladstone bag had been left unattended at Kings Cross Station. It had been found by a Mrs. Gladys Aberfoil who had opened the bag and become hysterical. A gentleman traveller who came to her aid had fainted at the macabre sight. A third person had screamed "murder" and begun a general panic on the platform. It was not until the police arrived that it was established that the head was not the result of a recent decapitation, but made of wax. Scotland Yard was investigating.

Rowland cursed. "I suppose we'll have to claim it."

"I don't see why." Clyde reached over to take the raspberry jam from Rowland and apply it to a slice of buttered toast. "We don't need Pierrepont back. Doesn't Scotland Yard have a museum where they put items like him?"

"The Black Museum," Rowland said, smiling. "It's probably not the worst place Pierrepont could end up."

"There you go...everybody happy. And we don't have to explain why you're wandering about London with a head in a bag."

Rowland was at least halfway convinced to let well enough be, when Menzies interrupted them. "Excuse me, sir, an Inspector Entwhistle to see you."

Entwhistle strode in before Rowland had a chance to respond to the announcement—in his hand, a Gladstone bag. Rowland and Clyde stood hastily.

Entwhistle dropped the bag on the table between them. "I believe this belongs to you, Mr. Sinclair."

Rowland nodded, thanked him and introduced Clyde.

"Can you explain why a grown man would be playing tasteless—my mother would say downright offensive, not to mention potentially dangerous—pranks?" Entwhistle demanded.

A little sheepishly, Rowland explained that the bag and its contents had been stolen from him the day before.

"Did you report the theft?"

"No, I didn't."

"Why not?"

"I wasn't entirely sure I wanted Pierrepont back. He was rather a bad penny."

"He certainly turns up like one," Clyde muttered.

"Why did you have the bag with you, Sinclair?"

"I had just been to see Lord Harcourt. I thought he might have wanted his brother-in-law's head."

Entwhistle accepted this with little show of alarm or surprise. "I see. I take it Lord Harcourt did not wish to have the head."

"That's right."

"And what was the purpose of your meeting?"

Rowland answered carefully. "He wished to convince me of Miss Dawe's guilt."

"And was he successful?"

Rowland glanced at Clyde. "No, not at all."

"Why would Lord Harcourt care who you thought was responsible for his brother-in-law's death?"

"You'd have to ask him that."

"Why do you have a wax head of the victim in your possession in the first place, Mr. Sinclair? Did Miss Dawe give it to you?"

"No…of course not. The poor girl doesn't even know it exists." Rowland stepped away from the dining table and invited Entwhistle to take a seat in the drawing room. He explained how the head had come into their keeping through Francis Pocock, who had been commissioned to make a statue of Lord Pierrepont by Lady Pierrepont. "She intended to use it to play tricks on the servants, I gather."

"I see." Entwhistle frowned. "I'm told that there was an incident at Holloway between you and the accused, Mr. Sinclair."

"A misunderstanding rather than an incident. I clumsily but quite unintentionally offended Miss Dawe. It was my fault entirely."

"The report stipulates that she became violent."

"I wouldn't say that. Miss Dawe became quite justifiably upset—that was all. The guards overreacted and I made matters worse by trying to intervene."

Entwhistle studied him. "I appreciate your candour, Mr. Sinclair," he said in the end. The inspector sat back, making himself comfortable. Clearly he had no intention of leaving just yet. "There was an altercation—what my mother would call a dust-up—just outside in Brook Street, I believe."

"Are you investigating me or the murder of Lord Pierrepont, Inspector?" Rowland asked calmly.

"Perhaps both, Mr. Sinclair, perhaps both. Would you mind telling me what in particular you've done to offend the B.U.F.?"

"Not so much the entire B.U.F. as William Joyce, I think." Rowland relented. "I presume, since you are so well apprised of my activities—"

"I am from Scotland Yard, Mr. Sinclair."

"—you are already aware that Joyce and I had a difference of opinion at the London Economic Conference."

"So, there was nothing more?" Entwhistle prodded.

"Not as far as I am aware."

"I advise you to be careful, Mr. Sinclair. Joyce is known to us for various incidents of brawling and assault. He is not a man to let bygones be bygones."

"Thank you for the warning, Inspector. We are taking precautions." Rowland paused. "How did you trace the bag back to me?"

Entwhistle smiled. "Elementary police work, Sinclair. The hotel's label is on the bag. It seemed too much of a coincidence that Pierrepont's head turns up in a bag carrying the label of your hotel. As I said before, we are Scotland Yard."

"Indeed."

"On that point, I must urge you in the strongest terms to leave the police work to us. I understand that you are anxious to help Miss Dawe, but really, Sinclair, you're flogging a dead horse, as my old mum would say, and doing so in a manner which may prove embarrassing, not to mention dangerous."

"Embarrassing to whom exactly?"

"I think you are aware that it is not just Scotland Yard interested in this case, Mr. Sinclair. Your belief in Miss Dawe is very gallant—my mother would say sweet—but it is not enough to stand against the weight of the objective evidence."

Rowland's eyes narrowed. "The gentleman who attended the crime scene with you…"

"Asquith?"

"Yes. Is he with Scotland Yard?"

"No. He's a civil servant."

Rowland persisted. "What part of the civil service attends murders, for God's sake?"

"He is with the Ministry of Health, I believe. I can assure you, Mr. Sinclair, it's all perfectly proper. I suggest you stop looking for conspiracies and reconcile yourself to Miss Dawe's situation."

"Again, I thank you for your advice, Inspector."

Entwhistle sighed. "But you have no intention of following it."

Rowland shrugged. "I find myself caring less about justice for the late Lord Pierrepont than for his niece."

Chapter Twenty-eight

Science of Eugenics

Improving Human Stock

A plea for greater interest in the science of eugenics was made in a paper prepared by Mr. A. Netzer and read by Mr. A. Ferguson at the Millions Club yesterday. It was stated that eugenists claimed to offer the only alternative to anarchy and the inherent disorders of Communism

Mr. Netzer pointed out that intelligence tests made on 1,700,000 physically fit men in the United States Army showed that only 13½ percent possessed superior intelligence. This small proportion represented a class which was failing to reproduce itself, while the others, of whom 45 percent would never develop mental capacity beyond a stage represented by a child of 12, were increasing alarmingly. Without an application of eugenic principles, persons of superior intelligence must eventually disappear, and with them the groundwork of civilisation and all it stood for.

Eugenics, he said, aimed at improving human stock by elimination of the unfit.

—*The Sydney Morning Herald,* 1930

By the time Milton and Edna returned, Entwhistle had departed.

"How's Allie?" Clyde asked as soon as Menzies closed the door behind them.

"She's still a little upset," Edna said carefully.

Rowland groaned.

"She'll settle down, Rowly. I suspect her reaction is coloured by disappointment—she thought you were proposing marriage, you know."

"What?" Clyde demanded. Rowland hadn't mentioned that part.

Milton laughed. "You're going to have to be clearer with your questions, comrade, or you'll find yourself betrothed to God knows whom!"

"Will she talk to me?" Rowland asked hopefully.

Edna shook her head. "Give her time."

"She may not have much time," Clyde said grimly.

"Did Allie say anything about her relationship with her uncle? Could what Harcourt said be—" Rowland ventured tentatively.

"She said it was vile and refused to speak about it."

"What does that mean?" Clyde asked. "Is she saying the relationship was vile or just the allegation?"

"I don't know." Edna shrugged. "We thought we'd best not press her lest she became hysterical again. Not surprisingly, she's overwrought at the moment."

Milton peered into the Gladstone bag. "I see our friend Bunky has found his way home."

Clyde tossed him the paper. "He didn't do it quietly."

Rowland told them of Entwhistle's visit.

"So, he's still convinced of Allie's guilt?" Milton asked.

"Surely the fact that he's even talking to you means something, Rowly," Edna argued.

Clyde snorted. "I suggest we find his mother and convince her."

Rowland smiled. Considering Entwhistle's deference to maternal homilies, it was as good a plan as any. He grabbed his hat.

"Where are you going?"

"Ennismore Gardens. With any luck, Mrs. Bruce might be able to find out where the Simpsons are residing. She telephoned earlier demanding we call and bring her up to date on the *investigation*."

Milton laughed. "You know, Rowly, I do believe I could be in love with Ethel Bruce. Why are all the best women unavailable?"

Rowland glanced at Edna. "I couldn't tell you, Milt."

Ethel Bruce was hosting a party for the children of Wilfred and Kate Sinclair. The garden, decorated with bunting and balloons, was overrun with girls in party frocks and ribbons and little boys in ties and short pants. Maids tended a table laden with bread and butter, cakes and ice-cream, and a footman distributed lemonade. Ernest was stumbling about blindfolded among a circle of children, while young Ewan was sitting in a bed of petunias trying to eat a snail.

Clyde picked up Rowland's godson and took the half-chewed snail out of his mouth.

Nanny Gray emerged with a washcloth and scrubbed the masticated snail from the child's cheeks. Kate joined them, apologising, clearly mortified that her son should be devouring garden pests when there was all manner of delicacy laid out.

Clyde laughed. "Your boy's obviously cultivated Continental tastes, Mrs. Sinclair."

"Ethel thought it would be nice for the boys to meet some of the neighbourhood children," Kate said.

"Where is Mrs. Bruce?" Rowland asked over the excited shouts of the small guests.

"Oh she's over there—with the egg and spoon race."

Kate pointed them towards an area of lawn which had been cordoned off with bunting into a track of sorts. Ethel Bruce stood in the middle of a group of giggling children, enunciating the care required to keep one's egg on one's spoon. Deciding to demonstrate, she ran the course with one hand on her silverware and the other clamping the hat to her head. The string of pearls around her neck swung wildly as she lunged this way and that to keep the spoon underneath the egg.

"That woman is magnificent!" Milton declared.

They did not interrupt the lesson, watching as the former Prime Minister's wife instructed her diminutive charges on the secrets of maintaining an egg aloft and intact. Eventually her own egg met a yolky end on the grass, and she joined Rowland and his companions still red-faced and breathing heavily.

"Heavens," she said, mopping her brow. "That was quite exhilarating." She glanced back proudly as the children raced. "Look at the little monkeys go! Oh, to have the energy of a child!"

"Did young people take their pleasure when the sea was warm in May? When they made up fresh adventures for their morrow, do you say?" Milton handed her an etched glass of chilled lemonade.

"Oh, Mr. Isaacs, you amaze me. Who but you would think to phrase that so beautifully?"

"Browning," Rowland murmured. "Though I believe Milt omitted a line." He studied Milton suspiciously, beginning to wonder if the plagiarist poet was reading *Paradise Lost* simply to throw him off the scent.

"You go back in and talk to Rowly, Ethel," Kate said, taking Ewan from Clyde's arms. "I'll keep an eye on proceedings here."

"Thank you, Katie dear. Remember, pin the tail on the donkey precisely at eleven, and the clown will arrive at half past."

"A clown?" Edna's eyes lit up.

Rowland laughed. He wasn't so keen on clowns himself, but Edna had always taken a child-like delight in their buffoonery. "We'll be back for the clown," he assured her.

Ethel Bruce led them into the sunroom which looked over the small but immaculate garden behind the residence. From there, they would still be able to see the party while they talked.

They told Ethel Bruce of their evening at the Winslow-Scotts'. Edna's face was merry as she detailed what Rowland insisted was a ludicrous version of their encounter with Prince George.

"Oh no, my dear," Ethel said. "I think you were both wise and brave to intervene. Prince George is so handsome that Mr. Sinclair might have forgotten himself!"

"I might have what?" Rowland demanded in horror.

Milton fell back against his chair laughing.

"Prince George is a famous ladies' man, of course, but there have been rumours about him for years...Noel Coward, you know...but let's say no more about it as Mr. Sinclair is looking quite distressed. Indeed, my Stanley would not be at all comfortable with this conversation. I'm sure he would have mentioned my hat at least a dozen times by now. Let us just be glad that you were there to protect Mr. Sinclair's virtue, Edna dear. It was a most valiant and selfless act."

Edna glanced at Rowland, recalling the kiss, the gentle intensity of it, and colouring almost imperceptibly. Perhaps it was not entirely selfless, but that, she kept to herself.

Desperate to move on from the proclivities of Prince George, Rowland recounted their conversation with Lady Furness.

Ethel nodded. "Thelma Furness—the Prince of Wales adores all things American."

"Lady Furness certainly appears to think that Mrs. Simpson is having an affair, and if your information linking Mrs. Simpson with Lord Pierrepont is correct, Mrs. Bruce, then that would give both Mr. and Mrs. Simpson, not to mention Lady Pierrepont, motive to kill him."

Milton shook his head. "It seems your friend Bunky was living quite dangerously in the end, Mrs. Bruce."

"My giddy aunt, he was," Ethel agreed. She paused, clearly remembering something of import. "I read in *The Times* that a wax head was found at Kings Cross. Are wax heads becoming a fashionable accessory? Or did you leave poor Bunky at the station, Mr. Sinclair?"

"He's been returned," Rowland assured her. He told her then of the meeting with Harcourt and the events which led up to the bag being stolen.

Ethel Bruce gasped. "He's suggesting that Bunky…his own niece…no that's just too abominable…it's preposterous! The man's obviously deranged."

"Do you know much about Lord Harcourt and his brother?" Rowland asked, leaving the allegation of incest, and worse, alone. He didn't want to believe it for many reasons.

"Stanley and I were introduced to both gentlemen once, when Herbert Wells dragged us to some presentation of the Eugenics Society."

"You know H.G. Wells?"

"Oh yes, he and Stanley rub along very well. Herbert was a great supporter of the League of Nations."

Rowland frowned slightly, wondering now if his chance encounter with the writer at the economic conference was as unplanned as it seemed. Not for the first time, he had an uneasy feeling that Wilfred was "managing" him.

"And he's a Eugenicist?" Milton asked.

"Indeed he is…determined to improve the calibre of the human race. Herbert is dismissive of selective breeding in a positive sense, but quite insistent that some people should be prevented from having offspring—for the sake of humanity. Stanley says it wouldn't be a bad idea to sterilise Labor voters, but I'm almost sure he doesn't mean it. We were just there to humour Herbert, really…it's all a bit of nonsense in my book."

"And Harcourt? What did you make of him?"

"Rather pompous, to be honest. Like Euphemia, he's quite mad on fauna—always talking of his African safaris and the adaptive genius of beasts."

Rowland remembered the mounted heads and various hunting trophies at Arundel House. It was difficult for any beast to adapt to a man with a shotgun, he supposed. "Harcourt seems very protective of his sister."

"Yes, they were both quite devoted to her. It's no wonder the poor girl is thirty and unmarried with her brothers hovering about her all the time!"

"Oh, the clown's here," Edna said, standing up and stepping towards the window. She looked again. "Mr. Sinclair and Mr. Bruce have arrived."

"Which one are you calling a clown?" Milton asked, grinning.

Without even pausing to look, Edna flung back her hand and hit him on the side of the head.

"Is there any way I could be introduced to Mrs. Simpson?" Rowland asked hastily as he realised they would soon be joined by Wilfred and Bruce.

Ethel faltered. "Oh dear, I haven't been formally introduced to the woman myself." Her face screwed up as she thought hard. "Leave it with me. I'll find out where she and her husband socialise. Perhaps we could arrange a chance meeting." She patted his arm. "Trust me, Mr. Sinclair. I'm a politician's wife. I've been arranging chance meetings for years."

They all rejoined the party then and the clown held the children and Edna in thrall with juggling and clumsy magic.

"Isn't he delightful?" She laughed as he threw a bucket of confetti at Stanley Bruce and winked at the sculptress.

Milton groaned. "You are not to step out with a clown, Ed! There's only so much we can take."

Clyde folded his arms across his chest, gazing thoughtfully at the entertainer. "You know, I worked as a roustabout once for Barnum Bros. Circus when they were touring the bush." He leaned over to Edna. "The clowns were mean," he confided, "and foul-mouthed."

Rowland laughed and Edna ignored them all.

"Rowland!" Wilfred motioned him away from the crowd.

"Dr. Pennyworth didn't mention that he'd been to see you recently," he said, glancing at his brother's forearm. Rowland no longer bothered with a sling and could, in fact, hold a glass in his right hand.

"Oh, this…" Rowland told his brother about the incident outside Claridge's and the recasting of his arm.

"You allowed a flaming doll-maker to perform a medical

procedure? For pity's sake, why didn't you just have Miss Higgins fashion you something out of mud and sticks?"

"Hardly dolls...and Ambrose was a doctor in Berlin." Rowland wondered how the sculptress would react to her work being described as mud and sticks.

Wilfred lit a cigarette and drew on it before he spoke again. "It could be that Joyce is pursuing some vendetta for your altercation at the conference," he said slowly. "He is a petty and vindictive wretch from what I gather, but, he is also a friend of Josslyn Hay."

"The Earl of Erroll?"

Wilfred nodded. "Hay has aligned himself with Mosley. He has not yet joined the B.U.F. officially, but his sympathies certainly lie in that direction. Mosley and Joyce have, of course, been doing their darnedest to court him."

Rowland frowned. "Do you mean to suggest that Joyce is targeting me at Hay's request?"

"I'm saying it's a possibility. I know you've had dealings with the man, Rowly. Have you offended him?"

"No...I don't believe so..." His eyes glinted then as a thought occurred. "Unless it's because I don't think Allie Dawe killed Pierrepont."

"Why would he care about that?"

"Maybe he killed Pierrepont."

Wilfred's eyes narrowed. He grabbed Rowland's arm and pulled him further away from the crowd. "Let me counsel you in no uncertain terms, Rowly, against making unguarded allegations against a peer of the realm!"

"Pierrepont was also a peer of the realm, Wil!"

Wilfred drew again on his cigarette. He shook his head. "Unless you have incontrovertible proof that Hay was involved, say nothing. Do you understand me?"

Rowland looked away, irritated.

"Rowly, bear in mind that if you appear to be slinging accusations left, right, and centre, then the chances of there being anyone willing to listen to your fears about Germany are significantly diminished."

Rowland turned back, frustrated. He hadn't forgotten Egon Kisch and the men of the German underground who had helped them escape. He'd promised to carry their story out of Hitler's Germany, but he had to do his best for Allie.

Wilfred dragged on his cigarette. "That character, Von Kirsch, is making a fuss—demanding you be returned to Germany to face justice."

"I see."

"I'm doing what I can, but it may be best if you left for Sydney, Rowly."

"I can't, Wil. Not now."

Wilfred sighed. Clearly Rowland's refusal was not unexpected. "There may come a time when you don't have a choice."

Rowland cursed under his breath. "We can't just leave Allie to hang…."

"No, I suppose not." Wilfred put a hand on his brother's shoulder. "Look, all I'm saying is don't go off half-cocked." He crushed the cigarette beneath his heel. His voice became a little harder. "I understand you're still wandering about with that wax replica of Pierrepont's head."

"Yes." Rowland did not try to deny it. "How did you know?"

"My eldest son has requested a wax head like Uncle Rowly's for his birthday."

"I see."

"I am not going to bother to ask why, because, frankly, I'm not sure any explanation would convince me that I shouldn't have you committed. But I insist that you get rid of it in a manner that does not end up in the newspapers!"

Rowland flinched. Apparently the article in *The Times* had also come to his brother's notice. "I'll return it to Madame Tussaud's," he said as an offering of peace. He had no use for the head anyway, and after his conversation with Harcourt he found himself unable to look at Pierrepont in the same way.

At first, Wilfred seemed surprised, as if he had expected Rowland to resist giving up the head. "Very well then," he said, "it's settled." He met Rowland's gaze sternly. "Try and be more careful, Rowly. It may be that whoever killed Lord Pierrepont will object to your poking about."

Chapter Twenty-nine

Wine and Alcohol—

FRENCH DOCTOR'S PRONOUNCEMENT

To the Editor.

Sir— On my return from a holiday on the Murray I find on my office table a number of prohibitionists' letters dealing with the question of "Wine and Alcohol". If the Rev. W. G. Clarke knew his subject, he would know that his quotations are in favour of wine. What the French call "alcoholiques" is best explained by Dr. L. Landouzy, Sen., member of the Faculty of Medicine, Paris, who said, "I refuse to range myself on the side of teetotallers, who, under the pretext of the abuse made of alcohol, unite in their uncompromising anathema to the alcoholism contained in wine. I refuse as a physiologist, a doctor, and dietist, to permit the proscription of this marvellous wealth of the soil of France—the wine."

H. L. PENFOLD HYLAND.

—*The Advertiser*, 1933

The terrace in Belgravia was shut tight. It was a house of scandal now. The old master was dead and Miss Allie Dawe had been arrested for his murder. Children threw stones and pointed until their nannies dragged them to the other side of the street.

The motor taxi pulled up and Rowland and Edna stepped out. They knocked several times before the door was finally answered, opened just a crack at first until the housekeeper recognised the young man who had brought Miss Dawe home before.

She let them in. It seemed the old housekeeper was the only servant who remained. Still the house was spotless, if unnervingly quiet.

"Mrs. Dawe is in the sitting room," the servant said curtly. "If you'll just wait here, I'll see if she's at home to visitors."

And so they waited. Less than a minute later, the housekeeper returned shaking her head.

Rowland had expected as much.

"Nonsense!" Edna declared. "Allie is in gaol and this is important." She side-stepped the housekeeper and strode towards the drawing room from whence the servant had come. Rowland removed his hat and followed.

The housekeeper cried "Stop!" and ran after them, complaining loudly.

Mrs. Dawe was reclined on a pale blue chaise lounge with a bottle of Scotch and a glass. There was an empty bottle on the floor beside her. Rowland could not recall having thought much about the nature of her illness before, but the scene did not surprise him. The loyal housekeeper was mortified, demanding they leave.

"Right, then." Edna removed her gloves and put down her bag. She turned to the housekeeper. "If you'd be kind enough to show me to the kitchen, I'll make Mrs. Dawe some coffee… Do you have coffee?"

For a while the housekeeper waivered and then, regaining her composure, she said, "Of course, we have coffee." She sniffed. "Do not trouble yourself, madam, I can see to it."

She shot Rowland a black look before she left the room.

"Take the bottle away from her, Rowly," Edna instructed, retrieving a couple of cushions from the armchair. She pushed the stupefied woman quite gently into a more upright position using the cushions to steady her.

Mrs. Dawe resisted the removal of her alcohol but was really in no condition to prevent it. Rowland blanched at the concentration of whisky on her breath. When the housekeeper returned, the sculptress poured a cup of black coffee and, blowing on it to cool the steaming liquid, insisted Mrs. Dawe drink it. After the second cup she asked the housekeeper to bring some bread and butter for her mistress and then, with the same gentle firmness, ensured Mrs. Dawe ate.

Rowland watched, a little awestruck by Edna's gracious command of a very difficult situation.

She caught his eye. "Mama used to drink a little before she died," she said, smiling wistfully.

After an hour or so, Allie's mother was sober enough to weep. It took another two hours before she was coherent enough to make any sense at all. All that time Edna plied her with coffee and water and food and spoke to her of Allie.

When finally the effects of the whisky had been sufficiently diluted, they spoke to her of Pierrepont's murder. Edna kept the smelling salts on hand in case Mrs. Dawe attempted to escape by fainting.

"Mrs. Dawe," Rowland said, "can you tell us how Lord Pierrepont might have obtained your nightie?"

"My frilly yellow nightie," she sobbed. "I always felt so beautiful in it…it has ribbon roses embroidered on the shoulders."

"Why was Lord Pierrepont wearing it?" Rowland persisted. He couldn't recall noticing the ribbon roses but he wasn't looking for embroidery at the time.

"He asked me if he could have it—we were in love, you know." She stopped blinking and steadied herself. "Bunky thought people would talk if he married his dead brother's wife… so he asked for the nightie so he could feel close to me. He was such a gentleman." She started to cry again. "I didn't know he was going to wear it."

"Did Allie know you and Lord Pierrepont were in love?" Rowland asked, frowning.

"Yes, of course. She thought it was wonderful…truly wonderful."

Rowland glanced at Edna. This revelation just made matters worse for Allie. She now had another reason to have killed Pierrepont.

"Mrs. Dawe," Edna asked patting the woman's hand, "did you know that Lord Pierrepont had married?"

"Oh yes…I was an actress once, you know…I had so many suitors…"

"Were you disappointed? That Lord Pierrepont had married someone else?"

Mrs. Dawe closed her eyes. Edna reached for the coffee.

"I suppose it's all right to say now," she said suddenly. "He was about to have that marriage annulled."

"Why?" Rowland asked, hoping she was still drunk enough to be indiscreet, but sober enough to be useful.

"Because we were in love, of course."

"But then why did he marry Euphemia Thistlewaite in the first place?"

"Because he was the kindest man and her child needed a father!" Mrs. Dawe clapped her hand over her mouth. "I shouldn't have said that…I'm not supposed to know that."

"It's all right, Mrs. Dawe, we already knew about the pregnancy," Edna said.

Allie Dawe's mother slumped into tears again. "My poor Allie…Why do they think she'd do this?"

Rowland tried to bring her back. "What do you know about Lord Pierrepont's marriage, Mrs. Dawe?"

"Nothing…nothing at all, but that he thought it a mistake…that he wanted out of the contract."

"The contract?"

"The marriage contract."

"Mrs. Dawe," Edna asked, "you do know that we're trying to help Allie?"

"Yes, I suppose you are."

"Is there anything you can think of which might help us to discover who might have wanted Lord Pierrepont dead?"

She shook her head. "Oh God, I need a drink."

Edna poured her another cup of coffee.

Mrs. Dawe sighed. She held the cup in both hands. "He said he'd been cheated. In the days before he died, Bunky was angry and out of sorts. He'd only say he'd been cheated."

Rowland applied the diluted paint in loose broad strokes, pulling out the shapes of two men and a woman at cards. His models talked of Allie Dawe, Euphemia Thistlewaite, Josslyn Hay, and every other person who'd crossed their paths in England since they'd arrived, as they attempted to sift the sands of Pierrepont's murder. Rowland painted not because he wanted to be distracted, but because the brush and canvas focused his mind in a way that nothing else could.

According to Mrs. Dawe, Pierrepont thought he'd been cheated. He'd spoken of a contract—was he talking about his dealings with the Earl of Erroll, or the marriage to Euphemia Thistlewaite…or both? And there was still the question of the elusive Simpsons. Ethel Bruce had promised to contact her networks as soon as Wilfred and Stanley Bruce departed for the economic conference the next morning. Until then, all they could do was wait.

"I wonder what interest the Ministry of Health has in Pierrepont?" Rowland mused out loud. Entwhistle had said the civil servant, Asquith, was from the Ministry of Health.

"Perhaps it's because Pierrepont's a peer. He was probably on some board or other connected with health," Milton suggested.

Rowland nodded. That was possible, but for some reason, Asquith's interest bothered him.

The following morning, Edna and Clyde set off to Holloway Prison to visit Allie Dawe. They returned with the news that she was still refusing to see Rowland but had become involved with a gardening project being conducted within the penitentiary. It seemed to have lifted her spirits a little, and of this news Rowland was glad. He feared most that Allie would fall into despair.

The telephone call finally came from Ethel Bruce at about midday. "Mr. and Mrs. Simpson will be having afternoon tea with some friends at the Ritz today at three sharp!" she said triumphantly. "Lady Furness will be among the party so you will need to resume the roles you took at the Winslow-Scotts. Good luck, Mr. Sinclair. I'll be waiting to hear all about it!"

Edna disappeared to change from the sober attire she had worn for the visit to Holloway into something more appropriate and cheerful for a sunny afternoon drinking tea at the Ritz. Rowland checked his clothes for paint and, finding only the smallest drops of vermillion on his waistcoat, decided that he would do. He was, after all, holding himself out as an artist. Checking his watch, he asked the butler to place a call through to the Ritz and make an appropriate reservation for afternoon tea.

"So how do you plan to orchestrate an introduction to Mrs. Simpson, Rowly?" Milton adjusted his cravat just so, and positioned a beret over the bandage on his head.

"If Thelma Furness is there, I'll simply walk over and say 'Hello again'...otherwise we may just have to become creative."

Edna emerged in a dress of rose beige silk. The colour brought out the green of her eyes. Her gloves were chocolate brown to match her hat and shoes. Rowland had always considered the sculptress too natural a spirit to look particularly sophisticated, but today she was breathtakingly chic.

She smiled—perhaps with too much warmth for the detachment required of the truly cosmopolitan—but Rowland thought her enchanting.

"Well, we'll have the attention of all the men at the Ritz," Clyde murmured with his own note of admiration.

A knock at the suite's door surprised them. The arrival of visitors was usually preceded by a telephone call from the reception to ask if they were receiving guests.

Menzies answered the door. "Please come in, sir."

"Quex!" Rowland said as the admiral strode in. "What are you doing here?"

"You are a hard man to please, Cousin Rowland—unhappy when I send for you, unhappy when I call personally." He shook Rowland's hand and nodded approvingly at the new cast. "Glad to see you're on the mend, old chap."

Rowland introduced Admiral Sir Hugh Sinclair to Edna, and then Clyde and Milton to the admiral. Hugh Sinclair greeted them all congenially, raising a brow at Milton's beret and telling Edna she was a vision.

Rowland glanced at his watch. "I'm loathe to be rude, Quex, but I'm afraid we have another engagement."

"You and your companions are not going anywhere, Rowly."

Chapter Thirty

Spies Over Europe

Startling Revelations

...The trial by court martial recently of a young British officer on the charge of espionage calls attention automatically to a startling state of affairs in Europe to-day. The truth is that practically all the Continental countries are spending more on espionage than before the War.

...More women are employed in the business of international spying to-day than ever before. Women who undertake the work think it an honour to accept great risks for the sake of their country. At the same time, the pay is excellent and liberal expenses are allowed.

—*The Central Queensland Herald*, 1933

"What the devil do you mean?"

"Now, before you become overzealous," Hugh Sinclair said calmly, "you should know that I have four men waiting outside the door and the authority to arrest you all, should it become necessary."

"That's preposterous!" Rowland pushed past his cousin and flung open the door. The four uniformed men who had abducted him weeks ago outside Allie Dawe's house, barred the doorway.

Rowland slammed the door, furious.

"What the hell do you want, Quex?"

"I intend to prevent you from making rather an embarrassing mistake, Rowland."

"What mistake?"

"Shall we sit down? I'm afraid you will not be having tea at the Ritz. Perhaps your man here can organise something palatable instead."

"Very good, sir," Menzies said, inclining his head.

The butler's acquiescence to the admiral's authority only made Rowland more incensed.

"How did you know we're going to the Ritz?"

"Sit down and I'll explain."

Rowland didn't move.

Eventually, Edna sat and pulled Rowland down beside her. "I suspect we do not have any choice, Rowly."

Hugh Sinclair smiled, motioning Clyde and Milton into armchairs before he commandeered one himself. "I wonder why you and your friends are having tea at the Ritz this particular afternoon?"

Nobody responded, perplexed that he would know their plans.

"Could it be because a certain Mr. and Mrs. Simpson are also having tea at that establishment, and that you wish to talk with them?"

"Obviously, you already know," Rowland fumed. "What has it got to do with you?"

"You're on the wrong track, Rowland. Lord Pierrepont was not having an affair with Mrs. Simpson, although I concede that he had gone to some lengths to make it look that way."

"Why would he do that?"

"Because he is loyal to the Crown."

"I don't follow you, Quex."

"I think I might," Milton interrupted, his dark eyes narrowing. "Would I be wrong to suggest that Pierrepont was covering for Mrs. Simpson's actual lover?" He tapped his forehead thoughtfully. "Someone who warrants a rear admiral to be mobilised in defence of his reputation…?" Milton slapped the arm of his chair. "Good Lord! King George is having an affair with the Simpson woman!"

Hugh Sinclair stared at the poet in horror. "Most certainly not! The King has never even laid eyes upon her!"

"Then what are you all working so hard to hide?" Rowland demanded.

"The King's sons don't always demonstrate the restraint and good judgement of their father," the rear admiral said carefully.

"Which son?" Edna asked. "Not Prince George?"

Rowland met Hugh Sinclair's eye. "No. The indiscretions of the youngest prince hardly warrant your personal involvement, do they, Quex?" He recalled the party at the Winslow-Scotts—the absence of Mrs. Simpson and Lady Furness' royal lover. "It's someone a good bit more important than George…Is the Prince of Wales having an affair with this Mrs. Simpson?"

Hugh Sinclair sighed. "The Prince of Wales and Mrs. Simpson have a close *friendship* which some quarters might consider inappropriate. The woman is, after all, American." He stroked his chin thoughtfully and chose his words carefully. "His Royal Highness, concerned that his old *friend*, Lady Furness, would similarly misinterpret his relationship with Mrs. Simpson, persuaded his loyal chum, Pierrepont, to play Mrs. Simpson's paramour. It was a naïve ploy perhaps, but well-intended. As you can understand there can be a great deal of competition for His Royal Highness' friendship. If you go poking your nose into all this, Rowland, you risk embarrassing the Crown."

"So, is this what you do, Quex? Clean up after the Prince of Wales?"

Hugh Sinclair's face became stony. "I've neglected you, Rowland. I really should have taught you manners at some point."

"Rowly..." Edna intervened as the tension in the room rose dangerously. "Sir Hugh has saved us a great deal of time and bother. We don't care who Mrs. Simpson's lover is if it doesn't help Allie's case."

Rowland looked down at her hand on his. She was right. As obnoxiously as the admiral had delivered the edict, he had saved them a wild goose chase they could ill afford.

"How do you know of our interest in the Simpsons, Quex?" Rowland asked. "Where we're going, when and why."

The admiral's face was unreadable.

"Menzies!" Milton exclaimed suddenly. "He's been spying on us! Our trusted butler has been keeping the admiral apprised of our movements from the beginning." He pointed accusingly at the manservant who had just re-entered the drawing room with a tray laden with tea and cakes. "What did you do with Beresford, you duplicitous fiend?"

Hugh Sinclair laughed. "You are letting your imagination get the better of you Mr. Isaacs. Mr. Beresford is very happily in the service of Lord and Lady Pugh in one of the other suites."

"But Menzies?"

"Mr. Menzies has been keeping a watchful eye on you," the admiral admitted.

"Good Lord!" Rowland groaned. "What is wrong with you?"

Hugh Sinclair regarded him frostily. "All things considered, Rowland, do you really think it surprising that I would take an interest in the activities of my Colonial cousins? Your sojourn to Munich was hardly innocent!"

Rowland sat forward, his eyes intense as things fell into place. "So, what exactly was your man Menzies sent to observe?"

"Initially, we were concerned that you may have been spying for the Germans."

"What?" Rowland was appalled.

"And then, you and I had our little chat, and I realised that was extremely unlikely, though I began to be troubled—" Rear Admiral Sinclair glanced at Milton and Clyde, "—about the influence of other parties on your allegiances. Mr. Menzies stayed on in the hope that you might have some information on the Germans."

Rowland did not bite. He was perfectly comfortable with his allegiances and not about to discuss them with Hugh Sinclair. "If you wanted to know about Germany, why didn't you just ask me?"

"I did, if you recall, but sometimes people don't realise what they know, what might be valuable. There is a lot of information in the background of holiday photographs, for example—a building or a person who just happens to be behind the picture's subject. It's the same for memories."

Pictures…His paintings…

"Murcott," Rowland said quietly. "Does Archibald Murcott work for you, Quex?"

"No."

"Ivy Murcott," Edna said, more to Rowland than anyone else. "Ivy's the spy."

"Of course." Rowland nodded. Ivy Murcott made sense now. "She's not Murcott's sister…thank God for that, at least. But Waugh knew her as Ivy Murcott. Is she Archie's wife or is Waugh a spy too?"

Hugh Sinclair said nothing.

"Did she take the paintings?" Clyde asked. "Rowly's paintings of Germany?"

Again silence.

Exasperated, Rowland dragged his hair back from his forehead. "Are you spying on Wilfred, too, then?"

"I hardly think you are in any position to get high-handed about spying and surveillance, Rowland. But no. Wilfred and I have an understanding."

Rowland shook his head incredulously.

"Look, Rowland," Hugh Sinclair sighed, "you seem to have once again taken me wrongly. I'm endeavouring to help you. At the moment, despite the horribly messy diplomatic incident which could result, my people are working tirelessly to ensure

Von Kirsch is not able to denounce you as a murderer and demand you be returned to Germany to face justice."

Edna poured tea, and passed a cup to the admiral. "For that we are sincerely grateful, Sir Hugh. Of course, Rowly didn't kill anybody."

The admiral glanced strangely at his cousin here. He spoke to Rowland again. "Prince Edward's reputation may seem trivial to you, Rowland, but in the current political climate, the leadership of Britain must be decisive, united, and devoid of scandal. And, as Miss Higgins has already pointed out, you would only have been wasting time digging into Mrs. Simpson's affairs."

"But does Mr. Simpson know?" Clyde asked. "If he too suspects Pierrepont—?"

"Simpson is well aware of the situation, Mr. Watson Jones. It may seem unusual, but it is not unheard of where a future king of England is concerned."

"So, how long are you going to keep us trapped in here, Quex?" Rowland asked.

"Until I'm sure you will stay well clear of Mrs. Simpson and say nothing of this conversation."

Rowland shrugged. "We no longer have any interest in Mrs. Simpson, and let me assure you that we've never cared in whose bed Prince Edward finds himself. For God's sake, Quex, you might have just told me."

"Getting you to listen is sometimes difficult, Rowland." The admiral sighed. "In any case, I wasn't aware you had any plans to pursue Mrs. Simpson…until just now."

Milton shook his head and wagged a finger at the treacherous butler. "You'll have to brush up on your eavesdropping, comrade."

"Very good, sir."

"Do you know who killed Lord Pierrepont, Sir Hugh?" Edna said suddenly.

"Of course not, Miss Higgins. Pierrepont is of no import in the greater scheme of things and certainly of no interest to us. I'm told he was murdered by that niece of his."

"What is the Ministry of Health's interest in Pierrepont's death?" Rowland asked.

"Health? I can't imagine, dear cousin…unless he died of smallpox or some such thing. What have they asked you?"

"Nothing really…they just had a man at the murder scene—he arrived with the chap from Scotland Yard."

"Did Scotland Yard call him?"

"I don't know."

"Well, someone must have. I suggest you ask them."

The afternoon wore on. Admiral Sinclair lingered, a civilised, genteel gaoler. He chatted quite amiably on all manner of subject, asking each of them their impressions of Germany. But it was clearly Milton and Clyde's accounts that interested him most.

They answered warily, knowing from Rowland that the admiral was a committed anti-Communist. The last thing they wished to do was expose the men who'd helped them escape.

Rowland looked on as his cousin talked with Milton, noting the slight stiffening in the admiral's shoulders when the poet spoke of anything that too plainly expressed his radical political beliefs. Artfully, Hugh Sinclair attempted to tease out details of Communist activity in Europe. Milton deflected the probing equally artfully, with poetry.

"So, are you ever planning to depart, Quex?" Rowland asked quite bluntly in the end. "Or must we be kept permanently under lock and key to ensure the Prince of Wales' reputation is unimpeachable."

"I don't see there's any need for anything quite so drastic, Rowland." Sinclair sipped the Scotch which Menzies—who for some reason remained in the guise of butler—had brought him earlier. "I've booked your passages home. You leave for Australia in a week."

Rowland's face darkened.

"But Allie…" Edna protested.

"Whatever you are doing for the girl, do in the next seven days because you will be boarding that ship." Sinclair looked at Milton. "I will ensure the charges against Mr. Isaacs are dropped."

"Unless Britain is having us deported—" Rowland began angrily.

"She isn't…yet, but you will be on that ship, one way or another." The rear admiral sighed. "There were other ways of doing this, Rowland. For your own sake, and that of your brother and your friends, take what I'm offering and go quietly, because the other ways will not end so well for any of you." He put down his drink. "It will be a great deal easier to dismiss Von Kirsch's allegations if you are no longer here."

Rowland simmered, cornered.

Hugh Sinclair regarded him quite sadly. "I'm not sure why you feel you need to fight me at every turn, Rowland. I am acting in your best interests, my boy." He shook his head. "It's no wonder poor Wilfred has always had such a job keeping you under control."

"For God's sake, Quex, they could hang that poor girl if—"

"Leave it in the hands of that solicitor you retained to represent her and trust the man to do his job!" Hugh Sinclair's voice became hard. "Make no mistake, Rowland, you will be leaving Britain in a week, one way or another. Consider yourselves lucky that I'm not having you all incarcerated until then." He checked his watch and stood. "Is that the time? I might be able to get on now. I'll have the details of your passages sent on to you." Glancing at Rowland's thunderous face, he smiled. "Chin up, old man. This is not good-bye—we'll meet again."

Edna grabbed Rowland's arm as he tensed forward. "Rowly, perhaps it's time we went home," she said gently, afraid he'd deck Rear Admiral Sir Hugh Sinclair then and there.

Milton stood. "Let me show you and Mr. Menzies out," he said coldly.

For a while after Hugh Sinclair and Menzies had departed there was nothing but tense, furious silence. Finally Edna rose from the couch. "You're all turning purple trying not to swear, so I'm going to change into something less fussy. While I'm gone you can get whatever you need to off your chests, and then we'll figure out what we're going to do." She left them, departing through the door which led to the adjoining suite.

Clyde groaned. He had been repressing profanity for Edna's sake. "Well, we can't very well swear now," he grumbled.

"Speak for yourself," Milton said before exploding into a string of curses ending in "Rear Admiral". But, by the time Edna returned in a simple frock with no hat or gloves, even he had calmed down sufficiently to be a gentleman again.

Edna settled on the arm of the couch. "What do you think?" she asked Rowland who had not yet said a word.

"I think," he said slowly, "that we have seven days to find out who really killed Pierrepont."

Chapter Thirty-one

Objection to Nude Figures

Theatre Drapes Them With Dust Sheets

The management of the Prince Edward Theatre, Church Street, Soho, London were officially informed that parts of the exterior decorations—four female figures devoid of drapery—must be modified.

The figures are 18 ft high and were intended to be symbolical of the spirit of the revue being presented at the theatre, "Un Vent de Folie".

As it was impossible at short notice to obtain painters to paint clothing on the figures, the producer of the revue, Mr. Jack Taylor, had them draped with the only material available—dust sheets which are usually used for covering seats when the theatre is closed.

Painters however began work on the figures next morning.

—*The Advertiser*, 1933

Rowland leaned casually against the lamppost with an open newspaper, waiting. A sudden turn in the weather had left the city cloaked in the famous London fog. It made him less visible but it also rendered more difficult the task of picking out a single man from among the crowd who entered the Geological Museum.

Delegates arrived in proudly flagged cars of state, and made their way in via a private entrance to the side. The mood was sombre—the conference was not going well. The American President had declared his hostility to its aims. It seemed there would be little outcome for all the hopes and money poured into this gathering of world leaders and economic minds.

But it was not the delegates who interested Rowland Sinclair. He watched the main entrance where members of the public and the media queued for access to the public gallery.

An old man joined the line. He was not tall, or remarkable in any visible way. Rowland folded the newspaper under his arm and approached.

"Mr. Wells."

Herbert Wells turned, squinted through the circular lenses of his spectacles for a moment before he smiled in recognition. "Mr. Sinclair, isn't it? Well, hullo, sir! Have you come to keep me company in the gallery again?"

Rowland offered the writer his hand, and Wells shook it. "Your wings are a little less clipped, I see. Perhaps today you will be able to draw the men who have so eloquently delivered nothing after days of talk!"

"Actually, Mr. Wells, I was hoping I could persuade you to have a drink with me instead. There is a matter about which I'd like to talk to you."

Wells' eyes narrowed. "You're not a hopeful writer are you? You haven't some manuscript you plan to foist upon me?"

Rowland smiled. "Not at all. But I would like to talk to you." He turned his head away quickly as a museum official walked past, lest he be recognised as the man banned after the riot involving Mosley's Blackshirts. "Just not here."

Wells hesitated.

"I assure you, I wouldn't trouble you if it wasn't important, sir. This is potentially a matter of life and death."

Now Wells was clearly intrigued. "I suppose today will be as much a failure as yesterday, and the day before that, and the day before that. Perhaps a drink is called for to toast what might have been if the world was not administered by fools." He nodded. "Do lead on, Mr. Sinclair."

Rowland took the writer to a small rather scruffy bar which catered for a bohemian clientele. He apologised that the venue was less than wholly respectable.

"Clearly you do not wish us to be discovered, Mr. Sinclair—at least by any gentleman of means," Wells said as they sat at a bare table decorated only with the remnants of a candle in the mouth of a wax-covered bottle. They ordered.

"I am told there was some excitement at the conference after our last conversation," Wells began.

"Yes, I'm afraid so."

"Would I be correct to infer that you are offended by Mr. Mosley's politics, Mr. Sinclair?"

"It's more than just his politics," Rowland said cautiously, unsure of where Wells stood. He knew from Milton that Wells was a bitter opponent of Zionism, but then the poet was not a Zionist either.

Wells sighed. "Nationalism," he said. "It is not till we leave such notions behind that there will be hope for mankind."

"Mr. Wells," Rowland began before Wells could embark on another subject, "I understand from Mrs. Stanley Bruce that you have at times attended functions of the Eugenics Society."

Wells nodded. "Indeed, I have, Mr. Sinclair. Do you have an interest in the subject?"

"Not so much the subject as the members of the society. I met Lord Harcourt recently. Are you acquainted?"

"Yes. I've met both Lord Harcourt and his brother, but I'm afraid I do not know them well. They are extreme."

"How do you mean, extreme?"

"Eugenicists do not hold a single position but hold a place in a spectrum of belief. Lord Harcourt and his brother are both part of a faction which advocates the most extreme form, which, frankly, is not only counter to social norms but to contemporary biological science. Personally, I have always thought that part of the movement more closely linked to the occult than science."

"I'm not sure I follow, sir."

"In animal husbandry, there is an established practice known as line breeding, I believe."

Rowland started. He knew about line breeding—the practice of joining related beasts to concentrate a desirable bloodline in stock. It had its adherents among Australian stud masters and graziers. While Rowland had never cared enough to have an opinion, he knew Wilfred considered it a dangerous practice in the longterm.

"Good God, are you suggesting the Harcourts advocate line breeding in human beings?"

"In theory, yes." Wells chuckled. "Do not be so shocked, Mr. Sinclair. The royal families of Britain and Europe have been practising an unofficial form of line breeding by default for a great many generations!"

In truth, Rowland wasn't shocked. Just appalled. He realised now that Lord Harcourt had accused Pierrepont of his own crime. Lady Pierrepont's unborn child…he winced…could the father be one of her own brothers?

"As I said," Wells continued, "their position is extreme—more mystical than rational. I believe Lord Harcourt has fostered some connection with the Thule Society and other organisations who promote ideas of racial purity, and whose excesses do not help the good case for Eugenics. As such, I have not pursued any form of intimacy with either of them."

Rowland signalled for the bill. "Thank you, sir. I cannot say enough how helpful you have been."

"You claimed this was a matter of life and death, Mr. Sinclair," Wells said almost petulantly.

"It is indeed, Mr. Wells. The life of a young woman depends on what you've just told me." He paid for their drinks. "I wish I could stop to explain but…"

Wells nodded. "A life depends on this information I have given you. One should not leave such a life waiting." He took out a calling card and handed it to Rowland. "Perhaps, Mr. Sinclair, if we do not meet again, you will write to me of the outcome of this mercy dash of yours?"

Rowland shook the writer's hand firmly. "I will, and with pleasure, Mr. Wells. Thank you, sir."

The suite was empty on Rowland's return. At his request, Claridge's had not replaced Menzies, and so the penthouses were tended by only the usual army of chambermaids.

As the Australians were now aware that remaining in London beyond a week would become, at the very least, difficult—more probably impossible—they'd decided to split up that morning and cover more ground. Edna had gone to Holloway Prison to encourage Allie Dawe to keep faith. Milton had set out to see Buchan to ensure that, whatever happened, Allie would have a champion in London. Meanwhile Clyde had headed for Scotland Yard to meet Entwhistle and pose a single question: had the inspector called the Ministry of Health?

Rowland was certain now that Harcourt had murdered Pierrepont. Yet he knew they would need more than accusations of links to extreme eugenics for the baron to be considered a more likely suspect than titleless, penniless Allie Dawe, who had been discovered with blood literally on her hands.

Rowland removed his jacket, which had become damp in the cloying fog. He rubbed his face, unsure of what to do next. He now considered Harcourt the most reprehensible of men, but the lord did seem to love his sister, however twisted that love proved to be. Euphemia, at the mercy of her brothers, and now possibly pregnant by one of them, would be utterly destroyed if Lord Harcourt's motives were exposed. And the future of her unborn child would be bleak indeed. Rowland was reluctant to destroy one innocent woman to save another.

He took Pierrepont's head from the Gladstone bag and placed it once again on the sideboard. The waxen face looked accusingly at him, as if it knew what he had almost believed about the man it represented. Rowland groaned as he recalled the same look in Allie Dawe's eyes when he had asked her if her uncle had been abusing her.

The telephone rang, and for the first time in weeks he was able to answer it himself without incurring the ire of a butler.

The reception redirected a call from a Mr. Asquith from the Ministry of Health.

"Mr. Sinclair, I understand from Inspector Entwhistle that you have been making enquiries with respect to the interest of the Ministry of Health in the death of Alfred Dawe, Viscount Pierrepont."

"I have."

"I can assure you, Mr. Sinclair, the ministry has very good reason to be involved. Perhaps we could meet and I'll explain… off the record as it were. Inspector Entwhistle tells me you have become something of a champion for Miss Dawe's innocence in the matter. I believe I may be able to help you with some hard evidence on that account."

"In that case, I would be delighted to meet with you, Mr. Asquith," Rowland said eagerly. All he had was conjecture at the moment. If Asquith had some sort of proof…

"Excellent. Can you come now?"

"Yes…of course…just tell me where." Rowland scribbled down the name and address of an establishment called The Bitter Pill.

"Mr. Sinclair," Asquith added, "you must understand that my speaking to you is somewhat unofficial. Can I ask you to come alone and not speak to anyone of this meeting? I cannot afford to be connected to the disclosure of this information."

"You have my word, Mr. Asquith," Rowland agreed.

He paused to dash off a note to his friends. "A breakthrough—much to tell. Back soon. R."

He pulled his jacket back on and grabbed his hat, farewelling Pierrepont's head with the hope that he would return with some valid corroborating evidence to help the desperate cause of Allie Dawe.

The club to which Asquith had directed Rowland was a few streets away from The Windmill Theatre, made notorious for its *tableaux vivants*. With acts titled as "Diana the Huntress," "The Birth of Venus," and "Nymphs Bathing," young women were displayed as classical nude statues, thus placating the censors while ensuring the patronage of the tiny but well-appointed theatre.

The Bitter Pill, in contrast, was a rundown, underground drinking house too decrepit to even qualify as bohemian. Its clientele were a step down from the men happy to pay for the more erudite spectacle of a naked woman pretending to be a naked statue.

Rowland was neither surprised nor alarmed that Asquith had chosen such an uninviting venue. He had himself taken H.G. Wells to a less than salubrious establishment to ensure they weren't seen. He assumed that Asquith, too, was wary of being noticed.

There was something clandestine, and anonymous, and forgotten about this part of Soho—the crowds were at the Windmill Theatre. Here the few passers-by kept their gazes averted and their business to themselves. In the fog, cloaked in coats and hats, every man became any man, indistinguishable and nameless. It was an apt place to pass secrets.

There were a few patrons at the grimy tables, smoking and drinking cheap wine from thick-walled glasses. They fell silent as Rowland entered, glancing furtively at the gentleman who'd descended into their squalid corner of the world.

Rowland spotted Asquith, who stood to shake his hand.

"There're too many people here," the civil servant muttered tersely as he fished some coins from the pocket of his long coat and tossed them onto the table, "and if you'll forgive my saying,

Sinclair, you stand out." He glanced around the tawdry premises nervously. "I know somewhere discreet," he said quietly. "We're going to shake hands and say goodbye. I'll leave; you stay for a drink before you follow. Turn left onto the street at the top of the stairs and keep walking. I'll be waiting for you at the corner."

With that he slapped Rowland on the shoulder and walked out. Rowland ordered a gin but, in truth, could not bring himself to take a sip out of the filthy glass. An ageing prostitute came in touting for business and spoke to him for a while. He let her have his drink, gave her a couple of shillings as he declined her services, and took that opportunity to leave.

Stepping thankfully out into the chilly day, Rowland turned up his collar and headed left as he had been instructed. The fog made it difficult to see whether Asquith was waiting for him on the corner as he had promised. With his eyes fixed ahead, he didn't notice the alley much less the men who waited in it. The sack which flew out over his head thrust the world into an immediate, suffocating darkness. A blow to the stomach winded him before he could make a sound and then, the distinctive click of a revolver being cocked and the press of its hard muzzle against his ribs.

Chapter Thirty-two

Waterloo Bridge To Be Reconditioned

(Australian Cable Service.)

LONDON, January 24

A letter from the Ministry of Transport was read at the London County Council meeting to-day, which stated that the Government had reached conclusions to proceed with the reconditioning of Waterloo Bridge at an estimated cost of £685,000. A grant of 60 per cent of the cost would be made by the Ministry. It was suggested that the question of colouring should be referred to the Fine Arts Commission.

—*Cairns Post*, 1933

Rowland blanched at the first onslaught of light, and gasped air as the sack was removed. The floor was cold, stone. The light produced from a single hanging bulb in a windowless room offered enough illumination to make visible an iron staircase which led down from a closed door well above the floor. It was a cellar of some sort.

Rowland's eyes adjusted and Asquith came into focus. The civil servant was seated on a chair, watching him. Rowland cursed. With Asquith captured, too, there was no one to raise the alarm.

It was only when he noticed the revolver in Asquith's hands that he realised the liaison at The Bitter Pill had been a trap.

"Don't move, Sinclair," Asquith warned as Rowland attempted to stand. "Theo will be back in a moment and he will be displeased if you've moved."

"Theo? You don't mean Harcourt? You're working for Harcourt? My God, man, he's the most reprehensible kind of pervert!"

Asquith smiled. A door creaked open at the top of the stairs and Harcourt descended. In one hand he carried several lengths of rope, in the other an Enfield rifle.

Rowland looked at the two men together. He cursed. Why hadn't he seen it before? Side by side their resemblance to each other was unmistakable. Asquith was Diogenes Thistlewaite—the other brother of Euphemia Pierrepont, nee Thistlewaite. And then he remembered, the portraits of the Baronets of Asquith among others at Arundel House…the subordinate title after which Diogenes had apparently fashioned his name.

"What do you want, Harcourt?" Rowland demanded.

Lord Harcourt regarded him curiously. "Odd tone for a man in your position to adopt. But then we didn't send our best and brightest to the penal colonies, did we? The breeding stock was arguably inferior in terms of intellect in the first place."

"At least our sisters were safe," Rowland spat.

Harcourt laughed. "Your horror is based in ignorance and twisted cultural norms, not science, Sinclair. If you were a man of science you would not be able to deny the argument for concentrating genetic success."

"Is that why you killed Pierrepont…in some warped act of genetic purification?"

Harcourt's face darkened. "Pierrepont reneged on our arrangement. When he discovered how special Euphemia's child would be, the fool said he would have no part of it. He wanted the marriage annulled. The closed-minded fool planned to denounce us and to ruin our sister."

Rowland decided to play his hand, weak as it was. "When this comes out, Harcourt, whatever the scientific justification, your sister will be ruined and her child a pariah. The only way to prevent that is to confess to the murder now."

"It's not going to come out, Sinclair," Asquith was unnervingly casual. "We're going to kill you."

"You were the last person seen with me, Asquith," Rowland said, sliding back as the gun was raised in his direction. "They'll work it out."

"Not in the condition they find your body," Harcourt said coldly. He trained the rifle on Rowland. "Tie him up, Diogenes," he instructed his brother. "We've only a few hours till dark."

Asquith bound Rowland hand and foot, then, dragging him to the base of the iron stairs, they secured him to that too, brutally subduing any resistance with their fists.

Rowland tried to reason with the brothers, but they only laughed as if they were part of some great joke to which Rowland was not privy.

The panic rose in Rowland's chest—and with it, fury. He swore at Harcourt and Asquith, calling them vile, inbred degenerates among other things less accurate but more profane.

Asquith kicked him until he couldn't speak anymore. Harcourt watched and when his brother was done, put down the rifle, removed Rowland's tie and used that to gag him.

It was quite late in the afternoon before Rowland's companions thought to worry about him. They had returned to find his note, which had promised he would return soon. In the first hours they simply assumed he was pursuing whatever breakthrough he had made in Allie's case. The sun penetrated the fog and the brightness of the day provided a kind of reassurance. Rowland was, after all, a grown man so they were initially more anxious to know what he had found than where he was.

As they waited they talked of Clyde's discovery that Entwhistle had not, in fact, telephoned the Ministry of Health, making Asquith's presence at Watts difficult to explain, unless he'd had some independent knowledge of Pierrepont's murder.

The daylight started to fade. Milton began to pace.

At five o'clock they reread and scrutinised Rowland's note more carefully—as if they could extract more information simply by reading it over and over again.

Milton squinted at the note under the concentrated light of a lamp. "Clyde, do you have on hand one of those art pencils you and Rowly use?"

Clyde tossed him the pencil. Milton placed the note onto the table and rubbed the flat of the lead over it. An impression became visible. Rowland's writing. "The Bitter Pill, Soho."

"What's that?" Edna asked, peering over the poet's shoulder.

"It's a rubbing of what was written on the previous page." Milton said grimly. "This must be where Rowly went."

"Why would he go to Soho?" Edna asked, already donning her gloves and looking for her hat.

Clyde grabbed his jacket from the back of the chair. "Let's go."

They took a motor taxi to Soho and alighted just outside the dissolute establishment whose name had been inadvertently impressed onto Rowland's note.

If Rowland had turned the odd head when he'd entered the bar, the three of them turned several more. A few drunken men called out to Edna. Clyde and Milton kept her protectively between them. They spoke to the establishment's dishevelled proprietor, describing Rowland.

The man was vague. He might have seen a tall man with dark hair and blue eyes but he didn't really pay that much attention to the punters. It was the woman who confirmed that Rowland had been there—a middle-aged prostitute who had been moved by the young man's manners, the courtesy with which he had spoken to her.

"That's Rowly," Milton declared. "He'd be polite to the devil himself!"

Edna swatted the poet as the prostitute reared in affront. "Do you know where he went?" Edna asked after apologising for Milton. "We're quite worried about him."

The prostitute looked a little sheepish. "I run out after him...I don't run after men, mind you, but the kind gentleman gave me five shillings. I thought he might have expected something fer that, if you know what I mean?" She took them up the stairs to the threshold of The Bitter Pill and pointed up the street. "He walked up there and then he disappeared into that alley. I figured then maybe he'd already arranged something, you know."

They had started towards the alley before she finished. Edna thanked the woman over her shoulder as she trotted to keep up with the long strides of the men.

Dark and dank, the alley ran behind a number of less prosperous businesses. They searched for any sign that Rowland had been there.

"Clyde, have you a light?" Milton asked, crouching by the rough brick wall of the building on one side of the alleyway.

Clyde flicked open his lighter and held it up to the wall. A fresh white mark—like chalk.

"Ed, could this be plaster?"

Edna nodded. She bit her lip.

"We'd better call Wilfred."

Rowland tensed as the door creaked open again and the bulb was flicked on. He was almost relieved, though he knew it meant his time had run out. Every muscle ached from the strain of the position in which he'd been secured. His left wrist was rubbed raw with his attempts to get out of the bonds, and against the cold stone floor his body had become chilled to the core.

Asquith and Harcourt ignored him for a while, sitting together companionably and sharing an apple. Asquith peeled the fruit with the gleaming blade of a hunting knife, before cutting segments. They talked of their sister, the progress of her pregnancy and their plans for her child. They discussed genetics, eugenic theories, and their own extreme position, which, it seemed, they were testing with Euphemia.

When the apple was consumed, Asquith wiped the knife and held it up to the light. He glanced at Rowland. Harcourt picked up the gun.

Instinctively, Rowland strained against the ropes as they stood.

Harcourt placed the gun against Rowland's temple and hushed him, as you would a child. "Sssshhh, it's all right. Don't move now, there's a good man."

Rowland froze, repulsed. The revolver's muzzle slipped on the cold sweat which had broken out on his forehead. Harcourt adjusted it, still hushing and crooning.

Asquith squatted over him with the hunting knife. Did they intend to murder him together? Or was Harcourt merely holding him still for his brother's strike? Pierrepont flashed into Rowland's mind...Was this how the viscount was killed: held under gunpoint until the blade was plunged?

Asquith cut the bindings on Rowland's ankles. "Get up," he said.

Rowland gasped into the gag.

Harcourt kept the gun trained on him but pulled it back so Rowland could struggle painfully to his feet.

Asquith sheathed his knife in a scabbard on his belt and took another gun from his pocket.

"Very well, Sinclair, we'd best get on. Theo is sitting at the House of Lords tomorrow morning—we don't want to be out too late."

Harcourt grabbed Rowland's collar, pressed the gun against his spine and shoved him up the stairs.

The cellar sat beneath a disused printing shop. Rowland concluded—by virtue of Harcourt's possession of the keys—that it belonged to the aristocrat.

A Vauxhall Cadet was parked in a narrow laneway behind the premise. It was dark now, as well as foggy. Rowland had no idea whether the fog had returned or simply not dissipated throughout the day.

As they approached the vehicle, Rowland made out another car parked at the end of the lane but close enough that he could see it was packed tightly with men. A prostitute peered into its window, plying her illicit trade to the car full of potential customers.

Before he could signal them for help, Asquith pushed him, still gagged and with his hands bound, onto the floor in the back of the Cadet. Harcourt sat in the backseat with the gun pointed at Rowland's head. Again the lord hushed and soothed as though he were calming a skittish filly.

Asquith slipped behind the wheel and started the engine.

On the floor, Rowland weighed his increasingly limited options. His panic seemed to have abated with the first reprieve, when Asquith had cut his bonds rather than stabbing him. Rowland was thinking more clearly now. He assumed the brothers were taking him out of London—to some rural manor—in order to shoot him and dispose quietly of his body. There would be his best chance. They had guns, but there were only two of them. Slowly but constantly, he rubbed his right wrist against the ropes. If he could wear the plaster back, the bonds might loosen enough to allow him to work free his hands. Aside from that, he could only hope the men in the other car had realised he was being abducted, and were not themselves doing something so unlawful that they dare not alert the police.

Rowland could hear very little traffic, though whether that was because of their location or the time, he was unsure. Cramped, with just the vibrating floor of the Cadet between him and the vehicle's whining differential, and with Harcourt's feet on his chest and a gun's muzzle pointed at his head, he found it difficult to judge the passing of time. Each minute stretched into a painful, tense age.

Quite unexpectedly, Asquith brought the Vauxhall Cadet to a stop. Rowland cursed silently…the bonds were no looser—the mannequin-maker's plaster cast had held.

Harcourt pulled him out of the car. It must have been late. There was nobody about at all and the moon was full and high. After the dark floor of the Cadet, Rowland's eyes were quick to adjust.

They were by the River Thames, near the entrance to a bridge. Rowland attempted to orient himself…there were so many bridges across the Thames. This one appeared to be undergoing some kind of maintenance and was closed to vehicles. The walkway for foot traffic was unbarred—not that there was any at this time of night. Then suddenly he recognised it: The Waterloo Bridge. They were standing on the Victoria Embankment.

The other motor car from the alley pulled up behind the Cadet. Rowland's spirits rose. They'd seen he was in trouble. Harcourt forced him onto his knees with the gun to his head as the men emerged from the vehicle.

They barely glanced at Rowland, moving only to clap Harcourt heartily on the back, greeting him with the words "*Epi To Beltion*".

Rowland groaned. These men were accomplices, not saviours.

Harcourt smirked, obviously enjoying his disappointment. "This, Mr. Sinclair, is the Kalokagathia—the best of humanity working to make humanity better."

Still gagged Rowland could say nothing. All hope of breaking away was fading fast.

Asquith grabbed a carpetbag out of the trunk. Almost ceremoniously, he and Harcourt hooked their arms through Rowland's, which were still bound in front of him, and dragged him to his feet. They walked him onto the deserted bridge with the five men of the Kalokagathia following closely behind. Once past the second recess they stopped.

Silently, with military order, they formed an arc around Rowland and backed him against the wall of the parapet. Asquith cut the bonds on his hands. The gag, they left in place.

"Undress, Mr. Sinclair," Harcourt commanded.

Rowland stared at him, sure that he had heard incorrectly.

"You heard me, Mr. Sinclair, remove all your garments, please."

Still Rowland did not move, shocked into a kind of fearless disbelief.

Harcourt backhanded him across the face. "Remove your clothes, Sinclair, or I swear Diogenes will remove them with his knife…in which case you may lose a yard of skin, as well."

Asquith pushed the blade against Rowland's throat to emphasise his brother's point. Rowland recoiled as the shallow cut reddened his collar with blood.

"Now," Harcourt warned.

Slowly, Rowland slipped off his jacket and then his shirt, and finally his trousers and shoes until he stood all but completely naked in the icy wind on Waterloo Bridge. Furious and cold, he watched Harcourt and Asquith, wondering what kind of perversion they had in mind, and looking desperately for any opportunity to escape.

Asquith surveyed the Australian's body thoughtfully, clearly but dispassionately assessing what he saw.

"In some ways he proves our case, does he not, Diogenes?" Harcourt said, moving to stand beside Rowland. His tone became professorial and he poked at his prisoner like some kind of exhibit. "The stature, the broad shoulders and lean, well-muscled frame of the Antipodean is, without question or doubt, the result of selective breeding. Only the strongest, fittest inmates were selected for transportation, you see and, once in the colony, the hardships of establishing a settlement in such an inhospitable wilderness picked off the weaker specimens."

Convinced now that he was among lunatics, Rowland attempted to pull off the gag so he could swear at his captor but Harcourt was not about to have his sermon disrupted.

"Leave it, Mr. Sinclair," he said, pointing his gun. "There will be time for your final words very soon. In the meantime, I will thank you not to interrupt!" Regathering his instructive poise, he continued. "Distance ensured that the blood of inferior peoples did not contaminate the superior genetics which had been established in the colony, and so we have here a strong, well-proportioned product of positive eugenics."

The Kalokagathia nodded in studious agreement. At that moment, Rowland would have traded his soul for the return of his clothes.

Harcourt paused as he considered the swastika of cigarette burns on Rowland's chest. "Interesting," he said, prodding the scar with his revolver. "A drinking game, perhaps…they are a somewhat primitive culture in many respects." He turned back to the Kalokagathia to complete the impromptu lecture. "Of course, convicts were selected for their physical strength and not their intellectual or moral powers—which has left us with a well-built monkey with criminal inclinations."

Too far. Rowland lunged for Harcourt. He managed to belt him once before he was brought down and subdued.

Harcourt mopped his bloody nose with a handkerchief. "And so you see, gentleman," he said, looking distastefully at Rowland, "the monkey proves my point." He motioned to his brother.

Asquith opened the carpetbag and took from it a lacy pink evening gown and a fox stole. He held it out to Rowland.

Harcourt smiled. "We'd like you to put this on, Mr. Sinclair."

Chapter Thirty-three

THEIR OWN RABBITS

Self-Sacrifice In Cause Of Science

By C.W.C.

A recent New York cable concerning Dr. Alan Blair's self-imposed agony when he allowed a poisonous spider to bite his finger, draws attention to the fact that such acts of noble self-sacrifice in the cause of medical science are not rare.

Dr. Houston, of the Metropolitan Water Board of London, drank raw Thames water, which contained approximately 218 million typhoid bacilli, to test a theory. "Every week there are similar instances of self-sacrifice in the interests of science but, as a rule, we hear nothing about them," Messrs. Bridges and Tiltman say.

—*The Advertiser*, 1933

Rowland reached around and pulled off the gag. Nobody stopped him on this occasion and he was able to speak for the first time in hours.

"What?" he said hoarsely. "What did you say?"

"We couldn't help but notice how awkward the constabulary finds dealing with a man in women's attire. You're going to put on this gown, Mr. Sinclair, and then throw yourself into the Thames—but don't worry, we'll knock you unconscious first—it'll all be very humane. When your corpse is found, certain assumptions will be made as to why you chose to take your own life. Most people will think it for the best and the matter will be closed and never spoken of again…So," Harcourt raised his weapon, "put on the gown, Mr. Sinclair. I think the colour will most become you."

"They'll find you in the reeds looking like Hamlet's Ophelia," Asquith laughed.

"There's no way my brother would believe—" Rowland began.

"Your brother will be so embarrassed he'll bury you with as little fuss as possible," Harcourt corrected.

Rowland gazed at the gun. He'd had enough now and rage supplanted fear and any form of caution. His voice seethed with fury. "You're going to have to shoot me, Harcourt, because I'm not trying on your bloody trousseau!"

Harcourt's face flushed. The forlorn bellow of a foghorn metered the stand-off.

"Very well, Mr. Sinclair. I'm sure we can manage, between us, to dress you ourselves. Any injuries will be, after all, attributed to your fall." Harcourt waved his revolver and signalled his comrades. The Kalokagathia closed in.

"Hullo, there! Are you all right?" In the distance, torches cut through the fog ahead of the voice. Unsettled, Harcourt turned towards the sound.

Rowland acted decisively, desperately, charging the Baron to the ground. The gun clattered onto the walkway.

"Get off, Sinclair!" Asquith discharged his own weapon in warning.

"You fool!" Harcourt turned upon his brother. "The whole world will hear that and descend upon us."

Rowland took his chance to run, but the Kalokagathia had regrouped and he was effectively penned.

"Just shoot him!" Harcourt demanded, scrabbling to retrieve his own gun.

Asquith hesitated.

Trapped against the bridge's parapet, Rowland could see only one way out…if it was a way out at all. Dying virtually naked was not ideal, but at least he wouldn't be wearing a pink evening dress. He hit the ground as Harcourt fired. The bullet splintered the stone capping just above his head. Rowland acted then before Harcourt could take aim again, vaulting the wall and plunging into the turbulent waters of the murky Thames.

"Are you aware of whom Rowland was to meet here, Mr. Watson Jones?" Wilfred bent to inspect the white marks on the alley wall under the light of a torch.

"No, sir." Clyde directed the torch so that Wilfred could see mark clearly. "We've already enquired at The Bitter Pill but nobody could place the man he met there. But there was a woman who saw him disappear into this alley."

"Why didn't she call the police?"

"She thought he might have had some business in the alley."

Wilfred frowned. "I see."

"She was not the kind of woman to readily seek out the police in any case, Mr. Sinclair." Clyde hesitated and then he asked, "I don't suppose Admiral Sinclair—"

"No. Quex hasn't got him this time." Wilfred frowned once again and shook his head. He glanced over at Edna, who had broken down in Milton's arms.

"And why is Miss Higgins crying?"

"She's scared, Mr. Sinclair. Rowly's luck has got to…" He exhaled. "I wish he'd simply waited for us."

"I fear such prudence is beyond my brother," Wilfred said angrily. "What were his movements this morning?"

"Rowly intended to speak to Mr. Wells. He hoped to find him at the economic conference."

"Why did he wish to speak with him?"

"He planned to make enquiries about Lord Harcourt."

"I can only presume this has to do with the Dawe girl?"

Clyde nodded.

Wilfred stared thoughtfully at the chalky marks on the brick wall. They were low down. Rowland must have been on the ground when his cast scraped the brick. "Dammit, Rowly," he muttered. He turned back to Clyde. "The London Constabulary are scouring the immediate area but, to be honest, Mr. Watson Jones, he could be virtually anywhere."

Rowland was unsure just how long he was below the surface. He had gasped water with the first shock of cold, before he remembered to hold his breath, to fight. There was a point when he became aware that he was no longer plunging downwards, deeper into darkness—that he had stopped. For what seemed an age, the water above him was too heavy, too pressing, to penetrate. And then some primal instinct to survive took hold and he began to claw his way to the surface.

His chest ached, his belly stung like it had been flayed, and he fought the urge to cough, to use his hands to block the screaming roar from his ears. He broke the surface vomiting water, his body cramping with cold as the current dragged him along. Unable to see anything Rowland began to doubt that he had come up after all…an overwhelming call to sleep beckoned him down into the Thames.

After a fruitless search in Soho, Wilfred had sent them back to Claridge's in the early hours of the morning. They had no doubt that despite Wilfred's often disapproving regard of his brother, he would search every room of Buckingham Palace itself, if that were what it took to find Rowland. Even so, they couldn't just wait without trying something—anything—themselves.

It was fortunate, then, that Wilfred did not call five minutes later or they might have already left their hotel on a search of their own accord.

Clyde answered the telephone.

Wilfred's voice was strained. "I'm afraid I have just received a report that a man jumped from the Waterloo Bridge a few hours ago."

"Jumped? Rowly wouldn't..."

"An officer...an officer advised me that Rowly's jacket, with his pocketbook and that bloody sketchbook of his, were discovered on the walkway. There was some sort of affray on the bridge...a gun was fired several times."

Clyde felt ill, sensing Milton's and Edna's hopeful eyes upon him. They thought it was good news.

"They'll drag the river at first light, Mr. Watson Jones." Wilfred stopped for several moments. "I'm on my way to the Victoria Embankment, on the off-chance—"

Clyde interrupted Wilfred's sentence. "We'll meet you there, Mr. Sinclair."

The beam of light caught him just as he was about to slip languidly back into the depths. A strong arm reached out and grabbed his shoulder. And then another set of arms and he was hoisted into the dinghy. He lay there, shivering violently and gagging the putrid river from his lungs. The men threw a rough blanket over him and the old soldier held his hand and spoke to him of salvation in case he should die before they reached the shore. "The Lord liveth; and blessed be my rock; and let the God of my salvation be exalted...."

Tea was the first thing other than cold of which Rowland became aware. Warm, sweet, tea in an enamel cup, being tipped carefully past his lips. He was wrapped in blankets, a hot water bottle against his chest. There was a soft supporting arm behind his head as the tea was pressed to his lips again. He drank obediently and the voice of the woman who tended him penetrated the fog of his mind.

"That's right, pet, drink. We thought the Lord had taken you for a while there when you first came in."

The bouts of shivering were less violent now. Gradually, as he warmed, full consciousness returned, and with it a disjointed recollection of what had happened on the bridge.

Rowland stared at the old-fashioned bonnet, which framed the young woman's plump rosy-cheeked face, secured in place by a wide blue ribbon. He felt he should recognise it somehow, but concentration was still fleeting.

The woman smiled warmly at him. He attempted to sit up, surprised by how much every part of him ached.

"Where am I, madam?" he asked, turning his head to take in his surroundings. He was in a small room attached to what seemed to be a dormitory. The walls were painted grey and green. There was a vacant bed next to his. Through the open doorway he could see at least fifty iron cots crammed into the adjoining hall in rows so tight that one would be able to touch the occupant of the neighbouring bed simply by reaching out. Almost every cot was occupied.

A few men gathered about the doorway between the dormitory and the small room, watching him curiously. Others went about their business or slept.

"Welcome to the Salvation Army Hostel for Men…in Blackfriars."

Rowland placed the bonnet then—the Salvation Army. Somehow he'd found his way into the care of the Salvation Army. "I must make a telephone call…."

"Don't try to get up yet," the woman cautioned looking at him strangely. "I've sent someone to find you some suitable clothes from the donation box."

"Yes, of course," Rowland murmured, remembering he'd left his clothes on Waterloo Bridge. He was recovered enough to feel embarrassed about his state of undress. Awkwardly, he introduced himself.

"Corps Cadet Martha Pratchett at your service," his nurse chirped enthusiastically, as she jotted his details on a form.

"I'm most pleased to make your acquaintance, Miss Pratchett. I can't thank you enough for your kindness."

Martha Pratchett studied him sternly in response. "I must say, Mr. Sinclair, you don't look or sound down and out…and you don't seem particularly despondent."

"I'm not." Rowland was puzzled that she would expect him to be so.

"Then why would you try to end it all?" she cried passionately.

"I didn't," Rowland sat up alarmed. Several of the men in the other room had looked up and were now listening intently.

"They said you jumped from the bridge."

"Yes…but only because people were shooting at me."

"Shooting?" Corps Cadet Martha Pratchett put her hands on her hips and regarded him in a way that made her scepticism clear. "Well, that may be, but surely you knew full well that you'd most certainly die jumping into the Thames with naught but your undergarments on!"

"But I didn't die," Rowland reminded her, "and I assure you the alternative was, by far, grimmer!"

"Well, you are very lucky, indeed, that we found you. The army patrols that bridge, because of all the suicides, you see. We keep a small launch boat ready to help anyone who ends up in the water…though most of the poor souls have gone to explain themselves to the Lord before we can fish them out."

"I am very grateful," Rowland said sincerely. "But I do need to get in contact with—"

"That can wait. I'm not sure you're ready to face the world yet." Martha patted Rowland's shoulder through the blankets. "Remember, Mr. Sinclair, it's when the world is darkest that your light can shine the brightest."

An old man in uniform came into the hall carrying a box under one arm. He greeted many of the men in the dormitory by name, making jokes and slapping the odd back as he wove through the narrow spaces between the beds towards the clinic in which Rowland lay.

"May I introduce your rescuer, Captain Leonard," Martha said. "He pulled you out of the river with the good Lord's help."

The smiling captain dismissed Rowland's gratitude. "It's nice to get a live one 'casionally," he said, placing the box down on the bed by Rowland. "You'll find somethin' to fit you in here, son. They won't be too stylish, but they're clean and paid fer."

"I'm sure they'll be more than adequate, Captain. Thank you. I do, however, need to access a telephone to let my friends know my whereabouts."

"Martha might step out while you change," the captain said, "and then we can talk about what you're going to do."

"I trust, Mr. Sinclair, that you will never consider doing anything so desperate again," Martha added. "Cast thy burden upon the Lord and he shall sustain thee. I'm sure your loved ones would be deeply grieved if they knew the terrible extents to which despair drove you. Self-murder is never the solution."

Rowland paused momentarily and then smiled. "I was trying to avoid being shot, Miss Pratchett."

"Sometimes it seems that way, Mr. Sinclair, and when it does you must let the Lord be your shield against the bullets of misery and temptation. Because of His strength will I wait upon thee: for God is my defence!"

Rowland gave up. "Yes, Miss Pratchett, I'll remember that… the Lord shall be my shield."

She beamed. "I'll let you get dressed, Mr. Sinclair, so you may begin the rest of your life." She trotted triumphantly out into the dormitory.

Captain Leonard winked apologetically as he shut the door between the rudimentary clinic and the dormitory. "The cadets can be overzealous about the salvation part of our work—their lights are sometimes a little dazzlin'," he said.

Rowland smiled. He climbed out of the low iron bed, still slow and unsteady. Leonard lent him a shoulder until he felt stable on his own legs.

The clothes, as the captain had warned, were old and patched and completely mismatched, but they were clean and they were *clothes*.

The outer layer of the cast on Rowland's right arm had disintegrated somewhat in the water, but he was otherwise intact. He buttoned the donated shirt, rolling up its right sleeve in the hope the plaster would dry out a little.

"In case you're concerned, Mr. Sinclair," Leonard said quietly, "we 'aven't told the Old Bill that you're 'ere."

"Why not?" Rowland asked, surprised.

"We felt it would not help your state 'a mind to be arrested."

"I don't understand, Captain Leonard. Why would I be arrested?"

"Attempted suicide is considered a very serious crime. But we don't judge, and we only want to help. Were it gamblin' debts that brought you so low…or a disappointment in love perhaps?"

"I was not trying to take my own life," Rowland said wearily. "I was trying to escape."

The old soldier smiled sympathetically. "Many people put it that way." He placed his hand on Rowland's shoulder. "It's all right, son. Lord 'arcourt has told us how it was. I'm told the poor man was distraught."

Rowland pulled away. "Harcourt? What did he say?"

Captain Leonard hesitated.

"Please…I really need to know what's going on."

Nodding finally, Leonard sat on the bed to explain. "The Salvation Army patrols Waterloo Bridge for people trying to jump, or just men in need. Our Sergeant Brooks and some young corps cadets were on the bridge last night, I was on shift with the dinghy. The foot patrol 'eard a disturbance from some ways away and went to see if anyone needed 'elp or comfort."

Rowland recalled the torches in the distance.

"They 'esitated, naturally, when they 'eard gunshots—but with the good Lord's 'elp, they found the courage to push on and investigate. When they reached the spot from where you'd gone and jumped, a gentleman—Lord 'arcourt, he said he was—told them what 'ad 'appened. He and the other gentlemen 'ad come across you trying to shoot yourself on the bridge. They'd wrestled the firearm from your hand after you'd discharged it wild-like. When they managed to seize the gun, you—being most determined to destroy yourself—vaulted the parapet wall and jumped. Sergeant Brooks says they were very concerned to see if you 'ad survived."

Rowland wanted to curse. He clenched his fist in his hair. "Do they know I survived, sir?"

"Poss'bly not. It were dark and the tides are so fearful strong in the Thames that we pulled you out a fair way from the bridge and we brought you straight 'ere. Sergeant Brooks didn't even realise we'd found you until he came in this last hour. According to 'im, Lord 'arcourt and his companions departed before the Old Bill arrived, they were so upset about what 'appened."

Rowland looked the kindly man in the eye. "Captain Leonard," he said urgently, "I promise you, sir, I wasn't intent on committing suicide. I didn't even contemplate it. Lord Harcourt and his insane associates were trying to kill me. Think, man! What would a peer of the realm and his companions be doing walking across Waterloo Bridge in the middle of the night?"

Leonard gaped at him, stupefied.

"Harcourt and his companions are vile and reprehensible murderers—they've already killed one man. I was to be the second. Please. God only knows what they're up to at this moment."

The captain bit his lip. "We thought…I'm so sorry, Mr. Sinclair."

"Please don't be. If it wasn't for you I would have drowned. I do appreciate your help, sir, but I desperately need to contact the police and my brother and friends. They could well believe me dead by now."

"Captain Leonard!" Martha Pratchett knocked insistently on the door. "Captain Leonard!"

"Yes, Comrade…We're nearly—" Leonard began.

Corps Cadet Pratchett burst in with her hands over her eyes in case Rowland should still be undressed. She was clearly flustered, by more than the thought of a naked man. "There are some gentlemen here, Captain Leonard, who are insisting that we hand Mr. Sinclair over to them."

Chapter Thirty-four

Salvation Army Bands

How They Began

...Soon after the founder, William Booth, had got his struggling little organisation going in London, said the speaker, an ardent worker named Fry, a resident of Salisbury, in the south of England, took his family of boys into the streets to play music as an aid to their work in spreading the influence of the Army, and about the same time a party of miners followed the same practice in the north of England. General Booth, ever watchful for a chance to increase the popularity of the Army and to attract the poor, Godless classes, saw a way in this idea to come in contact with the very people he was out to reform. Thus the Army bands began, and although they had improved greatly since those days, and were worthy of representation in musical festivals, their mission was still the same.

—*The West Australian*, 1933

Rowland tensed. Could the Kalokagathia have realised that he hadn't drowned? Had they seen the captain's dinghy and tracked him to the Blackfriars Hostel?

"Thank you, Corps Cadet," Leonard said. "I'll talk to them." He turned to Rowland. "Do not worry, Mr. Sinclair. We are the Lord's Army and you shall be defended!"

"Unto thee," Martha Pratchett cried, "O my strength, will I sing: for God is my defence, and the God of my mercy!"

"Captain Leonard," Rowland said quietly, "Harcourt and his companions are dangerous. I don't suppose the Lord's Army has weapons?"

"We have the Gospel, Mr. Sinclair."

"Then I'd best come with you, sir. I'll not have your comrades endangered on my account."

"As you wish, Mr. Sinclair, but stay behind me." The captain frowned thoughtfully. "Corps Cadet," he said to Martha Pratchett, "summon all our soldiers to the reception. Let us greet the enemy with a show of force…and Martha, per'aps you'd better send for the Old Bill now."

And so it was that when Rowland Sinclair walked into the reception room of the Blackfriars Men's Hostel to confront Lord Harcourt and his Kalokagathia, he did so surrounded by what seemed an entire regiment of the Salvation Army. A young cadet started to sing, and soon the hostel rang with full and earnest voices raised in "Even Greater Things."

From the midst of this extraordinary procession, did Rowland find his brother and his friends at the reception desk.

For a while their utter relief at finding Rowland alive stayed all questions as to why he would be leading a parade through the hostel. They could not have heard one another in any case, as the army continued to belt out, "Greater things! Greater things! Give us faith, O Lord, we pray, faith for greater things."

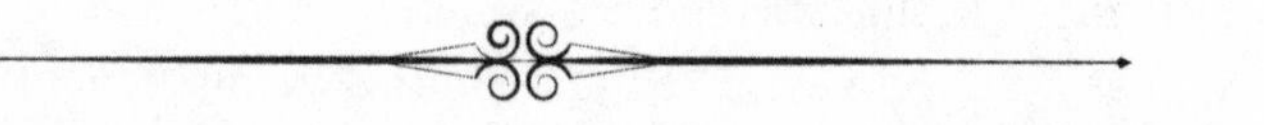

Edna glanced at the settee where Rowland had drifted off. The police had questioned him until well after dawn and, considering how he had spent the night, it was no wonder he was exhausted.

Not that any of them had spent the night well. There had been a while when all of them—even Wilfred—had been convinced

Rowland Sinclair was dead. Edna shuddered as she remembered the overwhelming horror of believing she would never see or touch or confide in him again. She thought of Wilfred Sinclair, staring out at the Thames in such deep and silent pain. Both Clyde and Milton loved Rowland like a brother, but Wilfred *was* his brother.

Edna had walked away from the men, unable to bear the sight of them struggling with their grief. She'd given in to hers. Seized by anguish, she'd wept like a lost child.

One of the many ragged men who slept on the embankment near the Waterloo Bridge had asked her why she was crying. He was dirty and muttered strangely but she'd talked to him anyway.

"I seen it," he said, looking wildly about. "He jumped, your sweetheart did. Went in dere...came up dere...and then the Sallies scooped him up in dere boat and took him. The Sallies take men from 'ere—it ain't right. The gov'ment should do somefink about it! It ain't right."

Edna knew she had frightened the poor man, screaming so excitedly for Clyde and Milton and Wilfred to come and hear his tale. By the time they'd reached her, he'd darted away and would not speak to any of them again.

But he'd told the sculptress enough.

Of course, when they'd finally located the Blackfriars Hostel, Wilfred had been perhaps too fervent in his demands for his brother's return. It had alarmed the young woman at the reception desk. But Edna could understand his impatience.

She mused on the manner in which Wilfred simply shook his brother's hand when at last Rowland emerged. Men said so much with their handshakes. Edna had embraced Rowland, clung to him and wept relief into his neck, but she was not a man and nobody expected her to hide so much.

The telephone rang. Clyde answered and after a brief exchange he replaced the receiver and woke Rowland.

"Your brother's on his way up, mate. He's got George Allen and Allie."

Rowland sat up and attempted to rub the fatigue from his

face. Edna uncurled herself from the armchair, smoothed her skirt, and put her shoes back on.

"Pierrepont!" Milton warned as they heard the knock on the door. Having established that the peer had been a victim of the Thistlewaites, tricked into marriage and then murdered to protect the secret of Euphemia's child, they had restored his wax head to the sideboard.

Edna grabbed her shawl from the back of a chair and draped it over the sculpture just moments before Clyde opened the door to admit Wilfred Sinclair, George Allen, and Miss Allie Dawe.

The solicitor had been despatched to Holloway to arrange the release of Allie Dawe as soon as the police had taken and accepted Rowland's statement.

Rowland was still unsure of how much Allie knew about the discoveries and events of the past days. She was quite withdrawn and seemed now to startle when anyone spoke directly to her. He wanted to comfort her, but was afraid that doing so would reopen old wounds. Rowland did not ask Allie Dawe whether she had forgiven him, but he hoped she would in time.

Allen informed them that Lord Harcourt had been arrested, as had his brother, who worked for the Ministry of Health under the name Diogenes Asquith. Three members of the Kalokagathia had panicked and were providing evidence of all the clandestine activities of the society and the Thistlewaite brothers. It appeared the impregnation of Euphemia Thistlewaite was a premeditated experiment designed to prove the extreme position of the Kalokagathia.

"Whilst Lady Pierrepont was, of course, *prima facie* involved," Allen concluded, "it is uncertain whether she possessed the requisite *mens rea* to be considered legally culpable."

Wilfred and his family, it had been decided, would join Rowland and his companions in embarking for Sydney in a few days. London's Economic Conference had stalled irretrievably.

"God, I'm sorry, Wil," Rowland said guiltily.

Wilfred sighed. "It was nothing to do with you, or the Blackshirts, Rowly. Roosevelt has set his mind against an agreement and, without the Americans..." he shook his head.

The American President, it appeared, had withdrawn support and then actively spoken against the conference's lofty aims. The result was bickering and very little else.

Allen nodded sagely. "I must say it all reminds me of a story from Cicero's dialogue—*De Legibus*—in which Atticus says: *me Athenis audire ex Phaedro meo memini Gellium, familiarem tuum, cum pro consule ex praetura in Graeciam venisset essetque Atehis, philosophos, qui tum errant, in lucum unum covocasse ipsisque mango opera auctorem fuisse, ut aliquando controversiarum aliquem facerent modum; quodsi essent eo animo, ut nollent aetatem in litibus conterere, posse rem convenire; et simul operam suam illis esse pollicitum, si posset inter eos aliquid convenire.*"

Clyde cleared his throat, casting a "what-the-Hell" glance in Rowland's direction.

"Got to hand it to that Atticus," Milton said, smiling and nodding. "He knew how to tell a joke!"

"What are your plans, Allie?" Edna asked before Allen could work out that Milton hadn't understood a single Latin word.

"Lord Bishopthorpe is arranging for me to take singing lessons!" She became a little less listless and a faint shadow of a her old vibrancy returned. "He's going to settle everything for mother and me, and says we mustn't worry because Uncle Alfred left us quite a lot of money."

Rowland smiled. Buchan was as good as his word. Pierrepont could not have left Allie and her mother anything at all, but clearly the Earl of Bishopthorpe intended to see them right while ensuring they did not feel too beholden. Allie's detachment, her reluctance to look at him, worried Rowland a little, but she had been through a great deal. Perhaps singing would help her as painting had helped him. Wilfred glanced at his pocket watch. "We must be going," he said, standing as he closed the timepiece. "I'm sure you could all do with an early night."

Edna smiled. "We'll have to wait till Dr. Ambrose finishes setting Rowly's arm again. He's calling tonight when he finishes at the factory."

Wilfred sighed and regarded his brother in exasperation. "Yes, Dr. Pennyworth mentioned you refused to allow him to attend properly to your arm. I suppose I should be glad that you chose not to tell the poor man it was because you'd prefer to be treated by a doll-maker!"

Rowland laughed. Pennyworth had removed the remnants of the old cast immediately, lest the moisture lead to some type of skin infection. Though the bone had clearly knitted, the physician had thought Rowland's refusal to submit to a new cast foolhardy. He expected full well that the still fragile bone would be rebroken in days. "Ambrose knows what he's doing—with bones, as well as plaster," Rowland assured his brother as he saw his guests to the door. "In any case, I find myself unexpectedly short of a suit."

"Yes, quite," Wilfred muttered as he stood back for Allie Dawe and Allen to proceed ahead of him. He glanced at the head-shaped lump on the sideboard which Edna had hastily cloaked with her shawl. "I thought I told you to get rid of that thing!" he growled.

"I've been a little preoccupied," Rowland replied tersely. "I'll take it back to the waxworks first thing tomorrow."

"See that you do!" Wilfred shook his brother's hand. "Ethel would like you all to come to supper tomorrow."

"Of course."

"Allen tells me that you asked him to arrange quite a substantial contribution to the Salvation Army?"

Rowland frowned. The size of the donation had obviously so alarmed the solicitor that he had alerted Wilfred. "Yes, I did."

Wilfred nodded. "I instructed him to double it." He patted Rowland's shoulder. "Return that head," he ordered as he walked into the hall.

Chapter Thirty-five

Mr. Churchill as Historian

£20,000 FOR NEW WORK

London, February 21

> The "Daily Telegraph" understands that Mr. Winston Churchill has agreed to write a "History of the English-speaking Peoples," running into 400,000 words. Cassells, the well-known publishers, are paying over £20,000 for the copyright.
>
> —*Kalgoorlie Miner*, 1933

Rowland and his companions arrived at Madame Tussaud's early, with Pierrepont in the Gladstone bag. They found Marriott Spencer in a terrible and vocal dither. It appeared his assistant had contracted what he called "some kind of pox" and he'd been left short-handed.

"I'm measuring today," he lamented. "The subject will be here in a few minutes and this is *not* something I can do alone!"

"Well, can't I help you, Marriott?" Edna volunteered.

"The chart is complicated. The measurements must be taken exactly and written into precisely the right column or it will mean nothing," Spencer wailed. "He will not be happy...not happy at all."

"Well, why don't you take all the measurements and I can record them," Edna suggested calmly. "You can show me how the chart works right now."

"But I can't take the measurements!" Spencer moaned, holding up his prosthetic and waving it about. "My hook...it scares the subjects."

"Too bloody right, it would!" Milton murmured as he ducked away from the path of the hook.

"Now don't get worked up, Marriott, dear," Edna said, grabbing his arm before he inadvertently stabbed somebody. "Show me how to use your measuring instruments and I'll measure. You can write the measurements down."

Spencer glanced at his watch. "Perhaps it might be done... you were always the cleverest of my students. Yes, let us pray that he is late and that there will be time to teach you."

Edna pushed up her sleeves. "Let's get started then. You don't mind waiting, do you gentlemen?"

"Of course not."

They settled themselves in the modest but well-appointed waiting room, while Edna accompanied the sculptor into the adjoining workshop. Milton and Clyde leafed through the out-of-date newspapers in the magazine rack. Rowland extracted from his breast pocket the artist's notebook that had been returned to him through Wilfred.

Ambrose had recast his right arm the previous evening with the same efficiency and economy of plaster. Rowland could therefore grip the notebook easily or, if he chose, use his right hand to draw. He began a sketch of Martha Pratchett. The lines were soft and round as he captured the warmth and generosity of her conviction.

A pair of gentlemen walked into the waiting room. The elder was easily recognisable, even by Australians; and, since he was Spencer's subject, not a surprising presence at Madame Tussaud's. Winston Churchill, whose illustrious political career had floundered since the Conservatives had lost government in 1929, removed his bowler hat to reveal the barren terrain of his rather large head. The second man was younger, scholarly, and deferential. Rowland guessed he was Churchill's private secretary.

Churchill checked his pocket watch and realised he was early. Taking the club chair beside Rowland, he tapped his walking stick impatiently.

Rowland looked up from his sketch. "Good morning."

"Yes, yes, good morning, good morning." The politician looked at Rowland. "Are we acquainted, sir?"

"I don't believe so." Rowland introduced himself, and then his companions, to the former Chancellor of the Exchequer. Churchill in his turn introduced his secretary without actually permitting the man to say a word on his own account.

"Am I to understand, by the presence of so many Australians in this room," Churchill said as he cut and lit a cigar, "that Mr. Spencer is planning some type of Antipodean display?"

"Not at all," Rowland assured him. "We aren't here as subjects."

Churchill scowled. "I expect I should be grateful that I won't be required to queue for the dubious privilege of being a wax exhibit!" He tapped his stick irritably. "I do hope this won't take long. Another five hundred bricks and my wall will be complete. I could lay two hundred bricks in the time I'm wasting here!"

Rowland's brow rose. He really had nothing to offer on the subject of laying bricks. That the aristocratic Winston Churchill was building walls was surprising, but he supposed the politician had a lot of time on his hands these days.

Rowland attempted instead to mitigate on Marriott Spencer's behalf. "Mr. Spencer is, I understand, a very particular and talented artist, sir. I'm sure the wait will be worthwhile."

Churchill snorted.

"Did I request thee, Maker, from my clay to mould me man?" Milton sighed. "Did I solicit thee from darkness to promote me?"

"That's Milton, isn't it?" Churchill said gruffly. "From *Paradise Lost*?"

Rowland smiled, relieved. Finally, the appropriation of Milton which he and Edna had been expecting for weeks. Now they could all move on.

Milton grinned and winked at Rowland. "Thought I'd put you out of your misery, mate," he whispered.

Rowland grimaced, realising he could no longer rely on what Milton was reading to help him pinpoint what exactly the poet was stealing.

Churchill was oblivious to this exchange as he peered over at Rowland's notebook. "I see you are a rather accomplished artist yourself, Mr. Sinclair."

"That's very kind of you to say."

"Kindness has nothing to do with it, Mr. Sinclair—I have no reason to be unduly kind to you. May I?" He clenched the cigar between his teeth and put his hand out for the sketchbook.

"Certainly."

Churchill looked thoughtfully at the sketch of Martha Pratchett. "Do you draw from memory or imagination, Mr. Sinclair?"

"Generally, only what I see or have seen, Mr. Churchill."

Churchill turned the pages, commenting occasionally on a particular picture, complimenting Rowland on the audacity of his style. He noted the absence of landscapes among the sketches. "I am myself quite captivated by the compositional challenge of a landscape," he said, puffing on the cigar. Churchill expounded for a while on the aesthetic reward of painting the lie of the land, the subjugation of the canvas through a strategic assault with paint, to produce hills and trees with dazzling effect.

Rowland might have deferred in that part of the conversation to Clyde, who did paint landscapes, but it was not really a conversation—more a monologue. Milton returned to his newspaper.

When Churchill turned to the sketches Rowland had made in Munich, he became particularly intrigued. "I assume you were in Germany only recently?"

"Yes, we were."

"And you saw all this?" Churchill asked, studying various drawings of brown-shirted Stormtroopers, of book-burnings and rallies. The artist's pencil had caught the rising nationalistic fervour in the eyes of Hitler's people. The Englishman paused over a sketch of Unity Mitford, the young British aristocrat obsessed with the German Führer, whom Rowland had encountered in Munich.

"This is Unity, isn't it?" Churchill said, surprised.

"Yes, I met Miss Mitford in Germany."

"She's a cousin of mine, did you know?"

"I didn't."

"Are you a Fascist, Mr. Sinclair? Fascism seems to have become fashionable among people your age. Unity is quite enamoured of it, I believe."

"No, I am not a Fascist," Rowland said coldly.

Perhaps realising he had offended the Australian, Churchill sat back and, after the tense silence that followed, tried to change the subject.

"Clearly, your injury does not inhibit your work, Mr. Sinclair." He nodded at the cast. "How did you damage yourself?"

Still smarting under the assumption that he was a Fascist, Rowland responded more bluntly and honestly than he might otherwise have. "Nazi Stormtroopers held me down and broke my arm because they didn't like the way I painted."

Slowly, Churchill pulled the cigar out of his mouth. "Are you a Communist, Mr. Sinclair?"

"Would the punishment have been appropriate if I were?" Rowland demanded. "No, I'm not. Nor am I Jewish, Mr. Churchill, in case you also believe that to be reason enough to ignore what's been happening in Germany!" Although aware that he was dealing harshly with Churchill, Rowland was—after weeks of listening to politicians make excuses for the Nazi atrocities, of having his concerns dismissed and ignored—unable to hold back.

Milton placed an old copy of *The Guardian* on the coffee table in front of Churchill, open at an article on the final speech given by Reich Minister Alfred Hugenberg at the London Economic Conference in June. The Nazi delegate had spoken of ending the Depression by allowing Germany to annex Northern Africa and Eastern Europe under the Third Reich.

"You will note, sir," Churchill said, "that Herr Hitler has since sacked Hugenberg from the ministry."

"Did Hitler sack him for the content of the speech or for letting the cat out of the bag?" Milton challenged.

"Some would say you sound like a warmonger, Mr. Isaacs," Churchill replied, though his tone was noncommittal. "Herr Hitler says he wants peace…and my parliamentary colleagues believe that we can appease the Nazis."

"Appease them? Rowly, show Mr. Churchill what else the SA did to you," Milton said bitterly.

Rowland hesitated, a little weary of being asked to undress yet again, but he could see that they had Churchill's attention. He loosened his tie, unfastened the first few buttons of his shirt, and exposed the swastika-shaped scar made up of dozens of cigarette burns.

Churchill flinched.

"Rowly's not Jewish, he's not a Communist, he's not even impolite and yet they did that to him," Milton said angrily, "after they'd broken his arm and just before they tried to shoot him. Rowly's an Australian, a British citizen, so perhaps we shouldn't all sit here comforted by the fact that this sort of thing happens to someone else…because I'm telling you, Mr. Churchill, the Nazis intend to burn their bloody cross onto more than just Rowly!"

Churchill's secretary cleared his throat.

Marriott Spencer had emerged from the workshop. He glanced at the occupants of the sitting room like a startled rabbit. "I'm so sorry to have kept you waiting, Mr. Churchill. We're ready for you now."

Churchill put the cigar back in his mouth and stood.

"Don't apologise, Mr. Spencer—I've had a most interesting conversation with the gentlemen loitering in your waiting room!" He handed the artist's notebook back to Rowland. "Do you paint, Mr. Sinclair? I should like to keep a weather eye out for your work."

"Rear Admiral Sinclair has his latest paintings," Milton said recklessly. "He might show you."

Churchill's brow rose. "Quex has them, has he? I might just ask him."

Rowland refastened his collar and adjusted his tie as Churchill disappeared into the workshop with Marriott Spencer. The startled secretary stood at the last moment and literally ran to join his employer.

Clyde grimaced at Rowland and Milton. "Spencer's not going to be happy if you've upset his subject—might throw the measurements out."

Rowland sighed. "I did lose my rag a bit…"

"Nonsense!" Milton declared. "We told him the truth. It's a pity he's such a spent force."

Rowland groaned. Milton was right. Churchill was in the wilderness politically—an anachronism of conservatism, alienated for his intractability on the subject of Indian self-government, among other things. They'd shouted at the poor old man for nothing. Even if they'd got through to him, no one would pay any attention to Winston Churchill.

Epilogue

The London Economic Conference finally closed on 27 July 1933, its purpose unrealised. The early denunciation of currency stabilisation by President Roosevelt of the United States of America rendered its objective of achieving that impossible. The Great Depression would continue.

Offended that his gift had been rejected, Francis Pocock refused to accept the return of the wax replica he had created of Lord Pierrepont's head. Unable to find any other suitable home, Rowland Sinclair gave it to Inspector Entwhistle of Scotland Yard who committed it to the collection of the Black Museum.

On 14 August 1933, Winston Churchill made his first of many public speeches warning against the ambitions of Adolf Hitler and urging Britain to rearm. He would be considered a warmonger by some and a prophet by others. Throughout his life, Churchill was remade in wax for Madame Tussaud's a total of seven times. Each time a little more wax was required.

In the latter half of 1933, H.G. Wells published *The Shape of Things to Come*, a science fiction which contemplated a Utopian world under a single global government. The point of divergence for this alternative history was the London Economic Conference which Wells covered with poignant disappointment in a chapter titled, "The London Conference: the Crowning Failure of the Old Governments; The spread of Dictatorships and Fascisms."

In September 1933, Prime Minister Joseph Lyons appointed Stanley Melbourne Bruce to the post of Australia's High Commissioner in Britain, a position Bruce would hold until 1945. In 1947, the Hon. S.M. Bruce would be made Lord Bruce, the Viscount of Melbourne. Ethel Bruce stayed in touch with the young people who helped her solve the mysterious case of Lord Pierrepont, and her hats continued to be a subject of comment by her husband.

Prince George became the Duke of Kent in 1934 just prior to his wedding to Princess Marina of Greece. In 1938, he was appointed Governor-General of Australia, but the appointment was postponed due to the outbreak of war in 1939. He did not survive to take up the role.

Thelma, Viscountess Furness, who had been the Prince of Wales' regular companion since 1929, returned temporarily to the U.S. in January 1934 to visit her sister in New York. She asked her close friend Wallis Simpson, who had recently returned from a tour of Germany and Norway, to look after the Prince in her absence.

In 1934, Josslyn Hay, the Earl of Erroll, joined Oswald Mosley's British Union of Fascists. The following year, Hay returned to Kenya and the Happy Valley Set, a group of Colonial expatriates notorious for their hedonistic lifestyles. In 1941, he would be found shot dead in his car at a crossroads on the Nairobi-Ngong Road.

The Ambroses prospered in London, establishing themselves as the makers of particularly lifelike mannequins. The eldest son of Ambrose the tailor left the family business to be apprenticed by Marriott Spencer at Madame Tussaud's.

In 1934, William Joyce was made Director of Propaganda for the British Union of Fascists and later appointed Deputy Leader. He spearheaded the B.U.F.'s shift from an economic platform to one based on anti-Semitism. Shortly before war was declared in 1939, Joyce and his wife would flee to Germany. During the war, Joyce was employed as a propaganda broadcaster by German Radio's English Service. His privileged British accent earned him the moniker "Lord Haw Haw." He and Rowland Sinclair would meet again.

The Blackfriars Men's Hostel run by the Salvation Army benefited from the quiet patronage of the Sinclairs. It continued to provide soup, soap, and salvation to thousands of hungry and desperate men. Martha Pratchett rose to the rank of General. Captain Leonard continued to patrol the Thames near Waterloo Bridge for those who found themselves floundering in dark waters.

The Waterloo Bridge was demolished and rebuilt in the early forties. Granite stones from the original structure were presented to various parts of the British world in order to further historic links among the British Commonwealth of Nations. Two of these stones now make up part of the Commonwealth Avenue Bridge which spans Lake Burley Griffin in Canberra, Australia.

Allen and Overy would grow to become one of the largest law firms in the world. The firm's reputation would be made by the role of its founding partner, George Allen, in advising to King Edward VIII during the abdication crisis of 1936.

Between 1923 and 1939, Rear Admiral Sir Hugh Francis Paget Sinclair KCB, (Quex) held the post of director, or "C," of the Secret Intelligence Service. In 1938, under the shadow of impending war, Quex would purchase Bletchley Park—which he had first come across in surveillance reports on the activities of his young Australian cousin. The rear admiral would buy the idiosyncratic mansion with private funds to use as a wartime intelligence station. He, too, would meet Rowland Sinclair again.

The Sinclair brothers and their respective entourages embarked for Sydney on the *SS Monterey* in late July. The outstanding charges for public indecency against Mr. Elias Isaacs were dropped. Quex Sinclair did in fact see them all off…though they had no idea that he was there.

Rowland Sinclair made a full and complete recovery from the various injuries he'd sustained in the months since he'd left Sydney. As much as he hated it, the scar on his chest caused him no problems, as long as he remained dressed. Of course that was not always possible.

Acknowledgments

Rowland Sinclair and his irrepressible companions have lived in my head for five books. So…one would think that by now I could write a novel on my own. But I can't. There are many people involved in the creation of my books. I'd like to acknowledge and thank them here.

My husband, Michael, who lives with me and the people in my head as if it were a perfectly normal thing to do, who edits manuscripts, discusses characters, and helps me understand the thirties. I would never have found Rowland without him.

My boys, Edmund and Atticus, who tolerate the whims and vagaries of a mother who writes, and who still steadfastly believe this series could use a werewolf.

My father, who reads every single one of my manuscripts immediately, and who is brave enough to tell me honestly what he thinks. He tempers an accountant's realism with a parent's unfailing belief in my work. My sister, Devini, who picks up the telephone even when she knows I'm just calling to talk about plots.

Leith Henry, who has been my friend since childhood and with whom I first began to write, who knows me well enough to step into my head and have a chat with Rowland. Jason Henry who sent me a toaster at a desperate time in my gastronomic life, when I really needed a toaster.

Alastair Blanshard, whose namesake does not appear in this book, but whose influence and advice does; who selflessly shared his memories of Oxford, partridges, and buckshot, and his hands-on knowledge of bow ties.

Wallace Fernandes, who values our friendship enough to pretend he's read my books (whilst I pretend I believe him); who explained to me the superiority of the Full Windsor knot and who makes me laugh when the practicalities of being a writer seem impossible.

Sarah Kynaston, nee Dabinett, who responds to my mad ideas with insane ones of her own, and then makes me put them into practice. Cheryl Bousfield and Lesley Bocquet whose enthusiasm for books is contagious and whose friendship is valued indeed.

All those writers I have the privilege to call my friends, who I won't mention individually because it'll look like I'm name-dropping, who have from the first, been generous and warm with their advice and their support. Amongst these, the Sisters in Crime, whose camaraderie and humour is reason enough to be a crime writer.

Rebecca Lochlann, who I came to know when we were both unpublished aspiring writers and whose work continues to enchant and move me.

Nigel E.S. Irvine, who sends me inspiration and ideas from his wanderings through archives and museums.

Poisoned Pen Press, who have brought my books to the U.S. and with whom it is both a pleasure and an honour to work..

Professor Carl Bridge of the Menzies Centre for Australian Studies in King's College who took the time to answer the queries of a complete stranger purporting to write a book. The public affairs desk of the Australian High Commission in London who directed me to Professor Bridge in the first place.

The booksellers and bloggers who have introduced Rowland to their customers, friends, and followers—thank you.

All the readers who have allowed me the privilege of their attention and their time. It is never taken for granted.

About Sulari Gentill

A reformed lawyer, Sulari Gentill is the author of the *Rowland Sinclair Mysteries*, eight historical crime novels (thus far) chronicling the life and adventures of her 1930s Australian gentleman artist, and the *Hero Trilogy*, based on the myths and epics of the ancient world. She lives with her husband, Michael, and their boys, Edmund and Atticus, on a small farm in the foothills of the Snowy Mountains, where she grows French black truffles and works in her pyjamas.

Sulari has been shortlisted for the Commonwealth Writers' Prize – Best First Book, won the 2012 Davitt Award for Crime Fiction, was shortlisted in 2013, 2015, for the 2016 Davitt Award, the 2015 Ned Kelly Award, the 2015 and 2016 Australian Book Industry Award for Best Adult Book, the NSW Genre Fiction Award, was commended in the FAW Jim Hamilton Award, and offered a Varuna Fellowship. In 2014, Sulari collaborated with National Gallery of Victoria to write a short historical fiction which was produced in audio to feature in the Fashion Detective Exhibition, and thereafter published by the NGV. She was an Ambassador of 2015 Emerging Writers' Festival and the inaugural Eminent Writer in Residence at the Museum of Australian Democracy. The *Rowland Sinclair Mysteries* have been released in print in the US, Canada, Australia, and New Zealand, and worldwide as audiobooks.

2017 saw international release of *Crossing the Lines,* a standalone literary novel.

Sulari remains in love with the art of writing.